Just in time for the holidays, fan favorite
Rhonda Nelson is giving Harlequin Blaze readers
two more books in her bestselling series

## *MEN OUT OF UNIFORM!*

These hot Southern heroes
have spent years taking on anything the military
could throw at them and they always came out on
top. So why do they get knocked off course by the
first sexy woman who crosses their path?

*Don't miss*

**#717 THE PROFESSIONAL**
(November 2012)

and

**#724 HIS FIRST NOELLE**
(December 2012)

*There's nothing like a man in uniform...
or out of it!*

Dear Reader,

To tell you the truth, I haven't given a lot of thought about where I'll spend my older years, but I sincerely hope that it's somewhere like the fictional Twilight Acres featured in this book. The residents are all young at heart, with enough money in the bank for the expensive things they couldn't afford in their youth. (And not all of it is strictly good for them!) They're an interesting bunch with lots of life experience, history and a whole lot of sass...which is more often than not directed at the hero and heroine.

When several residents of Twilight Acres realize that they've all had expensive pieces of jewelry stolen, one of the families calls in Ranger Security's Jeb Anderson to get to the bottom of the thefts. Having been given a brooch by one of the ladies, massage therapist Sophie O'Brien inadvertently winds up at the top of Jeb's suspect list.

Jeb is autocratic, irritating and unbelievably mysterious, and Sophie wants nothing more than to crack that cool reserve and tap into the heat she feels bubbling just below the surface. And once she does...*mercy.*

I love to hear from my readers, so please be sure to check out my website, www.readrhondanelson.com, like me on Facebook or follow me on Twitter @RhondaRNelson.

Enjoy!

Rhonda Nelson

# Rhonda Nelson

## THE PROFESSIONAL

&

## THE PLAYER

HARLEQUIN®

entertain, enrich, inspire™

ISBN-13: 978-0-373-79721-9

THE PROFESSIONAL

Copyright © 2012 by Harlequin Books S.A.

The publisher acknowledges the copyright holder of the individual works as follows:

THE PROFESSIONAL
Copyright © 2012 by Rhonda Nelson

THE PLAYER
Copyright © 2006 by Rhonda Nelson

Recycling programs for this product may not exist in your area.

www.Harlequin.com

**Printed in U.S.A.**

# CONTENTS

## ABOUT THE AUTHOR

A Waldenbooks bestselling author, two-time RITA® Award nominee, *RT Book Reviews* Reviewers' Choice nominee and National Readers' Choice Award winner Rhonda Nelson writes hot romantic comedy for the Harlequin Blaze line and other Harlequin Books imprints. With more than thirty-five published books to her credit, she's thrilled with her career and enjoys dreaming up her characters and manipulating the worlds they live in. She and her family make their chaotic but happy home in a small town in northern Alabama. She loves to hear from her readers, so be sure to check her out at www.readrhondanelson.com, follow her on Twitter @RhondaRNelson and like her on Facebook.

## Books by Rhonda Nelson

### HARLEQUIN BLAZE

# THE PROFESSIONAL

For quintessential Southern lady Jean Hovey, who makes me cornflake cookies and provides emergency plotting advice. Hugs, my sweet friend. Love you!

# *Prologue*

"You're certain they're twins?" the nurse asked as she peered skeptically into the bassinet.

Olga Montrose, the RN who'd assisted with the delivery, nodded, a smile on her lined face. "They most certainly are," she confirmed. "The blond one came first, then the dark-haired one less than two minutes after his brother. That's fast, particularly for a natural birth."

The nurse harrumphed under her breath. "They don't look like any set of twins I've ever seen," she said. "Even fraternal twins typically bear some sort of resemblance. These boys…don't."

Olga couldn't argue there, so she didn't try. She'd been working the maternity ward for over thirty years and had seen all manner of babies come into this world. Perfect and imperfect, big and small, identical twins and those of the fraternal variety.

But even she had to admit she'd never seen anything quite like the Anderson boys.

Weighing in at exactly seven pounds each—ordinarily one was smaller than the other—and both twenty-three inches long, they couldn't be any more different in appearance. The oldest boy, Jeb, was fair-haired, with startling especially blue eyes, even for a newborn, and had a visible dimple in his right cheek. The younger twin, Judd, had inky black hair and eyes that were so dark blue they already appeared brown and the same dimple as his brother, only on his left cheek. Exact opposites, but mirror images.

How inconceivably bizarre.

Both boys had thrashed around in their bassinets and wailed until, at a loss, Olga had put them in one together and the caterwauling had instantly stopped, as though a switch had been thrown. Presently the two lay facing one another and, though it was impossible, she got the distinct sense that they were somehow communicating. Ridiculous, she knew. Still…

She'd never seen a pair of twins more different or more distinctly bonded and knew a fleeting pang of sympathy for their parents.

For whatever reason, Olga suspected the two of them were going to be more than a handful to raise. Anyone charged with the dubious task of their upbringing would need lots of patience, fortitude and divine intervention.

With one last look at the pair and a shake of her head, she muttered a heartfelt, "Thank God it isn't me," then went on about the rest of her duties.

# 1

*THIRTY-TWO years later...*

Former Ranger Jeb Anderson was more accustomed to dodging bullets and IED's than a geriatric retiree with a Dale Earnhardt complex, on a tricked-out scooter, but luckily it took the same skill set.

"Move it, sonny!" an old man bellowed at him, narrowly avoiding Jeb's ankle with his back tire.

Interestingly enough, he wasn't certain what had been more dangerous—the potential bombs or these vision-impaired senior citizens on the only form of transportation they were legally allowed to drive without a proper license.

Sheesh.

Another older gentleman roared up next to him, his scooter candy-apple red with custom orange flames shooting down the sides, racing flags winging along behind him on the back. A cloud of Old Spice suddenly enveloped Jeb, making his nose burn and his eyes water.

"Psst," the older player stage-whispered, darting a covert look around them. He leaned closer. "You want to score some V?"

Jeb blinked. He wasn't altogether certain what V was, but he was relatively sure that he didn't need to score it.

"V," the man repeated impatiently, evidently in response to Jeb's blank look. "The Tent-Maker, the Rocket Launcher, Vitamin V, the Miracle of Manhood," he added with a suggestive waggle of his bushy brows.

*Ah.* That *V.*

"I get my next script in a few days and I can spare a couple of pills. Two for fifty. What do you say?"

Fifty dollars for two pills? Seriously? He'd say that was highway robbery. Of course, he wasn't familiar with the street value of Viagra, so for all he knew this was actually a bargain price. Fortunately—*blessedly*—he wasn't in the market for any sexual performance enhancement drugs, so he merely shook his head and the gentleman moved on.

Because Lex Sanborn—a fellow friend and former soldier—had warned him in advance that some of the jobs that came Ranger Security's way were a bit unorthodox, Jeb hadn't batted a lash when the three founding members—Jamie Flanagan, Brian Payne and Guy McCann—had told him that his first assignment with the firm would be to try and locate a jewel thief at an exclusive retirement home for those clients who needed specialized care.

Jeb considered working with the three legendary Rangers a real privilege. Known as The Specialist, Brian Payne's unmatched attention to detail, cool, unflappable confidence and keen observation skills had set the gold standard for every Ranger serving in Uncle Sam's army. With a supposed genius IQ and more brawn than even the traditional soldier, Jamie Flanagan was a force to be reckoned with, one who had married Colonel Carl Garrett's grand-daughter. He grinned. That sure as hell took nerve. And Guy McCann's almost providential ability to skate the fine line between sheer genius and stu-pidity and always come out on top was still locker room lore.

He couldn't be working with finer men—men who *got* him, who knew precisely why he'd gone into the military and why he'd ultimately elected to come out.

*After Mosul...*

Jeb released a tense sigh and battled the images back, the horror of his friends' broken bodies. *His* team, the one *he* was supposed to protect, and yet he was the only one to survive. He swallowed.

He'd be lying if he said there were moments when he sincerely wished he hadn't.

And then the inevitable guilt of that followed, imagining the pain his death would have caused his parents, his family, but most particularly his twin brother, Judd, who'd joined him in Ranger School and was currently still serving, but at present on a much-needed leave. Time hadn't permitted Judd a state-side visit, but he'd been able to manage a trip to Crete. It was odd being so far away from his brother, Jeb thought, as though he was missing an imaginary appendage.

Because they looked so different—Heaven and Hell more than one person had joked over the years—they'd never struggled with having their own identity, but the twin thing, the bond between them, had always been substantial. Had they not been so close, sharing that connection might have been a curse, but Jeb could honestly say he'd never resented the tie. Anything that Judd might have picked up from him was something he would have shared anyway.

They'd been more than brothers—they'd been best friends from the womb.

And this was the first time in either of their lives that their feet hadn't been on the same path. Or even the same continent, for that matter.

No doubt that was going to require more adjustment than anything else. Selfishly he'd hoped that Judd would make the switch with him, but that was hardly fair. Though his younger (by two minutes) brother had gone into the military initially to follow Jeb, Judd had thrived in the Ranger School and had developed a passion for serving that had defined his life just as much as it had Jeb's. Like himself, he knew Judd would stay there until he could no longer do the work to the best of his ability. He just hoped it didn't involve a tragedy, especially one that came with a heavy burden of guilt.

He wouldn't wish this hell on anybody.

Rather than linger on what he couldn't change, he sighed and tried to focus once more on the job at hand.

Twilight Acres looked more like a trendy resort than a glorified nursing home. The grounds were meticulously kept, featuring live oaks, sugar maples and weeping willow trees, lots of perfectly cut grass and flower beds bursting with blossoms. In honor of the Thanksgiving holiday there were potted mums, bales of hay, dried corn stalks and bunches of Indian corn artfully displayed around the grounds. Wrought iron lamp posts were positioned closely along the especially wide sidewalks and the heart of the community had been fashioned to look like an old town square. There was a beauty salon, a barber shop, several diners, a drug store and movie theater, a florist, a dentist and a doctor's office, a small grocery and what looked like a '50s era soda fountain.

A large gazebo with assorted benches, chairs and tables enabled residents to sit and play a game of chess or checkers or simply relax with a drink and talk. Uniformed staffers periodically refilled drinks and offered snacks.

For those residents who still liked to cook, there was a community center with a kitchen adjacent to the pool area and even a small, steepled white clapboard church at the end of the street. A community garden and greenhouse enabled residents to grow some of their own food and flowers, and the houses themselves were quaint and picturesque, all of them equipped with front porches and connected with a maze of sidewalks that encouraged access to neighbors. Meals were always available and the community provided cleaning and laundry services. Specialized vans carried the seniors to local attractions and made sure any off-site doctor's appointments were never missed.

All in all, the developers of the community appeared to have thought of everything and wanted their residents to genuinely enjoy their golden years. Jeb had been told the waiting list was a minimum of two years long and no amount of money, so-called donation or other motivation would move a person into a better position.

Given the seeming impartiality and incorruptibility, it seemed odd that they'd have a thief in their midst, but the facts didn't lie. Over the past three years more than a quarter of a million dollars in jewelry had been taken, more often than not from those residents who suffered with bouts of dementia. He grimaced, feeling his anger spike.

It took a particularly heinous sort of person to do that, in Jeb's opinion, and he looked forward to helping do his part to bring the perpetrator to justice.

Hired on by the most recent victim's family—

Rose Marie Wilton, who lost a diamond and emerald brooch which had been designed by the infamous Tiffany Company for Rose Marie's own grandmother—Jeb was coming in undercover and would be posing as the grandson of Foy Wilcox, whose central location and popularity would make it easy for Jeb to blend in and investigate. Foy had one of the few houses with a guest bedroom and had been considered ideal for Jeb's purposes.

Consulting the house numbers, Jeb located Mr. Wilcox's residence and noted the red scooter with the orange flames parked by the front door with a dawning sense of dread. His lips twisted. *Damn.*

Naturally, the Viagra pusher would be his host.

Jeb mounted the steps and with a resigned sigh, knocked on the door.

"Is that you, Mary?" Foy called, a happy note of expectation in his voice.

Jeb opened his mouth to reply, but was cut off.

"Come on in and make yourself at home, my dear," he said. "I'm changing and will be ready to go in just a minute."

Because he didn't see an alternative, Jeb opened the door and let himself into the spacious living room. A cursory glance revealed quite a bit about his pretend "grandpa." Foy was a fan of original art, high-end electronics, leather furniture and remote controls given the half dozen that lay on the stand next to his recliner. Jeb was strongly reminded of the so-called boardroom at Ranger Security, which had the same sort of man-cave feel.

The scent of fine cigars and some sort of disinfectant spray hung in the air and various photographs— some in color, some in black and white—lined the mantelpiece, presumably family, at least one a bride.

"I'm ready, Mary," Foy announced as he returned to the living room. His flirty, hopeful smile capsized when he saw Jeb and he blinked. "You're not Mary."

Jeb could state the obvious, too—Foy wasn't dressed.

At least, not in the traditional sense, and there was nothing conventional about the turquoise and black zebra-striped Speedo the older man was wearing. Even more disconcerting, evidence suggested that Foy was a man-scaper, because other than the slicked back hair on his head he was as bald all over as a newborn. A silk robe and a towel had been tossed over one arm and he wore a pair of rubber flip-flops. Jeb gave himself a mental shake and forcibly directed his gaze to Foy's face.

"I'm afraid not, Mr. Wilcox. I'm Jeb Anderson, the agent from Ranger Security looking into the jewelry thefts that have been taking place over the past few years. Rose Marie Wilton's family hired me. You were consulted by my boss, Major Brian Payne," he prompted.

Foy's eyebrows united in a dark scowl. "I know who you are and I know why you're here. I'm not a child, so don't talk to me like I'm one. I'm old, not ignorant."

*Shit*. He hadn't meant to cause offense. They certainly hadn't gotten off to a good start. "That's not what I—"

"Yeah, yeah," Foy said, ignoring him completely as he picked up his smart phone and loaded the calendar. He glanced up at him. "You're early," Foy announced. "You weren't supposed to arrive until four o'clock. It's three-thirty. Who looks like the dumbass now?"

Jeb felt himself blush. Foy was right. He'd incorrectly assumed that the older man would be waiting for him and, once he'd packed a bag, had decided not to delay his departure.

Clearly Foy, the resident Romeo, had other plans.

A knock at the door made them both turn and Foy's expression instantly transformed into a smile so smooth Jeb was hard-pressed not to admire the guy.

"Mary," Foy said warmly, striding forward. "Looking lovely as always. Is that a new cover up?"

Mary grinned, clearly pleased that Foy had noticed something different about her. She was an elegant lady, with carefully arranged blond hair, just enough make-up to hint at a more youthful beauty and finishing-school posture that made her appear taller than her true height. "It is," she said, nodding primly. Her gaze shifted to Jeb and she smiled expectantly.

"Mary, this is my grandson, Jeb. He's recently out of the military and is going to be visiting me for a few days. I'm working on my memoirs and he's kindly offered to take notes for me."

That was certainly news to Jeb. Memoirs? What sort of memoirs? Though Jeb would like to discount the remark as a good lie—and he suspected Foy Wilcox could spin a yarn with the best of them—there was a disturbing ring of truth to the announcement that made him distinctly uncomfortable.

"How nice," Mary enthused. A slight frown puckered her brow. "Oh. I hate to take you away from—"

"No, no," Foy was quick to tell her, shooting Jeb a black see-what-you've-done look over his shoulder. "He's going to settle in and take a nap. He's exhausted, poor lad. Had a nightmare layover in New York."

Jeb barely smothered a snort. Excellent liar indeed.

"Well, if you're certain," she said, still looking unsure.

"I am," Foy told her, herding her back out onto the porch, his fingers in the small of her back. "I'll be back after while, son," Foy told him. "Make yourself at home. There's food in the pantry and drinks in the fridge, but stay out of the liquor cabinet. I've got scotch in there that's older than you are." He settled Mary onto his lap, instructing her to wrap her arms around his neck in the process, then fired up his scooter and took off.

Jeb watched the pair hurtle down the sidewalk toward the pool area and knew a momentary flash of unhappy insight. He imagined his "grandfather" was getting laid with more enthusiasm and much more frequency than he was.

Rather than linger over that little nugget of disappointing information, Jeb decided he'd better call in. Charlie Martin, resident hacker for Ranger Security and new mother, had promised to have some information for him this afternoon.

Considering he was basically working blind, he'd take anything he could get.

BRIAN PAYNE REVIEWED the information in front of him and wished he could give his newest agent more to go on. "Sorry, Jeb. There's just not a lot here. Whoever is doing this has been at it for at least three years, chooses their items and victims wisely and, oftentimes, it's months before anyone even notices that their jewelry is missing. The only reason that Rose Marie noticed that the brooch was gone was because she'd been trying to make her will more equitable." No doubt a fact her heirs greatly appreciated, Payne thought.

Jeb laughed. "Maybe she should have a talk with some of my family," he said. "I'm anticipating all sorts of conditions to my inheritance when the time finally comes."

No doubt, Payne thought. Jeb's family had lots of old railroad money they'd parlayed into an even more lucrative real estate business. The fact that he and his twin had opted for a military career as opposed to the family business hadn't really bothered their parents, who'd only wanted their kids' happiness, but had angered their grandmother to no end. Twila Anderson's temper was legendary and her memory long. If she proved to be as spiteful, Jeb and his brother could find themselves cut out more thoroughly than they might imagine.

Not that either one of them would care. Payne was familiar enough with wealth to recognize greed and Jeb Anderson didn't have the look of it.

At the moment he merely looked haunted, but given the circumstances—those eerily close to his own—he completely understood the expression.

"Once my cover is completely in place with Foy, I plan on going over and talking to Rose Marie," Jeb continued. "As well as the others, of course. I need to know who has had any sort of access to their things. I also want to review who has lived and worked in the community for that length of time. See if I can find any sort of correlation there."

"That should be something Charlie can help you with," Payne told him. He studied Charlie's notes again and hummed under his breath. "Actually, she tagged a potential suspect based on a complaint she found in an online review of the community. Apparently, a Sophie O'Brien, who supplies one of the shops there on site with handmade soaps and lotions, was accused of taking a piece of jewelry from a resident. The family complained to the director, but nothing was ever done to their satisfaction."

"That sounds like as good a starting place as any," Jeb said. "I'll definitely check her out."

"Can you think of anything else I can get for you?"

"Some bleach for my eyes would be nice," Jeb drawled, chuckling. "Foy was wearing a Speedo when I arrived and the image is clinging determinedly to my retinas."

Payne laughed. "I guess modesty goes by the wayside at his age."

"He also tried to sell me some Viagra. I don't think modesty has anything to do with it. I think it's more like advertising."

Payne smiled. "Is it working?"

"He just left with a woman on his lap," Jeb told him, sounding equally bemused and impressed. "So, as incredible as it sounds, yes, I suspect it is."

"I don't know whether to be encouraged or appalled," Payne remarked, taking a pull from the drink on his desk.

"Me either and I've seen him."

Still chuckling, Payne told him to keep him posted and to let him know if he needed anything, then ended the call. A few more leaves lost their hold on the Bradford pear tree outside his window and drifted to the ground, revealing just a little more of the downtown Atlanta landscape. He spied a couple of utility workers fastening Christmas decorations onto the street poles and grunted in disgust. It was barely a week into November. Couldn't they enjoy Thanksgiving before giving way to the sadly over-commercialized Christmas season? Geez, he was beginning to sound just like his wife. He'd certainly never given a damn about one holiday or the other before he'd married Emma and started a family. He resisted the urge to do a ball-check, just to make sure he still had them, and then laughed.

Jamie and Guy had strolled into his office and both wore a questioning expression. "What's so funny?" Jamie asked.

"Nothing," Payne lied. Judging from his happy expression, Jamie must have won the most recent game of pool in the boardroom.

"Any trouble?" Guy said.

"Not trouble, really," Payne remarked, passing a hand over his face. "Just precious little to go on. I don't think this is going to be as simple as we'd originally thought."

"That seems to be a running theme of late," Jamie remarked with a grimace. He dropped into a chair and crossed an ankle over his leg.

"Not much we can do about that," Guy said. "How do you think he's going to do?"

Payne knew the question Guy was asking had nothing to do with Jeb's abilities—those were top-notch and without doubt. He was a Ranger, after all, and there wasn't a soldier alive who reached that level of expertise without possessing a keen mind, top physical form and a will of iron. It took more than being smart and in prime physical condition. It took mental endurance as well, which was often what broke before anything else did.

"I think that he'll make the transition simply because he knows that's what expected of him," Payne said. And with any luck, like him, he'd come to like it.

"He reminds me of you," Guy remarked thoughtfully.

Payne didn't betray a blink of surprise, but felt it all the same. That's exactly what Emma had said when she'd met Jeb Anderson earlier in the week. She said he was "intense" and "brooding" and she'd be willing to bet "autocratic," as well. She redeemed herself by adding the "but not quite so handsome as my husband" bit, but it was interesting all the same.

Because he'd noticed it as well.

Jeb Anderson had asked the same questions Payne would have asked had he been tasked with this particular case. And his reasons for coming out of the military were so very much like his own, only instead of losing one man on a mission he'd coordinated, Jeb had lost three.

After speaking with Colonel Carl Garrett, who'd been more disappointed to see him go than any other recruit he'd sent their way thus far, Payne had known that they were getting a Class A agent. Not to say that they all weren't, because they were. But even Payne had recognized the difference in Jeb, a do-it-or-die-trying mentality that marked him as a natural born leader with a determined, unshakable sort of resolve. It commanded respect, trust and loyalty.

Payne also knew the Colonel was sad to see Jeb leave because he fully anticipated losing his twin brother, Judd, as well, who was also purported to be an excellent soldier. He inwardly grinned.

No doubt Uncle Sam's loss would be Ranger Security's gain.

And as assets went, it was damned hard to beat the Anderson twins.

## 2

"Oh, Sophie," Clayton Plank groaned loudly as she kneaded his bony shoulders. "Sophie, Sophie, Sophie. You have *no* idea how good that feels."

Sophie O'Brien's lips twisted with humor. Oh, she believed she had some idea. Clayton certainly wasn't her most grateful client, but he was definitely the loudest. And to anyone who wasn't familiar with his noisy moans, groans, sighs and exaltations, those people would have undoubtedly imagined that Sophie was giving the eighty-seven-year-old man more than the traditional, strictly platonic massage.

Clayton, however, liked to put on quite a show and, because he had a standing appointment, local residents often dropped by Twilight Acres' General Store—where she sold her handmade lotions and soaps and kept a massage room—so that they could listen to him carry on.

Clayton, ever mindful of his audience, never failed to make it sound like he was receiving a variety of mind-blowing, imaginative sexual favors and never left her little room without looking hot, sweaty and pleasantly worn out.

She looked the same way, for that matter. But it was only because ninety-percent of her clientele were on blood thinners and required more heat than was ever comfortable, particularly during the summer months. She grimaced.

Georgia's zip code in August could easily be mistaken for Hell's.

"Same time next week, Clayton?" she asked, wiping the excess lotion from her hands and the sweat from her brow.

"It's a date," he said, his response predictable.

With a shake of her head, Sophie left the room so that he could redress and wasn't the least surprised to see several pairs of eyes dart in her direction. Most of the gazes were amused and familiar, though there were always a few more baffled ones that she didn't recognize. No doubt they thought she was a hooker, turning her tricks at the old folks' home as opposed to a seedy street corner. She mentally snorted.

As if the hookers didn't go directly to their houses.

She'd been around Twilight Acres long enough to know that the only difference between this place and a college campus was that everyone here was older and could better finance their vices. Pot, she'd learned, never went out of style, sexual enhancement drugs had replaced speed, and thirty year old scotch and fine wine had picked up where two-buck chuck and George Dickel had left off.

And considering that none of the residents had to cook, clean, work or hell, even drive for that matter, what was left to do there but get high or laid?

Golden years, indeed, Sophie thought, her lips sliding into a smile. She fervently hoped she'd be able to retire here as well.

"Oh, I'm so glad I caught you before you left," Cora Henderson said, hurrying forward. The older woman was practically quivering with excitement. Her long snowy white hair was loosely braided, the plait dangling just below her collar bone. A fan of jewel tones and bold jewelry, today she was wearing a white tunic shirt, a large turquoise necklace and matching earrings, multiple rings upon her long, elegant fingers and a skirt the shade of the Caribbean Sea.

Cora had been her grandmother's neighbor and dearest friend here at Twilight Acres. Since her grandmother's death two years ago, Cora had all but adopted her as another grandchild. She never forgot her birthday and insisted that Sophie spend the holidays with her and her family. She wasn't certain how Cora's relatives felt about that—especially after Cora had given her a cameo pendant her late husband had gotten for her while they'd honeymooned in Rome—but they were all too afraid of jeopardizing their inheritance to be anything less than polite.

Because she had no other family to speak of—or would speak *to*, for that matter—Sophie sincerely appreciated it.

Cora grasped her arm and leaned in excitedly. "Have you seen him yet?"

Sophie blinked. "Seen who?"

The older woman heaved a why-am-I-not-surprised sigh. "Of course, you haven't," she said. "You stay hidden away on that farm or in that massage room. Goats and old goats," she went on, a familiar refrain. "How do you expect to meet anyone if you're never out and about?"

If Sophie wanted to meet someone, then she'd go out and about. Since she wasn't so inclined, she was perfectly satisfied with the status quo. When and if she changed her mind, then she'd change her habits, but considering her last foray into the love department had netted her a two-week crying jag and a broken heart, she wasn't keen on revisiting Romance Land at the moment.

Sophie considered herself a relatively intelligent person, but to her eternal chagrin, she was nothing short of just plain stupid when it came to men. She'd been jilted just prior to the alter once and a string of broken relationships since had left her more than marginally gun shy. She never seemed to make the right choice, so she'd concluded that not choosing at all was her best bet. No more second-guessing herself, no more pining away for Prince Charming. Life was too short and she'd rather live it alone and happy than alone and miserable.

The "alone" part was the constant, but from here on out, she was in charge of the variables.

As for her goats, they provided the milk that she used to make her lotions and soaps—which she sold via the internet, here, and at several boutiques around Atlanta—and it was in her best interests to take care of them. Not that she wouldn't have anyway. Thanks to her grandmother, Sophie had always had a bit of a "Heidi" streak and loved animals. Growing up on a farm—the one she'd inherited when Gran passed away—would do that to a girl. In addition to her goats, she had chickens, geese, ducks, swans and peacocks. Then there was Antonio, the rogue raccoon who was forever getting into her garbage. He wasn't precisely a pet, but was around enough to feel like one.

The "old goat" comment didn't signify—she gave just as many massages to the women here as she did the men, possibly more. What had started as merely applying lotion to areas her grandmother and her friends couldn't reach had turned into an unexpected career path that had kept her here at the retirement village long after her grandmother had passed away.

Though she had a Business degree from the University of Georgia and had used her education to parlay her hobby soap-making—a craft she'd learned from Gran—into a lucrative career, she'd nevertheless gone back to school to get her massage therapy certification. Knowledge was power and she was a firm believer in doing things right. She grinned.

Another lesson learned from grandmother. Dozie O'Brien had been a force to be reckoned with. A war bride, she'd moved to the US with her grandfather at the tender age of seventeen. She'd left her family and country—Scotland—but, thwarting custom, had refused to give up her name, one that Sophie had ultimately taken. She hadn't appreciated what an honor her grandmother had bestowed upon her with that gift until she was in her teens and they'd visited Gran's family in St. Andrews. She'd always joked that she was a few pounds shy of an heiress—gesturing to her plump middle—but Sophie hadn't realized how close to the truth that was, joke or not, until they'd driven up to the gates of the family estate. It had been quite intimidating.

Sadly, she had few memories of her grandfather—he'd been thrown from a horse the year before Sophie had moved in with her grandmother, but through old photographs and the stories her grandmother would share, she'd always felt like she'd known him.

That her father could have been born of two such wonderful, kind people…

She grimaced and shook the thought away.

Naturally, Sophie hadn't been in favor of her

grandmother's move to Twilight Acres—selfishly she'd wanted her grandmother to stay at the farm they'd shared since she was six years old—but had to admit that, in the end, it had been the right decision. Her grandmother had flourished in the social setting, had made good friends and had the occasional romance. Sophie had been basically grafted in to the Twilight Acres family and the love and support she'd gotten from the community since the death of her grandmother had been unfailingly kind.

She cared about each and every one of the residents here—she had her favorites, of course, like Cora and Foy—but had come to know them all quite well and had developed an attachment to each and every one of them.

And to think that someone was stealing from them…

It made her blood boil.

Initially, Sophie had chalked up the misplaced necklaces, earrings, bracelets and brooches to nothing more than memory loss—this was a retirement village, after all, and many of the residents had a hard time keeping up with their teeth, much less other valuables. They were forever forgetting doctor's appointments, whether or not they'd taken their medication, things like that. But it wasn't until Rose Marie Wilton lost her vintage Tiffany brooch that Sophie had realized something much more sinister was going on.

In the first place, Rose Marie Wilton's memory

was tighter than a steel drum. She didn't misplace anything, let alone lose it or forget it. Secondly, when the odd pair of reading glasses was lost, then that was to be expected. But having several pieces of *especially* valuable jewelry go missing—at least a couple a year since she'd been on-site—then there was something more going on.

Sophie was determined to get to the bottom of it.

Evidently realizing that Sophie was treating the "out and about" question as a rhetorical one, Cora heaved a long-suffering sigh. "I have it on good authority that Foy's grandson is going to be here for several days. And Sophie, he's not just hot but *hawt*," Cora confided, using more of her newfound internet slang. "He's at the Four Square Diner in a booth against the window. If you walk by there right now, you can see him."

And if she had any interest in seeing him, she would do just that. As it was, she didn't and she had animals to feed. Furthermore, Foy didn't have any children. How could he have a grandchild, *hawt* or otherwise? Her friend had to be mistaken.

"Cora, I need to get—"

Cora tugged on her arm. "Just humor me, please. You can get a piece of pie to take home for dessert," she told her, shamelessly taking full advantage of Sophie's insatiable sweet tooth. Cora shoved open the door and propelled her into the chilly fall air. "Ethel made Japanese Fruit pie this morning. That's one of your favorites, right?"

Actually, yes. The raisin, pecan and coconut concoction was just about as perfect as a pie could be. Barring good old fashioned chocolate, of course, which would forever hold the top spot in her heart.

"Evidently he's a former Army Ranger," Cora pressed on. "I'm certain that he has at least one tattoo, but I haven't seen it yet. Don't all soldiers get ink?" she asked, more to herself than to Sophie. Cora typically liked to stroll, but Sophie felt more this was a power march. "I'm usually a tall, dark and handsome sort of girl," Cora went on. "But he's different. He's blond."

"Well, that's a deal-breaker then," Sophie told her with a matter of fact sigh. "I'm off blond guys at the moment. Luke was blond and you know what happened there."

Cora grunted indelicately. "Luke was an ass," she said. "Fake smile, fake tan and slicker than goose-shit. I warned you about him, remember? I told you he was a player, but would you listen to me? No. You were determined to see the good in him—determined to see the good in everybody and, while that's an admirable quality on the whole, it's not helpful when looking for a mate."

That was true enough, so Sophie could hardly argue there. Cora hadn't liked Luke from the onset. She'd said he reminded her too much of a bad used car salesman. Honestly, Sophie had just assumed that Cora hadn't warmed to Luke because he'd reacted poorly when her beloved parakeet, Jose, had landed on his shoulder and he'd smacked the bird away, when a simple shrug of his shoulder would have accomplished the same thing. He'd never particularly liked any of her animals either and the sentiment had definitely been mutual. She grinned. Her billy goat, Rufus, had never failed to nail him from behind when given the opportunity.

That definitely should have been a clue. After all, animals were generally a better judge of character than people were, weren't they? Perhaps that's what she needed to do? Introduce all potential dates to Rufus and see how he reacted. Anyone who got the head-butt didn't get a second date. The thought made her smile.

At any rate, Cora hadn't been the least bit surprised or unhappy when Sophie had told her that she and Luke had parted ways. In fact, she'd promptly lined Jose's cage with pictures of Luke she'd found online.

"Besides, Luke wasn't blond. His hair was brown with highlights. This guy, as you will soon see," she said, guiding her determinedly to the door, "is *blond*."

Indeed he was, Sophie thought, inexplicably stopping short at the sight of him. She hadn't walked into the door, but felt like she had all the same. An odd little thrill whipped through her middle and a tingling started behind her ears, making the hair on the back of her neck rise. Her belly clenched, no doubt to keep the bottom from dropping out of her stomach and her pulse suddenly hammered through her veins. Though she'd swear she'd never clapped eyes on him before in her life, an undeniable sense of recognition teased her, leaving her with the oddest sense of familiarity.

It was unnerving.

From the corner of her eye, she saw Cora's triumphant expression. "See. I told you. Man candy." She gave her a gentle nudge. "Move along, dear, and don't gawk. It's unseemly."

She'd just used the phrase "man candy" and had nerve to accuse her of being unseemly? Sophie thought dimly, shaken and out of sorts.

Though the restaurant was filled with its usual geriatric crowd—those early eaters who needed to take their medication with their meal—Foy's "grandson" would have stood out no matter where he was.

Blond, as far as a description went, was accurate. He *was* blond.

He was also forbiddingly large, gloriously muscled, impeccably dressed and unbelievably, *mouthwateringly* handsome.

His profile revealed cheekbones sharp enough to cut glass, an angled, well-defined jaw, a high forehead, a perfectly proportioned nose and a mouth that was so full it was almost sulky, for lack of a better description. His eyes were deep-set and heavy-lidded and, though she couldn't discern a proper color from this distance, intuition told her they'd be light, most likely blue. Though it was a cliché comparison, he put her in mind of a Greek God and she could easily see him holding court on Mount Olympus.

He was certainly holding court here, she thought, watching the hive of activity swirling around him. It was excessive, even for a newcomer and, though he hadn't so much as glanced in their direction, she got the distinct impression that he knew that she and Cora had entered the restaurant, that he was completely aware of everything that went on around him.

"Afternoon, ladies," Ethel said, beaming at them from behind the counter. She nodded at Sophie. "I expect you'd like some pie. For here or to go, dear?"

"For here," Cora interjected before she could respond. "I'll have a slice as well. Spiced tea for both of us."

Sophie leaned closer to her ear. "Cora, I told you—"

"Those animals aren't going to starve to death if you're a few minutes late with their feed," she interjected, heading toward an open table nearest the action. "Humor me. I've got a good feeling about this guy."

Sophie had gotten some feelings too, but whether they turned out to be good or not remained to be seen.

"Did you see those hands?" Cora asked under her breath. "They're huge and accustomed to hard work. That's rare these days."

Sophie determinedly avoided looking at the guy's hands, which took a galling amount of effort, then dropped into a chair. "For all we know he could have been hammering out license plates."

"Hogwash," she said, leaning forward. "I told you, he's former military. A Ranger," she added significantly. "Special Forces. That's impressive."

Yes, it was, she had to admit, particularly considering he'd served during a time of war. That took courage and a level of conviction and loyalty to a greater good that was becoming increasingly scarce. Both of her grandfathers had served in the military and even her father, possibly the most selfish man who'd ever walked the planet, had been in the reserves.

She considered it his one and only redeeming quality.

Thankfully, she hadn't heard from him—or her mother and brother, for that matter—in a couple of months. They'd always periodically terrorized her, even after she'd moved in with her grandmother. And since her grandmother's visitation service, when they'd cornered the family attorney and discovered she'd left them just enough to prevent contesting her will, and the rest of her estate to Sophie, things had only worsened.

Naturally the terms of the inheritance had gone over like a lead balloon and had resulted in a restraining order Sophie had faithfully updated every six months. The fear came from never knowing when they were going to strike. She'd been used to the occasional horrible letter, the unexplained vandalism of her car, the crank calls. Seeing them from a distance in a crowd.

But since Gran had died, they'd upped the viciousness with heart-breaking results.

When the restraining order had prevented them from coming near her or the house—they had just enough self-preservation to avoid jail—they'd lobbed poison over the fence and killed some of her animals. Did she have any proof? No. But she'd known it was them all the same. As a result, she'd had to build a fence within a fence to keep everything inside it safe. And while the three-hundred yards they were required to keep between them was enough to avoid physical injury, it wasn't enough to prevent her from hearing them. *"We're coming for you, Sophie, you little bitch."*

A bad seed, her grandmother had once confided, the heartbreak evident in her voice. Her father was living proof for the "nature" argument, that was for sure. He'd been nurtured by two loving, caring parents and had still turned out bad. The expulsions from school had started in the first grade, when he'd stabbed another child in the hand with a pencil just to see if he could pin it to the desk beneath. Having been permanently expelled from every public and private school in the area in his teens, he'd been sent to a "reform" school similar to a military boot camp. That's where he'd met her mother—who was even more…unstable—and the rest, as they say, was history.

They were bitter, twisted people, capable of horrible, horrible things, and she'd learned at an early age to steer clear of them. She absently rubbed the scar on the inside of her arm and shook off a sudden chill.

It was then that she caught him looking at her, a bold considering gaze that caught and held hers so thoroughly she couldn't have looked away if she'd wanted to. It left her feeling pinned and paralyzed, breathless and exposed, as though he were privy to each thought that tripped through her suddenly muddled head. Ridiculous, she knew, but the sensation held fast and quickly inspired…others. Impossibly, a spool of heat unraveled low in her belly and an answering warmth responded in her nipples, making them pucker behind her bra. She couldn't have been any more shocked if they'd caught fire. She'd never merely *looked* at a man and had that sort of reaction, much less in the form of the stranger-across-the-crowded-room scenario.

Thankfully, Ethel arrived with their pie, momentarily blocking his line of sight, and the brief interruption was enough to sever the bizarre connection.

*Good Lord…*

Right, Sophie thought, feeling a bit like a martini—shaken and stirred. Time to go, because this was as close to Foy's impossible grandson as she ever intended to be. He was off-limits. Out of bounds. Trouble in a pair of worn blue jeans. Sex on feet. And most definitely out of her league.

She waited until Cora put a bite of pie in her mouth, then abruptly stood and pressed a kiss onto the older lady's startled cheek. "I've got to get home. See you tomorrow."

Impulsively, she snatched her dessert—no point in letting it go to waste—and fled.

THANKS TO THE twin connection, Jeb was accustomed to a heightened sense of intuition. Though he and Judd weren't identical, the link was still there and unusually strong. As a boy he could remember having a sudden craving for strawberry ice cream, only to find his brother at the kitchen table, the carton in front of him, spoon in his mouth.

While in his teens, he'd been out on a first date with a girl when Judd had gotten a speeding ticket and the onset of panic and anxiety had ruined his evening. Even now, as early as last night, he'd felt a familiar spike of elation—much to their shared discomfort, an orgasm would do it every time—followed by a keen sense of loneliness. A text had arrived a minute later from Judd, a simple "I'm fine." No doubt the girl in the bed next to him prohibited a phone call.

At any rate, Jeb had learned to listen to his instincts and, after Mosul, would *never* ignore them again, regardless of "orders." Had he pulled back at the first prickling of his scalp instead of pushing forward as commanded, he would have avoided the ambush that had killed the rest of his team.

*He'd* been first, dammit. It should have been *him* coming home in a flag-draped coffin.

How he'd avoided the spray of bullets that had cut down everyone else was a mystery he didn't think he'd ever be able to explain. In fact, only the small camera attached to his helmet which had transmitted a live feed back to base—and had unequivocally proved his position—had kept him from an official inquiry.

Regret and remorse, his constant companions, pulled at him, but he beat back the sensation and focused on the unusual—even for him—intuitive cue currently yanking a knot behind his navel.

It had started the instant *she'd* walked into the diner.

She was a relatively unremarkable female, mid-twenties. Dark hair, dark eyes, average height and weight. Despite the chilly weather, her face bore the fading shade of a decent tan, suggesting she was fit and healthy. She wore a sensible jacket over a pair of orange scrubs, probably a nod to the Thanksgiving season, but put him in mind of a convict. His lips twitched. Undoubtedly, that wasn't the look she was going for. She was with an older woman with decidedly more style and a quick check of their body language revealed a certain reluctance in the younger woman and a sense of excitement from the other.

Odd.

The knot and jerking sensation intensified, then his fingers began to tingle and a ripple of awareness skidded down his spine. With effort, he resisted the urge to stare at her, though admittedly he didn't understand the impulse. Frankly, he could discern more from the corner of his eye than most men with the benefit of full-on vision and he didn't see anything remotely notable about her. She was neither beautiful nor ugly. She wasn't especially tall or short, thin or fat. Her hair was brown, not too dark or too light, but that basic common shade in between. It was shiny, he noticed, but the messy bun on the top of her head prevented him from recognizing the length. Based on everything else about her, he imagined it was shoulder-length. Again, not too…anything. She was rather plain, if he were honest.

And yet…

He shifted, determined to focus instead on the older couple who'd stopped to welcome him to Twilight Acres. He was of the opinion that the person he was talking to deserved the full benefit of his gaze. Looking elsewhere was rude.

"Yes, that's right. Foy's grandson," Jeb said for what felt like the millionth time in the last hour. He'd been greeted more out of curiosity than friendliness, but the more time he spent talking to people, the more information he was likely to be able to gather. As this was his first assignment for Ranger

Security, he wasn't too keen on the idea of blowing it.

The alternative had been working for his father—which really meant he'd be working for his grandmother—and that wasn't an option. The autocratic old biddy was about as warm as an ice cube, as sweet as a persimmon and better at giving orders than some of his former commanding officers.

And he was done taking orders.

"Carl," as he'd introduced himself, chuckled. "Foy's quite a pip."

His companion nodded. "And our reigning Scrabble champion." A hint of color bloomed in her lined cheeks and she patted her hair. "He's certainly got a way with words."

Hmm, Jeb thought, suppressing a smile. Clearly this lady had been for a ride on Foy's scooter as well.

Carl scowled, his wiry brows knitting. "Come along, Martha. We should let the boy finish his dinner."

At thirty-two, he was hardly a boy, but Jeb didn't take exception. The pair shuffled off, only to be replaced by another group. He smiled and nodded and repeated himself, and all the while his awareness of his mystery woman intensified, the compulsion to look at her causing a muscle ache in his neck from holding it in check.

Sheesh, Jeb thought, determinedly taking a sip of his iced tea. What the hell was wrong with him? When he looked up, another person had stopped at his table. The woman was in her mid-fifty's. Business casual dress, minimal jewelry and make-up. Short, no-nonsense hair.

"Let me guess," she said with an arch of a brow. "Foy's notorious grandson?"

Jeb chuckled. "Hardly notorious, but yes." He'd guessed her identity as well. "Marjorie Whitehall?"

She smiled. "That would be me. I'm the managing director, more affectionately known as the Drill Sergeant around here, but someone has to keep them in line."

He feigned a wince. "I don't envy you that." And based on what he'd seen so far, he really meant it.

"Your grandfather certainly doesn't make it easy, I can tell you that." She paused. "To tell you the truth, it would be especially helpful if he'd stop selling his Viagra pills. Everyone here is on some form of medication and the potential for a harmful combination is very real."

Jeb blinked, not altogether certain what sort of response was required. "I—"

"If you could have a word with him about it, I'd appreciate it."

*Ah.* He nodded. "Of course." Like hell.

She nodded her goodbye, then moved away and it was in that split second of unguarded disbelief at the turn this case had already taken—since when was he responsible for his faux grandpa's sexual enhancement drug racket?—that his gaze inexplicably moved to her.

The tug behind his navel jerked so hard it pulled the breath out of his lungs and, like a zoom lens, she loomed so clearly into focus that the rest of the room blurred. His mouth went bone dry and his pulse thundered in his ears as though he'd taken a shot of adrenaline directly into the heart. The forgotten fork in his hand clattered against the plate, revealing a slight tremor in his fingers.

*Bloody hell…*

He didn't get it, could not understand what it was about her that elicited this singularly insane reaction. She looked exactly the same as she had minutes before—perfectly ordinary—and yet something about her kindled a fire in his loins faster than he'd ever experienced. Heat slithered along his dick, making it stir, and his groin tightened.

She looked up then and caught him staring. The impact of her gaze when it met his made the hair on the back of his neck tingle, the soles of his feet vibrate and even more strangely, an odd sense of relief suddenly overwhelmed him, as though he'd found something presumed lost forever.

Predictably, his cell vibrated at his waist, but he didn't reach for it. No doubt Judd was picking up on his heightened emotional frequency. He couldn't begin to imagine what his twin was making of these feelings, because he sure as hell couldn't figure them out.

She continued to look at him, seemingly as trapped as he was. Her gaze was wide and startled and he'd been wrong, Jeb discovered. While the rest of her might be rather ordinary, her eyes most definitely were not. They were almond-shaped and large, the outer edges tilted just so to complement her cheekbones. And they weren't just dark, but a warm, melting brown, the color of good Swiss chocolate. He mentally frowned. How had he missed that before?

Before he could contemplate it any further a waitress arrived at their table, blocking his view. By the time she'd moved away, the object of his obsession was hastily kissing her friend goodbye on the cheek. He'd rattled her that much, had he? At the last second she snatched up the dessert, taking the plate and cutlery with her. For whatever reason, that made him smile.

The same waitress who'd serviced their table stopped by his. "Can I get you anything else, hon? A piece of cake? A slice of pie?"

He nodded at the woman making a beeline for the door. "I'll have what she's having."

The waitress followed his gaze and smiled indulgently, her grin fond. "Aw, that's our Sophie." She tsked. "Every tooth in that girl's head is sweet." She topped off his tea. "I'll be right back with your dessert. You might want to take a slice to Foy as well," she suggested. "It's his favorite."

Sophie? As in Sophie O'Brien? His one and only suspect?

That was…inconvenient.

# 3

"THANK YOU FOR the home visit," Lila Stokes said, looking pleasantly relaxed after her massage. Wrapped in a fluffy robe, a pair of satin slippers on her feet, she handed Sophie a cup of tea and a slice of orange cake.

"You're most welcome." She gestured to the plate and smiled. "I had an ulterior motive." Not really a lie, per se. She did have an ulterior motive, but it had nothing to do with this delicious cake.

After another restless night preoccupied with especially carnal thoughts of a certain blond former Ranger with big hands and beautiful lips—honestly, the man's mouth was hauntingly erotic, full and firm and just so damned sexy it made her long for it against her skin—Sophie had decided the best way to get him out of her mind was to occupy it with something else. While finding the thief had been a top priority for her, now it seemed almost essential.

Lila was one of the first residents who'd "lost" a

piece of jewelry and, though Sophie'd heard about it at the time, she hadn't really paid attention to the particulars. If she was going to get to the bottom of this, she'd need those facts along with a description of the item. Since gossip traveled faster than anything around here, discretion was key. The last thing she wanted to do was to tip off the thief and, considering all three burglaries had happened in the resident's home, then it was fair to assume the he or she lived on-site. Only someone with regular access could have pulled this off.

The idea made her a little sick at her stomach.

Lila settled into a wingback chair. "It was my mother's recipe," she said, smiling. "She made it every year for my birthday, even after I was grown. Said no matter how old I was, I was always going to be her baby."

"How lovely," Sophie said, flattening a moist crumb against her fork. It always made her uncomfortable when people talked about their mothers because she couldn't relate to any of their stories. Her mother had only ever had eyes for her father and her brother—the boys, as it were. She'd hated other women, other girls and always had to be the center of attention. She'd never had any use for Sophie and had made sure that the rest of them hadn't either. That was the thing about bullies, she thought. A lone bully was bad enough, but when a group of them lived together, they brought out the absolute worst in each other, a pack mentality.

Being their prime target had been sheer hell.

Sophie released a slow breath, pushing the memories back. The very best thing her father had ever done for her was dumping her at the end of her grandmother's driveway. She'd been six at the time. Bruised from head to toe, with a cut down the inside of her arm that had ultimately required twenty-four stitches to close.

"Get out," he'd said, glancing dispassionately at the bloody shirt wrapped around her arm. "I don't like you, but I don't want her to kill you either."

Terrified, but strangely relieved, she'd scrambled from the car, then had stood barefoot in the freezing December night and watched him drive away, back to Kentucky. After that night, her grandmother had completely cut him off, which had painted the ultimate target on her back.

Because, in their twisted minds, everything had become Sophie's fault.

"Can I get you a second slice, dear?" Lila asked.

Sophie blinked. "I'd better not," she said. "I've got to take some hand cream by Evelyn Hunter's when I leave here and she's sure to have a little something for me to try." Her stomach twinged. God help her.

Lila's eyes twinkled. "I'm sure she will. Just last week Evie made some sweet potato cookies for us to snack on during our bridge game."

Sophie hesitated. "That sounds relatively harmless." Lila was known for her rather unorthodox experimentation with flavor combinations. Sophie had recently bitten into a brownie the older woman had made, only to find a hidden layer of anchovies in the center. She squelched a gag, remembering.

"Oh, it would have been," Lila said, "had she not iced them with a salmon-flavored cream cheese frosting."

Sophie grinned and shook her head, then glanced at Lila. "She's really been on a fish kick lately, hasn't she?"

"Yes. I'd be wary of anything the size of a cake or pie if I was you." She hid her smile behind her teacup. "She could hide a catfish in one of those."

Chuckling, Sophie set her plate on the coffee table. "I'll be vigilant, I assure you." She paused. Time to get down to business. "Lila, did you ever find that necklace of yours that went missing awhile back?" she asked lightly.

The older lady blinked behind her glasses, evidently surprised at the subject change. She frowned, her face falling a bit with regret. "No, I didn't."

"Rose-Marie's brooch made me think of it," Sophie told her, which was true, of course, but not precisely why she was asking about the missing necklace.

Lila was thoughtful for a moment, her long elegant hands wrapped around her tea cup. She'd been a concert pianist in her younger days, traveling the world with various orchestras. Arthritis made playing difficult for her now, but she still sat down at her piano every morning, like clockwork, at seven. She'd once told Sophie that the music still itched in her fingers, desperate for the outlet.

Lila's gaze found hers and she released a small sigh. "To tell you the truth, I think my daughter might have taken it. Oh, she'd never admit to it, of course. But I have my suspicions. She was forever hounding me about putting it away in the safety deposit box with all my other jewelry, but that piece was so special I couldn't bear to part with it." A sad smile turned her lips. "It was a gift from my father, you see. My mother, too, to be fair, but my dad is the one who picked it out for me. It was a present for my coming-out party." She gestured toward the fireplace. "There's a picture of us over there."

Sophie stood and made her way across the room. Several photographs—some old, some new—lined the mantle, but the one Lila referred to was easy enough to spot. It was the one closest to her wedding photo. Black and white, and in a silver filigree frame, a sixteen-year-old Lila clung happily to the arm of her father. He'd been a handsome man, her father, and the proud smile on his face made an inexplicable lump form in Sophie's throat.

Standing at the foot of a grand double staircase, Lila was dressed in a white organza dress and white satin gloves extended to her elbows. She'd had dark hair then, black as a raven's wing, and it had been upswept into a sleek bun. She was radiant with happiness, her smile the epitome of youthful joy. The necklace circled her throat, a stunning sapphire and diamond choker. A pair of matching earrings glittered from her lobes.

Sophie turned and arched a brow. "Where are the earrings?"

"In the safety deposit box now," she said.

A jolt of surprise caught her. "They were with the necklace then?"

"Yes, I've always kept the set in the original box. Odd, isn't it?" she asked, looking baffled. "That the necklace went missing, but the earrings didn't."

Sophie felt a frown move across her face, then turned back to look at the picture once more. The necklace was memorable and she felt certain she'd recognize it if she ever saw it again. And, yes, it was most definitely odd that the thief hadn't taken the set, particularly when the earrings would have been worth a small fortune as well. Perhaps a set would have been more easily traced? Or was there another reason? Regardless, it was a terrible thing to do to someone. Lila had clearly treasured the jewelry.

"Monica was livid," Lila went on, referring to her daughter, "but she was only concerned about the reduction in her inheritance, which was foolish because the necklace was insured. She didn't lose anything, ultimately." Lila met her gaze, the older woman's suddenly sad. "But I did. An heirloom tied to a memory," she sighed. "To me, it was priceless."

Sophie swallowed. "I'm so sorry, Lila."

"Whatever for, dear? It's not your fault." She purposely brightened. "Aw, well. It's all water under the bridge now. I've accepted that I'll probably never know what happened to it."

Not if she had anything to do with it, Sophie thought, firming her resolve. "If you don't mind my asking, what makes you think that Monica is the one who took it?"

"Because, other than Marjorie, she was the only person who knew the combination to my safe. Marjorie's a tyrant, I'll grant you," she said with a dark chuckle. "But I don't think she's a thief."

Truthfully, Sophie didn't either. Marjorie ate, lived and breathed Twilight Acres and was a strict rule-follower. She was notorious for sending out her "Please don't" letters—please don't drive your power chairs on the lawn, please don't allow your dogs off a leash, please don't sunbathe naked by the pool. (Sophie had most heartily approved of *that* particular edict.) Overall Marjorie made sure that everything was strictly up to code and kept a close supervisory watch on everyone associated with the village. Though many of the residents complained about her rigid disposition and had even at one point considered taking up a collection to have the proverbial stick up her ass surgically removed, ultimately they knew Marjorie genuinely cared for their well-being.

As for the safes, much like those featured in hotels, they'd been part of the standard installation when the complex was built. Sophie was relatively certain every unit featured one. A thought struck.

"Did you set your combination or was it already coded?"

"It was coded, though I was assured when I moved in that the old code had been zeroed out and my new one set in its place."

Sophie supposed it was possible that someone could have broken into Marjorie's office and obtained the combinations to the safes, but if that was the case, why hadn't everyone been a victim? She knew for a fact that Arnold Hammerfield had an extremely valuable coin collection—he never failed to tell her about while he was on her table—and that several of the other residents liked to keep sizable amounts of cash on hand for emergencies. One resident was notorious for burying her stash in Mason jars around her lawn. The baffled groundskeeper had suspected a mole problem until the truth was revealed. Why not steal from them? Why was jewelry the only item taken?

"I suppose you've seen Foy's grandson," Lila remarked with a smile, seemingly ready for a subject change.

Sophie swallowed a sigh. "I have, at Cora's insistence," she added with a droll grin.

Truthfully, Foy's grandson was a topic she was getting mightily tired of—she hadn't talked to a single person over the past two days who didn't have something to say about the former Ranger. It was infuriating. And to make matters worse, like a bad penny, he kept showing up everywhere she went. Granted the village was relatively small, but it seemed like no matter where she was, he managed to be close by.

She'd avoided going to the diner for lunch yesterday because she'd been certain he'd be there again, laughing and smiling and looking all brooding and mysterious and sexy. She'd packed a lunch from home and, despite the chilly weather, had opted to dine al fresco on a park bench by the lake. She'd just spooned a bite of potato soup into her mouth when she'd looked across the water and spotted him. Evidently, he'd made the same choice and, smiling, had lifted his thermos in a salute to her.

Peevishly—hell, it wasn't his fault that she found herself wildly, inexplicably, horribly attracted to him—she pulled a book from her bag, stuck it in front of her face and pretended to read. While hiding in plain sight, she'd inadvertently dropped a glob of soup on her right breast and accidentally let her cake slide off her plate. She was so annoyed she'd abandoned the rest of her meal, gathered up her things and left in a foul mood.

And realizing that she'd let him put her in a foul mood had only angered her further. Where was this newfound control she was supposed to be exercising? What the hell had happened to it?

Just because he had the unique ability to make her body mutiny and melt like a popsicle on the

Fourth of July, and she'd caught him staring at her several times with that microscopic gaze as though she were an exotic specimen in a Petri dish didn't mean that she was destined to fail at celibacy.

It simply meant she needed to try harder.

Honestly, for a man who was supposedly here to visit his grandfather and make notes for his memoir—that little tidbit had made its way to her this morning—he certainly didn't spend a lot of time with Foy. If he wasn't in the diner, then he was in the general store. If he wasn't in the store, then he was at the pharmacy. If he wasn't at the pharmacy, then he was at the barber shop. Or the fitness center, or the recreation room, or simply visiting someone else. She frowned. It was odd and, combined with it being physically impossible for him to be Foy's grandson, she suspected he wasn't being completely honest with everyone about his purpose here.

Granted she didn't know every branch of Foy's family tree and if Foy said he was his grandson—which he did—then who was she to question it? Furthermore, Foy was shrewd and, of the residents here, he was the least likely to be taken advantage of.

Ultimately, though, it didn't matter. She just knew she needed to stay the hell away from him.

"Speak of the devil," Lila said, a smile in her voice.

Sophie blinked. "Pardon?"

A knock suddenly sounded at the front door and with a sense of impending doom, she turned and followed Lila's gaze. The devil, indeed, Sophie thought, her mouth parching at the sight of him. He wore a black cable-knit sweater which accentuated every impressive muscle from the waist up, and a pair of faded jeans which did the same thing from the waist down. Black boots and black sunglasses completed the look. A silver watch encircled his wrist and though she couldn't isolate a brand name on any particular item, everything he wore looked well-made and of quality.

In a word, expensive.

In her discount scrubs and worn tennis shoes, she suddenly felt like a slob. It wasn't that she couldn't afford nice clothes—she could—she just preferred to spend her money on other things. Like food for her animals, farm equipment and new furnishings for her house. She'd be willing to bet her tractor cost more than his, Sophie thought with an inward smile.

At any rate, his arrival combined with the sudden racing of her heart and the absurd impulse to lick him from one end to the other was her exit cue.

Thankfully, she'd already packed up her massage table and bag, and was ready to go. Trying not to look like she was in a hurry, she casually crossed the room and hefted the bag onto her shoulder. "I'd better get going, Lila," she said.

Rather than wait for an invitation into the house, to her chagrin Foy's grandson—Jeb, she'd heard—opened the door, came in and stood in front of it. Purposely, she was sure. Panic and irritation surged through her, impossibly heightening her awareness of him.

"I hope I'm not interrupting anything," he said, his voice a warm baritone with a cool, raspy finish. A shiver hit her middle, sending goosebumps over the tops of her thighs. He fastened his gaze on hers once more and, while it had been unnerving at a distance, this close it was practically debilitating. His eyes were so very blue, Sophie thought dimly. Vivid and clear. Mesmerizing. Deep. A girl could drown in them. *She* was drowning in them.

"Not at all," Lila trilled, obviously happy to be included on his visitation circuit. "Sophie humored me with a home visit this morning."

"Lucky you," he murmured so low Sophie was certain she was the only one who heard it. Latent humor glinted in his gaze and his sulky, sexy mouth lifted in a faint grin.

She swallowed, stunned. He was flirting? With her? "I did," Sophie said with a nod. Did that squeaky voice really belong to her? She cleared her throat. "And now I've got to get going. Mustn't get behind schedule," she continued with a brittle laugh and started toward the door.

Rather than move out of the way like anyone else would have done, he stood firm and extended his hand. "Jeb Anderson," he said. "I'm F—"

"Foy's grandson," she finished, unable to keep the skepticism out of her voice. "I've heard." She shook his hand for all of half a second, then snatched it back, ignoring the fire that streaked down her arm and the instant weakening of her knees at the contact.

Though she was certain he picked up on her tone, his expression didn't change. He smiled, revealing a deep dimple in his right cheek. A dimpled badass? Really? She smothered a whimper. How unfair was that?

"I imagine word travels fast through here."

"It does," she agreed.

"Can I get you a cup of tea, Jeb? A slice of orange cake?" Lila asked, seemingly unaware of the tense undercurrent humming between them.

"I'd love that, thanks." He arched a brow. "It's Sophie, right?"

"Yes." She didn't elaborate because she desperately wanted to leave. He smelled *really* good, too. Like a loamy forest and musk. It was a rich smell, very masculine and it suited him perfectly. She could feel her reflexes slowing, becoming sluggish, which was odd considering she felt like her insides were about to vibrate out of her body.

"You're the resident masseuse?"

She shifted her bag as though it were too heavy, hoping he'd get the hint. "Among other things, but yes, that's right."

"Excellent," he said with a nod. "I should set up an appointment while I'm here. I could use a good working over."

Whether the innuendo in that comment was real

or imagined—probably imagined, Sophie told herself—it had a devastating effect all the same. Visions of his large, magnificent, naked body sprawled out on her table, his skin slickened with oil and glistening in the low light while she rubbed his shoulders tripped rapid-fire through her mind, eliciting an odd little noise from the back of her throat.

She suspected it was a moan.

His suddenly humorous gaze confirmed it.

If only a hole would open up beneath her feet, Sophie thought, mortified. With effort, she attempted to salvage the moment by attempting to be a professional. She cleared her throat. "You're welcome to call and set up an appointment."

"She works wonders," Lila interjected. "She might be little, but she can get in there and work a knot out in nothing flat."

His lips twitched and his gaze drifted over her from head to toe, as though confirming Lila's description of her size. Her nipples beaded behind her bra and a flush of heat skidded over her belly. "I've got a few knots she could work out."

Sophie nearly swallowed her tongue. Oh, yes. He was definitely flirting with her. As impossible as it seemed, the suggestion in his tone wasn't open to misinterpretation. And the temptation to flirt back was almost impossible to resist. She got the impression that he was purposely trying to rattle her, that he enjoyed watching her wiggle like a worm on a hook.

Fine. She'd play along.

"Oh, I'm sure it's nothing a little time on my table couldn't fix," she said. "You'd be amazed how much good a little oil and a deep tissue massage can do."

Gratifyingly, a little of the satisfaction clinging to his smile dimmed.

"I like to heat the oil up," she went on. "Get it really hot so that it slides more easily across the skin."

He swallowed, the muscles working along his neck, and his jaw went a little slack.

"Peppermint is my favorite," Lila interjected, returning to the living room, her arms laden with more tea and cake. "It smells good and it tingles."

Sophie chewed the inside of her cheek to keep her smile from widening any further.

Jeb's eyes twinkled and he hummed under his breath. "Indeed. I'm tingling now just thinking about it."

She was, too. In inappropriate places. Right here in Lila's living room. When she was supposed to be avoiding him and catching a thief. All-righty then.

Time to go.

JEB WATCHED HER go and felt his shoulders shake with a chuckle. Sophie O'Brien had been doing her dead level best to avoid him since the first time she'd clapped eyes on him. From her hasty retreat from the diner night before last, to the book she'd pretended to read to keep from looking at him yesterday at lunch—her performance might have been more convincing if she'd remembered to turn the page, he thought drolly—to, as early as this morning, seeing him on the street and purposely changing directions.

Though irritating—as his prime suspect, it was imperative that he talk to her—it had been endlessly entertaining. She had the most expressive, animated face he'd ever seen. Take this morning, for instance. When she'd looked up and noticed him coming in her direction, both her eyes and her mouth had rounded—though he knew it was impossible, he could have sworn he heard her swear—then she'd stopped short and wheeled in the other direction. And it wasn't even a good short stop, like a "Darn, I must have forgotten something and I need to go back and get it." It was more like a dreaded, "Oh, hell, there he is again."

Initially, her reaction had baffled him. Women, on the whole, didn't purposely avoid him. Quite honestly, it was ordinarily the other way around. Though Jeb liked getting laid as much as any man— probably more so than some—he'd never let his appetite for sex get in the way of being selective. When he chose a woman to bed, several key factors came into play. In addition to him finding her attractive, she had to be smart, self-sufficient, healthy—he didn't want any diseases, thank you very much, and a condom wasn't foolproof—and, equally important, she'd have no expectations of a permanent relationship.

If and when he ever decided to settle down, he was just old-fashioned enough to want to do things the same way his parents had. His father had always said that he'd known by the end of his first date with his mother that he was going to marry her. Jeb didn't necessarily expect that kind of fanciful certainty, but he liked to think he knew his own mind well enough to know when he'd found the right girl.

Presently, he wasn't looking for a girl—right or otherwise, though admittedly, Sophie O'Brien was proving to be much more intriguing than was strictly professional—he was looking for a thief. Barging uninvited into Lila's this morning was the closest he'd managed to get to her and that was only by happy coincidence. He'd seen her bicycle outside, an aqua blue retro number with a wicker basket attached to the front and his anticipation had spiked with victory.

She'd bolted from her chair as though she'd been hit with a cattle prod upon seeing him, then had started immediately gathering her things, preparing to escape once again. It had been horribly rude to block the door, but as a momentary trap it had worked beautifully.

Right up until he'd started flirting with her—he couldn't have been any more shocked if he'd started speaking Swahili—and then, in another turn of unpredictable events, she'd started flirting *back*. After avoiding him like the plague.

It boggled the mind.

And spoke directly to his groin.

Nothing a little time on her table couldn't cure, indeed. Her soft hands, hot oil… He'd gotten the sudden mental image of her naked body riding him on that table, both of them slick with *tingling* oil and he'd gone rock hard.

And that wasn't even the most significant reaction.

That bizarre yank behind his naval had given another significant pull, the balls of his feet had vibrated and a powerful bolt of heat struck his already tortured groin. Coupled with the irrational sexual attraction, he'd been hit with an even more illogical urge to protect her. From what? Who the hell knew? But the inclination to stand between her and harm's way was undeniable. There was something distinctly vulnerable lurking in that warm, chocolate gaze, a hidden hurt she couldn't fully conceal. He had no idea what had triggered the notion, but it was there all the same and, since he'd decided to never again disregard his gut instincts, clearly more intel on her was needed.

He made a mental note to ask Charlie to dig a little deeper into her background. The preliminary report he'd received on her revealed that she was financially secure, having inherited a farm from her grandmother and running her own successful business. He'd spotted her soaps and lotions in the General Store—Wisteria Grove Farms—and had been impressed with the simple packaging and product.

According to her website, her soaps were all organic and handmade and any scents were derived from essential oils. Completely natural. It was impressive.

Judging from the soft-looking silky glow of her skin—up close he'd been better able to appreciate it—she undoubtedly used her own products. He'd never made particular note of a woman's skin before, but Sophie's was especially luminous. It seemed to shine as though illuminated through some sort of inner light, one that he was unaccountably drawn to.

Had she not been his only suspect—though intuition told him she was not his thief—her avoiding him would have probably been best for both of them, Jeb thought grimly. For whatever reason, he suspected Sophie O'Brien—or better still, his mind-bogglingly severe reaction to her—was a game-changer.

And didn't have the time nor the inclination to play.

Gratifyingly, though, he thought he'd isolated why she'd been so determined to avoid him and it was the same reason he'd been so curious about her—good old-fashioned sexual attraction.

While her mind had been formulating a retreat, her body had been betraying her. Those lovely eyes had darkened further as her pupils had dilated and the rapid pulse hammering at the base of her equally lovely neck were hard and fast clues to what was really going on with her. Add to the fact that she'd swallowed several times—dry mouth, another

sign—and had been covertly checking him out…
It was a no-brainer.

Evidently—for reasons as fascinating as she was,
ones he would *have* to learn—she didn't *want* to be
attracted to him. Jeb grimaced.

He felt her pain.

And, courtesy of Ranger Security and the job he
had to do, he grimly suspected that they were both
about to get even more uncomfortable. He was here
for the duration and staying away from her was out
of the question.

Because, even if she wasn't the thief, he didn't
think he was going to be able to help himself.

# 4

"AH, THERE you are," Cora said happily, peering through the wrought iron gate. "I've been looking all over for you." She frowned. "What are you doing out here? You know this is Marjorie's private Garden of Contemplation. She'll pop a blood vessel if she finds you out here."

"I got special permission," Sophie told her.

Cora's carefully drawn on brows furrowed thoughtfully. "I'd never thought to ask." Looking more than a little intrigued, she lifted the latch and took a tentative step into Marjorie's forbidden area as though she were trespassing on holy ground. She glanced around, taking in the water garden, flowering plants, shrubs and bird feeders. Water gurgled from a nearby fountain and the tinkling of wind chimes sounded on the breeze.

"Wow, this is nice," Cora murmured. "So quiet, so peaceful."

Yes, it was. Or it had been, Sophie thought with

a rueful sigh. Much as she loved Cora, Sophie had hidden away here because she'd wanted to be alone. Due to a last minute cancellation—Jeanie Wilson's vertigo was acting up again—she had an hour between appointments and it wasn't like she could just dash home and come right back. Wisteria Grove was a thirty-minute drive from Twilight Acres. She'd no sooner get there than she'd have to turn around and come right back.

Better to cool her heels here and wait, but considering the fact that Jeb—when had she started thinking of him as Jeb instead of Foy's Grandson?— managed to magically *friggin'* appear everywhere she went, citing a headache, she'd prevailed upon Marjorie to let her use the garden. If he was going to flirt with her—and she was going to stupidly flirt back—then, clearly, hiding was her only option. She snorted inwardly. Work the knots out, indeed.

Her whole body had become a knot after that little exchange.

At any rate, the director had relented, albeit reluctantly, then purposely shut the curtains across the French doors which led into her office. Honestly, Sophie thought. She hadn't been interested in spying on her—at least not right now, anyway—she'd just wanted a few minutes to herself, particularly after this morning's run in with the handsome irritant. She glanced at Cora and swallowed a sigh.

An effort in futility, it would seem.

Seemingly enchanted, Cora flitted from bloom to

bloom like a starstruck butterfly. "She must really have the touch," she said. "Some of these roses are temperamental. And rare," she said bending down to peer more closely at one bush. She straightened, then turned to Sophie and smiled. "No wonder she won't let anyone back here. I wouldn't either, if I was her."

"You said you were looking for me?" Sophie prompted.

Cora's eyes rounded. "Oh, right. Yes," she said, beaming. "Guess what we're having tomorrow night?"

She couldn't begin to imagine, but a sense of dread had descended all the same. "I don't know. What?"

"A dance!" Cora enthused. "Marjorie has given her approval and the party planning committee is on top of everything. Good food, good wine, and dancing. We're calling it the Fall Ball."

Uh-oh. She had a feeling she knew where this was heading. The community was notorious for hosting themed parties, which she'd always been able to avoid by playing the old I-don't-have-any-thing-to-wear-card, but that excuse was likely wearing thin. "I'm sure you'll have a wonderful time."

"I'm sure you will, too, because you're coming."

Sophie winced regretfully. "Sorry, I can't. I'm busy tomorrow night."

Cora scowled at her. "Watching reruns of The Office doesn't make you busy, Sophie."

That was a matter of opinion, but as it happened... "I hadn't planned on watching reruns of The Office."

"Watching old episodes of All Creatures Great and Small doesn't make you busy either."

Dammit, she should have known better than to tell Cora about those. "But they make me happy," she countered. "And that's what's important."

"Piffle. You can watch those any time."

"That may be true, but—" She hesitated, feigning disappointment. "—I wouldn't have anything to wear. No formal gowns lurking in the back of my closest, I'm afraid."

Cora's smile became uncomfortably triumphant. "No worries, dear. I've already bought you a dress."

She blinked, stunned. "What? When?"

"Two actually, so you'll be able to choose which one you like the best. Betty is on standby to do any alterations, so I want you to scoot over to her house before you leave this afternoon. You're finished with appointments at three—I checked with Curtis—so you don't have to rush home to the farm. Betty says it'll only take a few minutes." She stood. "I've got shoes and accessories for both dresses as well, so once you've made your choice then let me know. You can get ready at my place," she said. "I'll help you with your hair and make-up."

Sophie's head was whirling. Two dresses? Shoes and accessories? Hair and make-up? And she still hadn't answered her question. "When did you buy me these dresses?"

"Immediately after the last time you wriggled out of coming to one of our parties," she said archly. Her gaze softened and she laid a hand atop hers. "I promised your grandmother that I would look after you, dear, and I take my promises seriously."

Sophie swallowed, touched. She knew and she appreciated it, she really did. But she failed to understand how coming to a dance where she wouldn't have a single person—in her generation, at least—to dance with fell into the "looking after her category." Not that she expected—

Sophie stilled as realization dawned and her gaze swung to Cora's. Oh, but she would have someone to dance with, wouldn't she?

Foy's cursed Grandson—Jeb.

Which was no doubt why Cora and her Band of Merry Matchmakers were going to such great lengths to host a *ball*, for pity's sake, at such short notice. Oh, for the love of all that was holy, she thought, equally mortified and horrified. She felt like the good-hearted but homely friend who was always tragically looked over in those teen-targeted made-for-TV movies. It was a good message for a high school girl, but pretty damned pathetic at her age. Disgusted, she glanced at Cora, who looked innocently back at her.

Sophie wasn't buying it. And she sincerely doubted that her well-intentioned but seriously misguided friend had bought those dresses months ago. She'd be willing to bet Cora had called one of the boutiques she liked to frequent and had something appropriate and in Sophie's size delivered this very afternoon. Renewed misery washed through her.

She'd become their pity-project.

One that was going to be paraded like a prized animal in front of the best-looking, most lethally attractive man she'd ever encountered in her life.

"Indulge an old woman, would you?" Cora said, smiling softly. "It would mean a lot to me."

If she'd issued the I-Could-Die-Tomorrow warning like she typically did when she was trying to get her way, Sophie might have been able to resist. As it was—her cheeks puffed as she exhaled heavily—she couldn't, because the sentiment was sincere. For whatever reason, Cora was certain Foy's Grandson was crucial to Sophie's future happiness. She'd be proven wrong soon enough, so what was the harm in humoring her?

"All right," she sighed. "I'll come."

Cora's lined face lit up. "Excellent, my dear. You won't regret it, I promise."

Sophie sincerely doubted that, but refrained from commenting. Though she didn't relish the idea of being so obviously pimped out, as it were, the ball would actually give her a chance to do a little more investigating. Though she'd spoken to both Rose-Marie and Lila, she hadn't been able to catch the other two victims—Pearl McIntosh and Nanette

Hearst—at home. Pearl had been visiting family in the city and the last time she'd dropped by Nanette's, she'd been at the salon, getting her weekly set. Neither woman, Sophie was certain, would miss the Fall Ball.

Neither would Marjorie, for that matter—she'd have to patrol the festivities, make sure none of the rules were being broken—and, while Sophie didn't suspect the administrator of any wrong-doing, she'd like the opportunity to take a peek into her office, to see how accessible those safe-codes really were. Though she didn't know at this point where Pearl or Nanette kept their jewelry, both Lila's and Rose-Marie's had disappeared from their safes. It was an incriminating common denominator, one that definitely needed investigating. Once the party was in full swing, there was no reason why she couldn't duck out for a few minutes and do a little poking around.

Once the alcohol and music really started flowing, none of the seniors would miss her, she was certain. Though she'd deliberately avoided these formal affairs, she'd been to enough of their other parties to know that inhibitions went by the wayside quickly with this lot. Foy and a couple of his cronies had done their own version of The Full Monty at last month's British Invasion party—which Cora had secretly renamed The Twig and Berries Show—and Hortensia Forsythe hadn't let the fact that she needed a walker keep her from doing a table dance. She shook her head and chuckled at the thought.

Come to think of it, Foy's Grandson was in for an eye-opening experience. No point in only one of them being uncomfortable, Sophie thought, marginally cheered. And, while she definitely dreaded going to this ill-conceived dance, a vain little part of her actually looked forward to looking good in front of him for a change. Because if Cora was going to the trouble to pull all this together on her behalf, then no doubt the dress would be spectacular.

And what girl didn't dream of having a Cinderella moment?

JEB DIDN'T KNOW what had surprised Payne more—that he hadn't gotten any further along on this case than he had, or that he'd had to abandon the cause long enough to come home to retrieve, of all things, his tux.

"Why on earth would you need a tuxedo at a nursing home?" Guy asked.

"In the first place, it's not a nursing home. It's a retirement village and let me tell you, these people take their retirement seriously," he said, chuckling darkly. "It's like Spring Break around that place year round, only better because, unlike most poor teenagers, these folks have the cash to do things up in style. Do you know what they're planning next month? They're bringing in a *snow machine* so that they tube down the south hill of the village," he said, feeling his eyes widen. "Foy said where Mother Nature couldn't provide, money and ingenuity could. A snow machine," he repeated. "To go tubing. Probably while drunk and high. And *yesterday* they decided to host a ball, which is why I'm here this afternoon picking up my tux. Black tie only, I'm told, or they won't let me in the door, Foy's notorious grandson or not."

"I'd never thought about getting a snow machine," McCann said thoughtfully, evidently intrigued. He sent a speculative look at Payne, who also, incredibly, seemed more interested in that little part of Jeb's speech than anything else. "This Foy has a point. Instead of packing up the kids and heading to Colorado next month, we ought to get a snow machine and set it up near your cabin."

"That north slope is all but clear," Payne said, his gaze thoughtful. "And there's plenty of room since I built the addition."

"We could use the ATVs to bring the kids and tubes back up the hill."

"Or install a cable. There's time, and it shouldn't be too involved. Jamie could do it, I'm sure."

McCann grinned, anticipating their new toy. "We'll need to clear it with the wives."

"Emma won't mind," Payne remarked. "She can bring the animals."

"I'll check with Julia and give Jamie a call, to see if he and Emma would be on board with a change of plans."

Had he vanished? Jeb wondered, watching the conversation play out in front of him. Granted the snow machine was a cool idea, but this wasn't exactly the reaction he'd been expecting when he'd mentioned it to them.

"Sorry," Payne said, turning back to him. "Didn't mean to get sidetracked."

McCann nodded his goodbye and retreated to his own office, presumably to nail down a snow machine.

"So, other than needing a tux, how are things going?" his boss asked.

Naturally, this was the question he'd been dreading, because truthfully things weren't *going* at all. Jeb hesitated, then rubbed the back of his neck. "Much as it pains me to admit it, not well," he finally confessed.

Jeb had never seen the point in learning how to bullshit. He'd just always figured his time was better spent making sure it wasn't necessary. On the rare occasions he could have employed the tactic, honesty still prevailed.

He settled into a chair. "On the surface going in as Foy's grandson was a good idea, but in practice… it's not really helping me all that much. I've learned family histories, medical histories, heard old stories and new stories and eaten everything that's been put in front of me for the past two days, but—" He shrugged helplessly "—that doesn't make them trust me. And the questions I need to ask aren't coming up in polite conversation."

Payne winced. "I see." He arched a brow. "What about Foy? Can he ask the questions?"

Jeb snorted. "Foy's too busy dating and playing cards and getting massages to be of any assistance. I mentioned my dilemma to him last night and his response was, 'Tough, sonny. That's your problem, not mine.'"

Then the old guy had promptly told him to get lost, that he had a date coming over and that he'd turn the porch light off when it was safe for him to come back to the house.

That damned light didn't go off until two o'clock this morning. His date—who Jeb strongly suspected got paid by the hour—had left at ten, but Foy'd forgotten the light and had only remembered when he'd needed to get up to "drain the lizard."

Sheesh.

Jeb had used the time to the best of his ability, attempting to break into Marjorie's office, but the locking mechanism required better tools than he'd had on hand—rectified now, of course—and he hadn't dared risk ruining the door and leaving evidence behind. He planned on slipping away tonight during the party and giving it another go. On the surface, everything about the director seemed above board and suspicion, but at this point he couldn't afford to strike a single person off his list.

"What about the O'Brien woman? Have you gotten a read on her?"

Not in the way Payne thought, but… "She's universally adored out there," Jeb said, which was true. "The residents treat her like an honorary granddaughter. The cook at the diner makes her favorite pie at least once a week, Foy services her bicycle—"

"Her bicycle?"

"She uses it to make home visits around the village," he explained. "It's easier to negotiate around the scooter traffic." He sucked in a breath, then released it slowly. "She's certainly close enough to everyone there to have pulled it off, but my gut says that she's not our thief. And intuition aside, on the surface I don't see any motive. She's successful in her own right. She wouldn't have needed the money."

"That's assuming the jewelry has been sold," Payne added. "This could be something else." He shrugged. "Maybe the thief just wanted the jewelry."

"It's possible." At this point, *anything* was possible. But if that was true, why take the high-end stuff? Why not take the costume jewelry? Why not target other valuables? Other people? Though the thefts had definitely been deliberate, something about it all felt odd and haphazard. Off. He couldn't quite put his finger on it yet, but he couldn't deny the suspicion all the same.

Payne was thoughtful for a moment. "If your gut says she's not involved, then odds are, she's not.

But perhaps she would be willing to help you," he finally said. "If she's universally adored, then it only stands to reason that she's universally trusted as well."

Jeb's pulse gave an involuntary leap. Under ordinary circumstances that would have undoubtedly been an excellent suggestion. Sound, well-reasoned, spot-on. But these were hardly ordinary circumstances, because there was nothing ordinary about the way he reacted to her—hell, even the *thought* of her, given how his groin was tightening right now. Were that not problem enough, there was the tiny issue of her not wanting to be within one-hundred yards of him.

Not that she couldn't be persuaded…

Strictly speaking, he didn't *want* to be attracted to her. But he was.

She might not *want* to want him. But she did.

And that universal adoration in the village was reciprocated. It was obvious that she adored them all, that she'd do anything and everything for them. If he asked for her help, he was certain that she would give it.

That Payne hadn't questioned his instincts, had even told him to go with his gut, meant more than Jeb could have ever hoped for. It was proof that he'd made the right decision, evidence that the instinct to leave the military had been spot on.

He needed to reward that trust with a positive result, and if that meant asking the most extraordinary ordinary woman he'd ever met for her assistance, one that he wanted more desperately with each breath…then so be it.

# 5

Unaccountably nervous, Sophie looked into the mirror and gulped.

*Holy crap.*

When Cora had told her that she'd bought her a dress for this evening's event, Sophie had immediately known two things. One, that it would be exquisite, because Cora's taste was faultless. Two, that it would be expensive. She'd nearly choked on her own tongue when she'd glanced at the price tag, but Cora had insisted that it was worth it.

What Sophie hadn't counted on was a third description, one that was easily the most notable about the beaded, sequined chiffon gown she presently wore.

It was *sexy.*

So sexy, in fact, that it felt a bit like false advertising. This wasn't her real body, not one she recognized, anyway. Her breasts weren't this plump, her waist this small, her hips this curved.

Cora clapped her hands together delightedly. "You look wonderful! Simply wonderful!" she enthused. "My goodness, who knew you were hiding such a lovely figure beneath those shapeless scrubs?"

"My scrubs are comfortable," she said, feeling duty-bound to defend her practical, serviceable clothing. She smoothed her finger over the delicate beading, turned this way and that as the sequins caught the light.

"Maybe so, but they're criminally unflattering. Of course, it would help if you'd buy the right size. They're too big and boxy. They give you all the dimension of a kitchen sponge." She thrust a small purse into her hands and dropped a black, fringed shawl over her shoulders. "Come along, we need to get going."

"I need to be able to move," Sophie told her as Cora quickly herded her out the front door. A gust of cold wind scattered leaves across the porch, making her long for a more substantial coat. "I do a lot of bending and stretching. I'd be miserable in tight clothing."

"We'll take the golf cart tonight and save our feet for dancing," Cora told her. "And being tight and fitting are two different things, dear. No worries." She started the cart and backed out of the driveway. "Now that I know your proper size, I'll have some made for you."

"What? No, I—"

"I knew when I saw that dress it would be the one you'd choose," Cora said. "The peacock design is especially gorgeous, isn't it? And those colors look fabulous with your skin."

She didn't know about the colors and her skin—skin was skin, wasn't it?—but the dress was definitely stunning. It was a black halter-style design with jewel-toned beaded peacock feather embellishments which snaked over the bodice and down over her right hip. The lower half of the gown was accordion-pleated chiffon with a ruffled, flirty hem. The dress feathered around her feet with every step she took and felt good against her legs.

True to her word, Cora had insisted on doing her hair and make-up. Rather than loading her hair up with a lot of goopy spray, her fairy godmother had rolled it on huge rollers to give it a little extra body, then let it fall loosely around her shoulders. She'd gotten a little more dramatic with the make-up—had insisted the dress deserved it—but, rather than forcing every feature to make a bold statement, she'd focused most of her attention on Sophie's eyes. "It's eyes or lips, dear," she explained. "Never both."

Sophie had known a little dart of panic when she'd watched Cora whip out the green eye shadow, but she had to admit that the finished effect was noticeable, but not garish. She should have known not to worry, she thought, darting a glance at her older friend, a wry grin curling her lips.

Cora might be willing to hastily host a dance to

put her on display for Foy's Grandson—she got the sudden mental image of Cora leading her around a rink with a leash attached to her neck, feeding her chocolate treats every time she did something right, just like a dog show she'd watched recently, and smothered a laugh—and buy her a tasteful but sexy dress, but ultimately she'd draw the line at tacky or inappropriate.

And it was hard to stay annoyed with her when Cora so clearly thought she was being helpful. So determined to find her a man. Come to think of it, she'd been particularly relentless about it since Gran died. That, and making sure that she was safe. Gran had confided in her about the "family" problems and Cora had insisted on alerting the guard at the front gate after the incident with her animals. It meant a lot.

Sophie cleared her throat. "Thank you," she said. "For all of this." She gestured to the dress, feeling suddenly awkward.

Cora grinned. "You are more than welcome, dear." She pulled up to the community center and, ignoring the "No Parking" signs nearest the door, did just that.

"Cora, Marjorie will—"

"Some rules beg to be broken, dearest." She shrugged, unconcerned. "I'll leave the keys in the ignition and if she's that upset about it, she can move it herself." She glanced at the doorway and gasped delightedly. "Doesn't that look lovely? Joy and Martha have certainly outdone themselves."

They had, Sophie thought, following her gaze. Corn stalks wrapped with twinkle lights stood on either side of the door and a swag of Indian corn, mums and black-eyed Susan's hung in an arch above the entrance. Music and laughter rang from inside, indicating that they were fashionably late, just as Cora had planned.

"Never go anywhere without making an entrance," she'd said.

Though she'd been relatively indulgent of Cora's mechanizations up to this point, Sophie suddenly found herself very nervous. Her empty stomach fluttered with unease and her hands trembled, betraying her anxiety.

"You look absolutely beautiful, Sophie," Cora told her. "You're going to knock him dead."

*Him. Jeb. Foy's Grandson.* The man whose bottom lip she wanted to suck. He was inside and they were making an entrance. And she had on green eye shadow and a sexy dress. *Oh, sweet heaven.* What the hell had she been thinking? She couldn't do—

Cora snatched her arm an instant before Sophie would have dug in her heels, dragging her forward. Though the room didn't stand still when they walked inside, several appreciative glances turned in their direction.

*His*, of course, was the one she felt most keenly. It slid over her body like a caress, lingering along her neck, her breasts, the curve of her hip. Though she knew it was insane, she could practically feel that blue heat, felt a rush of color burst beneath her skin everywhere his gaze touched. It was unnerving. Thrilling. Terrifying. Electrifying. If he glanced at her crotch, she'd undoubtedly embarrass herself with an immaculate orgasm, Sophie thought, her sluggish blood pounding through her veins.

She resisted the almost overwhelming urge to look at him and followed Cora deeper into the room. The tables had been draped with gold and plum colored table clothes and candlelight glittered behind hurricane lamps. Fall flowers and stalks of wheat tied with satin ribbon decorated the food and beverage tables, and the scent of mulled cider hung in the air. The only discordant note was the band, which was currently playing Adam Levine's "Moves Like Jagger."

Badly.

And none of the participants on the dance floor possessed the skill to move like Mick, but what they lacked in proficiency, they made up for with enthusiasm. Especially Foy, Sophie thought, watching him work a walking stick like a microphone.

"It's disturbing, isn't it?" Jeb said, materializing at her side. She jumped a little and her heart stuttered. How the hell had he done that? "You don't want to watch, but you can't look away."

She smiled in spite of herself, her pulse racing

through her veins as desire and adrenaline flooded her system. "Sort of like a train wreck, you mean."

He leaned closer, still seemingly mystified. "And he knows every word. Watch him," he said, gesturing with his glass at Foy. "He doesn't miss a single syllable. I don't know what's worse—that his hips actually move like that or that he's more acquainted with popular music than I am."

"Look at it this way," she said. "You know exactly what to get him for Christmas."

He chuckled, the sound warm and deep. "Yeah. An iTunes gift card."

She shrugged negligently, feigning a nonchalance she didn't feel. "Or Maroon 5 tickets."

A startled laugh broke up in his throat and his mouthwatering shoulders shook with humor. She knew because his shoulder was so close to her head. She'd realized that he was tall, but this close his size was particularly noticeable. At five foot four inches, she was of average height and wasn't used to feeling short, but next to him she felt positively petite. Even in these heels. She rather liked it.

And naturally, he looked fabulous, she thought, covertly studying him. The tuxedo he wore was obviously not rented, further confirming her suspicions about his clothing. Clearly it had been custom made, tailored precisely to accommodate his glorious frame. The material draped flawlessly over his massive shoulders, down his trim middle and his trousers hit the tops of his gleaming shoes at that difficult but magical point to prevent bunching.

"You're right," he said with a sigh. "No doubt he'd like the tickets better."

The song drew to a close, much to the chagrin of Foy and his audience, and another slower one took its place. Lady Antebellum's "Just a Kiss." A quick glance toward the band revealed a hastily retreating Cora, who'd obviously just made a request.

No doubt everyone in the room had noticed it as well and they were all looking on at the pair of them with expectant smiles.

Sophie felt more heat creep up her neck, heaved an inward sigh and tapped the dwindling reserves of her patience.

Left with little choice, Jeb turned to her and, smiling, offered his hand. "Would you like to dance, Ms. O'Brien?"

"Yes, thanks. Better to go ahead and get it over with, I suppose." With as much reluctance as anticipation, she carefully put her hand in his—there it was again, that almost crippling sizzle—and, wobbly-legged, followed him out onto the parquet floor.

His smile didn't waver, but something in his gaze shifted as he pulled her into his powerful arms. "I'm sorry?"

Sophie clamped her mouth shut to keep from moaning aloud. He felt *wonderful*. Big and hard and muscled and warm and the scent of him flooded her senses, that woodsy, musky fragrance. A hint of something else reached her—oranges, maybe?—but the impression fled as others filled her. Tendrils of heat wound through her middle and spread vine-like through her limbs, settling hotly in her womb. The only thing that kept her from nuzzling his neck was physics—she couldn't reach it. She should have worn the higher heels, Sophie thought absently, feeling his chin brush the top of her head.

"I only meant that we wouldn't want to disappoint everyone," she finally explained.

"Disappoint everyone?" He drew back and looked at her, his gaze brooding and slightly confused. "I'm afraid I don't follow."

She could tell by the tone of his voice that "not following" wasn't something he was accustomed to and admitting it even more so. For whatever reason—insanity, probably—she found that oddly endearing.

She grinned, pleased, then gestured covertly toward the rest of the room. "They're all watching us," she said. "And, as I'm sure you've figured out, this crowd never misses the opportunity to throw a party, but this? This is a little much, even for them."

Though he didn't visibly look around the room for confirmation, she felt his muscles stiffen when realization hit. "No," he said disbelievingly. "Surely they didn't— Foy, er…Gramps told me this dance had been in the works for months."

Sophie chuckled. "Gramps lied. This party was manufactured out of thin air because Cora and her

Party Planning Posse are in full-throttle match-making mode, and the men are going along with it because there's food, alcohol and the potential for mischief. Like pieces on a chess board, we've been well-maneuvered."

"Matchmaking? Us? But I…" He glanced around again, as though needing additional confirmation. Cora and her group were all huddled together, looking on with self-satisfied smiles. Foy danced by, waggled his brows meaningfully at the two of them, and then winked at Jeb.

"Don't worry," she said. "Asking me to dance was enough. I don't expect a proposal."

He drew back once more, looked at her again with that shockingly blue gaze as though she were some sort of foreign entity or a riddle he couldn't quite figure out. "You're teasing me."

It was a statement, not a question.

Ah, Sophie thought, as pleasure warmed her chest. Something else the badass former Ranger wasn't accustomed to. "About the proposal? Yes. The matchmaking bit and this party being hosted solely for our benefit? No." She winced regretfully. "That's all true, I'm afraid."

"I'm…shocked," he said, giving his head a small shake.

She rolled her eyes. "Hang around a little while longer. You'll get used to it."

Heaven knows she could get used to this, Sophie thought, feeling his masculine thighs brush against her body as they swayed to the music. Despite the just-a-kiss theme of the song, Sophie concluded she must be more slutty than she'd ever realized, because at the moment she'd be monumentally disappointed with just a peck. Anything less than a proper back-against-the-wall, legs-around-his-waist screaming orgasm would leave her heartbroken and miserable.

And the kicker? She'd never been a sex-against-the-wall kind of girl. She'd always been a clean sheets and controlled lighting kind of girl.

Of course, she'd never been this attracted to a man either. She'd never felt so consumed with awareness that it had literally infected her, made her itch for the remedy. Fantasize about the cure. Crave it. Be her own best friend, as it were.

He chuckled softly. "Thank you."

Sophie frowned, perplexed. "For what?"

"You said I smelled good."

She did? Out loud?

Evidently seeing her confusion, he laughed again and humor lit his gaze. His wicked mouth tilted at one corner, making the dimple appear in his cheek. "You smell nice as well."

"It's soap," she said, mortified, sucking on the insides of her cheeks. Good Lord, how long was this song, anyway?

He hummed under his breath, leaned in and took a breath. "Ah, yes. The cherry vanilla, right?"

Shock bloomed through her and she looked up at

him. He'd been smelling her soaps? Had paid close enough attention to be able to differentiate one scent from another? That was a first. Men typically didn't appreciate her work. Though he'd never been stupid enough to say it, she'd been able to tell that Luke thought it was frivolous. That this man evidently had been interested enough to smell each one pleased her more than she would have ever imagined.

Smiling, she inclined her head. "I see you've been checking out my display in the general store."

"I have," he admitted. "I like the packaging. It's simple and wholesome and allows the product to speak for itself. I bought a bar of the citrus and sandalwood," he said, then leaned down so that she could smell him, putting her mouth in dangerous proximity to his neck. Unable to help herself, Sophie's eyes fluttered shut and she breathed him in. Her insides melted.

"I'm surprised you didn't notice," he said, his voice not quite as level as it had been a moment ago. He straightened and she felt his fingers flex against the small of her back.

"I'm so used to them," she lied. No wonder she'd smelled oranges, Sophie thought. That hint of something else had been familiar because she'd designed it. Something about knowing that his big hands had used something she'd touched—she'd made—on his wet, naked skin made her belly clench and her feminine muscles contract. Warmth seeped into her panties and she resisted the urge to squirm against him.

If she didn't get away from him soon, she was really going to embarrass herself. Hell, she'd already told him he smelled good, for pity's sake, without even realizing it. Heaven only knew what she'd say next. "I want to lick you all over." Or "You could lick *me* all over." Or even, "Why don't you bend me over that chair and take me until my eyes roll back in my head."

Her poor nerves couldn't take it and the stress of the unrelenting attraction—the seemingly endless pull of his gaze—was wearing down her resolve.

At long last the song ended and he reluctantly released her. She immediately missed his warmth, wanted him to draw her closer again.

"Would you like something to drink?" he asked, gesturing toward the refreshment table. Another smile twisted his lips and he leaned forward and lowered his voice. "Since they've gone to all this trouble on our behalf, we should probably make a good show of it. I don't mind if you don't."

Wonderful. So much for making an escape. At least one with any dignity. And now, if she said she did mind, she'd just look ungrateful and bitchy. What had happened to her plans? The one where she avoided him and lusted from afar, most specifically. Sophie heaved a resigned sigh.

But she'd pretty much thrown that plan under the bus when she'd agreed to come tonight, hadn't she?

Yes, she had. And she grimly suspected it was a

decision that was going to haunt her later, with unforeseen but far-reaching consequences.

"I don't mind at all," she lied, her mouth stretched into an unnatural too-bright smile. But… She gestured wordlessly toward the foyer, where the restrooms were located. "I'm just going to run to the…" She purposely left the sentence unfinished so she wouldn't have to tell another fib. Honestly, she'd been telling so many untruths of late she was surprised her nose hadn't started to grow.

He nodded knowingly. "Right. I'll see you in a few minutes then."

Sophie merely smiled and took off, dodging Cora with the same bathroom ruse. She might have been willing to change her Avoid Jeb plan for the evening, but she wasn't about to change the other one. Mere seconds ago, Marjorie had been dance-napped by Fred Holcolm and would easily be occupied for the next twenty minutes. Fred was a slow talker—he gave a whole new meaning to the phrase "Southern drawl"—and could turn a trip to the mailbox into a drawn out event.

This was her chance. That the timing gave her an opportunity to regroup and gird her loins, as it were, was just a happy coincidence. Right? Right.

With one last glance into the ball room, Sophie zigged toward the restrooms for appearance sake, then zagged and ran out the side door.

# 6

JEB WATCHED SOPHIE'S retreating back as she exited through the double doors and released an agonizingly slow breath. He felt like he'd been holding it since she walked in this evening and his stomach ached with the effort.

But how was a man supposed to breathe when she looked like *that*?

He'd known the instant she'd walked in, of course, because the tell-tale knot behind his naval had given its warning and the hair on the back of his neck had prickled with awareness. He'd only turned around to confirm it and the second he'd caught sight of her in that dress he'd damned near choked on his tongue.

Because Sophie O'Brien had a body that wouldn't quit.

He didn't know why he hadn't noticed before. How he could have possibly missed it even beneath those plain unisex clothes she typically wore?

Clearly he needed his eyes examined, because her breasts were full and lush, her waist so small he could span it with both hands—he knew because he'd done just that while they'd been dancing and he'd gone so hard he'd had to put a little distance between them to keep from embarrassing himself. And her hips... Mercy. Her hips were mouthwateringly generous and curved. Hips like those put a man in mind of how he'd fit between them, how they'd cradle him as he plunged into her silky welcoming heat.

Rather than her usual ponytail, her dark hair had been left down and loose and had brushed over the tops of her slim shoulders. Those melting brown eyes had been outlined with a smoky green, giving her an exotic, sexy look which had only enhanced her appeal.

Oddly enough, he'd never paid particular attention to her mouth before tonight—another sign he needed to see an optometrist, he thought with a dark chuckle—but one look at her ripe cupid's bow lips had left him so turned on his hands had actually begun to shake. They were a natural rosy color, pillowy soft, with a distinct extremely sexy V in the middle of her upper lip. He'd wanted to taste that V, trace its outline with his tongue.

Ultimately, though, how she looked was negligible to the way she *felt*.

Simply taking her hand to lead her onto the dance floor had left him oddly shaken. The blistering zing of awareness aside, there was something about the way her small but delicate fingers felt against his, the fleshy vulnerability of her smooth palm nestled against his bigger one that made an odd sensation wing through his chest. A curious mix of expectation, *familiarity*, of all things, and longing. That irrational urge to protect had swelled again as well, coupled with the even more disturbing need to possess.

Jeb didn't need a degree in psychology to understand the significance of these caveman-like inclinations. They were easily enough, alarmingly deduced. Had he been a dog, he would have merely pissed a circle around her, marking his territory.

That was a singularly unique development, one that had evidently reached his twin because his cell phone had vibrated in his jacket pocket. He hadn't checked the message yet, but was certain it contained a call back request.

It would have to wait.

Jeb cast a glance toward the doorway and frowned when Sophie didn't emerge back through it. She'd been gone for several minutes—typical, he imagined, she was a woman, after all—but, because he was a glutton for punishment, he wanted to dance with her again. He wanted to hold her sweet, curvy body next to his, feel her small hands wrapped behind his neck, her lush breasts against his chest. He even liked the way her hair tickled his chin, the scent of her wafting up around him.

She felt…right.

Gratifyingly, her petite frame had hummed with the same sexual energy, the same hammering need, the same helpless desperation. It had taken every atom of willpower he possessed to keep from leaning down and kissing her, tasting the desire on her tongue.

Because he knew it wouldn't be enough. He wouldn't be content with just a kiss. He'd want to devour her. Taste every part of her—the arch of her neck, the curve of her hips, the swell of her belly, the fluted edge of her spine, the dimples in her lower back, the plump crowns of her pouting nipples, the soft moist skin between her thighs. And when he'd finished feasting on her, he'd want to take her so hard that their resulting release would tilt the friggin' world off its axis.

For a start.

Jeb felt his lips quirk, exhaled mightily, then shifted to relieve some of the pressure behind his zipper.

On a personal level, suggesting that they spend the rest of the evening together for the benefit of their senior citizen matchmakers probably hadn't been the wisest decision, one that was no doubt going to result in a perpetual hard-on, chronic sexual tension and the inability to relieve himself without soaking a ceiling tile, but…

If he was going to ask for her help, as Payne had suggested, then this was as good a time as any. Since the seniors were determined to matchmake, they'd undoubtedly grant him and Sophie the privacy necessary to hold the conversation.

Privacy, with her, was a tricky bit of business, but if it meant that he could get the job done, then he was simply going to have to make it work.

He knew that Colonel Carl Garrett—one of the toughest old bastards Jeb had ever had the pleasure to serve under—had recommended him for his current position. Not until he'd given up trying to get Jeb to change his mind, of course, but he could hardly blame the veteran soldier for that. The Colonel had been convinced that a promotion and the benefit of time would alleviate the damage of that bedamned mission in Mosul, but Jeb had been equally certain that it wouldn't.

Recognizing a stalemate when he saw it, the Colonel had reluctantly let him go.

While coming out of the military wasn't ever going to wash the blood off his hands—there wasn't a day that went by when he didn't think about his fallen team—Jeb had consoled himself with the fact that he'd never again have to execute orders against his better judgment. That Payne had made a recommendation instead of an edict was a monumental relief and gave him the benefit of his own judgment and experience.

And while he'd never *experienced* anything close to the myriad of feelings Sophie O'Brien's presence elicited, instinct told him that she wasn't the thief and that she was the key to solving this mystery. A single look around the ballroom—at all the trouble this group had gone to on her behalf—was only further confirmation that she was the perfect person to help him catch the perpetrator. Hell, they'd put together this event for her in less than twenty-four hours. She'd said they'd done it for *their* benefit, but Jeb certainly didn't think so. Admittedly, everyone seemed to like him well enough and he supposed that he should be flattered that they all thought he was good enough for Sophie, but this was *her* party, not his.

Which begged one important question…

*Why?*

Why was she still single? Why was the Metamucil Brigade doing her match-making for her? Why were they so determined to see her with someone?

"Haven't lost her already, have you, son?" Foy asked, sidling up next to him. Looking distinguished in his tux, a Mason's ring winking on his finger, his pretend grandfather pulled a small silver flask from his inside pocket and took a drink, wincing with the burn.

Jeb bit back a wry grin. "She's gone to the restroom."

Foy inclined his head. "Women," he breathed with a smile. "Aren't we lucky?"

Jeb didn't know how one related to the other, but nodded all the same.

The older man's gaze followed Mary around

the room, a fond glint in his eye. "They're soft and sweet-smelling. They can be tender and nurturing one moment, and fiery and fierce in the next. Younger men don't appreciate that," he continued. "They're too slick, determined a girl's not going to get their hooks into them, and can't see past the end of their peckers."

In the process of taking a sip of his own drink, Jeb choked.

"That's because they're weak and stupid," Foy continued, darting him a concerned glance. "Only a real man, one with an evolved mind and a firm sense of self can appreciate the complexity, the strength and vulnerability—the *sheer magnificent beauty*—of a woman." He turned to Jeb, arched a graying brow. "Have you ever witnessed the birth of a baby?"

The question took him by surprise. "No, I haven't."

"No children then?"

Jeb shook his head. Much to his parents' lament. They'd been singing the settle-down-and-give-me-a-grandchild song for several years now.

Foy's gaze turned inward and unexpectedly somber. "I have," he said. "My one and only, a boy. Back then it wasn't customary for the fathers to be in the delivery rooms with the mothers, but hell would have frozen over before they'd have kept me out of that room."

Given what he knew of Foy thus far, that seemed perfectly within character, Jeb thought.

"For hours and hours, it went on, her labor," he continued, his voice strangely even, absent of its usual enthusiastic inflection. "I have never seen anyone in my life in that much pain and never felt more helpless in the face of it. She bore it all, my Annie. She squeezed my hand so hard she broke two of my fingers."

Like a badge of honor, he held them up for Jeb's benefit. They were crooked, bent in two different angles and had obviously healed without a proper setting first.

"Limp with exhaustion, soaked with sweat, she'd smile at me between contractions—*smile*," he emphasized wonderingly, "because she'd fallen in love with our baby the instant she'd learned she was pregnant and she understood the reward waiting at the end of the agony." Foy paused, swallowed, his expression grave. "I didn't, at that point. All I could see was her suffering and, with every cry of pain, I just knew she wasn't going to survive it, that I was going to lose her. It didn't matter that the doctor told me that everything that was happening to her was perfectly natural, that she wasn't in any danger. I didn't see how her little body could go through all of that and not fail." Foy hesitated, bit the inside of his cheek, and a sense of unease slid up Jeb's spine. "She was the first to notice that something was wrong," he said. "Because he didn't cry, you see. He never made a sound."

Jeb inwardly swore. *Jesus…*

"I was too busy looking at my boy—my *son,* blood of my blood, flesh of my flesh—and falling hopelessly in love." A soft smile caught his lips and he shook his head, clearly lost in the memory. "It's true that men are visual, because I can tell you that, while I was excited about having a baby and made all the right noise and said everything that was expected of me, I just didn't get it. I didn't recognize the wonder and awe and significance of what that meant…until I saw him, and the world changed." He released a slow breath, took another pull from his flask. "All of that happened in the space of a few heartbeats, and then, in a few more, that new world crumbled." Foy glanced up, held his gaze. "It broke me," he said simply. "And my wife, whose own heart was broken, whose body was spent and bleeding, turned and held on to me so that *I* wouldn't fall to pieces. *That*, my friend, is strength." He looked away, surveyed the room once more. "They'd wanted to take him away, didn't want to let her see, let alone hold our son, but Annie wasn't having it. She insisted that they give him to her—" He frowned thoughtfully, hesitated again. "—and I'll never forget the look on her face, the bittersweet longing in her eyes as she slipped her fingers over his cheek…" Foy cleared his throat. "We named him Beau, after her father. She sang him a lullaby, thanked the Almighty for the privilege of carrying him, then dressed him in the clothes we'd bought to bring him home in so that he could be properly buried. They're side by side now, the pair of them, and my name has already been cut into the stone." He shrugged, blew out a breath. "All it's waiting on is for me to die. She made me promise to live until then—*really live*—so that's what I'm doing. I never broke a promise to her and I never will."

Jeb swallowed. "She sounds like an amazing woman."

Foy chuckled, inclined his head. "That she was," he said fondly. "Let me tell you, any man who thinks of them as the weaker sex is a fool, and any man who thinks he doesn't need one is an idiot. We weren't designed to live alone. There's a reason Tab A fits into Slot B."

Er… While Jeb appreciated that Foy had shared his story with him—it certainly gave him more insight into his pretend grandfather—he sincerely hoped this wasn't going to segue into the birds and the bees discussion. Admittedly, Foy had the benefit of wisdom and experience when it came to women and relationships, but when it came to sex Jeb was confident that he didn't need any direction. A subject change was in order.

"Sophie tells me that this ball was only set into motion yesterday. That it hadn't been in the works for months."

"She's right. I lied."

Jeb blinked, stunned that he'd admit to it so readily. "Why?"

"Because Mary told me to."

That's it? Really? "Did Mary tell you why she wanted you to lie to me?"

"No, and I didn't ask. These ladies know how to put on a party and Mary gets frisky when she's been into the sangria." He grinned up at him. "If I can get the band to play some John Legend, it's going to be a win all the way around for me." He leaned in as though sharing a secret. "Word of advice. Don't just dance to the slow songs. Get out there on the floor and put a little hip action into it." He gave a little swivel of his own for demonstration. "Do a little advertising, if you get my drift. You save the slow tunes for the end of the evening, when it's time to close the deal."

Before Jeb could formulate a reply—not that he could think of one off the top of his head—Foy waved at Mary and took off. Determined to live. Keeping his promise.

Another look around the room confirmed that Sophie still hadn't returned from the ladies' room. He frowned. Granted her clothing probably made a trip to the bathroom more time consuming than it did for him, but he really would have assumed she'd be back by now. A thought struck.

Had she left? he wondered. Had she changed her mind about staying for the evening for appearance's sake?

Given the way she'd been dodging him, it was entirely possible, Jeb thought grimly, a dart of disappointment mushrooming in his chest.

Feeling suddenly ill at ease and twitchy, he walked out into the hall, looked in both directions and, while there were several people huddled in clusters of conversation, she wasn't among them. He didn't want to linger outside the bathroom door like some sort of pervert, but at this point he didn't know what else to do. As luck would have it, Lila emerged from the ladies' room.

"Evening, Lila," he said, smiling at her.

She inclined her head, eyes twinkling. "Jeb. I hope that you're enjoying yourself. I couldn't help but notice that you were dancing with Sophie earlier," she said. "Sweet girl, our Sophie. And so pretty, too."

"Yes, she is," he agreed, recognizing another sales pitch. He looked pointedly at the restroom door and hesitated awkwardly. "She, uh... You didn't happen to see her, did you?"

Lila frowned at first, then finally took his meaning. Her eyes rounded. "No, I didn't, sorry. It's empty."

He straightened, smiled, though it felt weird on his face. "Right."

*She'd bolted.*

Left him here horny and miserable, in a tux, the lone actor in this two-person play they'd been forced to perform. The idea of going back into that room, alone and pitiable—an odd sound emerged from his own head and he realized it was his teeth grinding against one another—while the rest of the attendees got hammered and paired off made him want to howl. He could cheerfully throttle her, Jeb thought, stunned at how quickly his irritation surfaced and how ineffectual his attempts to tamp it down were.

Ordinarily he didn't allow himself to get worked up over things he couldn't control. Emotion was the number one enemy of common sense and could cloud judgment faster than the blink of an eye. When life or death decisions were on the line, one learned to ignore those impulses and soldier on.

Literally.

It was only years of practice that allowed him to nod politely at Lila, take a quick look into the ballroom to confirm Marjorie's whereabouts, then get about the job he was here to do.

And if he cursed under his breath all the way to her office and kicked a stray ear of Indian corn that had fallen into his path, then by damn, he'd earned it. His cell vibrated again and, with a grim "Not now, Judd," he plucked it out of his pocket and hurled it into a nearby pond where it landed with a satisfying plunk.

Shit, he thought, eyes widening in shock as he stopped short. That wasn't his phone. It was Ranger Security's phone.

In a fit of temper, he'd just destroyed company property.

*Him.* Jeb Anderson, decorated soldier, former Army Ranger, West Point graduate. Nicknamed Shades in Jump School because he'd been so cool and enigmatic. Unreadable, he'd been told. The ultimate poker face.

And he'd let *her* do this to him. Wind him up so tightly that all he could do was spin. He felt his expression blacken.

It was intolerable.

Women might be strong, they might be able to endure much more than he'd ever realized, they might be kind and nurturing, fierce and fiery. Hell, they might be everything Foy had said about them.

But they were also trouble.

And only a fool wouldn't realize *that*.

He rounded the corner, noting the golf cart parked near the fence as he passed, then silently opened the gate into Marjorie's courtyard. The Forbidden Garden, as Foy liked to call it. Jeb had just put the pick in the lock on one of the French doors leading into the director's inner sanctum when a flash of light from inside made him still. He lowered himself to the ground, nearer to a gap in the curtains, and peered in. A small pen light hovered over an open filing cabinet, putting off little helpful illumination, but the large aquarium nearest the intruder was much more accommodating.

Jeb blinked, certain his eyes had deceived him. Shock detonated through him.

*A shimmer of black chiffon, a wink of turquoise beading...*

What in hell was she doing in there? What possible reason could she have for breaking into the director's office? Could he have pegged her that wrong? Could his instincts be that off?

No, he didn't think so. But clearly a little reconnaissance was needed.

SWEARING SOFTLY UNDER her breath, Sophie carefully slid the filing drawer closed and moved on to the next one. Like its predecessors it, too, revealed nothing out of the ordinary and certainly no easily accessible safe codes. Marjorie's computer was password protected and, though she'd tried a few possible codes—drill sergeant, task master and boss woman, just for kicks—she knew she wasn't going to be able to gain access.

In all probability, if the codes were on file in this office, then they were on the hard drive.

The only other possibility was a locked drawer in the bottom of her desk. Sophie had crawled up under it and tried to access the locking mechanism from the back, but with no success. Other than a questionable bottle of nail polish—blood red, which was hardly Marjorie's style—and a pop-on clown nose under her credenza, she hadn't found anything of note at all in the director's office.

Unsurprisingly, she kept good records, notating every last detail about each resident. Trips to the doctor's office, which prescriptions they were on, any allergies, family relations, religious and political affiliations, even their likes and dislikes. At the bottom of Lila's file she'd written "Loves salt water taffy."

Residents who'd passed away were put into a separate drawer, their folders marked with a pretty sky blue heart. Sophie had gotten a little choked up when she'd come across her grandmother's file and had run her finger across the beloved name.

Theodosia Grace O'Brien. Friends and family called her Dozie. She'd been a wonderful woman, her grandmother. The kindest person she'd ever known, with a heart for people and animals alike. She never passed a person in need without offering to help and she never noticed a stray without taking it in. Her lips quirked sadly.

Like her. She'd been the ultimate stray.

Marjorie had marked "estranged" next to her father's name on her grandmother's file, along with "Needs a pet," and "Excellent gardener." Both were very astute observations.

In addition to the files on the residents, Marjorie also kept files on all the employees. Hank, who manned the barber shop, each of the beauticians at the salon, even the onsite postal worker. Sophie learned that Hank was a medium who hosted ghost tours in downtown Atlanta on the side, that one of the grounds crew was a recovering alcoholic, and that Ethel had "coulrophobia." She made a mental note to look that up.

Naturally, she'd taken a minute to review her own file as well. Marjorie had denoted all the primary stuff—name, age, date of birth, business on site, the relation to her grandmother. "Works well, universally liked, poor taste in clothes and men." Honestly, she'd pegged her with the poor taste in men comment, but was beginning to get a bit of a complex about her scrubs. Didn't people understand the concept behind her work wear? She didn't select them for their style, dammit. They were comfortable.

Her cheeks puffed as she exhaled and, with one last look around to confirm that she hadn't left any evidence of her visit behind, Sophie stood, blew a kiss to Marjorie's beloved Kissing Fish, Emma and Mr. Knightley—Lizzie and Mr. Darcy had tragically gone to the big aquarium in the sky last year—and made her way quickly back outside.

The codes had been a long shot, but they'd at least given her a starting point. Now she wasn't certain what she'd need to do next. Find a way to get Marjorie's computer code? Break into Marjorie's house and search for the jewelry?

Eek. She was a soap-making goat farmer who moonlighted as a masseuse—she wasn't a cat burglar. Before she committed any additional crimes, she needed to talk to Pearl and Nanette. She needed to know exactly how their jewelry was stolen and, more importantly, where it was stolen from. If—

and this was a big if—their items had been removed from their safes as well, then she'd be left with no other choice than to take a closer look at Marjorie.

But if that meant she might be able to recover Lila's necklace and Rose-Marie's brooch and whatever else had been taken, then so be it.

Sophie had no idea how long she'd been gone, but knew that it had been longer than the traditional bathroom visit. With any luck, Jeb would have been too occupied by everyone else to notice anything remarkable about her absence.

Anticipation spiked as she drove the golf cart back across the grounds, off the lighted paths, of course. A flash of white caught the corner of her eye as she rounded the big elm tree nearest the pond, but a closer look revealed it was only a swan. Her face chilled from the speedy drive, she pulled the cart right back into position near the door—silently thanking Cora for leaving the keys in the ignition—and snuck back into the recreation center.

Foy, Clayton Plank and several other of the men were on the dance floor reenacting Lady Gaga's Bad Romance—hilariously well, actually—and Hortensia Forsythe was more than halfway through her table dance. She was down to her slip and heels, and Martin Howard was standing in front of her, wolf-whistling and shouting "Take it off, Teensy!"

Cora and a group of her friends were huddled together in the corner of the room, giggling like school girls, a suspicious cloud of aromatic smoke drifting up above their heads. No doubt they'd have the munchies soon, Sophie thought, with a chuckle.

Looking exhausted and past caring, Marjorie was slouched in a chair near the band, drinking champagne directly from the bottle.

Clearly she'd been away much longer than she'd realized, Sophie thought, scanning the crowd for a head and shoulders which would stand well above the others. Her own shoulders drooped dejectedly when her search proved futile.

He'd left.

It was just as well, she told herself. Really. There was no reason for her to be upset, for her to even care that he'd given up on her and made his exit. It wasn't like they'd made a real date. It had only been for the benefit of everyone else, right? Isn't that what he'd said?

So why was she suddenly so depressed? Why did she feel like she'd been shown a present only to have it snatched out of her grasp when she reached for it? Why, for the love of all that was holy, was she on the verge of tears?

She knew why.

Because, at one point, while they'd been dancing, she could have sworn she saw the same raw and ragged desire that had been tearing her up for days, clawing at him as well. The tension in his touch, that brooding inscrutable gaze...

Hope, that easily kindled insidious builder of expectation, had sprouted.

Clearly she'd been mistaken. Once again.

Sophie swallowed tightly, laughed as Foy and his crew reached the "zombie shuffle" portion of the iconic dance, then smiled her goodbyes at everyone and pushed back through the double doors out into the night. The music and laughter faded and the silence closed in around her, making her even more keenly aware of being alone.

A weak, resigned chuckle bubbled up her throat and she shook her head. *That's* what Marjorie should have written at the bottom of her file, Sophie thought.

"Will die alone."

# 7

HIDDEN BEHIND A massive magnolia, Jeb watched as
Sophie left the party. She'd barely stayed five minutes upon her return and, though he hadn't been
able to clearly see her face, everything about her
body language suggested that she was unhappy. Her
shoulders were rounded, her step slow. He heard
her chuckle, but there was no humor in the sound.
It rang hollow, almost defeated. Then she'd shaken
her head, tightened the wrap around her shoulders
and, rather than take the cart again, began walking
toward Cora's.

Cold and confused—an admittedly unfamiliar
state for him—and plagued with the irrational urge
to comfort her, to right her wrongs, Jeb frowned into
the darkness, trying to make sense of what had just
happened. Was she disappointed that she'd missed
him? he wondered. That he'd left? Was that the reason for the sudden onset of unhappiness?

But if she'd wanted to spend the evening with

him, then why in the hell had she snuck away? Why had she left? Better still, what had she hoped to find in Marjorie's office? What had she been looking for? The jewelry? Was it possible that she knew there was a thief among them? Yes, he thought, his stomach clenching. Who knew this group better than Sophie? Who interacted with all of them? It was entirely possible that she was aware that something was going on.

But if that was the case, then why look in Marjorie's office? There certainly wasn't any high-end jewelry in there, Jeb thought. The director wasn't the type and a quick look into her financials had revealed a frugal spender and faithful saver. Big purchases were planned, not impulsive. In fact, other than the cost of those exotic fish he'd spotted in her office and the garden attached to it, Marjorie didn't splurge for anything.

He glanced at Sophie again, watched the lovely swing of those heavily rounded hips and felt another stab of desire land below his belt. Moonlight gleamed off her dark hair and a gentle breeze teased at the ends, lifting them away from her creamy neck. He swallowed thickly, his mouth parching as he appreciated the sheer feminine perfection of her body, the achingly sweet slope of her cheek, the ripe fullness of her mouth. How in the hell had he ever thought her ordinary? he wondered, his chest suddenly tight, when she was clearly the most beautiful woman he'd ever clapped eyes on.

Though he didn't know when he'd made the conscious decision to continue following her, Jeb found himself doing that all the same. Careful to stay hidden behind various trees and shrubbery along the way, he stayed close enough to reach her quickly if needed, but far enough away to prevent detection. Against all reason and better judgment, irritation had given way to curiosity and the insatiable need to figure her out. To find out why she'd abandoned him to break into Marjorie's office.

As soon as she'd climbed into her vehicle, he'd dashed a block over to Foy's, slid behind the wheel of his Jeep and, staying a few car lengths away, fell in at a comfortable distance behind her truck. Fifteen minutes into the drive, traffic thinned and streetlights vanished. Withering Kudzu creeped along the embankments and he narrowly missed a deer.

Finally, she made a right turn onto Shady Springs road, drove along another mile, then stopped at a gated entrance to a long graveled driveway. With the beam of her headlights, he saw the gate swing open—remote access?—then he purposely drove past the entrance to her farm. Still puzzling over the gate, he waited until he was certain she'd had time to go inside, then backtracked and killed his headlights. He pulled past her entrance once more and parked in the driveway of an old barn.

Though it was pitch black without his headlights, his eyes soon adjusted to the darkness and he made his way toward her farm. The gate was ground level, easily ten-feet high, with slats too narrow to wiggle through and the surrounding fence proved just as impenetrable. Just as high as the gate, it was clearly custom designed, a cinderblock wall which had been covered in stained and textured concrete stamped to look like an old rock wall. He whistled low.

This wasn't a fence devised to keep things in—it was erected to keep things *out*.

He frowned, staring at it, and wondered who or what had frightened her to the point that she felt like she needed it. Who or what was she afraid of? Because one didn't go to the trouble and expense to build something like this without good reason. He'd come here looking for answers and so far he only had more questions. A cursory glance revealed that any trees or limbs close to the fence had been cut away, obviously to prevent someone from finding a way over. The only thing that stood in his favor was his training, otherwise he wouldn't have been able to clear it without a ladder.

Thirty feet inside he encountered another fence— barbed-wired—which he'd completely missed in the darkness. He toppled end over ass, felt the metal bite into his skin and tear his clothes and landed flat on his back with an undignified grunt. Stunned, he laid there for a minute, in what he gloomily sus- pected was goat shit, and felt a laugh swell in his chest. Unbelievable, he thought, wheezing quietly

as his shoulder shook. Could he possibly Barney
Fyfe this anymore?

He feared the answer to that question.

With a small grunt, still in his tux, he stood and
dusted himself off, then dropped into a crouch and
made his way into the low valley below her house,
which sat on a small knob overlooking a pond. He
could hear the occasional bleat of a goat, the rustle
of feathers. Lights burned from the front porch and
several windows downstairs, casting a decent glow
across the front yard.

Lots of flowers bloomed from various planters
around the yard, and whimsical whirly-things made
out of multicolored metals dangled from the bare
tree branches and swirled in the breeze. Obviously
a fan of metal artwork, a red pig with a pink snout
and blue wings stood next to her front door. He
smiled and shook his head. Before he could move
any closer, an unexpected noise registered and he
immediately froze.

*Oh, hell.*

Jeb didn't need extensive Army training to recognize the tell-tale, dreaded sound that emerged
roughly ten feet behind him. He was Southern, after
all, and any born-and-bred Georgia boy worth his
salt would recognize the distinct metallic click and
slide of the cock of a twelve gauge shotgun. And
given the decided assuredness and rapidity of the
action, he knew whoever had him in their sights
was familiar with the gun and knew how to use it.

"On your feet and hands where I can see them," she ordered. He had to hand it to her. Sophie O'Brien was cool as a cucumber. Her voice was smooth and steady, not betraying the slightest bit of fear. Which, irrationally, irritated him. He was a strange man trespassing on her property—she ought to be afraid, dammit. Granted, he didn't wish her any harm, but how was she to know that? Why hadn't she stayed in the house and called 911 like a normal woman would have done?

Oh, right, he thought sarcastically. Because she wasn't a *normal* woman. When compared to other women he'd met, anyway. She was kind and confident, fiendishly clever and sexy as hell. Mother Earth and Rosie the Riveter all wrapped up in a lushly curved '50s pin-up era body.

He wanted her.

And the hell of it? Aside from the conflict of interest and tiny matter of her name at the top of his suspect list?

She didn't like him. Or didn't *want* to like him. All arrogance aside, that was novel. And galling.

"Move," she said again, her voice firmer. "I'd rather not shoot you—my ice cream is melting— but I will if you don't do as I say."

Beautiful, Jeb thought, feeling extraordinarily stupid. He'd been an Army Ranger, one of the fiercest soldiers among Uncle Sam's finest…and he'd been bested by a goat farmer with an Annie Oakley complex. One that, to add insult to injury, was more concerned with her melting ice cream than finding a man lurking in the bushes outside her house.

With a sigh dredged from the depths of his soul, he did as she asked and flashed a grin at her. "Evening, Sophie. Your shrubs need mulching."

She gasped, betraying the first bit of surprise. It was ridiculous how much that pleased him. "You?" she breathed, her eyes wide. "What the hell are you doing out here?"

He pasted a reassuring look on his face and gestured to the gun still aimed at his chest. "Would you mind lowering your weapon? It's a bit unnerving."

She did as he asked, bringing the barrel down until it was aimed directly at his groin. "There," she said, a smirk in her voice. "Feel better?"

"Not particularly, no." She was still in her evening wear, but had obviously taken off her shoes because a pair of purple and black muck boots had replaced her strappy pumps. Between the shotgun, the dress and the boots, she looked like a beauty queen gone rogue. The thought startled a chuckle out of him.

"You think it's funny that I've got a loaded gun pointed at you?" she asked.

"No, I don't think it's funny at all—I used to get shot at for a living." He shrugged, his gaze tangling with hers. "But when you've been a target for as long as I have it loses the power to scare you."

Some of the starch left her spine and she swallowed, the delicate muscles in her throat working.

He glanced pointedly at her feet. "I was laughing at your shoes. They don't exactly match the dress."

She started, blinked and then a smile bloomed over her lips and she lowered the gun. "They were by the door. I didn't have time to color coordinate."

He shoved his bleeding hands into his pockets, looked out across the pond, watched the water ripple in the moonlight. "All right," he said, because he had to know. "What gave me away?"

Satisfaction clung to her grin and she cocked her head toward the edge of the property. "There are height sensors near the inside of the primary fence. I don't have anything here taller than I am, so anything above six feet trips an alarm."

He nodded consideringly. Smart and sophisticated. Given the breadth of the fence he should have anticipated something like that. "Any particular reason you've erected a fortress around your house?" he asked lightly. "Or why there's another fence inside of that one?"

A shadow shifted fleetingly behind her gaze, but she merely lifted an unconcerned shoulder, then turned and walked toward the house. "To keep people out, obviously," she said, her voice droll. "Come on. I'm looking forward to hearing why you were skulking in my shrubs."

As an enemy captured behind the lines, as it were, he'd expected an interrogation, but he had a few questions of his own he wanted answered first. "In my line of work we don't call it skulking, Ms.

O'Brien. We call it surveillance." He mounted the steps. "And I'll be happy to tell you why I'm monitoring your behavior as soon as you tell me what you were looking for in Marjorie Whitehall's office tonight."

Sophie felt her eyes round and bit back a curse. He'd seen her? But how? Why? Surveillance, he'd said. Dread ballooned in her belly. Had she been under surveillance this whole time? Was that why he'd been conveniently popping up everywhere she went? Why she hadn't been able to make a move without practically running into him? Why he'd been…so attentive? Flirty, even?

*Ah…* Her chest squeezed. Of course, it had. And she'd been so blinded by her uncustomary, ridiculously potent attraction to him that she'd missed it.

Right.

And to think she'd been relieved when it had been him she'd caught. For a moment she'd been terrified that one of her so-called family members had gone crazy enough to risk going to jail.

Feeling like she'd been kicked in the gut, Sophie squared her shoulders and pushed through the door. Her kitty, Boo—named for Boo Radley, of course—yowled and wound around her legs. He cast a haughty look at Jeb, his yellow eyes unblinking, then rather than bow up and hiss like he'd done upon meeting Luke, he strolled over to Jeb and sniffed tentatively at his leg.

Traitor, Sophie thought, scowling at her beloved pet.

"Ah," Jeb said, seemingly delighted. "Who's this?"

Sophie toed off her boots and returned the gun to the cabinet. "Boo. He's had diarrhea lately, so I'd be careful if I were you."

Predictably, Jeb grimaced. "Oh. Bad luck. I hope it's nothing serious."

"It's not." Because it was a lie. Her patience at an end, her nerves frayed to near-breaking, she turned and crossed her arms over her chest. "Listen, this is my house, so we're going to have this conversation on my terms. Any questions you have for me are optional. The ones I have for you are not. Why the hell have you been following me and what the hell are you doing trespassing on my land?"

He'd scared the hell out of her. She'd always lived by the adage better safe than sorry, so she was prepared for anything, but she'd grown so tired of living, constantly looking over her shoulder, that she'd been trying not to do it anymore. Being afraid had felt too much like a victory for them, a loss for her. She wanted the power back.

But she'd realized tonight that she was much more frightened than she'd ever realized. It was unnerving.

In the process of shrugging out of his coat—clearly he'd meant to stay awhile—Jeb paused and shot her a wary look. She didn't know how she knew it was wary—naturally, nothing about his expression shifted, but she could feel the difference, almost like an atmospheric change.

Suddenly Heathcliffe cried from the front porch and Jeb's eyes widened in shock. He jumped as though something had bitten him, and whirled around. "Bloody hell," he breathed. "What was *that*?"

Sophie was too busy convulsing with laughter to tell him. Watching GI Joe meets James Bond spin Matrix-style around her living room looking for the boogey-man because of a bird was simply… priceless. Eyes streaming, her sides heaved and she couldn't catch her breath.

Jeb glared at her. To her delight, his cheeks actually turned pink. She'd be willing to bet that didn't happen often.

"Yeah, yeah. I'm sure it was funny. You didn't run for your gun, Annie Oakley," he drawled. "So I can assume we're not in any immediate danger."

Still chuckling, she shook her head and wiped her eyes. "Ah, wow. I needed that," she said. Poetic justice.

He shrugged a mouthwatering shoulder, his expression droll. "I live to entertain."

"It's good to have goals."

Seemingly weary, he dropped onto her couch and started loosening his tie. It was such a man thing to do, she found herself momentarily dumbstruck.

"Are you going to tell me what that was or not?"

*Have a seat, Jeb. Make yourself at home, Jeb.*

*Take off your shirt, Jeb.* Wait, no… She gave herself a shake. It was then that she noticed the state of him. His coat was covered with dirt and debris and tiny tears rent his shirt. Blood oozed through the linen from a couple of cuts on his chest and visible gashes marred his hands.

She frowned, seized with the irrational urge to nurse those minor injuries. "What happened to you?"

"Fence number two. Stupid me, I left my night-vision goggles at home." He lifted his hand, inspected the damage, then grimaced as though it didn't signify. "It's nothing. The noise?" he prodded.

"It was Heathcliffe, one of my peacocks." She arched a brow. "You've never heard one cry before?"

The corner of his sulky mouth twitched with a grin and he cut a look at her with that bright blue gaze. "Obviously not."

"It takes some getting used to."

He snorted. "It's creepy as hell."

That, too, but she'd grown to like it. She snagged her ice cream from the table and settled into her chair. "Your tux is ruined."

He laughed softly, watched her spoon a bite of ice cream into her mouth. "So is my pride, but I'll recover." He heaved a dramatic sigh. "I don't want anything to drink, thanks."

She smiled unrepentantly. "I'm only polite to invited guests."

He tsked. "What would Emily Post have to say about that?"

"Nothing I'd care to hear, I'm sure. Please tell me what you're doing here."

He sighed softly, the sound seasoned with dread, then he looked up at her, that bright blue gaze pinning her once more. "Were you looking for me when you came back to the ball?"

Sophie opened her mouth, closed it. What an odd question. Why would he want to know that? What difference did it make to anything? She licked her lips. "I… Does it matter?"

He leaned forward, resting his arms on his knees, his hands dangling between them. He studied her carpet, then gave a little resigned laugh, as though the answer surprised him. "It does."

She couldn't imagine why, but rather than dance around half-truths and lies, it was time for a little honesty. She'd give it with the hope that he'd reciprocate. She released a small breath. "I was," she admitted. "I'd told you that I would come back, and I happen to appreciate that old antiquated notion that people should do what they say they will. But by the time I'd gotten back, you'd already left." She purposely avoided looking at him, swirling the melted ice cream around the bottom of her bowl. "So I left, too."

"But why did you leave to start with?" he asked. "Why did you go to Marjorie's office?"

Oh, no. She'd answered a question. Now it was

his turn. She set her bowl aside, then looked up.
"Why have you been following me? Either you tell
me or you leave. The choice is yours."

"It's part of my job," he said.

She felt her forehead wrinkle and renewed fear
washed through her. "You're being paid to follow
me? Who hired you?" Surely to God her father
hadn't— Or her mother— But why? What could
they possibly want? Beyond making her miserable?
She absently rubbed her arm, struggling to control
the irrational panic. She was an adult. She was protected. She didn't have to be afraid. She could take
care of herself, dammit.

Evidently something in her expression caught his
attention. Concern lined his otherwise smooth brow,
reflected almost tenderly in his gaze. "Sophie? Are
you all right? Nobody hired me to follow you, specifically," he said, still staring at her. "You just got
swept up in the net of my investigation, that's all."

Swept up in the net? His investigation? What did
that mean? She nodded, the rush of adrenaline spent,
making her insides tremble. Geez. She couldn't take
much more of this.

"Right," she said, trying to sort it out amid the
mess in her head. "But you obviously suspect me
of something, or you wouldn't have been following me, you wouldn't have danced with me, and
you wouldn't have come over my fence," she persisted. She arched a brow and might have whim-

pered. "Could you please just stop talking in cryptic circles and tell me what's going on?"

He released a heavy breath. "Okay, let's get something straight. I haven't *followed* you anywhere until tonight, after I caught *you* skulking around Marjorie's office. Up to that point, I have been conducting an investigation, which like it or not, you've been a part of. Because I don't think you're the person I'm looking for and because you are so well-liked and trusted in the village, I'd planned on asking for your help. Tonight. At the Fall Ball. Then you left and didn't come back and you broke into Marjorie's office and, well—" He laughed darkly. "—for obvious reasons, that sort of changed things."

"If by 'changed things,' you mean 'moved to the top of your list,' right?" Wonderful. Just brilliant. Several things suddenly clicked into place. "Listen, I know damned well that you aren't who you say you are—Foy doesn't have any children, so a grandson is pretty much out of the question. You've spent more time wandering around the village, visiting with other people than you have spent with your so-called grandfather, so it's obvious to me that you are investigating something or someone related to Twilight Acres. Here's a thought," she said, sarcasm rising right along with her temper. "Why don't you just ask me if I've done what you think I've done? Just ask me, Sherlock, and I'll tell you the truth. I won't lie."

He shrugged, then shot her a sardonic grin. "That simple, eh?"

"You're the one making it complicated."

"How am I supposed to know whether or not you're lying?"

She lifted her chin. "If you were following me so that you could eliminate me as a suspect and then ask for my help, then you're already half-convinced that I'm not the person you're looking for."

His gaze searched hers and that Petri dish sensation commenced again. She resisted the urge to squirm beneath that probing stare, that singularly intense, unwavering regard.

"Tell you what," she said. "In a show of good faith, I will tell you what I was doing in Marjorie's office first, then you can decide whether or not you want my help."

He blinked, seemingly surprised. "That's...generous. You had me on the ropes. Why are you backing down?"

She chuckled low. "Oh, I'm not backing down. I'm showing mercy. Sometimes that takes more courage, wouldn't you say?"

Jeb grinned, the dimple appearing in his cheek. Seemingly impressed, his gaze drifted across her mouth, making her lips tingle. "All right. Show me what you've got, badass."

*Mercy.* If he looked at her again like that, more than her lips were going to be tingling.

Time to put up or shut up. She released a slow

breath. "Over the past couple of years, several of our residents have supposedly misplaced some of their valuable items. Four, that I'm aware of. Losing things is common enough among the residents of Twilight Acres. It comes with the territory." She hesitated, bit her lip. "But losing stuff from their *safes* isn't. Two of the four who have supposedly 'lost' their valuables had them go missing from their in-home safes. I believe someone is stealing from them, taking advantage of them," she said, her voice hardening with anger. "And I want to know who."

A slow grin had begun to spread across Jeb's face—which he tried unsuccessfully to smooth away with his hand—and his eyes twinkled with knowing humor. Almost like she'd confirmed a suspicion.

Sophie paused, lifted a brow. "What?"

"Nothing," he said lightly. "Please continue."

Why did she get the sensation that he knew as much or more about this than she did? She shot him a wary look. "These safes were installed when the complex was built and new codes are programmed when a new resident moves in."

His smile faded and he leaned forward. "Who has access to the codes?"

"Other than the resident, only Marjorie."

"I see."

No doubt he did. "Personally, I don't think Marjorie is guilty of anything—she's utterly devoted to the residents and the village."

That blue gaze sharpened. "Then why did you break into her office?"

"Because I wanted to see how accessible the codes were, to see if perhaps someone could have looked at them without her knowledge."

"You're a whole helluva lot better at this than I am," he muttered grimly.

"Sorry?"

"Nothing. Go on. Did you find anything?"

She winced, shook her head. "Not the codes, anyway, which was what I was looking for. Her computer is password protected and there's one locked drawer in the bottom of her desk, which I couldn't get open. It's possible that the code file is in there, but I doubt it. In all probability, it's on the computer, but the likelihood of someone knowing her password is slim to none." Boo leapt into her lap and she stroked his silky fur. "She keeps good records though," Sophie added. "She's got detailed files on everyone."

He made a moue of agreement. "That could come in handy."

"That's what you're doing here, isn't it?" she asked, wondering why it had taken her so long to put it together. "You're investigating the thefts."

He nodded, gave his head a small wondering shake. "I am. Rather poorly, it would seem." He passed a hand over his face. "Geez."

"Ah, I doubt that," Sophie told him, eying him

consideringly. "You'd never tolerate a poor performance, most especially out of yourself."

He glanced up, a hint of surprise lighting his gaze. He studied her again, his eyes narrowing slightly in bewilderment, as though he was not only interested in trying to figure out what was going on in her head, but that it was somehow imperative. Necessary. "What makes you so sure?"

She lifted her shoulder, didn't just meet his gaze, but held it. "Intuition. I'm good at reading people."

A beat slid to three. "I've been told I'm not easily read."

Ah. So that was it. *She* was getting into *his* head and he wasn't used to it. For whatever reason, that little bit of insight settled warmly around her heart. She hummed under her breath. "Perhaps the person who told you that didn't speak the right language."

There, Sophie thought. Chew on that.

# 8

"So, AM I still at the top of your list?" Sophie asked, absently stroking the cat sprawled across her lap.

He envied that cat.

Jeb swallowed a sigh, suddenly exhausted, still disturbed by her speak-the-right-language comment. What did she mean? That he'd just never met anyone capable of understanding him? That couldn't be right, because even Judd couldn't always get a bead on him. Granted it was rare, but it did happen. He winced, remembering his phone, and made a mental note to call first thing in the morning to get a replacement.

Was she still at the top of his list? she wanted to know. She, of the double fence and sexy dress and melting eyes and hot mouth.

"No, not that one, anyway," he said, resting his head against the back of her couch. She'd never truly been there to start with, but now didn't seem like the time to tell her that. Her house smelled like cinnamon and yeast and a low fire burned on the hearth, crackling merrily.

"Oh? There's more than one list?"

"You've been officially moved to the top of my pain-in-the-ass list, but you are no longer the prime suspect in my investigation." Eyes closed, he laughed softly. "Happy now?"

"I was the prime suspect? Really?" she asked disbelievingly. "Why?"

"Because in the preliminary search, one of our agents found a complaint about you in an online review of the community. The reviewer accused you of taking a piece of jewelry from a resident."

She inhaled sharply.

He turned his head and cracked one eye open. "You don't ever Google yourself?" He winced. Shit, that sounded dirty. "I didn't mean... Er..."

Her ripe mouth curled into a wide grin and her eyes twinkled with humor. "My grandmother would threaten to wash your mouth out with soap."

"You know what I mean," he said.

"I do," she admitted. "And no, I have never Googled myself," she said, giggling. Her face fell. "But clearly that is something that I need to start doing if there are slanderous allegations against me being reported in cyber space."

"They didn't say that you'd *stolen* it, only that you'd *taken* it," he pointed out.

Her shrewd gaze narrowed. "Ah. Accepted it, you mean?" She sighed. "Well, in that case, I am guilty. Cora gave me a cameo pendant. It had been a gift from her husband, one he'd bought her during their honeymoon in Rome. I suspected that her family didn't like it, but since it wasn't theirs and Cora wanted me to have it, I couldn't refuse."

Jeb smiled. "I can see where that would have been difficult. She doesn't seem like the type to take no for an answer."

She snorted. "I'll say. How the hell do you think I ended up in this dress?"

Jeb let his gaze drift slowly over the dress in question and, by default, the body beneath it. Naturally, his own body reacted accordingly. Heat flooded his groin and his fingers itched to touch her. "I can't fault her for that, I'm afraid. You look beautiful."

He could see the pulse hammering in her throat from where he sat, watched her gulp, her gaze sliding along his thigh. "Thank you," she murmured. A frown suddenly marred her brow and she winced, then nudged the cat off her lap and stood. "I'd better put some antiseptic on that," she said, nodding at his fingers.

He shook his head. "Nah. Don't trouble yourself. I'm fine." He'd had much worse. *Much*, much worse, as a matter of fact, but was touched that she seemed so concerned. He wasn't used to having anyone make a fuss over him—anyone except his mother, of course—and it felt odd…but nice.

"It's no trouble," she said, heading toward the

door. Just as she would have went through, she grabbed the jamb, stopped short, wheeled around and looked at him. A sheepish smile tugged at her lips. "Can I get you something to drink, Jeb?"

He grinned, chewed the inside of his cheek. So he'd been upgraded to guest status then? Sweet. "Do you have any liquor?"

"Johnny Walker."

He lifted a brow. Annie Oakley knew her scotch. "Red?"

She nodded haltingly. "I've got Red. I've also got Blue."

He whistled low, pleasantly astonished. Blue was as legendary as rare. "You're willing to waste your good scotch on a trespasser?"

She lifted her chin. "I'm willing to *share* my good scotch with a partner."

"You'll help me then?" He'd assumed that she would since she'd already taken it upon herself to look into the thefts, but he hadn't officially asked her yet.

"In any way I can," she told him, determination ringing in her tone. "This person isn't just taking a piece of jewelry, they're taking a memory. Lila's father had given her that necklace for her coming-out party. She's heartbroken that it's gone and she suspects her daughter, which has undoubtedly caused resentment."

"Do you think the daughter took it?"

Sophie considered the question before responding, which he liked. "I don't know. Lila said Monica had only been concerned with the monetary value of the piece, but that it had been insured." Her brow puckered. "She never said if Monica knew the necklace was insured."

"That's something we're going to need to know."

"I can ask her."

Jeb grinned at her. "I'm counting it on it."

She returned his smile, then disappeared into the other room. While she was gone, he put a few more logs on the fire, pleased when the timber took flame. He liked that she'd opted for a working fireplace instead of gas. Gas might be more user-friendly, but there was nothing so satisfying as the scent and sound of a real blaze.

A cursory glance around her living room revealed a good deal about his new "partner." She had a keen eye for good electronics, comfortable furniture—some of it repurposed, like the antique traveling trunk that doubled as her coffee table—and vintage prints. Some he recognized—the Parrish's, for instance—but others he couldn't place.

A handmade quilt lay folded over the back of the couch, suggesting she spent a lot of time curled up with a blanket, and a stack of books rested on the end table. Everything from the classics to current popular fiction. He browsed her DVD collection and felt his lips twitch. A fellow Dr. Who fan.

A fellow Dr. Who fan with a double fence around her place, who'd looked momentarily terrified when she thought he'd been paid to follow her, almost as if he would have done her harm. And she knew her way around a rifle. He'd also noticed that she'd absently rubbed her arm, or more specifically the five inch scar on the inside of it. Up until this point she'd been wearing long sleeves, so he hadn't caught a glimpse of it until tonight. It was faded, which indicated she'd had it awhile and it would have hurt. The unconscious reaction coupled with the fear told him that it hadn't been an accident—it had been deliberate—and she was terrified of the person who'd given it to her.

The urge to protect had been plaguing him since he'd met her, but it was a living, breathing thing inside him now. He wanted to pummel the hell out of whoever had hurt her. He wanted to make them afraid. He wanted to pay them back in kind for what they'd put her through.

Though he desperately wanted to probe her about it, to ask more questions, he couldn't bring himself to do it. Some pains were too difficult to share, a fact he knew all too well himself. Some burdens weren't lifted with a conversation, they were lanced, like a boil.

He couldn't ask that of her. Wouldn't.

She returned to the living room then, the first aid kit under one arm, the whiskey beneath the other, and a pair of crystal tumblers in her hands.

He hurried forward. "Here, let me help you with that," he said, rescuing the whiskey first.

"Thanks," she murmured. She set everything else down on the trunk.

He gestured to the bottle. "Mind if I pour?"

She shook her head, her lips twitching. "Not at all. You're really excited about this, aren't you?"

"'Pleased' is the word I think you're looking for," he said. "I've never had the Blue."

"Then you're in for a treat. It was my grand-mother's favorite," she said. "She was Scottish. A war bride. She was only seventeen years old when my grandfather brought her over here. She said she was willing to leave her country for him, but she wouldn't give up her name." A sigh slipped through her lips. "And she never did. She was an O'Brien until the day she died."

"So she was your maternal grandmother then?" Jeb took the top off and carefully distributed the liquor into their tumblers, then handed one to her.

"No, paternal." She raised her glass and clinked it against his. "To a new start."

Paternal? Wouldn't Sophie have taken the grand-father's name then? After all, it would have been the same as her father's. How could she be an O'Brien. Unless she'd chosen to be…

His gaze tangled with hers. "To a new start," he repeated. He lifted the glass to his lips without ever taking his eyes off of hers. Anticipation spiked as the whiskey settled smoothly on his tongue, smokey and sweet. Just like her, he thought, watching her savor the rich amber liquid.

He hummed appreciatively, winced as the fire sizzled pleasantly down his throat. "Nice," he murmured. "Thank you."

"You're welcome." She smiled, almost shyly, then gestured to the couch. "Take a seat and I'll work on those cuts."

He did as she asked, shifting his tumbler to his other hand. She settled in next to him, opened the first aid kit, then reached for his hand, wincing as she inspected the gash in his palm. "I'll try not to go too Nurse Ratched on you," she said, her small fingers inspecting his damaged skin.

He stared broodily at her, unable to help himself. "Hey, I'm just glad you didn't shoot me."

Her lips twitched. "Me, too. Mild abrasions are within my scope, but a gunshot wound is beyond my talents." She carefully cleaned the negligible wound, chewing absently on her bottom lip while she worked.

He wished she wouldn't do that. Her mouth was distraction enough, without her sinking her teeth into it. And watching her mouth while she was touching him, even if it was only to bandage a few shallow cuts, was…provoking.

"Was being Foy's grandson the only untrue part of your cover story?" she asked.

Firelight brought out the red in her hair, Jeb noticed, and cast a warm glow over her face. This close he could see a series of ginger freckles across her pert nose and he found them strangely adorable. He was a freckle man. Who knew?

"Depends," he said. "What did you hear?"

Finished with one injury, she moved onto his fingers. "That you were former military. A Ranger."

"What do you think, Nancy Drew?" he drawled, interested in her response. What did she see when she looked at him? Aside from those disturbing bits of insight she'd already exhibited.

She nodded at his glass, indicating that he should move his drink to his other hand. He did, and shifted closer to her on the couch, so that she could more easily reach him. "Oh, I never doubted that part," she told him. "I was just looking for confirmation."

He took another drink, felt the warmth of the alcohol burn through his blood. "It's true," he said. "I came out a few months ago and went to work for a private security company in Atlanta. Rose-Marie Wilson's family hired us and I was assigned to the case. It's my first, as it happens, so I'd like to make a good impression."

"I'm sure you did or they wouldn't have hired you." She made a nonsensical noise under her breath, then frowned at his hand. "This one is worse. I'm going to have to put a bandage on it."

He was past caring. At this point he would have let her wrap his whole damned arm in gauze if it meant she'd keep touching him. Funny how something so seemingly innocuous could elicit such a strong reaction.

But her fingers were cool and tender, her profile achingly sweet, and every bit of desire—every last fiber of this unholy attraction—seemed to boil up from beneath his skin. Heat slithered into his groin, tightening his balls.

"There," she said, looking up at him. She stilled at his expression and her smile faltered. "All d-done."

No, he was the one who was done, Jeb thought fatalistically. No doubt he'd been done the day he met her. He'd just been too ignorant to realize it.

SOPHIE'S HEART SKIPPED a beat in her chest and, though she'd finished tidying up those scratches, she still kept Jeb's hand in hers. She should probably let it go—and had intended to, really—but when she'd glanced up and caught him looking at her like *that*…

No man had *ever* looked at her like that.

Like he wanted to lay her out like dinner on the ground and lick her up with a spoon. Like he wanted her as much as she wanted him. Like every depraved thought that had flitted through her mind the last couple of days hadn't been original at all, because he'd thought of them first and more often.

Impossibly, it made her hotter.

Longing twisted through her, tying her up in knots, and her mouth watered while the rest of her body had decided to liquefy and simmer. She longed to touch more of him, to slide the tip of her thumb across the slope of his brow, to taste the skin on the highest part of his cheek, where she knew it would be the softest.

She had never, ever wanted a man more than she did him right now.

Ever.

And she instinctively knew she never would again. He had some sort of mystical power over her, an appeal that called to her on a purely visceral level. Not that she didn't find him fascinating, because she did. She liked being able to predict those inscrutable faces—the man behind the mask, as it were—and she especially liked that she appeared to be the only person who could do it. Take now, for instance. For all intents and purposes, he still looked every bit as lethal and intimidating as always.

But she could tell that the alcohol had mellowed him out, easing some of the tension from his shoulders and his eyes—that purely remarkable shade of blue—had gone all heavy-lidded and sultry-looking. Combined with that perpetual sulky, sensual mouth he looked especially hot...wicked, even.

And if he didn't stop looking at her like that, she was going to be in serious trouble.

"It's getting late," he said, his gaze dropping hungrily to her mouth.

"I'm sure Foy is worried about you."

He snorted, a chuckle startled out of him. "Foy locked me out of the house until two a.m. last night. He had a guest over," he drawled. "And he was especially hopeful about Mary and her inability to hold her sangria tonight."

Sophie grinned, not the least bit surprised. "Foy is definitely the resident Romeo."

He passed a hand wearily over his face. "Foy is a pain in the ass."

She grinned. "But he's not at the top of your pain-in-the-ass list, is he? Cause that's my spot. Undeserved," she said with a feigned, wounded shrug. "But what can a girl do?"

He hesitated, arched a hopeful brow. "A girl could give me her couch for the night."

The idea of him spending the night at her house made her belly clench. Too much temptation, too easily accessible. Too close. But the idea of saying no never occurred to her. It *was* late, and it was a thirty minute drive back into the city. For him to make the trip not knowing whether or not Foy was going to let him into the house seemed absurd when he was already here.

"You're welcome to the couch, but I've got a guest bedroom upstairs."

He released a sigh. "You're an angel of mercy."

More like a glutton for punishment, Sophie thought, but warmed at the compliment all the same.

"An angel of mercy with excellent taste in alcohol," he added, gesturing to the bottle. "And one who knows her way around a twelve-gauge shotgun." His twinkling gaze snagged hers and he grinned. "If you can fry an egg without letting the edges get all crispy and gross, you'd be a top contender in The Perfect Woman contest."

"Ah, I see why you've asked to spend the night," she said. "You're drunk. Off three inches of scotch."

"I'm not drunk," he said, smiling. "I'm…warm. A couple of ticks behind buzzed maybe, but not drunk." He inclined his head. "That's good stuff."

She was "warm" too, but could only attribute a minor portion of it to the alcohol. Of course, she hadn't finished hers, so…

"Come on," she said. "Let me show you upstairs." She released his hand, immediately missing its warmth, then stood and headed toward the hall. A thought struck and she shot him a look over her shoulder. "Shouldn't you call Foy and let him know not to expect you?"

"Can't," he said matter-of-factly. "My phone is in the pond."

Sophie felt her eyes round, started mounted the stairs. "What? Why? How did it get there?"

"It's not important," he said. "It wasn't my finest moment. But if I could use your phone to send a text, I'd appreciate it. Judd's going to flip a bitch if he doesn't hear from me soon." His tone was a bit grim and held a degree of certainty.

Sophie opened the bedroom door, ushering him inside. "Who's Judd? Your boss?"

Jeb glanced around the room, made a moue of approval. "My twin. This is nice, thanks. I've been sleeping on a futon at Foy's."

Another jolt of shock moved through her. "You're a twin. There are two of you?" she asked faintly. She gulped. That was hardly fair to the world, was it?

He grinned. "We're not identical," he said, humor lighting his gaze. "But we're closely bonded."

"A twin connection, you mean?"

He nodded, didn't elaborate further.

"That's cool," she said. "So you're close?"

A dark chuckle emerged from his throat. "Uncomfortably, at times."

She envied him that. Her brother was two years older, but she never remembered being anything but afraid of him. He'd been the perfect blend of the worst of her parents, a sociopath with a violent streak.

Sophie nodded, unable to contribute. "Right," she said. "There are clean linens on the bed. You can use the hall bath—I've got my own—and there are towels and washcloths in the linen closet and a spare toothbrush in the drawer next to the sink. Let me just go and grab my phone. And I'm going to lock up while I'm downstairs. I'll only be a minute."

By the time she'd arrived back upstairs, he'd removed his shoes and socks, set the heels against the wall and had stripped off his shirt. He stood, barechested, his slacks unbuttoned, but not unzipped, and was in the process of hanging his shirt on the bedpost when she walked in. Lamplight glowed over his gleaming skin, casting shadows over the muscled planes of his body. He was glorious, a living, breathing testament to the ultimate male form. There were scars, too, of course—evidence of war—and she ached to kiss each one, to thank him for bearing them for their country.

A tattoo encircled his right bicep, which at first glance looked almost tribal, but a closer peek revealed it was the sign of the Gemini, repeated over and over. She felt a grin curl her lips.

"I'll have to tell Cora," she said, handing him her phone.

A question appeared in his gaze as he accepted it, the muscles rippling beneath his skin. Her stomach clenched and heat flooded her womb. "That you've got a tattoo," she added a bit unsteadily. She shook herself, blinked, determined to look at something besides his splendid abs. "She said you've have ink," she explained.

He glanced at the tattoo, as though he'd forgotten that it was there. "Right. Yes. Judd has the same one, but it's on his left arm. We got them after we graduated Jump School." He keyed in a few lines of text, sent it, then handed her phone back over.

"He was in the military as well?"

"He's still in the military," he said, an odd shutter falling over his gaze. He glanced away—so that she couldn't see his face?—and smoothed a finger over the coverlet. "He's on leave right now, in Crete, which is why he's had access to a cell phone, otherwise communication is spotty."

She winced, wondering what had made him

suddenly shut down. The wall had come down so quickly, she'd nearly recoiled. "That must suck."

He met her gaze once more. "It does," he said, expelling a breath. "But it is what it is. We'll adjust."

Meaning they hadn't yet. Interesting. Jeb had told her earlier that he'd come out of the military a couple of months ago and gone to work for a security company. At the time it had seemed like such an innocuous statement, one that didn't signify...but it clearly did. Why had he come out of the military? Why had he abandoned what should have been a life-long career? Particularly when his brother— his twin—was still serving?

Something horrible had happened, Sophie thought, studying him. Because only something substantial would have made this man switch course mid-stream. She knew it as well as she knew that the world was round, that the sky was blue, the grass green.

To her surprise, he took a step forward, lessening the distance between them, putting his bare skin within arm's length of her fingers. Too close. Startled, Sophie swallowed.

"Do you remember the song we danced to tonight?" he asked, his voice low, a little rough and unsteady. He sidled a little closer. Or had she moved? She couldn't be sure. Either way she could feel the heat coming off his skin, could smell the tang of the orange in the soap he'd used.

"I—I do."

His gaze slid hungrily over her face, along her cheek, her eyes, lingered on her mouth. "Remind me of the title, please."

She moistened her lips, her own gaze dropping inexplicably to his mouth. Her knees wobbled. "Just a Kiss."

"I agree," he said, closing the distance between them. He framed her face with both hands, his thumbs sliding over her jaw, then drew her to him and lowered his mouth to hers. Sophie went up on tiptoe, vibrated like a tuning fork, then looped her arms around his neck and…melted.

A tornado of energy, of sensation, whirled from the bottoms of her feet to the top of her head, wrapping her in an eye of unparalleled joy, infinite desire. Longing bubbled up inside of her, bittersweet and curiously sacred, and she clung to him, feeling the power in his touch, the desperation in his lips. His were soft against hers, but firm and his tongue expertly probed the inner recesses of her mouth.

A low moan hummed against her lips and she smiled when she realized that it was his. He seemed to tense against her, almost as though he'd been shocked into stillness—in awe—then he'd pushed his hands into her hair, angled her head and deepened the kiss. Like he was drowning. Like he couldn't breathe. Like he needed her. He tasted like good scotch whiskey, spring rain, a new beginning…familiar. Hauntingly so, which was impossible and yet..the sensation was there all the same.

Warmth flooded her womb, tingled hotly in her nipples, made her breasts heavy with longing. Her stomach fluttered, the backs of her thighs quaked with a shiver and she could feel the pulse beat hammering between her legs.

Jeb wrapped her closer, one massive hand on her face, his thumb sliding reverently over her cheek, while the other hand slid down her back and settled hotly on her ass. He gave a little squeeze, lifting her up so that the evidence of his arousal rode high on her belly.

*He was...*

*That was...*

*Oh, sweet heaven.*

His fingers trembled against her face, proof that she affected him as much as he affected her. He groaned softly, the sound ringing with regret, then slowly ended the kiss and rested his forehead against hers.

His brooding gaze burned with longing, a hint of futility and something else, something she couldn't quite decipher. Wonder, maybe?

"Just a kiss," he murmured, his breath and tone equally, gratifyingly, unsteady. "For now."

Quivering from one end of her body to the other, Sophie nodded.

Because that sounded like a promise.

# 9

DESPITE THE FACT that he'd been wound tighter than a spool of thread, Jeb slept like the dead in Sophie's guest bedroom. Sleep had eluded him for a couple of hours after she'd retired to her own room—probably because he'd imagined he could hear the whine of the zipper when she'd removed her dress—followed by the sound of her shower starting immediately thereafter. The hard-on he'd been fighting delivered a knock-out punch with that one, because he couldn't think about her being in the shower without thinking about her being naked. And wet.

He shifted and continued his trek to her barn. Though he hadn't heard her get up or go out of the house—mildly disconcerting, all things considered—she'd left a note taped to the coffeepot citing her whereabouts should he wake and find her gone.

That kiss must have done more than scramble his loins—it must of fried his brain as well. Honestly, he'd been thinking about kissing her for days—looking at her mouth, longing for the taste of her. He'd wanted it with an intensity that had left him nothing short of baffled.

But nothing could have prepared him for the act itself, or more significantly, the feelings it would provoke. The instant he'd touched her lips to his, felt the sweet slide of tongue into his mouth, that jerk behind his naval had given a massive yank he'd felt to the soles of his feet…then the knot he'd been carrying around in his belly—the one that had grown tighter every time he'd clapped eyes on her—suddenly loosened and unfurled, relaxing with a release so achingly perfect he'd felt the relief of it all at once. It was like his middle had slipped an unknown tourniquet and the feeling of happiness and contentedness, desire and need had welled up within him, filling him so completely he was hard pressed not to collapse beneath the weight of it.

If merely kissing her did this to him, then he couldn't imagine what it would be like when he finally bedded her. And, he would. He had to. It wasn't a matter of exercising restraint or using good judgment or even the power of his baser instincts.

He needed her. He *needed* to get inside of her, to hold her and taste and feel her greedy little body beneath his. And every beat of his heart, every determined, rhythmic push of his blood through his veins, only intensified the sensation, only heightened his awareness of it.

It was terrifying.

Other than failure, Jeb had never been afraid of anything in his life. He'd walked into battle a dozen times over, had been as close to death as anyone was capable of being just as often and yet, he'd never been afraid. Wary, maybe. Careful? Always. Hell, he didn't have a death wish. But one didn't join the military without coming to terms with their own mortality pretty damned quick. Fear could get you killed.

That he was afraid of this woman—this extraordinarily ordinary, gun-wielding, soap-making, goat farmer—was nothing short of inconceivable. He released a pent-up breath.

But there it was.

Jeb smothered a laugh and shook his head. Clearly he'd lost his mind. Rather than lingering on that thought, he took a moment to survey her property with the benefit of daylight. Ducks, geese and swans glided along the top of the large pond in front of her house and chickens clucked from a nearby pen. Farther down the lane nearest the barn, half a dozen goats gobbled feed from a trough, while a lone one struggled to get its head out of the fence.

Not the brightest of animals, goats, Jeb thought. Tsking under her breath, Sophie emerged from behind the pen, a cup in her hand. Dressed in a long-sleeved flannel shirt, a pair of jeans and her now infamous muck boots, she looked adorable. Her cheeks and nose were pink from the morning chill and a pink camouflage hat covered the top of her head.

"Come on now, Jenny," she called. "I don't have time for this."

"Why not?" Jeb asked, setting a foot against the fence railing. "Are we in a hurry?"

She started and her gaze found his. A smile slid over her lips, lighting her whole face. Something in his chest squeezed almost painfully.

"Not particularly, but she does this every morning. She's not as smart as the other goats and they pick on her. That's why she won't eat with them." She bent down and carefully angled the goat's head back through the fence, then put the cup up under its nose and rubbed its head. "Here, sweetheart," she cooed indulgently. "Fight back today, would you? Give 'em hell."

Jeb grinned. "I didn't know being a motivational speaker came along with this job."

She shrugged, gave the animal one last pat. "I'm always a cheerleader for the underdog."

Because she'd been one? Jeb wondered. Because she had firsthand experience of the inequity? Or, like him, was she just wired that way? Possibly both, he imagined. He cast a sweeping glance around her farm, noting the tidiness of everything. No weeds, no debris, no downed trees or old stumps. A pair of peacocks—one male and one female—walked slowly by, pecking at bits of leftover grass in their path. Despite their "cry"—he suppressed a shudder, remembering—they were truly beautiful birds.

"You've got a lovely place here," he said. It was warm and inviting, nice and lived in.

"Thank you," she said, coming over the fence. "It's a lot of work, but I enjoy it and it's home. I couldn't imagine living anywhere else."

"You're awfully isolated out here," he remarked, scanning the front edge of her property, eyeing the fence.

She peeked into the cup in her hand, to avoid looking at him, he suspected. "I've got everything I need to take care of myself."

"The fence—both of them—look relatively new." He was fishing and she knew it.

"I put them in after Gran died. Some of the family wasn't happy with the terms of her will." She arched a brow and smiled. "I see you found the sweatshirt I left out for you." Her lips twitched. "It almost fits."

Ah, yes, he thought, poking a tongue inside his cheek. The sweatshirt in question was John Deere green, with the infamous logo on the breast. It was a large. No doubt it would have swallowed her, but it was admittedly a little tight on him. Paired with his tuxedo pants and dress shoes, he looked ridiculous. But his shirt was ruined and without another to go under the equally torn tuxedo coat, he'd no doubt look like a male stripper.

He'd elected for ridiculous instead.

And as a diversionary tactic, bringing it up had worked well. It had almost made him forget that she'd actually revealed something. Some of the family wasn't happy with Gran's will? And that had required this sort of fortification? A fence inside a fence. The first fence he could understand—it was the first line of defense, designed to keep people out. The motion sensors were a brilliant touch. They alerted her to an intruder and gave her ample time to either ambush them—like she had him, which still boggled the mind—or to alert the authorities and lock herself out of harm's way.

He'd noted the locks on all the doors and windows—the sensors there as well—and the loaded gun cabinet next to the door this morning. She was ready. She was prepared. And she was clearly determined *not* to be a victim.

But from who? A member of her family? An image of her rubbing that scar suddenly emerged in his mind's eye and his stomach tightened with dread. She'd taken her paternal grandmother's name, had presumably changed it from that of her father's. A tingling eddied through his fingers, across the back of his neck.

*Her father? That's* who she was afraid of? It was and he knew it. Every bit of intuition he possessed told him that it was true. Shock and anger rocketed through him and bile tickled up the back of his throat. He'd already asked Charlie to do some deeper study into her background, but she'd been looking under the wrong name. No wonder she hadn't found anything that threw up a red flag. As soon as he went in this morning to get a new phone, he'd update her and see what she could find out. He had to know why Sophie was this spooked, what had happened to make her so afraid of the one man who was supposed to love and protect her. He couldn't imagine the betrayal, couldn't wrap his head around it.

But he knew this—nobody was going to lay a finger on her on his watch.

Hadn't he felt it all along? The vulnerability? The baffling urge to protect? It's because she needed it. Desperately.

"I did find it, thanks," he said, pulling at the shirt in an attempt to stretch it a bit more. "An old boyfriend's?" he asked, dreading the answer to that question. The idea of her kissing anyone else—he couldn't push his mind past a single kiss, because it flatly refused to go there—made him want to tear his hair out by the roots and howl.

She shot him a look. "No," she told him. "Come on, I need to get a few things from the shop." She gestured toward a building behind her house. A miniature version of the house, it sat roughly thirty feet from her back door. Convenient, but separate. "They gave me the sweatshirt when I bought my tractor," she explained. "Large and Extra Large were my only choices."

He winced. "I would have preferred Extra Large."

Her lips twitched. "I'll bear that in mind next time."

"You know how to drive a tractor?" he asked, shoving his hands into his pockets. Why was he not surprised? "You just scored another point in The Perfect Woman contest."

"I try," she said, laughing softly. She pushed through the front door of the little building and the scent of citrus and vanilla immediately rose up to meet him. A quick look revealed a showroom of sorts, with lots of different soaps and lotions arranged around the room, grouped according to scent. Sophie slid behind the desk at her computer, clicked through a few screens, then the whine of the printer reached his ears. "Right," she said. "Feel free to take a look around." She picked up a basket. "I've got to pull a few orders together."

Taking advantage of the chance to learn more about her, he strolled around the room, then made his way to the back, where the actual work took place. Soaps in different stages of production filled large square molds, little round molds and a big knife, similar to a paper cutter sat in the middle of one table. Bits of precut fabric, satin ribbon and her label on another, obviously where the finishing work happened. Various ingredients lined shelving attached to one wall, lots of essential oils and things he didn't recognize. A stove and refrigerator rounded out the room and her iPod docking station sat on the window sill. There was no chair, even at the finishing station, indicating that she was on her feet for the entire process. It was much more labor intensive than he'd realized, obviously, Jeb thought, impressed.

"This is incredible," he told her. "You do everything yourself, from start to finish."

She nodded, seemingly pleased. "I do," she said, then darted him a sheepish look. "It's the only way to ensure quality control."

He smiled and inclined his head. "Ah, I see. Control issues, huh? Is it because you're the only one who can do it right or because you don't want to let anyone else help you?"

She considered him for a minute, her melting brown gaze fixed on his. Reading him. Seeing things no one else could see. "Hmm. Do I detect the voice of experience in that question?"

Unnerved, a bark of laughter rumbled up his throat. She *had* to quit that. "It's vaguely familiar," he said, rubbing the back of his neck.

She laughed, the sound low and knowing. "Oh, I don't think so. *Hauntingly* familiar, more like. Taking orders must have been sheer hell for you," she said, her tone thoughtful. "I'm honestly a little surprised that you ever went into the military at all. But where else are men with honor, a sense of duty and the belief in the greater good supposed to go, huh?" The corner of her ripe mouth lifted in a grin, as if it was a foregone conclusion.

As if she hadn't flipped his world on its end.

In a couple of sentences, after having known him for three days, she'd just summed up his entire military career, as well as his motivation for pursuing it.

He was so stunned, his feet turned to lead and panic punched his heart rate into overdrive.

Was nothing safe from her? Was she going to be able to read every insight into his soul, every carefully locked down secret, every unformed thought that flitted through his head?

Because if that was the case, more than his sanity was in trouble. Gut instinct told him his heart was as well.

SOPHIE WASN'T EXACTLY sure what she'd said that had rooted him to the floor, but clearly she'd rattled him. "Jeb?"

He blinked, seemingly coming out of stupor. "Sorry," he said, his smile strained. "I was woolgathering."

She set the basket on her hip and reached for the door. "Come on," she told him. "I'll fix a little breakfast and we can talk strategy."

"Strategy?"

"For catching the jewel thief," she went on. He closed the door to the shop for her, then beat her to the back door so that he could open it for her, ever the gentleman. In his too small John Deere sweatshirt and tuxedo pants, she thought, stifling a snicker. He should have looked ridiculous—like a proper fool, to tell the truth—but, naturally, he didn't. His shoulders were mouthwatering beneath the too tight fabric and now that she'd seen them bare, in all their muscled glory, she didn't think he could ever look anything short of perfect to her.

She'd relived that kiss a million times since last night, still shivered when she thought about it now. And while he might have been talking to her because she'd been an initial suspect in his investigation, that's *not* why he'd been flirting with her.

She didn't know when anything had ever pleased her more.

This glorious specimen of masculine flesh, this honorable, duty-bound, sweet, funny, frustratingly inscrutable former Ranger wanted...*her*.

She'd be lying if she said she wasn't surprised.

Sophie knew her own worth—she knew that she was a catch, that she was hardworking and clever, devoted and loyal to those she loved, honest and trustworthy. She had many good qualities. But those good qualities and her mind—probably her best one—were packaged beneath a completely ordinary face. She owned a mirror. She knew what she looked like. She was passably attractive, her eyes being her best feature.

But men didn't look at her and swoon, they didn't whistle when she walked by, and they certainly never looked at her and lusted.

But Jeb had.

And it thrilled her to her little toes.

She set her basket on the counter, offered him a

seat and quickly set to work on their food. "Tell me what you know so far," she said. "What have you been able to find out?"

She felt his brooding gaze as it followed her around the kitchen. The back of her neck prickled beneath that unwavering regard. "Not much," he said. "We know from Rose-Marie's family that her brooch was taken from her safe, so that's in keeping with what you've told me about Lila. That pattern holds with Nanette Hearst as well. I was able to talk to her yesterday and, though it took a little bit of effort—she had me looking at every picture she'd ever taken of her cat—" he drawled with a wry smile "—she finally revealed that she'd been certain that the piece had been in the safe."

"Were you able to get a picture of it?" she asked. "So we'll know what we're looking for."

"Not of hers, no. I have one of Rose-Marie's."

Sophie flipped the bacon, then began cutting up a bit of melon. A quick check of the eggs revealed they weren't quite ready. "I don't have a picture of Lila's, but it would be easy enough to get. She's wearing it in one of the photographs on her mantle. I would know it if I saw it again."

"It should be easy enough to snap a picture of it with a cell phone," he said. He released a breath. "That still leaves Pearl McIntosh. Unfortunately, I haven't had any luck finding her."

"She's been visiting family in the city. She's supposed to be back today. Her book club is meeting and she's not going to miss that."

"Do you think you could talk to her?"

"I can." A thought struck. "Does Foy know about all of this?"

"He does," Jeb told her.

"I'm surprised he didn't offer to help you."

Jeb hesitated. "I'm not convinced that he actually believes that anything has been taken."

"You should have told everyone that you were his nephew," she said. "It's pretty much common knowledge that he and Annie didn't have any kids."

He winced. "Actually, they did. A boy, but he was stillborn."

Shocked, Sophie turned to look at him more fully. "What?" she breathed. "How do you know that?"

"Because he told me. Last night, while I was waiting for you." He swallowed, then gave his head a regretful shake. "Sad stuff. Tragic."

She'd known Foy for years, considered him one of her closer friends at Twilight Acres and, though she'd heard many stories about his Annie, the one he'd shared with Jeb, obviously, was one she'd never heard. She didn't think anyone else on site had heard it either. Foy was the reigning king of Twilight Acres. News about him travelled fast. Tragic news would have travelled faster.

Jeb arched a brow. "You didn't know?"

Sophie shook her head, bit her lip. "No, I didn't, and I doubt anyone else does either."

Her handsome guest mulled that over. "Oh. Wow."

"Yes, wow. He must have had a reason for sharing something so personal, something he hadn't confided in even his closest friends."

"Would Marjorie know?" he asked.

Sophie chewed the inside of her cheek. "I don't think so. It wasn't in Foy's file."

He grimaced. "I really need to get into her office."

"That's how you caught me, isn't it?" she breathed. She hadn't thought about it last night, but clearly he'd been coming to Marjorie's office for the same reason she had.

He grinned, shrugged. "Yes. When you didn't come back to the dance, I decided that, rather than waste the rest of the evening, I should try to do something proactive, something I was actually getting paid to do. So I left and went over there." He leaned forward, considered her. "How did you get in exactly?"

"Through the French doors in her garden. There's a hide-a-key rock next to the fountain." She grinned at him. "How were you going to get in?"

He sighed softly, eyes twinkling, and shook his head. "By picking an unlocked door, evidently."

"We can go back tonight, if you'd like."

He nodded. "When does Marjorie normally leave?"

"Not until around six, usually," Sophie told him.

"Why don't we grab a bite to eat at the diner?" he suggested lightly. "Then when we leave together, everyone will assume that I'm coming home with you and my absence at Foy's won't seem so notable."

His plan made perfect sense, logical and well-reasoned, but she couldn't help but feel like he was angling for an invitation to spend the night. A thrill whipped through her, swirling around her middle, that "for now" promise ringing in her ears.

She smiled, then turned back to the stove. Ah, the eggs were ready. "Be sure to bring an overnight bag. You can follow me through this gate this time instead of coming over the fence."

"Right," he said, chuckling. "I wouldn't want to risk another injury that required a Band-Aid." He held up his hands, gesturing to the Disney princess one across his knuckle. "I've got to take this off before I get back to Foy's. He'll revoke my Man Card."

Sophie chuckled, plating their food. "Hey, that's all I had on hand. I love Mulan. She's a warrior, too. Carried a sword. Defeated the Huns. I thought she was appropriate."

"Bullshit," he said. "You thought it would be funny to put a girly Band-Aid on my hand."

Sophie laughed, outed, and slid his plate in front of him. She'd already set butter and jam, salt and pepper on the table. "That might have a teensy, insignificant part of my motivation."

"Ha."

She sat down, draped her napkin over her lap and

added a smear of butter to her toast. She peeked over at him, noting the grin on his face with a hefty dollop of satisfaction.

"You made eggs," he said. "With no crispy, gross edges."

Yes, she knew. "The trick is to cook them slowly."

"That settles it. You are The Perfect Woman."

Pleasure bloomed through her chest, pushing a smile it took effort to contain over her lips. "Oh, I doubt that. Perfection is too hard to live up to. I'd rather be ordinary, but skilled."

"Trust me," he said. "You're not ordinary. You're…remarkable," he said, his voice strangely thick, a hint of unmistakable wonder and admiration.

Sophie blushed to the roots of her hair. "I'd argue with you, but that would be stupid. So thank you." She swallowed a bite of fruit. "I think you're pretty damned remarkable, too."

She did. And if the tightness in her chest and the happiness tripping through her veins were any indication, she was half in love with him already.

So much for swearing off men, Sophie thought with a fatalistic sigh. It had been a bad idea from the start, one doomed to failure. And if she was going to fail, better it be *spectacularly* with him than with anyone else.

# 10

"HERE YOU GO," Payne said, handing over a new cell phone. "What did you say happened to yours again?"

"It got wet." True enough, if not completely accurate. He arched a brow. "Is Charlie around?"

"I think she might be in her office. If not, then you can look for her at the bakery down the street. Raw Sugar. Her sister-in-law, Mariette Martin, owns it and she and the baby spend a good bit of time down there." He leaned back in his chair. "Any progress?"

"Yes, a bit. I've talked to Sophie and she's going to help me," he said. He felt a smile tug at his lips. "She was actually investigating the thefts on her own. I caught her in the director's office last night."

Payne's gaze sharpened with interest. "Really? What was she looking for?"

Jeb explained briefly. "She's going to talk to Pearl today, secure a picture of her missing jewelry, and find out if her necklace was taken from her safe. If so, then that narrows things down a bit."

"Yes, it does," Payne said. "And the director is the only person who has access to the codes?"

"Other than the resident, yes, that's the way it looks."

"I'm sensing a but."

Jeb released a small breath and winced. "But I don't think she's guilty," he admitted. "The village is her life. She's intimidatingly efficient. I can't see her rolling through a stop sign, much less stealing jewelry from her residents."

"Is it possible that someone has gotten access to her codes?"

"That's what Sophie was looking for last night, but she didn't find anything. The codes are not easily available, but it's not impossible that someone has managed to get to them. We suspect that the file might be on her computer, but it's password protected."

"Charlie should be able to help you with that." He chuckled darkly. "We all changed the passwords to our computers recently—I changed mine to pure gibberish—and she still managed to get into each one. I had an electronic post-it on my desk top when I turned it on the following morning. 'Nice try, but no cigar, Chief,' she'd said."

Jeb chuckled. Actually, that wasn't why he'd wanted to talk to Charlie—he wanted to talk to her about Sophie—but Payne had an excellent point. "I'll find her."

"Keep me posted."

Jeb promised to do just that, then left Payne's office and went in search of Charlie. Luckily, she was in. He knocked on her doorframe. "Do you have a minute?"

"Sure," she said, smiling in welcome. Married to one of the other agents, Jay Weatherford, and being the first female non-Ranger hired on by the company, Charlie was an interesting woman, one they all seemed to respect. "What can I do for you?"

"Remember how I asked you to dig a little deeper into Sophie O'Brien's history?" he asked, settling into a chair in front of her desk.

"I do," she said, hesitating smally. "I've got to tell you, there just isn't that much to go on. From everything I can tell, she's squeaky clean. She's never even had a traffic ticket."

"That's what I wanted to talk to you about. I've found out a little more about her myself and…I wondered if you could do a little more poking around for me."

"Of course," she told him.

Jeb leaned forward, trying to find the right words to explain his request. "She's clear of any suspicion as far as my case goes," he explained. "In fact, she's helping me."

Charlie's eyes widened. "Oh."

"This would strictly be for my own benefit." He

cleared his throat, feeling heat climb his neck. "It's personal."

Impossibly, her eyes rounded further and when she "oh'ed" again, no sound emerged from her mouth.

"I think she's in some sort of danger, only I can't get it out of her," he added. "Every time I ask her a question, she finds a way to avoid telling me anything. I don't want to press her, but—" He shook his head. "—something's not right. She's afraid of someone. Her father, I think, quite honestly." He told Charlie about the scar on her arm, the double fence, the near panic attack when she thought he'd been hired to spy on her. "She told me last night that her grandmother had kept her maiden name and that she'd taken it. The grandmother she's talking about was her paternal grandmother, so—"

Understanding dawned in Charlie's eyes. "So she purposely abandoned her father's name." She nodded once. "Right. I'll look into it and get back to you."

He breathed a small sigh of relief, caught her gaze once more. "Thanks. And I'd appreciate it if you wouldn't mention this to—"

"Mum's the word," she said. "I could blackmail every one of y'all if I was a dishonest woman. There isn't a man working here who hasn't had me do something similar." She smiled and waved him off. "Don't sweat it."

"There was one other thing," he said. "I need to

get into a password protected computer and I was told that you were the woman to see about that."

"Piffle," she said. "It's child's play." She reached into her desk and handed him a simple USB drive. "Plug this little baby in and it'll do the rest."

He whistled low. "Really?"

"Really. I wrote the program myself. You can even save the files you're looking for onto it."

He looked at it once more, then glanced at her and smiled. "You're a little scary, you know that?"

She preened. "Thanks."

Confident that things were finally moving in the right direction, Jeb left the building and made his way to his truck. Because he knew he couldn't put it off much longer, he decided to go ahead and let his brother know that he was fine. He punched in the number, called up the message screen.

*Other phone is dead. New number. I'm fine.* He paused, winced. Swore.

*It's a woman.*

There, Jeb thought with a smile. That ought to explain everything.

And it wasn't just any woman, either. It was possibly *the* woman. Because he grimly suspected that she was going to ruin him for anyone else, that after everything was said and done, she was going to be the one he wasn't going to be able to let go.

He'd just shifted into reverse when his cell phone rang. "Dammit, Judd, I don't have…" He frowned, not recognizing the number. But it wasn't Judd. "Jeb Anderson," he answered.

"Yes, yes, I know!" Foy snapped. "I called you, didn't I? Why wouldn't I know who I was calling?"

Foy? "But I just got this—"

"Phone," Foy finished. "I've been trying the other number for hours, but you didn't ever answer, so I just called your boss and got the new number from him."

Brilliant. "What did you need, Foy?"

"I need you to get over here and figure out who has stolen my Annie's engagement ring out of my safe, that's what I need! It's gone." Panic and despair made the older man's voice break. "Gone," he repeated. "Someone's taken it. Someone's taken her ring."

Jeb felt his expression darken. "Have you told anyone, Foy?"

"No," he said. "I thought it was best to talk to you first."

"That's right. Keep it to yourself and let me do my job. Sophie's helping me now and we're going to get to the bottom of this."

"Do you have any idea who it might be?"

"Not yet, no," he admitted, unwilling to lie. "But I know who it's not and sometimes that's more important. We'll get Annie's ring back, Foy. I promise."

"You shouldn't make promises it's not in your

power to keep, son," Foy told him, his tone weary. "It only makes you feel helpless when you break it."

"I have no intention of breaking it," Jeb said determinedly. "I'm on my way. Stick around the house because there are some more questions that I need to ask you."

Foy sighed heavily, the sound laden with heartache. "I'm not going anywhere."

He wasn't either, Jeb thought, until he'd nailed this bastard to the wall.

UNABLE TO EAT, Sophie pushed her food around her plate and kept glancing toward Marjorie's office, waiting for the lights to go out.

"Looking every few seconds isn't going to make her leave any faster, Sophie," Jeb told her, shooting her an indulgent smile.

She grinned, tucked her hair behind her ear. "I know. I'm just impatient."

She still couldn't believe that Foy had been a victim. Everyone knew and loved Foy and more importantly, everyone knew how much he'd loved his late wife. It was a shameful thing to take her engagement ring from him. Utterly horrible. She glanced around the diner, took in the beloved faces around her and realized with a sickening since of dread that, more than likely, one of these people was responsible.

Looking more than a little pleased with herself, Cora strolled up to their table. "Evening, Sophie, Jeb."

Sophie nodded at her, returned the grin. "Evening, Cora."

"Y'all are looking like quite the pair," she remarked. "I couldn't help but notice that both of you left the dance a little early."

Sophie was surprised Cora had been able to notice anything at all from last night, all things considered.

"We did," Jeb said. "We ended up at Sophie's place so that we could have a proper chat." He made "a proper chat" sound wicked and depraved, as though they'd done things Cora had only ever read about.

Cora's brows winged up her forehead and she shot a knowing look at Sophie. "*Really*?" she drawled knowingly. "Well, isn't that nice?"

Jeb glanced across the table at her, his gaze so hot she felt her skin scorch. It might have been for Cora's benefit, but it was sending her heart into arrhythmia. "Oh, it was," he remarked, his voice rife with innuendo. "I don't know when I've enjoyed an evening more."

Though there was a hint of truth in that last statement, Sophie nevertheless grinned and kicked him under the table. He grunted with pain and his eyes widened. "It was harmless, really."

"I spent the night," Jeb confided, evidently to punish her for the kick to his shin.

Before Cora's eyebrows completely disappeared, Sophie quickly interjected, "In the guest bedroom.

He spent the night in the guest bedroom and I slept in my own room. We did not sleep together, at all."

Her older friend's expression fell, clearly disappointed. "Oh."

Jeb gestured to Cora, who leaned down and he whispered something in her ear.

Cora gasped delightedly, drew back and shot him a wink. "Atta boy," she said. "I knew you had it in you."

Smiling happily, Cora grinned at her and then twinkled her fingers in goodbye.

"What did you say to her?" Sophie asked suspiciously, her smile taking the heat out of the question.

"That's between me and Cora," he said. "It's a secret."

"You told her you were spending the night again tonight, didn't you?"

His blue eyes twinkled with devilish humor. "I might have said something like that."

She lifted an unconcerned shoulder. "Oh, well. I might have told your brother the same thing, so it's all good."

He choked on his tea. "What?" he wheezed. "My brother? Why are you talking to my brother?"

"Strictly speaking, we're not talking." She popped a fry in her mouth. "We've been texting."

His expression went comically blank. "You've been texting my brother. But—" His eyes widened as understanding dawned. "I texted him from your phone," he said with a resigned nod. "Right."

"He's concerned about you," she told him, eyes twinkling. "He says he's been picking up some weird vibes."

Jeb chuckled darkly. "Oh, he did, did he? Wonderful. Brilliant. I appreciate that."

"I couldn't ignore him," Sophie protested. She withdrew her cell phone from her purse and held it up so that Jeb could see. "See? He even sent me a picture. Isn't this gorgeous?" she said. "That's the view from his apartment. Look at that water. It's so blue. It reminds me of your—" She stopped short. *Oh, hell.*

Naturally, he hadn't missed the slip. A grin tugged at both corners of his lips, making that increasingly dear dimple wink in his cheek. "It reminds you of my what?" he asked.

She took a sip of her drink, looking at a speck on the table. "S'not important."

"What?"

Oh, geez. "It's not important."

"That's cruel," he said. "I sense you were on the verge of paying me a very sincere compliment and now you're refusing." He tsked under his breath, as though he was heartbroken.

"Oh, please," she said with an exasperated sigh, feeling the tops of her ears burn with humiliation. It was a constant state where he was concerned. "I was just going to say that the color of the ocean there reminds me of your eyes." She met his gaze, drawn in, as usual. "You have the bluest eyes I've ever seen." Her breath thinned in her lungs. "They're quite…compelling."

He swallowed. "See? I knew it. A compliment." He looked away and drummed his fingers on the table, almost as if he was embarrassed. "Thank you."

She leaned forward, studied him a little closer. A hint of pink stained his cheeks, confirming her suspicions. For whatever reason, that little bit of color cheered her, made her feel like she wasn't alone in *this*—whatever it was—happening between them. If she could make this badass former Ranger blush with a little compliment about his pretty eyes, then anything was possible, right?

"Can I get you anything else?" Ethel asked, her plump face wreathed in a smile. She looked particularly happy for them, as though she, too, had been a part of the match-making scheme. "A slice of cake? A cup of cobbler?"

Jeb shook his head. "Nothing for me, thanks. I'm fine." He glanced at Sophie and lifted a brow. "Would you like something?"

Sophie shook her head. "No, thanks."

Ethel frowned at her, put a hand against her forehead, checking for a temperature. "You all right, Sophie? You're not getting sick, are you?"

"Er…no," she said, mortified. "I'm just full." Geez, it wasn't like she'd *never* turned down dessert before. Granted, it wasn't often, but it wasn't such a damned phenomenon either.

"But you love my chocolate cobbler," she persisted.

Jeb's lips twitched with humor, the wretch. "I do," Sophie admitted. "But I'm going to pass tonight, all the same."

Ethel tsked. "Nothing to share, even? I could bring two spoons."

"How about an order to go?" Jeb suggested, an odd gleam lighting his gaze. It was almost…wicked. A shiver slid down her spine as his gaze fastened on her mouth and lingered. Remembered heat bloomed on her lips, the taste him of him on her tongue.

"Excellent," Ethel enthused, beaming. "I'll fix that right up for you."

Sophie shook herself and considered him for a moment, her gaze narrowed in thought. "You like chocolate cobbler?" she asked.

He shrugged a single massive shoulder. "I don't know, I've never had it."

She grinned. "Then why did you order it?"

"Because I like chocolate. It reminds me of your eyes," he confided, leaning forward so that he could better look at them. "Melting and sweet and a little sinful."

*Holy hell*, Sophie thought, feeling her jaw go marginally slack. She blinked, almost drunkenly, taken aback at this description, then dredged her vocabulary for some sort of response. She finally settled for, "Oh."

"It was one of the first things I noticed about

you," he said. "They're quite lovely. And so expressive."

She cleared her throat. "Thank you."

"You're welcome. Do you know what else I noticed about you?" he asked, lowering his voice. It was a little rough and foggy and sexy as hell.

She tried to respond, but squeaked instead.

"Your skin. It's beautiful," he said, his gaze tracing her face. "It practically glows with an inner light, one that's just yours. And it's *so* soft," he added, issuing a soft masculine growl. "It makes me wonder what the rest of you feels like, if there are bits that are even softer."

She was going to drool all over herself if she didn't close her mouth, Sophie thought, feeling suddenly under the influence of...something.

*Him*, she realized. *This* is what he did to her. With a few words, he'd turned her body into a puddling pool of heat, her brain to mush.

Need contracted her muscles, vibrated along her nerve endings and warmth mushroomed in her belly, spread up into her breasts, making her nipples tighten behind her bra and her feminine muscles clench. She squeezed her legs together in an effort to alleviate some of the mounting pressure, the desire to squirm.

"Oh," she managed to say again.

Looking entirely too pleased with himself, masculine humor clinging to his grin, he reached across the table and took her hand, pressing a lingering kiss into her palm. Who would have ever thought that was such a sensitive area, that it would have been mysteriously linked to her core? Certainly not her, she thought, sinking her teeth into her bottom lip as sensation flooded her.

"Guess what?" he asked.

Probably, she didn't care. She moaned a little, squeezed her eyes shut, then opened them in a vain attempt to regain some sort of control. "What?"

"Marjorie left five minutes ago."

# *11*

JEB WATCHED AS she blinked the desire out of her eyes, then chuckled as she started and gave her head a shake. "Come on, then," she said. "Let's go."

"Ethel still hasn't brought my to-go order." More to the point, he couldn't get up without everyone noticing that he was...*up*. He should have known better than to taunt her, that it would only result in his own frustration, but he just couldn't seem to help himself.

It was just too damned easy.

And knowing that she wanted him, that he made her hot, that he made her lose control, was so damned powerful it was difficult to ignore. Impossible to resist.

"Forget the to-go order," she said, sliding out of the booth. "Let's go."

Thankfully, Ethel arrived and handed over his container. "Here, darlin'," she said. "If you've got a little ice cream to add to it, then all the better."

Grinning his thanks, Jeb left enough cash to cover the bill, plus a generous tip, then followed Sophie's lead and exited the booth. He was still hard enough to upend the table, but he tugged his sweater down and prayed that no one would notice.

Naturally, she did.

Her eyes dropped below his waist, rounded, then she visibly swallowed. "Oh," she said. "I see."

He chuckled grimly. "Just walk in front of me, would you?"

Seemingly unable to tear her gaze away from his crotch—which, naturally wasn't helping matters—she nodded distractedly and licked her lips. "Right. Sure."

He groaned. "Sophie, you're killing me."

She gave herself a little shake, then blushed. "Sorry. I'm just— That's—"

He wheeled her around and nudged her toward the door. "—distracting," he finished. "Believe me, I know," he added drolly.

Having already agreed upon a strategy for getting into Marjorie's office, Sophie had parked her car close to the director's building in order to make it look like they were simply getting ready to leave. At the last minute, they veered off the lighted path, then snuck into the garden.

Sophie went unerringly to the hide-a-key rock, slipped it from the bottom of the enclosure, then carefully opened the door. She dropped down into a crouch once they were inside the office, then he closed the door, locked it behind him and adjusted the curtain until there wasn't any discernible opening anyone could see through.

"All right," Jeb said. "First things first." He withdrew the USB device he'd gotten from Charlie and plugged it into Marjorie's computer. The screen immediately glowed to life, prompted for the password, then a series of asterisks streaked across the text box and, like magic, they were in. The home screen loaded, revealing a picture of the Twilight Acres sign. He clicked through a few desktop files, grimacing when they revealed nothing.

"Well?" Sophie asked. "Do you see anything suspicious?"

The light from the aquarium glowed touched the side of her face and she was so close, her sweet breath whispered across his ear. "No," he said, trying to concentrate on the task at hand. "Nothing yet."

He loaded her documents and scrolled through them, then felt a smile curve his lips. "Ah," he said. "Bingo."

Finding a file marked simply "Benchmark," which was the name of the safe company, he clicked on it, his anticipation spiking. It withered, deflated, when he was once again prompted for a password.

"Shit," he said. "This file is password protected."

"The little thingy won't work?" she said gesturing to the device. Her terminology made him grin.

"I don't know." He was tempted to remove it, then

install it again just to see what would happen, but was afraid that it would shut the whole computer down, or at the very least, alert Marjorie to the fact that she'd been hacked. The director was obviously very concerned about protecting her privacy and that of her residents, but something was beginning to feel off. Why password protect the document? He attempted to open another file, only to have the same thing happen again.

She protected *every* file? But why? It was almost overkill. Everything couldn't be sensitive, right?

Jeb released a breath. While they were here, he might as well give it a go. He closed out of that screen, launched the document files once more, then removed USB, waited for the tell tale ding, then plugged it back in, opened the file and held his breath.

Once again the little asterisks did their thing and the document materialized on the screen.

Sophie squeezed his shoulder. "Wow, that's handy."

Jeb grinned. Yes, it was, he thought, making a mental note to thank Charlie. He immediately saved the file to the drive, then looked for others that might prove useful.

"I'm going to try to get into this drawer again," she whispered.

He nodded distractedly. "Okay, I'm going to keep poking around in here."

Sophie dropped to her hands and knees, then

crawled up under the big desk, nudging his legs over in the process. His gaze dropped to her luscious rump, displayed to mouthwatering perfection in a pair of worn jeans. Muttering something about Cora and her scrubs, she'd opted for a different outfit today, one that was infinitely more feminine and flattering.

Trying to ignore the sudden flash of heat in his loins, he determinedly directed his attention to the task at hand. He clicked through a few more document files, then on a whim, moved to her pictures. A file called My Happy Place caught his attention. It, too, was protected, but thanks to Charlie's little miracle of technology, it was no match for him.

The first picture loaded and Jeb felt his eyes bug and his jaw go slack. "Holy mother of…"

Sophie stilled. "What?" she asked. "Did you find something?"

"Er…you could say that." He was going to need some bleach for his eyeballs and some sort of memory modification charm, like you'd find in a Harry Potter book.

She abandoned the drawer and wiggled back out from under the desk, then popped and peered at the computer screen.

She inhaled sharply. "Is that…"

"It is," he confirmed tonelessly. "It's Marjorie. In a leather corset, fishnet hose and thigh high boots."

Sophie peered closer, her eyes squinted in confusion. "She looks like she's in some sort of...dungeon."

"Well, the guy she's with is in chains, attached to a wall," Jeb said.

"And she's got a leather riding crop in her mouth." She swallowed, released a sigh. "That explains the red nail polish, anyway."

Jeb clicked through a few pictures, each one more graphic than the next, showcasing Marjorie as an enthusiastic and competent dominatrix. "What nail polish?"

"I found a bottle of red nail polish under her desk last night. It's not anything I've ever seen her wear. Around here, anyway." She blinked owlishly. "Clearly she wears it...other places."

"In her happy place," Jeb told her. "That's the name of the file."

"Wow. I would have never suspected her of something like this. It's..." She shook her head. "I can't even wrap my mind around it."

"And if you didn't imagine she could be a dominatrix, then what does that say about whether or not she could be a thief?"

She paused, shook her head. "I still don't—"

Suddenly a noise from the foyer reached them, a distinct sound of the door opening. Sophie gasped and they shared a look. Jeb gestured under the desk, where she quickly scrambled, then killed the power to the computer. He grabbed the USB, then crowded in under with her, dragging the desk chair into place just as the door swung open.

If that was Marjorie, then they were screwed. And she'd probably beat them, Jeb thought, stifling the inappropriate need to chuckle.

Feeling him shake, Sophie turned her head toward his and shot him a questioning look. He could just make out her perplexed expression and it made him want to laugh all the more. She glared at him significantly, then put her hand over his mouth.

"Stop it," she mouthed silently.

He kissed her hand again, this time touching his tongue to its center.

She stilled, went a little boneless and smothered a moan.

But whoever had come into the office clearly wasn't Marjorie. They didn't turn on the light and didn't come near the desk. Instead, humming lightly under their breath, the person opened the cabinet beneath the aquarium and the sound of lightly splashing water resonated like thunder in the quiet room.

"Hello, my lovelies," the person trilled. It took a second to place the voice—Ethel.

Sophie noticed it too, her gaze finding his once more in the dark. A frown marred her brow, suggesting that it wasn't Ethel's job to clean Marjorie's aquarium.

It would be easier to focus on that little tidbit of information if her breasts weren't pressed right up against his chest. Plump and ripe, the sensual weight

of them sizzled through him, making another part
of his anatomy take notice.

It swelled accordingly.

She noticed.

Jeb shrugged helplessly. What could he say? He
wanted her. He'd made that plain enough over the
past few days. Him having a hard-on, particularly
when she was nuzzled so closely up against him,
shouldn't come as any real surprise.

She bit her bottom lip, smothered some sort of
noise, then dropped her head against the curve of
his shoulder. Her warm breath fanned over his neck,
eliciting another burst of reaction and he felt his
dick stir against her, seeking her like some sort of
carnal divining rod.

To his everlasting joy and torment, she scooted
up and slid her nose along his throat, breathing him
in, then pressed her lips against him, tasting his
neck. And the hell of it? He couldn't move, not without making a sound or knocking something over.
He had to lay there and take it, and the she-devil
knew it.

Jeb bit back a curse as she slipped farther up
along his body, but somehow managed to get an arm
around her, then slip his hand up under her sweater,
touching her sleek, warm skin.

So soft… Softer than he'd dared to imagine.

She answered him with another retaliation of her
own, sliding her hand along his jaw, then turning
his head and pressing her lips against his. Her kiss

was slow and thorough, laced with an undercurrent of desperation and urgency. Her entire little body hummed with it, vibrated like a struck piano wire. She shifted, drawing herself more closely to him and ran her hand down over his chest, then lower still as she cupped him through his jeans.

He would have come up from beneath the table if she hadn't held him down, stilling him with a deeper kiss. Stroking him through his jeans, she sucked his tongue into her mouth, mimicking a more intimate act, and he felt an ooze of pleasure leak from his dick, a warning of what was to come.

Literally.

It seemed impossible that Ethel was in the room with them, messing around with that damned aquarium, but the periodic hum or splash of water would confirm it.

It was mind-boggling. But strangely thrilling, he had to admit.

Not content to merely touch him through his clothes anymore, he felt Sophie's hand at the button on his jeans, felt it give. She couldn't lower the zipper without it giving them away, but she'd used the silent breath he'd sucked in as an opportunity to slide her hot little fingers over the head of his penis, coating him with his own cream.

Jeb set his teeth so hard he feared they would crack.

She was trying to kill him, he decided. Trying to make him have a heart attack.

Rather than let her torture him, Jeb decided a little torment of his own was in order. He carefully nudged her onto her back, then followed her down with a kiss. She tasted like French fries and sweet tea, like seduction, like heaven and he wanted to sink into her so desperately his hands shook from the effort of holding back. He wanted to slide his dick deep into the heart of her, nestle his own hips into the perfect cradle of her wider ones and slake his lust in her soft, welcoming body.

He just *wanted*.

He found the hem of her shirt, then edged it up, pushing his up over her warm, silky skin until he found the lacy edge of her bra. He expertly popped the clasp in the middle, silently thanking the brilliant designer who'd thought of that plan, then felt the cup give way and snag on her nipple.

A brush of his fingers and it was out of the way and her plump, lush breast was in his hand, the beaded nipple thrusting against his palm. He ached to taste it, to feel it rasp across the roof of his mouth.

From the dimmest recesses of his mind, he heard the office door close, felt the silence close in around them once more. They both stilled, then looked at each other. Waited. Heard the exterior door whoosh shut, the tumbler in the lock click into place.

Then he was on her.

Jeb shoved Marjorie's desk chair out of the way,

rolled into the space behind the desk, taking her with him.

She shrugged out of her shirt, removing the bra in the process, then lifted her hips so that he could get her jeans off. Good Lord, she was beautiful. Full, lovely breasts, crested with rosy crowns, the sweet curve of her belly, a thatch of dark curls nestled between her thighs.

He didn't know where to start, which part he wanted to taste first. Rather than wait on him to figure it out, she leaned forward and drew the shirt over his head, then bent forward and pressed her hot mouth against his chest, licking a path along the upper ridge of his right pec. She hummed appreciatively, slipped her greedy hands over his belly and around his back.

Jeb groaned, lowered his zipper and shucked his pants and boxers. She moaned when she saw him, a tiny little mewl of feminine affirmation, of desire, and something about that sound tripped an internal trigger.

"I'm healthy," he breathed, sliding a hand down the middle of her belly, dipping his fingers into the honey pot between her thighs, gratified when she inhaled sharply and arched up into him. He palmed her right breast, then bent and pulled her into his mouth. "You?" he whispered blowing over it, making her shiver.

"Clean and protected," she said, spreading her legs, a silent, desperate invitation.

Jeb nudged her weeping folds, found her gaze and fastened his on it. "Look at me," he said, his voice raw and broken. Every muscle in his body was clenched and ready, bracing him for the unknown. Because this coupling was different—she was different—and every iota of understanding and intuition he possessed told him that when he took her, when he made her his...that was it.

He'd be lost. There'd be no him without her.

Her melting brown eyes caught his and clung. Desire, hunger, fever and something else, something tender and gentle—affection, maybe?—glinted back from him, reflected in her gaze. A soft smile shaped her lips and she sighed as she arched up and pushed herself against him.

"I need you," she said, her voice anguished, desperate. "Please."

*I need you...*

Not just want, but *need*.

And need he understood, because he needed her as well. He had to have her. It wasn't optional. It never had been.

With a guttural groan and a sigh of relief, Jeb pushed into her, slid home, burying himself to the hilt in her heat. Sensation rocked through him, the balls of his feet tingled, his stomach shook, every hair on his body stood on end and his chest squeezed so tightly he could scarcely draw a breath. The world dimmed to black and white, then zoomed back into colors so bright he wondered if he'd ever really seen them before.

She tightened her feminine muscles around him and rocked up, drawing him farther into her body. Her breasts grazed his chest, her soft hands slipped over his back, greedily eating up his skin, and she bent forward and kissed him, her mouth soft and inviting.

She was gorgeous, simply, heartbreakingly beautiful. And above all else, she was *his*.

# 12

OH, HALLELUJAH, Sophie thought as Jeb, hovering above her like a Greek god, poised at her center, the silky head of his penis sliding against her weeping folds. *At last*.

Though it had only been a few days, it felt like she'd been waiting forever for this moment, that her whole life had hinged on the next few seconds, the instant his body met hers.

His tortured gaze bored into hers, pinning her thoroughly. Desire had dilated his pupils, making his eyes a glorious midnight blue and the way he was looking at her, the possessiveness she saw in his gaze as he stared down at her as though she were the most beautiful woman he'd ever seen…

It was enough to make one a little emotional and she found herself blinking back tears, her throat tight.

She'd begged. She'd said please.

And she wasn't ashamed.

With a low moan that sounded as if it had been wrenched from his soul, he pushed into her…and the rest of the world faded away. Sophie sucked in a breath, instantly tightening around him, holding on to him.

He felt magnificent. Right. *Huge.* She arched her hips, meeting his torturously slow, rhythmic thrusts, savoring every thick inch of him as he invaded her body. He bent his big blond head and suckled her breast, pulling at her nipple with his lips, licking it with his tongue. And with every determined sensual assault against her breasts, he plunged into her, seemingly trying to sever the invisible chord that ran between the two.

"You have damned near driven me crazy," he said, thrusting into her over and over again. She could feel the rug at her back, his hot body at her front and her breasts bounced on her chest, absorbing the impact of his magnificent frame as it slid repeatedly into hers. "I've wanted you since the instant I saw you," he confided, as though it were somehow her fault. "Then the want turned to need and I knew—I *knew*—that I wouldn't be able to help myself. That nothing would keep from taking you, having you."

She wrapped her arms around him, bent forward and licked his male nipple, anchored her legs on his hips so that he could come closer, hold her tighter. "I've wanted you, too," she said. "Needed you, too. I looked at you and…melted," she said, laughing softly. "I wanted to lick you from head to toe, fantasized about sucking on your bottom lip."

He moved faster and faster, pistoning in and out of her, his tautened balls slapping against her tender flesh. "Do it now," he said, lowering his head so that she could do just that. She pulled that sulky lip into her mouth, slid her tongue over the soft, plum-like skin and sighed with satisfaction as another wave of sensation bolted through her.

Fire licked through her veins, burning her up from the inside out and she bucked frantically against him. She could feel the first quickening of release as it sparkled deep inside her and every thrust of his body acted like a bellows, fanned the flame, building it higher. She clung to him, arched into him, whimpered and thrashed as she came closer and closer to the inferno that waited for her. And then, without warning, the blaze swept through her, sucking the oxygen out of her lungs, tearing a long, keening cry from her throat as she convulsed around him.

Jeb pounded into her, milking the release, drawing every bit of pleasure from her body. His lips peeled away from his teeth, his beautifully muscled chest heaved and then suddenly, she felt him tense, felt every muscle in his body atrophy as his seed flooded her womb. It pulsed inside of her, spasm after spasm, triggering belated delight deep in her core. He angled deep, held steady, his shoulders shaking as the orgasm broke over him.

He bent and kissed her, his eyes soft, his smile sated and her heart gave an involuntary little squeeze.

"Definitely the perfect woman," he said. He carefully rolled off of her, grabbed a few tissues from the top of Marjorie's desk and handed one to her. Decidedly moist, she appreciated it and did a quick clean-up job, then tossed it into the trash can conveniently located near her head.

The thought made her chuckle.

"What's funny," he asked, dropping down beside her. He propped up on his elbow and peered at her through the darkness.

She gestured to where they were. "Just this," she said. "It's not far off from how I imagined we'd, you know," she trailed off.

She could see his eyes twinkling in the faint light, the dimple in his cheek. "Really? How did you imagine the first time?"

"With my back against the wall, dress around my waist, your pants around your knees, at the dance last night. I kept thinking about it the whole time we were dancing. How I just wanted you to grab hold of me and take me until my eyes rolled back in my head." She rolled her head toward him, smiled and lifted a brow. "Turns out I'm a proper slut."

He swallowed, his jaw a little slack. "You are not a slut," he said. "You just find me irresistible, that's all."

She laughed. "Oh, is that all?" she said drolly.

"It is," he said. "But don't worry, because I'm suffering from the same affliction. While you were thinking about me pinning you up against the wall, I was thinking about dragging you under one of the tables. I'd say that makes us about even, wouldn't you?"

"It makes us crazy," she said. She turned and peeked at him beneath lowered lashes. "But I kind of like it."

"Do you know why I really wanted that chocolate cobbler?" he asked, his hand coming up to play with her breast. He circled her nipple with his thumb, making goose-bumps pebble over her skin.

Sophie released a faltering breath. "Why?"

"Because I want to paint you in it and lick it off. I want to put it here," he said, circling her breast. "And here." He slid a line down to her belly button. "And here," he added, sliding a finger down her cleft, over her still-sensitive clit. His gaze tangled with hers. "Any objection?"

She shook her head, quivering in anticipation. "N-none at all."

THANKFUL THAT HE'D put his phone on silent, Jeb checked the display and shook his head.

*Atta boy. My spidey senses are telling me this one is special. Really special. My congratulations, brother. I like her.*

He'd missed another message as well, this one from Charlie. A simple "Call me ASAP." Evidently she'd found something, Jeb thought, wondering what sort of information would require an "as soon as possible" response. His gaze slid to Sophie, who was bent over putting her shoes back on.

Good Lord, had anything else felt as wonderful as being inside her? Had anything ever made him feel more powerful? More alive? More…everything.

She was utterly and completely remarkable. She was sweet and kind, full of fire and loyal, hardworking and…adorable.

This one is special, his brother had said.

Mild understatement.

This one wasn't just merely special—she was a game-changer. She was it. His undoing. He couldn't imagine taking another step forward, ever again, without her by his side. Was he in love with her? Honestly, he didn't know. He'd never been in love before, so he had nothing to compare it to. He only knew that he needed to breathe the same air she did. He needed to be near her. He needed to hold her. To protect her. To ensure her happiness.

She looked up and caught him staring and a slow smile slid over her kiss-swollen lips. "What?" she asked.

"Nothing," he lied. "I just like looking at you."

"You've got to quit saying stuff like that," she said. "You're going to ruin me for other men."

"Good."

She blinked, seemingly startled.

"It's only fair, don't you think?" he asked. "You've ruined me for other women."

Another one of those refreshing blushes painted her cheeks. It was mind-blowing, genuinely remarkable that she didn't recognize her own appeal. That she didn't know how astonishingly fabulous she truly was. Humility was a little thin on the ground these days, but Sophie O'Brien had it in spades.

Or was it doubt? he wondered, his belly tightening. Had her father done such a number on her that she was incapable of seeing her true value? Had her confidence been undermined to the point that she didn't know that she was the most amazing creature he'd ever clapped eyes on?

"Did you want to look at anything else here before we go?" she asked.

Jeb shook his head. They'd already gone through the files she'd reviewed last night and made pictures with his cell phone of everyone's pertinent details. To his surprise, she'd even started a file on him. She'd noted his name, his "adoptive" relationship to Foy, who had evidently explained things to her with that little white lie, that he was a former Ranger, but present employment was unknown. She'd notated his social style, his affable ability to start a conversation and his height, which she'd dubbed "substantial," along with the added note, "Would look good in my happy place."

Jeb had about choked when he'd read that little

tidbit and Sophie, to his delight, had become quite annoyed on his behalf.

"How dare she think she could chain you to a wall and whip you and do…other things," she'd finished, unable to go on.

"You going to shoot her?" he'd teased.

"Please," she'd said, rolling her eyes. "I'm not going to jail for a man, even one as hot as you."

Careful to make sure that they'd destroyed any evidence of their visit, Jeb took one last look around the office. The desk was tidy, the USB tucked safely away in his pocket, her chair was in its place. All of their clothing was on and accounted for, though there had been one frightening moment when Sophie hadn't been able to find her panties and they'd discovered them hanging from a low branch of an artificial ficus tree.

They were thongs. Who knew?

Satisfied that everything was as it should be, he made his way over to Sophie, who was staring at the aquarium, a line furrowed on her brow.

"What's wrong?" he asked.

"Something's different," she said. "I can't put my finger on it, but something isn't right."

Jeb glanced at the aquarium. He'd never looked closely at it before, so he couldn't say whether anything was different or not, but he knew enough about instincts and heeding them, to give her a minute to let her take a proper look.

"Ethel's not supposed to clean this either," she

added. She bent down, looked closer. "Marjorie has a company that comes in to do it for her. I've seen their van here before."

That's right, Jeb thought. He'd seen the notation on her financials.

"Do you know what coulrophobia means?" she asked.

"Not off the top of my head, but I can look." He withdrew his phone, loaded the dictionary app. He chuckled. "It's the fear of clowns," he said. "Why?"

"Because Marjorie had noted it on Ethel's file. And…" She was thoughtful, considering.

"And what?"

"And I found a red clown nose under Marjorie's desk when I noticed the nail polish."

Jeb cocked his head. "What would one have to do with the other?"

"I don't know, but it's too odd to be a coincidence, don't you think?"

Yes, he did. He just didn't know how they could possibly be connected. He bent down and watched the fish circle the tank, their pale pink bodies glimmering in the artificial light. Water bubbled from an air filter in the back and ornamental grasses swayed with the current. Coral formations provided cover should the pair wish to hide and a white castle and bubbling treasure box rounded out the décor.

Jeb's gaze narrowed as something caught his eye. His stomach clenched and his fingers tingled as he drew closer, peered at the treasure chest. It had been moved recently, the gravel beneath it disturbed and it hadn't closed properly, because something had gotten in the way.

"Sophie, could you describe Lila's necklace to me please?"

"Sure," she said, shooting him a look. "It's a diamond and sapphire choker. Each little piece is set like a flower, a pansy, I think, and very closely set."

Jeb chewed the inside of his cheek, pointed to the treasure chest. "Like that, you mean?"

She started, her eyes rounding, then bent down and followed his finger. "What?" She inhaled sharply. "Yes," she said. "Exactly like that. Oh, my goodness," she breathed. "Look at that. I bet it's all in there."

He'd bet it was, too. Jeb found a long glove in the compartment below the aquarium—wet from recent use—and pushed his hand into it so that any germs that were on his skin wouldn't get into the water and harm the fish. He reached in and snagged the treasure chest, then carefully opened it up.

Sophie's breath caught. "Lila's necklace, Rose-Marie's brooch, Nanette's diamond earrings, Pearl's string of pearls." She held up the last item. "Annie's ring. Oh, Jeb," she sighed, disappointment weighting her shoulders. "Why would Ethel do such a thing? Why would she take these things and then plant them in Marjorie's office?"

He didn't know, but it was past time to find out. "Let's call Marjorie," he said.

"Call Foy, too, and let him know that you've got it. We can alert the others after we've talked to Marjorie, but Foy..." Her face crumpled with sympathy.

Jeb nodded. "You call Marjorie and ask her to come down here. Tell it's urgent, but nothing else. I'll call Foy."

The old man answered before the end of the first ring, indicating that he'd been waiting by the phone. "Jeb?"

"I've got it," he told him. "It's safe. I've got to tie up a few things here first, then I'll bring it to you."

"You've found it? You're sure?"

"Positive. And we've found everyone else's things as well."

"Well done," Foy told him, his gruff voice thick. "I knew you had it in you."

"Thanks, Foy," Jeb told him, though he didn't feel like he'd actually done all that much. It was pure dumb luck that they'd come back tonight and heard Ethel in the aquarium. Had they not broken back into Marjorie's office, it could have been weeks, possibly months, before they'd had any sort of significant break in the case.

His gaze slid to Sophie, who just ended the call with Marjorie. A wondering smile slid over her ripe mouth as she stared at her friend's jewelry and something about that smile hooked him right in the heart. He felt it snag in his chest and tug. This was good, right?

Only his excuse, his ticket into her world, was disappearing. It was over.

So now what? Jeb wondered, his cheeks puffing as he released a breath. What sort of reason was he going to have to manufacture to keep her in his life? Because he grimly suspected that she'd just become the center of his universe.

# 13

NOSTRILS FLARED, eyes blazing, Marjorie marched into her office, sniffed delicately, obviously noticing the scent of sex in the air, and narrowed her gaze.

Sophie wanted to fall through the floor, but ignored the heat rushing into her cheeks and held her ground.

It helped that her ground was next to Jeb's.

"I want to know just what in the hell you think you're doing in here," she demanded. "This door was *locked*. My computer was *off*. You've got exactly three seconds to tell me or I'm—"

"Going to nail us with your riding crop, Ms. Whitehall?" Jeb asked, his lips quirking dangerously.

She gasped and all the color drained from her face. "Now, listen here. I—"

Jeb strode forward. "I'm Jeb Anderson with Ranger Security," he told her. "And I am *not* Foy's grandson. I was hired by Rose-Marie Wilton's family to investigate the theft of her vintage Tiffany brooch, as well as several other missing pieces of jewelry from other residents on site, most recently a diamond engagement ring that had belonged to Annie Wilcox, Foy's late wife, which was stolen from his safe this afternoon."

Marjorie blanched. "What? But—"

"The missing jewelry—all of it—was found hidden in the treasure box of your aquarium."

Looking as if she might be ill at any moment, Marjorie's disbelieving gaze darted to her aquarium, then she gripped the edge of her desk. "I didn't take it," she said. "I swear, I have no idea how it got there. I—"

"We know how it got there," Jeb told her. "Because we were here when the engagement ring was put into the box tonight." He arched a brow. "Do you have any idea why anyone would want to frame you for these thefts? Anyone holding a grudge against you? Anything at all you'd like to share before the authorities get here?"

She swallowed, pressed a hand against her throat. "You know who did it?"

Jeb nodded. "We do. The 'why' of it is still a bit of a mystery. We were hoping you could enlighten us."

She glanced up, her gaze darting nervously between the two of them. "How did you know about—"

"Your happy place?" Jeb asked. "I hacked into your computer," he admitted. He lifted a shoulder.

"You were a suspect in my investigation. It was necessary to clear you." He arched a brow. "She found out, didn't she? And you retaliated by using her phobia against her."

Sophie blinked and swiveled to look at him. When had he figured that out?

"She was blackmailing me," Marjorie finally admitted. "I've always kept a decent supply of cash put aside, but she was determined to drain me dry, to take it all, just because something in my personal life isn't precisely in character for a director of a retirement home." Marjorie swallowed. "How dare she. It's no one's business but mine. And Twilight Acres is my home. These people, as infuriating as they can be," she admitted with a significant eye roll, "are my family."

Sophie certainly understood that. She felt the same way about all the residents here.

"How did she get the codes to the safes?"

Marjorie grimaced. "Undoubtedly the same way you did," she said. "By figuring out my password."

"I didn't figure out your password. I used a customized program that did it for me. I wouldn't think Ethel would have access to something like that."

"Could she have figured out your password?" Sophie asked.

"She could," she said. "She knew my other name. My handle. The Whippet." She squeezed her eyes shut. "Stupid," she muttered. "I should have changed it. I just never suspected she'd do anything so heinous."

The Whippet? Really, Sophie thought. Like the dog? She got the "whip" part, but… Oh, she thought, understanding dawning. Female dog. Bitch. Whippet. Double meaning. Quite clever, actually.

"Any idea why these specific people were targeted?" Jeb asked.

Marjorie rubbed a line from between her brows. "Any person who ever had anything negative to say about her cooking could have been a target," she said. She frowned. "Foy's ring went missing today?" she asked.

Jeb nodded. "It did."

"Cora had mentioned that Ethel was having a tantrum today because Foy had suggested her mashed potatoes didn't have enough salt." She rolled her eyes, looked up at them. "Did you recover all the missing items?" she asked.

"We did," he said.

"Then I'd like an opportunity to handle this in-house," she said. "You can ask them all first and I'll abide by whatever they decide. But I can fire her for this with the threat of going to the authorities if she ever harasses any of us again."

And she'd have the leverage to get Ethel completely off her back, not that Sophie could blame her for wanting that. Granted pain was not part of her pleasure process, but to each his own. If Marjorie got her jollies by beating the crap out of people who liked it, then who was she to judge? Hell, she'd just had sex with a man right here under her desk. She certainly didn't have the right to hurl any stones.

Jeb considered her request. "I'll talk to everyone and get back to you. In the interim, change your safe codes and your passwords and don't let her know that we're onto her."

"You saw her, you say?" she asked, lifting a brow.

"We did."

"But she didn't see you?"

"We were hiding," Jeb told her.

Her eyes twinkled with knowing humor. "I'll just bet you were." She glanced at Sophie. "Your sweater's on inside out, sweetheart. Might want to correct that before you leave."

Sophie felt her eyes widen in alarm, glanced down at her shirt and winced. "Damn."

"And if you ever find you can't keep him in line, let me know," she added. "I've got a few toys I could lend you."

Sophie cleared her throat. "I don't think that'll be necessary, thanks."

Marjorie merely shrugged, then predictably settled down and got to work.

"Do you think they'll go for it?" Jeb asked her. "Do you think Foy and the rest of them will let Marjorie handle Ethel?"

Sophie chuckled darkly. "Oh, I think they're definitely going to be more in favor of Marjorie meting out justice than anyone else."

Jeb slung an arm around her shoulder and pressed a kiss against her head, the treasure chest in his hand. "Come on," he said. "Let's go give these people their belongings back."

She grinned. "I like the sound of that."

"And then we're going to go to your house and I'm going to do some finger painting. With chocolate. And you're going to be my canvas."

Sophie grinned. She couldn't think of a better way to end the day.


"WHAT DO THE letters ASAP mean to you?" Charlie asked Jeb the next morning when he finally got around to returning her call. They'd returned the jewelry last night, confirmed that Marjorie would be responsible for Ethel's punishment, then gone back to Sophie's and played paint by number with chocolate cobbler on each other's bodies.

It had been wonderful. The best. He'd awoken this morning to her sweet rump squashed against his aching groin, her plump breast his hand and a smile of bone deep contentment on his face. For the first time since he'd left the military, since that horrible business in Mosul, he felt…hopeful about the future.

Guilt had accompanied it, of course, but admittedly it wasn't as debilitating as it had been before.

"Sorry," he said. "I haven't had time."

"Are you with her?" she asked.

He watched as Sophie threw feed out to her

chickens. "I am, but she's not right here with me at the moment so I can talk, if that's what you mean."

"Yes and no," she said, letting go a breath. "Listen, I'm not even sure where to start, so I'm going to give you an abbreviated rundown, okay?"

Unease nudged his belly and he felt his attention narrow. "Okay."

"Sophie's family is as screwed up as they come. With the exception of both grandparents, who are both deceased, she doesn't have a single relative who isn't certifiably crazy. Seriously. Her father never attended a school he didn't get kicked out of. He stabbed a kid in Kindergarten through the hand with a pencil and that's the least violent thing on record, although certainly not the least disturbing. His teacher's note said, and I quote, 'The boy scares me. There's a darkness in his eyes, a pure lack of remorselessness that makes me fear for my safety as well as the other children's.'"

Jeb whistled low. "Damn."

She laughed grimly. "And that's not even the half of it. He met Sophie's mother in reform school. Her mother had already been diagnosed with Borderline Personality Disorder, with an unnatural predisposed hatred of other members of her sex. So the sociopath meets and marries the psychopath and they have a boy, whom they adore. But when Sophie came along…"

"Oh, geez," Jeb said, passing a hand over his face.

"They terrorized her, Jeb. I widened the net to

a three state radius and found hospital records that would break your heart. The last one I found was right here in Cobb county. She'd been six, taken to the hospital by her grandmother. Multiple cuts and bruises and a gash inside of her right arm that required twenty-four stitches to close. She took her grandmother's name less than a month later, but the grandmother kept a restraining order against her son until the day she died. Sophie has been renewing one for both her parents and her brother every six months for the last two years. She's called the police department several times, reporting disturbances around her house, crank calls and vandalism to her car. They even poisoned her animals. Bastards."

*Ah, Jesus.* He lowered his head, stared at the porch decking beneath his feet. The fence inside the fence—it had been to protect her animals. Anger tightened his fingers, made them ache and he had to unclench his jaw in order to respond.

"Do you know where they are now?" he asked.

"That's why I'm calling," she said. "They're holed up in a cheap hotel less than three miles from her address and they've been there for three days. I don't know what they want or what they're planning, but she needs to be on guard. They're dangerous."

Yes, they were, Jeb thought. And they were going to play hell trying to get past him. "Thanks for everything, Charlie. I appreciate it."

"Keep her safe," she said. "I don't know her, but I like her already."

Smiling, her cheeks pink from the cold, her muck boots on her feet, Sophie mounted the steps to the porch. Her expression faltered when she saw his face.

"What's wrong?" she asked.

What to say? He knew she was going to be angry that he'd asked Charlie to dig around in her past, but her family, who seemed hell-bent and determined to hurt her, were an immediate threat. She needed to know. And, unfortunately, it was his job to tell her.

"That was Charlie," he said. "Our resident hacker, remember?"

"The one who designed the password breaker program?"

He nodded. "One in the same." He hesitated, trying to find the right words, or if not the right words, then at least the ones that would piss her off the least.

She frowned, concerned. "Jeb, what it is?"

He looked up, caught her gaze. "Your father, mother and brother are in a motel less than three miles from here. They've been there for three days."

She stilled and a flash of fear raced across her face. "How do you know this?" she asked faintly. She frowned. "I don't understand..."

"I know because I asked Charlie to look," he said. "I knew that you were afraid of something, I knew that you'd built a fortress around your house and kept a cache of loaded weapons next to your door." He paused, swallowed, glanced at her arm. "I knew that someone had hurt you. Badly," he added. "But I didn't realize, until you'd made that comment about some family members being unhappy with the terms of your grandmother's will, that it was by someone who was supposed to love and protect you."

She sank down onto the top step. "They've been there for three days?" she asked. "That's unusual. They usually never stay here that long." Her tone was wooden, lifeless, but the fear was unmistakable all the same. "They'll breeze through for a day, make a crank call or slash my tires, or try to poison my animals, or taunt me from the distance allowed by the protection order," she said. "But they never stay. They leave."

It was heartbreaking to watch her, to see the sadness round her shoulders, the fear make them tense. "When was the last time you saw them?"

"A couple of weeks ago. In the parking lot of the grocery store. They told me they were going to get me. Called me a 'thieving bitch' because Gran left me everything. She raised me," Sophie said. "She wasn't just my grandmother. For all intents and purposes, she was my mother. She nursed me through childhood illnesses, she braided my hair, she taught me how to cook, helped me with my homework." She swallowed, her voice cracking. "She was all I ever had."

Jeb pulled her into his arms. "I wish I could have met her. She sounds like another perfect woman," he said, giving her a squeeze.

The comment had the desired effect and she managed a wan smile. "She was," she said. She nodded toward the end of the driveway. "He left me there," she said. "At the end of that drive. Bleeding, bruised, scared, no shoes. In the middle of December. I was six."

Bile rose in the back of his throat. "He's not right, Sophie. He's sick. They all are."

"I know that now," she said. "And I guess a part of me knew it then, but I still wondered what was wrong with me, why was I so hard to love?"

She was killing him, Jeb thought. Absolutely killing him and her pain made him want to pummel the ever-loving hell out of her father.

She slid a finger over the scar on her arm. "My mother did this," she said, shocking him. "He brought me here and left me to keep her from killing me. I should thank him for that."

"You don't owe any of them anything."

"They're coming for me," she said. "They wouldn't have hung around otherwise."

Jeb tilted her chin up and stared into her woefully familiar eyes. "They won't get near you, sweetheart. I'd die first."

Her chin trembled and she leaned forward and pressed a kiss against his lips. "Don't you dare," she said fiercely, her voice cracking. "Don't you dare."

Jeb swallowed the lump that formed in his throat. "I know all of your secrets," he said. "It's only fair that you know one of mine."

# 14

SOPHIE STILLED, then turned to look at Jeb. "You don't have to do that," she said. "You haven't found out anything that I wouldn't have eventually confided. It would have taken more time, because it's painful, but I would have told you."

His gaze searched hers. "I want to tell you. I *need* to tell someone," he said, his voice strained. He hesitated. "You pegged it when you said you didn't know how I ever stood being in the military because I liked being in control. It was a struggle, I'll admit. But I liked the sense that what I was doing made a difference, that I was part of something bigger than myself, that I was doing my bit for Uncle Sam."

"I can understand that," she said, snuggling in closer to his side. She loved the way he felt next to her, as if this niche inside his arms had been made expressly for her.

"I've always had good instincts and, when I've

followed them, they've never let me down. Not once."

She had a terrible suspicion she knew where this was going.

"Six months ago I took a team into Mosul. I felt like something was off, wrong, and that I didn't need to move forward." He paused, his gaze turning inward. "I conveyed my feelings to my commanding officer, who was sitting safely back at base, maneuvering us like pieces of a chess board. He told me to press on. To follow orders."

Ah, Sophie thought. She'd been wrong. His instincts had been right, not wrong. And he'd ignored them.

"I did," he said. "And even though I led my men in, when the bullets started flying, I was the only one who survived."

Sophie's heart squeezed and she wrapped her arm around his waist. "Oh, Jeb, I'm so sorry."

"That's why I came out," he said. "That's why I pulled the plug on my career and found a new one. I decided that I was never going to follow another order that put me at odds with what I felt was right."

"I don't blame you," she said. "You were on the ground, in front, in the line of fire. That officer should have listened to you. Should have trusted your instincts." She grimaced. "No wonder you couldn't stay," she said. "How could you after your commanding officer showed so little confidence in you? Especially since ignoring your expertise resulted in the death of your friends."

He turned to look at her, that wondering expression on his face once again, the one that said she'd just taken another peek inside of his head and he'd been unprepared for it. "That's unnerving," he said. "You…get me, you know it? You really do."

Sophie grinned. "Do you know what I'd like to do right now, soldier?" she asked, arching playful brow.

He chuckled low. "What?"

"Get *on* you."

"I CAN'T TAKE this waiting," Jeb told Payne days later. "And it's wearing on Sophie's nerves too. She's constantly looking over her shoulder and is taking a pistol with her everywhere she goes." He blew out a breath, rubbing the bridge of his nose. "I'm sick of it. Sick of watching her suffer."

"What are you going to do?"

"I'm going to go scare the hell out of them," Jeb said. "I'm going to frighten them so terribly and threaten them so thoroughly that they'll never look cross-eyed at her again, much less violate the protection agreement."

At this point, the issue of Sophie's family was common knowledge, as were Jeb's feelings for her. He'd known the first day that she'd walked into the diner that she was special. He'd felt it in his gut.

She was it.

His.

"Wait for us," Payne told him. "I'll get Jamie and Guy and we'll be there in less than half an hour. No point in going in alone and, between the three of us, I think we'd make a formidable team."

Touched, Jeb swallowed. He wouldn't have asked, but sincerely appreciated the offer. Had Judd been here, Jeb knew his little brother would have had his back. It was heartening to see that these men would, too.

"Thanks," he said. "I appreciate it."

Thirty minutes later, dressed in black swat outfits and packing enough artillery to level a small town, the four of them burst into Sophie's family's dingy motel room and went Special Ops on their ass.

Her father had scrambled from the bed and curled into a ball against the wall, her brother had literally pissed himself and her mother had screamed like a wild woman and launched herself at Payne, who'd held up his gun and coolly informed her that it had been awhile since he'd gotten to shoot someone and she'd do as good as anybody.

"Leave immediately," Jeb had told them. "Don't call her, don't send her any letters, don't look at her, don't come within a hundred miles of her. Stay the hell away from her, or make no mistake, I'll hurt you." He meant it. "And believe me, I know how. I can make you feel pain you've never imagined in your worst nightmares. Do you understand?"

"Fine," her father snarled. "The bitch isn't worth it."

Jeb drew back and slammed his fist into his jaw,

# GET 2 BOOKS

We'd like to send you two *Harlequin® Blaze®* novels absolutely free. Accepting them puts you under no obligation to purchase any more books.

## HOW TO GET YOUR
## 2 FREE BOOKS AND 2 FREE GIFTS

1. Return the reply card today, and we'll send you two *Harlequin Blaze* novels, absolutely free! We'll even pay the postage!

2. Accepting free books places you under no obligation to buy anything, ever. Whatever you decide, the free books and gifts are yours to keep, free!

3. We hope that after receiving your free books you'll want to remain a subscriber, but the choice is yours–to continue or cancel, any time at all!

## EXTRA BONUS

**You'll also get two free mystery gifts!**
**(worth about $10)**

# FREE!

◄ DETACH AND MAIL CARD TODAY! ▼

HB-2F-11/12

knocking him out cold. "Don't you talk about my future wife like that," he said.

The four of them sat in the parking lot and waited for the three to load up their stuff and leave. Looking appropriately frightened, they had, spinning gravel as they aimed their car away from her farm.

"You're going to marry her, huh?" Jamie asked, stuffing a snack cake into his mouth.

"What?"

"In there," he said. "You told her father not to talk about your future wife like that."

He blinked. "I did?"

The three of them chuckled and shook their heads. "You did. Sounds like a Freudian slip, doesn't it, boys?" Guy remarked.

Payne arched a brow. "Do you want to marry her?"

Jeb felt a bemused smile slip over his mouth, tugging the corners of his lips. He did. Sweet heaven… he did. He laughed, shook his head. "Yes, I do."

"Well, get on with it then," he said. "Didn't that group host a ball in less than twenty-four hours? A wedding is even more romantic. I'll wager they could pull one of those together in half that time."

A spark of an idea formed and he nodded, feeling the rightness of it settle over him.

"I've got to go," he announced, pushing from Payne's car and heading to his own.

"I imagine you do," Jamie called out. "Let us know when and where and we'll be there."

Jeb grinned. "You got it," he said. "And brace yourselves, boys, cause these senior citizens know how to party."

"Sophie, someone's here to see you," Carl called.

She frowned and checked her appointment book. She didn't have anyone down. How could she have missed…?

Jeb ducked into her massage room and smiled when he spotted her. "Hey," he said. "You owe me a working over, remember?"

She chuckled softly. "I seem to recall something like that. Get undressed and get on the table."

He did, revealing the body she'd come to think of as hers, the glorious muscles, the sleek skin. Her living playground. She warmed the oil and dropped it on his chest, then swirled it over his slickened skin.

He groaned. "Oh, that feels good. You really know what you're doing."

"Did you ever doubt it?" she asked, smiling as her heart rate tripped into over-drive. Her breasts grew heavy with want, hungering for his touch. Her womb flooded with a familiar heat and soaked into her panties, readying for him.

"You know what would make this massage even better?" he asked.

She bit her lip, trailing her fingers down the front of his thighs, watching his dick leap to attention. *Hers*, she thought. *All hers*.

"What would make it better, Jeb?"

She took him in hand, had the pleasure of watching his back come off the table, a hiss of pleasure move between his clenched teeth.

"If you'd get naked and get up on this table…and slide around on top of me."

Unable to resist him, Sophie did just that. She threaded her fingers through his, frowning when something didn't feel right. She drew back.

"What happened to your hand?" she asked, staring at the bruised knuckles.

"It ran into your father," he said, his gaze searching hers. "They're gone, Sophie. And they're never coming back. Ever."

Her heart skipped a beat and she blinked, confused. "What?" she breathed.

"Me, Payne, McCann and Jamie went over to the motel and explained things to them," he said. "They could leave and never bother you again, or we were going to show them what would happen if they didn't." He cracked his knuckles and grinned.

"What?"

"It wouldn't have come to that, but as bluffs go, it worked well. Bullies only respond to force. We were forceful."

Her chest squeezed and emotion clogged her throat. "You did that for me?"

"I would do that and a whole lot more for lesser reasons," he said.

She melted, resting her forehead against his.

"How am I supposed to resist you when you say things like that?" she asked helplessly.

He drew back, smiling. "I didn't know you were trying to resist me."

"Well, not very hard, I'll admit," she said, "but I should be trying. I shouldn't be so damned easy."

"Why the hell not?" He grabbed her bare rump, lifted and pushed up into her, making her eyes roll back in her head. "It's working brilliantly for me," he said. "God, you feel good. I feel like I'm going to die every time we're together like this and still, I look forward to it."

She tightened around him, leaned back and put her hands on his chest, undulating her hips. His big hands anchored either side of her waist and he pushed up, meeting her as she rode him, catching her rhythm and going with her for the ride. He leaned forward, pulled a nipple into his mouth. "Marry me," he said, thrusting harder.

She started, certain she'd misunderstood him, felt the flash of impended release boiling up inside her. "Marry me, Sophie," he repeated, his voice raw, desperate. "I need you." He bit back a curse, then groaned as she clenched around him once more. "Marry me. Please. I love you."

She came, hard. Her neck went boneless, too weak to support her head, and a long cry of release ripped from her throat, happiness permeating every cell.

Her release triggered his and he joined her there,

his glorious body quaking beneath hers. "Marry me," he repeated, those blue eyes beseeching. "Say yes. Be mine."

Sophie smiled, melted against him. "I've been yours since the day I met you," she said.

"Then let's make it official. Cora's got your dress."

She straightened and pulled away from him. "What?"

"She's got your dress and the church is ready," he said, grinning like a fool.

*Her* fool.

"You're joking."

"Do I look like I'm joking? You're the one who said they could host a party in no time at all. Why would a wedding be any harder?"

"They're all waiting? Right now?"

"Every last one of them." He stood, retrieved a small box from his pants pocket and withdrew a ring. "Here," he said, his hands trembling. "Let's make it official, shall we?"

A lump welled in her throat. "It's Annie's ring."

"It was," he said. "Foy wanted you to have it. He's giving you away. Threatened to plant a conker on Clayton Plank if he had a problem with that."

She chuckled, her eyes welling with tears. "I can't believe you did this," she said. "I don't know what to say."

He tipped her chin up and kissed her. "'I do' will suffice."

Thirty minutes later, dressed in a designer gown she couldn't have been more happy with had she picked it herself, surrounded by her surrogate family and friends, Foy walked her down the aisle and he and Cora gave her away.

Cora gave her a squeeze, her eyes brimming with tears. "Your grandmother would have been so happy to see you today," she said. "She made me promise that I'd see you settled, and I have," she said. "I never break a promise."

Sophie's throat clogged with emotion and she hugged her dear friend. "Thank you, Cora. For everything."

"Love you, sweet girl," Cora said. "He's a lucky man."

Sophie turned to Jeb, who stood waiting patiently for her. Those vivid blue eyes glowed with happiness and pride and, God help her, love.

He loved her.

With his brother serving as best man via the face-time feature on his phone, the preacher officiated the service, then asked the all important question.

"Do you, Sophie, take Jeb to be your lawfully wedded husband, to love and to cherish, to have and to hold, in sickness and in health, for richer or for poorer, for as long as you both shall live?"

Her gaze tangled with his and her chest ached with joy. "I do."

He breathed an audible sigh of relief, much to the merriment of their guests.

"I love you," she whispered, because she hadn't said it yet. "You're the winner of my Perfect Man contest."

\* \* \* \* \*

# THE PLAYER

This book is humbly dedicated to all men and women past and present who have served and are currently serving in our Armed Forces, and to their families, who keep the home fires burning.

# Prologue

"With all due respect, sir, that's bullshit."

Colonel Carl Garrett lifted his gaze from the report he'd been pretending to study and determinedly squashed the smile that tried to curl the disapproving line of his lips.

Best not to tip his hand.

Instead, he leveled a cool stare at the three men seated on the wrong side of his desk, most particularly at Guy McCann, who'd issued the comment. The other two, Majors Brian Payne and Jamie Flanagan, sat stony-faced but, predictably, had a better grasp on their tempers.

"Bullshit or not, Lt. Colonel, brawling off-base is an Article 15 and, as I'm sure you're aware, puts a flag on your clearance papers." He paused, purposely injected a little more piss and gravel into his voice. "I'm not sure you're seeing the gravity of the situation."

Not a threat, per se, but a reminder. Hell, he knew perfectly well they understood what was going on. They hadn't been handpicked for Project Chameleon—a special forces unit so secretive that there was absolutely no evidence of its existence in any military file, computer-generated or otherwise—because they were stupid. Garrett suppressed a grimace. In fact, they were too damned smart, which had made trying to get them to rethink leaving the Army with the usual methods—re-upping bonuses, flattery, better posts, etc.—useless.

Unfortunately guilt had a better grasp on them than any form of greed—feeling responsible for the death of a close friend would do that. Through no wrongdoing on their own part, Project Chameleon had lost one of its own during its last mission, and so far, no amount of lecturing and reviewing what had happened could ease their sense of guilt. They'd gone in as four and come out as three.

They'd failed.

Major Payne—a name he'd understandably taken considerable grief for over the years—released a weary breath. "Permission to speak freely, sir?"

"Granted."

"Rutland's an asshole," he said, his voice a barely controlled mixture of irritation and hope. "You know that." He snorted. "Hell, everyone knows that."

"The bastard needed his ass kicked a long time

ago," Flanagan chimed in, leaning forward in his seat.

All true, he knew. And he secretly applauded them. Still… "If Rutland needed an attitude adjustment, it was not up to the three of you to give it to him."

"He mouthed off about Danny," Flanagan said, as though that should explain everything.

And it did.

McCann swallowed and the other two grew quiet at the mention of their late friend's name. Silence thick with the weight of grief and regret suddenly expanded in the room, causing a twinge of remorse to prick Garrett's resolve.

Major Daniel Levinson had been a good man, a better soldier, and an original member of this unit's college crew. Each of them had come out of the ROTC program at the University of Alabama. "Roll Tide" was a frequent cheer amid their set and Bear Bryant was revered with the sort of exaggerated regard worthy of a fallen saint. It wasn't merely football—it was a religion.

Though their military careers had taken them on different paths over the years, they'd remained close. Closer than any band or so-called brotherhood of buddies Garrett had ever known. He'd always admired them for that. Truth be told, he'd envied them as well. The military was a boys' club, its very nature a breeding ground for camaraderie and lasting friendships. But these 'Bama boys were different, had shared a special connection that made them more like family than friends.

When Project Chameleon had come along, it had been a no-brainer to reunite the four. They'd all been at the top of their field, each one of them successful in their own right. Each one of them different enough to offer unique qualities to the unit, making it one of the most balanced and effective special forces teams the Army had ever known.

Though he had a reputation for being a bit of a ladies' man—a *player* in today's slang, if Garrett remembered correctly—at a little over six and a half feet, Flanagan not only had the brawn but also sported a genius-level IQ which made him the brain of the unit. Honestly, it had surprised him to learn that Flanagan had thrown the first punch in this recent scuffle. Ordinarily he wasn't quite so rash. Though they'd all taken Levinson's death hard, Garrett suspected that Flanagan was having a harder time dealing with the loss than the other two at the moment.

Understandable, of course, given how Danny had died. Still…

With nerves of steel and an attention-to-detail that had landed him the nickname "The Specialist," Major Brian Payne—who only went by his last name—didn't do anything in half-baked, half-assed measures. He was a man you could count on to not only get the job done, but get it done *right*.

Guy McCann was a bit of a smart-ass with an

endearing penchant for being able to bend a rule just shy of the breaking point, but with good enough instincts that he always landed on his feet. And Levinson... Well, Levinson had been the best of all three, and what he'd lacked he'd made up for in heart.

On their own they'd been formidable defenders of Uncle Sam—together they'd been lethal.

Naturally when the powers-that-be had heard rumors of their intent to leave, he'd been given strict instruction to prevent it. Garrett ran a finger over the flag attached to the topmost file. They'd inadvertently given him the power to do it, and yet, when it had come down to the nut-cutting, he'd been unable to follow through. Better to have them in his debt than have an unwilling unit too bent on leaving to be effective. Better a grateful man than a bitter soldier. If they were bound and determined to leave—and they were—then if he could wring one more mission, be it personal or professional, out of them, then he'd still be better off. Fortunately the brass above him had thought so as well.

"So what's going to happen?" Guy asked. "How long is this going to hold us up?"

"That depends," Garrett told them, leaning back in his chair.

Guy's green gaze sharpened. "On what?"

"On whether or not you agree to my terms."

The three of them stiffened and shared a guarded

look. "*Your* terms?" Guy asked warily. A muscle ticked in his tense jaw.

At last…the heart of the matter, Garrett thought. "That's right. You want out. We can do this one of two ways. The hard way… Or my way."

Flanagan muttered a hot oath, leaned back and shoved a hand through his dark brown hair. "I knew this was going to happen," he said, shooting Guy a dark look. "We're *so* screwed."

"Sonofabitch," Guy muttered angrily.

Payne swallowed what was most likely a similar statement, but managed to hold his temper. Just barely, judging by the vein throbbing in his forehead. "And what, exactly, would *your* way entail?" he asked.

"Nothing complicated," Garrett told them smoothly. "You'll just owe me."

"Owe you?" Guy repeated, with equal amounts of surprise and trepidation.

Jamie frowned, his hazel eyes wary. "Owe you what?"

Garrett shrugged, but his tone belied the casual gesture. "A favor." He cast them all a steely look in turn. "From each of you. When I call it in, I want no questions asked, no excuses. Just do it."

Guy considered him with a measuring, probing look. "That calls for a lot of trust."

"I've worked with you for the past four years, McCann. It's either there or it isn't. The choice is yours."

A beat slid into five while the three of them shared another one of those unspoken looks of communication. Garrett watched closely, but didn't detect a single indication of yea or nay from any one of them. Yet Payne evidently got the message because it was he who ultimately spoke for the group. "One favor from each of us? That's it?"

Garrett nodded, anticipation spiking.

Payne released an even breath. "Then we accept your terms, sir. We want out. If you can make that happen quickly, then a favor won't be a problem."

"Excellent," Garrett told them, his lips curling into a belated smile. "Consider it done."

The three stood, preparing to leave. Garrett found his feet as well and extended his hand to each of them, sealing their bargain with a handshake. An old-fashioned gesture, but one that was better than a contract with men like these. They were men of courage, dignity and honor. A rare breed in this day and age.

He let go a sigh, fully absorbing the fact that they would no longer be under his command and found himself quite startled to realize that he'd... miss them. He cleared his throat. "Gentlemen, it's been a pleasure."

"Likewise, sir," Flanagan told him.

"An honor," McCann added.

A man of few words, Payne merely shot him a look which aptly conveyed the same sentiment, then added, "Until later, sir."

Garrett felt a grin tug at his lips. "Oh, don't worry," he told them. "I'll be in touch."

"WHAT THE HELL WAS THAT all about?" Guy asked as they made their way down the hall away from Garrett's office.

"Leverage," Jamie said grimly, feeling an immeasurable amount of relief regardless of the bargain he'd just made. It was over. Finished. Ranger Security—their postmilitary plan—was, at most, a mere month away, and it couldn't come a day sooner. In fact, he would have just about promised Garrett anything—a firstborn, his left nut, hell *anything*—to have pushed those clearance papers through.

He wanted out. End of story.

Jamie shot Payne a look. "What's your take on this favor bargain?"

Payne cocked a brow and shoved open the front doors, revealing the beautiful natural landscape of Fort Benning proper. Georgia, he thought. God's country. "I think Garrett's a crafty bastard who just secured three freebies for Uncle Sam."

"Or for himself," Guy drawled. "He wasn't very specific. Hell, for all we know we could end up being his personal errand boys."

"What? And waste all our special training?" Jamie chewed the inside of his cheek and shook his head. "He might have something personal in mind, but you can bet your sweet ass it's going to be something which requires our particular set of skills."

Guy inclined his head at the point, then blew out a breath. "Well, frankly I don't give a damn what he wants—I'm just glad it's over."

Now that was a sentiment they all shared. Jamie felt a crooked smile slide across his lips, looked over and caught the vaguest hint of a grin transform Payne's usually impassive countenance.

"Boys," Guy said meaningfully, "I say it's time to celebrate."

Payne nodded once in agreement. "I wouldn't say no to a cold one."

Jamie hesitated, wincing. He was about to severely tick off his friends and he knew it.

Guy glanced at him and frowned. "Let me guess," he said, his lips twisted with sarcastic humor. "I'm going to take a shot in the dark here and say that you've got a date."

"With Michelle," Jamie admitted.

"Date three, right?" Payne asked.

Jamie chewed the corner of his lip and nodded.

"Ah," Guy sighed knowingly. "Then she'll be getting the Sayonara Serenade?"

"Of course." Rather than linger and feel their censure—Payne, in particular had become annoyingly vocal on the amount of time he chose to spend with the opposite sex of late—Jamie turned and started walking backward toward his jeep. "Cold beer or a warm woman?" He chuckled, lightening the moment. "It's an easy choice, guys."

Or at least it was for him.

GUY MCCANN WATCHED AS Jamie cranked his jeep and, wearing a cocky I'm-getting-laid grin, drove off.

How Jamie got a woman to sleep with him *after* he'd officially cut her loose was a phenomenon that both Guy and Payne had marveled over for years. Especially since it had been Jamie's love life that had necessitated setting up some rules. After a particularly bad breakup, Guy, Payne and Jamie had sat down over beers and decided on three hard and fast mandates for preserving their bachelor status.

Frankly, he and Payne had personal reasons for wanting to remain single, but Jamie had always been the romantic of the three. At least until he'd caught Shelly Edwards, the so-called love of his life, balling their landlord in lieu of rent.

In their bed, no less.

At any rate, after that particularly humiliating episode Jamie had changed. Instead of looking for the love of his life, he'd merely started looking for the love of his *night*. Following their rules—never spend the entire night with a woman, never let her eat off your plate, and after the third date, cut her loose—he'd pretty much perfected what they'd dubbed "kamikaze romance." After all, every relationship was destined to crash and burn.

Payne watched him drive away as well, then glanced at Guy. "Is it just me, or is he getting worse?"

"Getting worse?"

"More women, more often."

Guy mulled it over, rubbed the back of his neck. Actually, he hadn't noticed, but now that Payne had pointed it out, it did seem like Jamie hadn't been around as much lately. Aside from making plans for Ranger Security, Jamie hadn't had much time for their usual pursuits—beer, poker, target practice, etc... In fact, now that he really thought about it, Jamie's dating schedule had taken a dramatic upswing in the months since Danny's death.

He looked up and caught Payne's knowing gaze. "I see you've come to the same conclusion that I did," Payne told him.

Guy nodded, his mood suddenly somber. "Getting out will help," he said. It had to. And God knows that was the truth for him. There wasn't a day that went by that he didn't think about Danny, about the part he played in his friend's death. If he'd only... Aw, hell, Guy thought, abruptly shutting down that line of thinking.

He could "if-only" until hell froze over and the outcome would still be the same—Danny Levinson, best friend, beloved son, brother, uncle and cousin to a family which still grieved his loss, would still be six feet under in Arlington National Cemetery.

He'd still be gone.

And no matter what Garrett, Payne or Jamie ever said, Guy knew he'd never stop believing that it was his fault. As the senior officer, he'd been in charge. He couldn't take credit for the success of the mission without also taking blame for the loss. And no one would ever convince him otherwise.

It was that simple…and that complicated.

For the time being, they were each three days and three favors away from freedom—a brand-new life devoid of mistakes and if-onlys—and God knows they all needed it. Especially Jamie, who seemed to be taking it the hardest. An image of Danny's crooked grin suddenly rose in his mind, causing a barbed-wire of tension to tighten around his chest.

They all needed it, all right. They needed it badly.

# 1

"IT'S HAPPENED," Jamie Flanagan announced grimly. He snagged a chair from a nearby table, whirled it around and straddled it with a dejected whoosh of air that effectively caught his best friends' combined attention.

In the process of licking the hot wing sauce from his fingertips, Guy looked up. "Dammit, we both warned you about this. Which one is pregnant? Christy? Liz? Monica?"

"My money's on Monica," Payne said easily. "She was clingy."

"Had to change the security code to the building because of her, remember?"

Payne nodded, absently taking a pull from his beer. "She was a pain in the ass, I remember that."

Guy shot Jamie a pleading look. "It isn't her, is

it, Flanagan? Say it isn't her. She's, er… She's not mother material."

Equally annoyed and horrified, Jamie swore hotly. He should have known they'd leap to the wrong damned conclusion. Considering they'd both been riding his ass about his "serial" dating, it only stood to reason that they'd immediately suspect a woman problem.

"Nobody's pregnant, dammit," he snapped. "How many times do I have to tell you bastards that I'm careful?" He exhaled loudly. "I know how to apply a friggin' rubber, for chrissakes. It's Garrett. He's calling in my *favor*."

Guy blinked. "Oh."

Payne stilled and his ice-blue gaze sharpened. "What does he want?"

Jamie let out another long breath, uttered a short disbelieving laugh and shook his head. "He wants me to go to Maine for a week to guard his granddaughter."

"Guard his granddaughter?" Payne repeated. "Guard her from what?"

That had been the first question he'd asked as well, and the answer he'd gotten had been irritatingly ambiguous. Not that he hadn't taken and followed orders on less information. He'd been trained to obey, to trust in the authority of his superiors, and yet something about this felt…*off*. He'd tried to chalk it up to his new civilian mentality, but he suspected that this gut hunch had more to do with intuition than new programming.

"Garrett says there's evidence that a personal enemy of his might be targeting her."

Guy frowned. "Personal enemy?"

"What sort of personal enemy?" Payne asked. "I mean, I don't doubt that he's got one—a man doesn't get to his level without pissing people off. Still…" he added skeptically.

Jamie couldn't help scowling. "That's just it. He wouldn't say. Evidently he's got someone in place through the weekend, but needs me to step in on Monday."

"We'll have to rearrange some things," Payne said, predictably jumping into logistics mode. "Guy and I will have to split your cases."

"It's piss-poor timing, that's for sure," Jamie said, signaling the waitress for a beer. A midtown staple, Samuel's Pub had quickly become their traditional beer and sandwich haunt. Good Irish whiskey, good prices, Braves decor. What more could a guy want? Jamie muttered a hot oath. "Hell, some notice would have been nice."

Guy rocked back in his chair and grinned. "But that would be completely out of character for Garrett."

Too true, Jamie knew, but it didn't change the fact that he'd be leaving his friends and partners in the lurch three months out of the gate in their new business venture. Thanks in part to all three of them, Ranger Security had taken off better than any one of them could have expected. Jamie inwardly grinned. Turns out hi-tech personal and professional security was in high demand—and quite lucrative.

Thanks to Payne's investment capital—though he seemed to resent his impressive portfolio at times, Payne had "come from money" as Jamie's grandmother used to say—they'd secured top-of-the-line equipment and a prized office building in downtown Atlanta. The lower level housed the offices and the other two floors had been converted into apartments. Since he and Guy had no aversion to sharing space, they'd taken the second floor and Payne had moved into the loft, or the Tower, as they'd come to call it.

Since Payne had taken on so much of the financial burden, it only seemed fair that he have a place to himself. Not that Jamie and Guy weren't paying their way, but their money had come from a sizable mortgage whereas Payne had merely "transferred funds." Regardless, provided business continued to grow, he and Guy should be operating in the black within a few years, and in his opinion, that was pretty damned good.

"So the granddaughter is in Maine," Guy remarked. "What does she do?"

Ah, Jamie thought, inwardly wincing. Here came the fun part. He passed a hand over his face and braced himself for sarcasm. "She, er… She runs a de-stressing camp for burned out execs—Unwind, it's called—and well, Garrett's, uh…" He conjured a pained smile. "He's already arranged for my 'stay.'"

A disbelieving chuckle erupted from Guy's throat. "A de-stressing camp? He's sending *you*— Captain Orgasm—to a de-stressing camp?"

Payne coughed to hide his own smile. "To guard his granddaughter, no less. Talk about sending the fox in to guard the henhouse." He snorted. "Garrett must have lost his mind."

"Oh, no," Jamie corrected. "He's as crafty as ever. He issued a curt guard-her-but-no-funny-business order and promised to—" Jamie pretended to search for the exact phrase, though he remembered the ghastly threat verbatim. "Ah, yes. 'Cut my dick off with a dull axe and force-feed it to me' if I so much as looked at her with anything more than friendly interest."

Payne grinned. "So your reputation precedes you, then."

Jamie winced. "He might have mentioned Colonel Jessup's daughter."

And honestly, there had been no need. After that horrid debacle, Jamie hadn't needed any additional threats to stay away from daughters—or any relative, for that matter—belonging to superior officers. And it really wouldn't be hard. There were plenty of other available women around.

Neesa Jessup had seduced *him*, not the other way around, and yet when Date Three had rolled around and he'd attempted to break things off, she'd gone to her father and cried foul. It had been a huge ugly mess and, given his particular reputation, no one was readily inclined to believe him. Guy, Payne and Danny had, of course, but they'd been on a short list. Needless to say, since then he'd been a lot more...selective.

Payne took another mouthful of beer and swallowed. "So I take it you're going in undercover?"

Jamie nodded. "That's the plan."

"I still don't get it," Guy said, his shrewd gaze speculative. "How are you supposed to guard her if you don't know where the threat is coming from?"

Precisely, Jamie thought, still smelling a rat. "He told me he'd give me an update once I'm in place, but the gist of the order was to stick to her like glue."

Guy scowled. "And that's not going to look suspicious?"

Jamie shrugged. Just thinking about it made his head hurt. "Hell if I know," he muttered tiredly. It sounded odd, but not altogether difficult, so that was a plus, right? In all honesty, it would be a relief to simply be done with it. This favor was his last niggling tie to a life he'd left behind. Had to leave behind to preserve his own sanity.

Even as early as last year, if anyone had told him that he'd wanted to be anything other than a United States Army Ranger, he would never have believed it. The military had given him purpose, manned him up and given him an outlet for what he now recognized as disappointment toward an absentee father.

Thanks to a hardworking mother and a hot-headed Irish grandmother who weren't averse to boxing his ears when the need arose—an unexpected smile curled his lips, remembering—Jamie had been a lot better off than a lot of the boys he knew whose fathers *had* been around.

Like Guy, Jamie thought, covertly shooting a look at his friend. Guy's old man had been a royal bastard, a hard-assed proponent of the "spare the rod, spoil the child" mentality. Unfortunately that had been the extent of his religious tendencies. He'd been a mean-spirited drunk who, on more than one occasion, had sent his son to the Emergency Room. Guy hadn't heard from the man since he was in his late teens. Frankly, Jamie had toyed with the idea of looking the old man up and thrashing the shit out of him. Someone needed to, at any rate.

Jamie's gaze slid to Payne. Payne's father had been at home while Payne was growing up, but from the little things that his friend had shared over the years, he might as well have not been. Payne's father had always had one eye on the door and the other on another woman. His parents had apparently stayed married for Payne's benefit, but Jamie suspected Payne would have had a lot more respect for both of them if they'd merely divorced and done away with the infidelities.

They finally ended the marriage when Payne graduated from high school and since then, Payne's father had systematically married and divorced women who were craftily garnering another portion of his inheritance. He needed to be thrashed as well, Jamie decided, but for different reasons.

Quite frankly, all three of them had been raised in unconventional households and the older Jamie got, the more he suspected that no one's family was normal. Normal was as real as Santa Claus and the Tooth Fairy.

Normal didn't exist.

And after Danny's death, he wasn't so sure that the ideas of *right* and *just* weren't myths also. If they existed, if they were true, then why hadn't Danny walked away from that ill-fated mission with the rest of them?

Being in the military, death was a distinct possibility. One didn't enlist without knowing—without *believing*—in the greater good and being willing to die for that cause. Jamie, Guy, Payne, Danny— they'd all felt the same way.

Being a Ranger was more than a career. It had been a labor of love. Brave men had essentially committed treason when they'd formed this country. Thomas Jefferson had been in his early thirties when he'd penned the Declaration of Independence. That still amazed him, Jamie thought. So young and yet so wise. A vastly different world and set of values from where they were today. But that was a whole other issue.

At any rate, their very freedom was based on bravery, on loyalty and on a belief in a cause that so many, quite frankly, didn't appreciate and took for granted. There were thousands of men in marked and unmarked graves all over the globe who'd boldly gone to war and sacrificed their lives for this country. Jamie would gladly give his own…and yet living with the grief of a fallen friend somehow seemed more difficult than dying himself.

Something had changed that night. Not just for him, but for Guy and Payne as well. Rationally they'd all known the risks. But knowing it and dealing with it had turned out to be two completely different things. Did Jamie still believe in his country? In his service? In the merit of even that particular mission?

Yes, to all of the above.

He just didn't believe he could watch another friend die.

Danny, a brother to him in every way that counted, had taken his last breath in Jamie's arms. He'd watched the spark fade from Dan's eyes, felt his life slip away like a shadow…and Jamie had felt a part of himself die on that sandy, blood-soaked hill as well.

The familiar weight of grief filled his chest, forcing him to release a small breath. Whatever Garrett wanted him to do had to be easier than that, by God. It had to be.

"Look at it this way," Guy finally said in a blatant attempt to lighten the moment when the silence had stretched beyond the comfortable, a still too often occurrence. He shrugged. "She could be ugly."

Payne nodded, smiling encouragingly. "It'd definitely be easier for you to guard an ugly woman, Flanagan. Less temptation." He selected a celery stick. "What's her name?"

Smiling in spite of himself, Jamie rubbed the bridge of his nose. "Audrey Kincaid."

"Pretty name," Guy remarked thoughtfully. "But that doesn't mean anything," he added magnanimously, the smart-ass.

"Right," Payne said. "She could still be ugly."

Not even with the luck of the Irish, Jamie thought, but it didn't matter. She could look like a friggin' supermodel and he wasn't going to touch her with a ten-foot pole.

Actually, he had a grim suspicion who the granddaughter might be and he knew for a fact that not only wasn't she ugly, but in fact, she was drop-dead instant-hard-on gorgeous. The Colonel only had two pictures of family in his office—one Jamie knew for a fact was Garrett's wife because he'd met her several times.

The other was of a young blue-eyed beauty about the right age with long curly black hair. It was a candid shot of her and an enormous brindled English Mastiff. Considering the dog wasn't lunging for her throat, but sitting docilely by her side, Jamie could only assume the animal was hers.

His lips quirked. Quite frankly, if that was who he was being sent to protect, he imagined the dog could do a better job of it than he could. Furthermore, he hoped like hell it wasn't her, because for reasons he'd never really understood, he'd always been drawn to that picture, of the woman in it specifically. Every time he'd visited Garrett's office he found himself staring at it—at *her*. There was an inherent kindness in her eyes, a softness about her that he found particularly compelling. That trait combined with the obvious intelligence and just a hint of mischief made her face the most interestingly beautiful one he'd ever seen.

No doubt guarding her would be absolute torture, particularly given Garrett's orders. Jamie felt a grin tease his lips. He was pretty attached to his penis, thank you very much, and there wasn't a doubt in his mind that Garrett wouldn't make good on his threat if Jamie put so much as a toe out of line.

Furthermore, if he botched this favor, he'd just end up owing Garrett another one and moving on would be that much further away. Jamie tipped his tumbler back, felt the smooth amber taste slide down his throat.

And there wasn't a woman alive who could make him risk that.

# 2

CELL PHONE SHOULDERED to her ear, Audrey Kincaid stood at the cashier's stand of her local grocery store, absently pulled a tampon out of her purse and tried to write a check with it.

The thin, pimply-faced teenager behind the register sniggered. "Er… That's not going to work, ma'am."

Mortified, Audrey closed her eyes and, blushing furiously, awkwardly shoved her hand back into her bag in search of a pen. Ordinarily she thought it was incredibly rude of people to use their cell phones while in the checkout and, had she been talking to anyone but her grandfather, she would have cut the call short, or merely asked the person to call back.

But one didn't do that with her grandfather.

*The Colonel* didn't abide interruptions.

He was accustomed to being listened to and the idea that she—or any one else for that matter— might not be interested in what he had to say was unthinkable. A military man through and through, he was a surly, autocratic, occasionally ill-tempered pain in the ass who thought that an untucked shirt-tail was an abomination and rap music a crime against nature. His vehicles were American made, his lawn an immaculate work of art where the grass didn't dare offend him by growing out of sync, and his home office an inner sanctum of dark wood, Old Spice and the scent of cherry cigar smoke.

Though he was the unquestioned leader of their family, most of the members of their clan could only tolerate him in small doses, her mother included. But for whatever reason, he and Audrey had always shared a special bond. For all of his grit and grump, from the time she'd been just a little girl she'd loved listening to his stories. While the other grandchildren had gravitated to their grandmother's sewing room and kitchen, Audrey had preferred playing chess in the Colonel's office and coaxing orchids and other finicky flowers in his greenhouse.

Was now a bad time to talk? Definitely. She was standing in the checkout, feeling the murderous eye of a harried mother behind her, trying to write a damned check with a tampon, for pity's sake… but she had no intention of letting him know that. She had neither the nerve nor the disrespect to pull it off.

"I need a favor, Audie," her grandfather said, using the nickname he'd given her shortly after she was born.

Audrey handed the cashier a check, accepted her receipt and one-handedly wheeled her cart-with-the-cockeyed-wheel toward the door. No small feat, she thought, suppressing an irritated grunt. Trying to sound as though she wasn't the least bit inconvenienced, she said, "Sure, Gramps. What can I do for you?"

"I'm sending a guy to you who's in need of special attention."

Her grandfather referring someone to Unwind— her camp for the stressed-out from all walks of life, whether it was high-powered executives who'd logged in too many hours and consumed too many antidepressants, or strung-out mothers who'd doled out too many juice boxes and covered car-pool one time too many—wasn't the least bit unusual. She'd had many a weary soldier through her camp, many an overwhelmed officer's wife ensconced in one of her little lakeside cottages.

But this was the first time he'd ever asked her to give anyone *special* attention. Clearly, this was no ordinary person. Whoever this guy was, given her grandfather's line of work, he'd most likely been through hell. Her heart inexplicably squeezed for both the unknown man and his unknown pain.

Empathy, dammit. Her biggest weakness.

Four years into a high-powered job on Wall Street as a commodities broker, Audrey had had the ultimate wake-up call—at the ripe old age of twenty-six, she'd had a heart attack. A small one, but still a heart attack nonetheless. She'd been healthy—a regular at the gym—with no prior history of any cardiovascular problems.

In the weeks preceeding it, however, she'd had multiple stress-related panic attacks, had started filling her regular thirty-two-ounce java cup with straight-up espresso and her snack of choice had been chocolate-covered coffee beans. Hell, she'd been wound so tight it had been a miracle that she hadn't snapped completely.

To make matters worse, she'd been in a bad relationship which had ended with a restraining order. Unfortunately, Audrey had a knack for attracting damaged men who needed a lot of attention—emotional vampires, she'd come to call them, because they tended to suck the life right out of her.

But no more.

She'd promised herself after Jerry that she'd never get involved with another damaged, life-sucker again. A wry smile curled her lips.

And her present boyfriend was anything but that.

At any rate, she'd had to seriously rethink her life path and the first thing that her family—and her grandfather, in particular—had insisted she do was give up the job. Initially Audrey had protested. What the *hell* was she supposed to do? But one teary-eyed look from the Colonel, when she would have sworn the man had had his tear ducts surgically removed, had been all it took to make her seek an alternate, less stressful career.

After her own heart attack, Audrey had learned that there were many more like her—young Type-A professionals who were burning the candle at both ends and essentially stressing their healthy bodies beyond their limits. When a well-meaning friend suggested that she make a list of things that relaxed her, then take it with her to a soothing vacation spot, a lightbulb went off for Audrey and Unwind was born.

She took a risk, cashed in her 401-K, and bought a somewhat run-down thirty-two-acre summer sleep-away camp up on Lake Bliss in Winnisauga, Maine. A year later Unwind was a fully renovated quaint, but comfortable getaway with custom luxuries for each of its visitors.

Two years after that, it was operating fully in the black.

In order to personalize each experience, campers were required to fill out a lengthy questionnaire, which detailed the reason for their visit as well as personal preferences for their ultimate relaxing stay. She had a fabulous kitchen crew on staff as well as a fully-equipped spa. The library sported hundreds of books and movies for campers who craved brain candy and mindless entertainment.

For those who liked to work out their frustrations in a more physical manner, there were the stables, a state-of-the-art gym, various hiking trails and a multitude of water sports compliments of the lake. Between the amenities which were automatically provided and the accommodations she made as a result of the campers' requests, Unwind provided a calm, soothing atmosphere of escape and relaxation. In short, it was the baby of her own rebirth and she loved it.

Audrey opened the back gate of her SUV and began loading her grocery bags into the cargo area.

"I've already spoken to Tewanda," her grandfather said, "and took the liberty of filling out all the necessary paperwork."

In the process of awkwardly moving a twenty-pound bag of dog food—which would last all of one week the way that Moses, her English Mastiff, ate—Audrey frowned. "*You* filled out the paperwork?"

He hesitated. "Flanagan will be there on my orders and I'm not altogether sure he would have been completely truthful regarding the nature of his visit."

That made sense, she supposed. Despite her best efforts to draw people out, they were often purposely vague about the reason for their visit. Still, part of the Unwind experience was customization. How was she supposed to customize this visit if the participant hadn't filled out the form? Tewanda knew this, Audrey thought. Surely her crackerjack assistant hadn't simply let that slide. Even for her grandfather. Oh, hell. Who was she kidding? *She* wouldn't have called him on it. How could she expect Tewanda to?

Thoroughly intrigued now, Audrey closed the back gate and climbed into the driver's seat. "And what exactly is the reason for his visit?"

"He lost a good friend eight months ago," the Colonel said somberly. "Let's just say that he's having a hard time getting through it."

Audrey's heart squeezed. "That's certainly understandable."

Her grandfather cleared his throat. "Right. Well, it would probably be better if you didn't mention it to him. He just needs some TLC and no one can give him that quite the way that you can, Audie. You have a rare gift for making people feel better."

Gift or curse? Audrey wondered, more often feeling like it was the latter. She'd always been a very empathetic person, to the point that she often absorbed so much of another person's pain that she made herself physically ill. Even as a little girl she'd managed to attract the downtrodden, the kids everyone picked on. In her teens, things had pretty much stayed the same—the rebels, the outcasts, the shy and withdrawn. Basically anyone with a problem.

But with maturity came a different set of issues, bigger obstacles, and she found herself staying emotionally wrung out. She'd given so much to other people—usually, and to her detriment, to a significant other—that she hadn't had anything left for herself. Unwind had been the perfect solution because it had afforded her the opportunity to capitalize on her strengths, but enabled her to share the load, so to speak.

"What was his name again?" she asked. She wanted to make sure to look for the paperwork when she got back to camp.

"Major Jamie Flanagan. He was a Ranger in a special forces unit of mine. A damn fine one," her grandfather added with obvious pride.

"*Was* a Ranger?"

"Er... He and a couple of other friends left the military a few months ago."

Audrey paused. She didn't understand. If he'd left the military, then how could her grandfather *order* him into Unwind? "But—"

Accurately following her line of thinking, the Colonel chuckled. "What?" he joked. "You think a soldier who leaves the military automatically leaves my command, Audie?" She could almost see him shaking his head. "Surely you know me better than that?"

One would think so, Audrey thought. Her grandfather...you had to love him.

"Anyway, enough about Flanagan. He'll be arriving Monday and I've made sure that I've listed activities which should—" he cleared his throat of a distinctly wicked chuckle "—*appeal* to him. All I ask is that you keep a close eye on him. Spend as much time with him as possible. I'll call for regular updates on his progress."

This conversation was getting weirder and

weirder by the second. One minute her grandfather sounded genuinely concerned, the next he sounded downright…gleeful. She'd better take a look at that questionnaire, Audrey thought with a curious sense of foreboding. Something definitely wasn't right.

"So tell me what's happening with you?" he asked briskly, effectively ending that line of conversation. "Still seeing David?"

"It's Derrick," Audrey replied, repressing a smile. Her grandfather knew this perfectly well. He just couldn't stand the guy. "And yes, I am."

"More's the pity," her grandfather said glibly, never one to mince words. And unfortunately he had many where Derrick was concerned.

Audrey exhaled a long-suffering sigh. *"Gramps,"* she chided.

"You could do so much better, you know. You're a smart, pretty girl. Why you'd want to shackle yourself to that self-absorbed blowhard for the rest of your life is a mystery to me."

A frown wrinkled her brow. She hadn't told her family that Derrick had proposed. "Who said I was getting married?"

"No one," he said. Almost too easily, Audrey thought, wondering if she was being a tad paranoid. "I just assumed that since you're still together, marriage has to be on the horizon. What's the point of a prolonged relationship if you aren't moving toward a more permanent arrangement? If there's no goal, there's no point, right?"

For someone who didn't like Derrick, her grandfather had an alarmingly similar thought process. Derrick had used the same argument just last week when he'd issued his ultimatum—marry him or break up.

Quite frankly, she didn't want to do either.

For reasons she knew better than to explore, marrying him right now was out of the question... But she didn't want to break up either. Sure Derrick had his faults. He spent too much time on his hair, he laughed too hard at his own jokes and, the biggest turnoff of all, he screamed like a girl when he came. This high-pitched, rupture-your-eardrums screech would be right at home in a bad B-movie. Honestly, it was awful.

In addition, he was *a bit* self-absorbed, but that only meant that he wasn't dependent upon her to fill him up, right? After a succession of life-suckers, that had certainly been a welcome change, one that she'd desperately needed.

While she could admit that his confidence might get on other people's nerves, most of the time it didn't bother her at all. Really. She told herself that it was refreshing, that confidence was an admirable trait and Derrick... She grinned in spite of herself. Well, Derrick had that particular characteristic in spades.

Which is why her grandfather hated him.

Her lips curled with wry humor. Evidently her grandfather didn't think Derrick had the necessary qualities to back up the confidence. But it didn't matter what her grandfather thought. It only mattered what Audrey thought, and most of the time Derrick's somewhat exaggerated ego didn't bother her at all. There was something to be said for a guy who wasn't dependent on her opinion. Compared to her other relationships, Derrick was a walk in the park. He was easy.

Was she in love with him? Probably not. Her heart didn't skip a beat when he touched her hand—or any other part of her, for that matter—and, though he traveled frequently with his job, she couldn't exactly say that she'd ever truly missed him.

But there was a consistency and predictability to their relationship which she found quite comfortable, for lack of a better explanation. And she had no desire to change the status quo. Hopefully by the end of next week she'd be able to come up with a convincing argument for her cause. That was the plan, at any rate, as far as she had one.

"Well, you know what I think of him," her grandfather said. "He's a—"

Audrey chuckled softly. "Yes, Gramps, I certainly don't have to wonder about that." Ever. In fact, she could confidently say that not many people *ever* had to wonder what the Colonel thought. It was part of his charm.

"Don't be fresh, young lady," he scolded. "I only

have your best interests at heart. And he's not one deserving of yours," he added gruffly.

Affection swelled, making Audrey smile. Now how could she stay mad at him when he said things like that? "I know you do."

"Yeah, well, always be sure and keep that in mind," he muttered darkly, causing a momentary premonition of dread.

Audrey scowled. "Why would I need to keep that—"

"Gotta go, sweetheart," he said briskly. "Your grandmother's got dinner on the table and you know how she gets if the roast gets cold. I'll talk to you next week. Take good care of my boy." A resounding click echoed into her ear, signaling the end of their bizarre conversation.

Baffled, Audrey stared at her cell before closing it, then gave her head a little shake. Men, she thought. Even the older, so-called wiser ones were incomprehensible.

*In future, keep that in mind,* he'd said. Clearly he intended to give her a reason to do just that.

The question was…*what?*

# 3

"LET ME GET THIS STRAIGHT," the young Halle Berry look-alike on the other side of the reception desk said. "*You're* the Colonel's friend?" She had an "oh-hell-no" look on her face, as if she couldn't quite believe him.

Jamie smiled awkwardly. "I am," he repeated, verifying the fact.

Her dark brown eyes widened in what could only be described as shocked disbelief, then her gaze turned consideringly crafty and a secret smile curled her lips. "That sly old dog," she muttered under her breath, flipping through a stack of large white envelopes. "He said he had an ace up his sleeve, but I never dreamed…" She trailed off.

"I'm sorry?"

She looked up and handed him a packet. "Oh, nothing." She smiled warmly. "Welcome to Unwind. I'm Tewanda. If you have any questions, you can reach me by dialing zero from the phone in your cottage. Here's your welcome information as well as your itinerary and key. You're in number eight, a nice secluded little hideaway with a beautiful view of the lake. It's also got a pier, should you decide you'd like to swim or fish." She leaned forward and pointed to a laminated map attached to her desk. "You'll find a map of the property in your packet as well, but things are clearly marked so you shouldn't have any problems. We'll have an informal meet and greet in the lodge at six. It isn't mandatory, but we urge you to come. In the meantime—"

Jamie sensed movement behind him and watched Tewanda's warm brown gaze turn frosty. He glanced over his shoulder and saw a man strolling toward them across the room.

"Where's Audrey?" the guy asked, interrupting them rudely. Jamie scowled.

Though he knew it was ridiculous, he instantly disliked the guy.

"I'm with a guest right now, Derrick," Tewanda said coolly. "As I was saying Mr. Flanagan, settle in and—"

"I can see that," Derrick interrupted again. He shot Jamie a condescending look, one that somehow managed to be pitying and patronizing at once. It was a "you-poor-weak-bastard" look, which made Jamie's blood pressure rise and his right fist involuntarily clench.

"But I'm in a bit of a hurry and I need to see Audrey before I go." He paused. "She hasn't returned any of my calls, which can only lead me to assume that you haven't passed along any of my messages."

Tewanda's nose flared as she drew in a breath. "Oh, I've passed them along, all right. Maybe she just doesn't want to talk to you."

He smiled as if the idea was out of the question. "Oh, I doubt that. Page her," he ordered. "I'm pressed for time."

With a tight "excuse me" and a murderous look, Tewanda lifted a walkie-talkie from the desk.

The man leaned over to Jamie, as though he were an ally. "Good help's hard to find these days," he said, shooting a look at Tewanda. "I've tried to tell Audrey that she should let her go, but does she listen to me?"

He certainly hoped not, Jamie thought, sidling away from him. What a prick.

"Audrey, Derrick is here disrupting a check-in and won't leave until he speaks with you. Could you come up here and get rid of him— Er, I mean *talk* to him, please?" she asked with faux sweetness.

"See," Derrick said. "Such impertinence. If I ever have any say-so—and I will," he added with a confident smile, "—then she'll be the first of many changes I make around here."

Tewanda merely rolled her eyes. "Oh, don't worry, Derrick. The day you have any say-so will be the day I quit."

"Where's she at?" he asked, ignoring her comment. He checked his watch again and glanced impatiently toward the door.

"I don't have her on GPS," she snapped. "How the hell should I know?"

A startled laugh clogged Jamie's throat and he and Tewanda shared a smile. "Sorry," she mumbled.

"It's all right," he told her, waving it off.

"What are you apologizing to him for?" Derrick asked, seemingly offended. "It's me you were rude to."

She tidied a stack of papers on her desk and grunted. "In a perfect world, you wouldn't exist."

Jamie had only been in the man's company for a total of thirty seconds and found that he wholeheartedly concurred.

Derrick scowled and readied his mouth for a comeback, but before he could utter a sound, the woman from the photo on Garrett's desk walked in.

*Sonofabitch,* Jamie thought, his suspicions confirmed. *Oh, this was not good. Not good at all.*

As an elite graduate of Ranger School, Jamie had been trained to notice every detail. For instance, the minute he'd walked into this room, he'd noted everything from the exits—doors and windows—to the half-eaten jelly doughnut hidden behind a potted plant on the desk. In a pinch he could describe the pile of the carpet, the picture hanging on the opposite wall and could cite the programs currently running on the computer. It was this very training that enabled him to quickly catalogue Audrey Kincaid's every feature.

In the time it took her to cross the room, Jamie had noted that her hair wasn't black as it had seemed in the picture, but rather a very dark brown just a degree shy of black. Espresso, he decided. Her eyes were the same, a clear intelligent blue that shimmered with wit and warmth. She was petite—five-four or under, he imagined—but with an athletic build that was surprisingly curvy. She had a small mole just up and to the right of her lush mouth and when she smiled, an adorable dimple winked in her left cheek. She was sexy and enchanting and delicious and he found himself fighting the inexplicable urge to lick her all over.

Which wouldn't be good because she was totally off-limits. Garrett would kill him. After he cut his pride and joy off and force-fed it to him, Jamie reminded himself grimly.

He'd do well to remember that.

"Derrick," she said in a softly chiding voice. "I thought you'd be on your way to the airport by now."

Derrick grinned, gathered her into an awkward hug and said, "I couldn't leave without giving you a proper goodbye." He nuzzled her cheek and, though it could have only been wishful thinking on Jamie's part, she winced as if she didn't particularly care for his attention. Looking ready to retch, Tewanda rolled her eyes.

"You didn't have to do that," she said, disentangling herself from him. "You, uh… You don't want to miss your flight."

"No, no, of course not. I just wanted to give you a reason to miss me."

Audrey smiled, rather weakly, it seemed, but didn't say anything.

He ran a finger down her nose. "And I also wanted to remind you to think about what I'd asked you."

This time she chuckled, but there was almost a sick-sounding quality to it that Jamie was certain both he and Tewanda had heard, but that had completely gone unnoticed by Derrick. In fact, he got the distinct impression that Derrick missed a lot.

"Er…no worries," she told him. "I'm not likely to forget."

"I guess not," he said, smiling smugly. "All right then. I'd better be off." He bent down and kissed her on the cheek. "I'll see you Sunday…and I'll expect an answer," he added ominously. Without so much as a backward glance to the rest of the occupants in the room, he strode out.

"Want me to give him an answer?" Tewanda offered hopefully when the door closed behind Derrick.

Audrey's shoulders sagged with a sigh of obvious relief. "No," she told her. "That won't be necessary." She pushed a hand through her hair, then looked up and for the first time her gaze landed on

Jamie. "Oh," she said, her eyes widening in obvious embarrassment.

Tewanda grinned. "This is our newest guest—Jamie Flanagan," she said. "The Colonel's friend," she added significantly.

Impossibly, her eyes widened further, then another "oh" slipped from between her lips. Three beats passed, then she gave her head a small shake. She smiled and hurried forward to offer her hand.

Against his better judgment he took it and, to his immediate chagrin, his palm tingled where it touched hers. Heat detonated in his loins and a curious warmth expanded in his chest.

Now that was novel, Jamie thought, somewhat startled by the singularly disturbing reaction. His dick had stirred the instant he'd seen her—no surprise there because it nodded at almost every woman of the right age with a halfway decent rack—but this was the first time he'd ever gotten a charge out of merely touching a woman's hand. While the picture of her might have been compelling, seeing her in the flesh was nothing short of magnetic. Jamie gritted his teeth as more prophet-of-doom musings rolled through his head.

"It's a pleasure, Mr. Flanagan."

"Jamie, please," he told her, smiling, as a litany of curses reeled through his head.

"Jamie, then. I'm Audrey. Welcome to Unwind."

Hell more like, Jamie thought, because guarding this woman without seducing her was going to be an exercise in restraint which would result in the most perverse sort of torture he could imagine.

Unwind hell.

He'd be lucky if he didn't come un-glued, un-hinged, un-wound, or un-manned by the time this week was over.

"SINCE MR. FLANAGAN IS a special guest, why don't you show him to his cottage personally?" Tewanda suggested sweetly.

Unable to tear her gaze away from the man in question, it took Audrey a few seconds to respond. "Er…sure. I'd be happy to. If you'll just come with me," she said trying to sound more professional than the half-wit she'd undoubtedly just appeared to be.

Sheesh, Audrey thought, resisting the pressing urge to fan herself as they walked outside into the cool autumn air. You'd think she'd never seen a good-looking man before.

But this man wasn't merely good-looking, she thought with a covert peek from the corner of her eye—he was *pure* take-your-breath-away nipple-tingling flash-fire-across-the-thighs *eye candy*.

*This* was her grandfather's friend? *This* was the guy who needed special attention?

Quite frankly, she couldn't imagine that he didn't get all the attention that he wanted.

Of the female variety, at least, she thought with a quirk of her lips.

He had that look, that cocked, locked, ready to rock sexuality that instantly put a woman in mind of warm massage oil and thigh-quaking orgasms.

Unfortunately, to her immeasurable chagrin considering she'd only been in his presence a mere sixty seconds, that included herself.

That certainly didn't bode well for a week of what her grandfather had insisted should be intense one-on-one attention. Particularly as she was supposed to be considering a marriage proposal. But that was a whole other problem she'd simply have to think about later, she decided, channeling a little Scarlet O'Hara.

Right now, she was finding it hard enough to regulate her breathing, much less anything else. She was too distracted by the disturbingly masculine line of his jaw, those sleepy hazel eyes which managed to be both wise and wicked and that shock of adorably curly brown hair.

He was clearly an alpha—from the jut of that jaw to the swagger in his step, everything about him screamed *merited* confidence—but that hair softened him up, made him approachable and gave him a beta boy-next-door quality that mysteriously added to his overall sex appeal. Audrey felt a smile tug at her lips. No doubt he could make an orchid bloom in an arctic winter or charm the habit right off a nun if the mood struck…then convince her it was her idea.

And she'd bet he didn't scream like a girl when he came, either.

*Mercy.*

Jamie paused next to what was clearly a rental sedan. "Do I drive up to the cottage?" he asked.

Audrey shook her head and indicated an area to the side of the office. "Up there will be fine. If you'd like to leave your bags with me, I'll wait here while you park."

"Bag."

"I'm sorry?"

"You said 'bags.'" An interesting display of muscle action rippled across his back as he reached into the back seat, pulled out a small duffel and, wearing a lazy smile, handed it to her. "It's bag. Singular."

Audrey chewed the corner of her lip, eying the duffel skeptically. "You have almost a week's worth of clothes in *this* bag?"

"With a couple of changes to spare."

She chuckled and inclined her head. He certainly had the art of packing light down to a science. Of course, given his military training she supposed that was habit as much as necessity. The more they packed, the more they had to carry. Too bad that some of the other people who came here didn't have that same mentality. If they had to schlep their weighty Louis Vuitton everywhere themselves, they might rethink packing everything but the kitchen sink.

Feeling herself intrigued beyond what she

to be prudent, Audrey waited while Jamie moved the car. He made quick work of it, locked up, then loped with easy grace back down to where she stood and took the bag. "All right, then," he said, casually taking in their surroundings. "Where to?"

Audrey set off and pointed toward the lake. "Right down there."

"This is a beautiful place," Jamie remarked, seemingly enjoying the fall landscape. Tall trees dressed in their finest foliage soared overhead and painted a mirror image on the lake's rippling surface. New England asters bloomed in a purple perfusion of color along the various winding stone paths throughout camp and a couple of bickering squirrels squabbled over acorns. Stark white steep-roofed cottages were tucked along the lake and deep into the tree line, giving the impression of an old Colonial village.

"Thanks," she said. "I'm proud of it. It was in pretty bad shape when I first bought it. Beautiful land, of course." She slid him a glance. "It's not called Lake Bliss for nothing. But the buildings and landscaping were all in need of serious repair."

"How long have you been in business?"

"This is our fourth season."

"Season?"

"We don't operate year-round," she explained. "The winters are too intense and frankly, we don't have enough business to merit being open beyond

Christmas. We run camps March through November."

Jamie nodded. "So what do you do those other months? Hunker down here?" He glanced around. "I'm assuming you live on site."

"I do," Audrey confirmed with a smile. She gestured toward her own place, a slightly larger variation of the guest cottages. "I usually spend a month recuperating, a month vegging out and another month traveling and visiting family. In February, we're gearing up toward a new season, so even though we aren't technically open, we're here getting things in order."

He smiled and she felt that grin all the way down to her little toes. "Sounds like you've got things down to a science."

Audrey chuckled, shoving her hair away from her face. "Not really," she said. "But we've found a system that seems to be working for us." She mounted the steps to his cottage. "Ah. Here we are."

Jamie inserted the key into the lock and let himself in.

"It's fully stocked," Audrey told him, stepping in behind him. Which was quite nice because she got a wonderful view of his delectable ass—the ass she was not supposed to be noticing. She grimaced. Somehow she imagined this was not the sort of *special attention* her grandfather had in mind. "Linens, pantry—everything. Naturally, we've met any special requests, which were on your application form, but if you've forgotten anything, there's a general store just up the hill. If you can't find what you need there, let us know and we'll take care of it. No worries. That's our motto."

Jamie dropped his bag into a recliner. "Special requests?" A line wrinkled his forehead. "I didn't make any special requests."

Audrey forcibly flattened a smile and cleared her throat. "Er...my grandfather made several on your behalf."

"I'll just bet he did," Jamie muttered darkly with a comical grimace.

"You'll find Guinness beer in the fridge and Jameson whiskey in the cabinet." She cocked her head. "Tribute to your Irish heritage, I presume?"

Jamie nodded and grinned. "It's the best."

Audrey'd had Guinness before, but had never been much of a whiskey drinker. She confessed as much. "It's too much," she said. "I don't care for the burn."

*"Uisce beatha."* He sighed, absently scratching his chest.

"Come again?"

*"Uisce beatha.* It's Gaelic for 'water of life.'"

"Oh."

He chuckled. "Trust me, the Irish know how to make a good whiskey. You'll have to try it. It's smoother. It's got a sweet honey flavor and slides like silk down your throat."

Audrey resisted the pressing urge to fidget and

let go a small uneven breath. Well, when he put it like that, who wouldn't want to drink it?

Jamie crossed his arms over his chest and leaned a heavily muscled shoulder against the wall. His too-sexy lips quirked with droll humor. "What other special requests did the Colonel make for me?"

"Oh, just a few things," Audrey told him lightly. "Books, medications. The usual."

Liar, liar pants on fire. There'd been nothing *usual* about the things her grandfather had specifically asked for on Jamie's behalf. And in fact, now that she'd met him, she couldn't imagine that he'd need any of them.

Jamie frowned. "Books? Med—?"

"Anyway," Audrey smoothly interrupted before they could get into any of that. She moved toward the door, preparing to make a swift exit. "You'll want to get settled, I'm sure. Take your time, but do be sure and come up to the lodge at six. It's informal, but we like to go over everything that Unwind has to offer. I'll be taking care of you personally this week."

"Personally, eh?" he asked with a grin that would ignite water.

Audrey blushed. "That's right." She cleared her throat. "Anyway, be sure and bring your schedule—"

"Schedule?"

"Yes. It's in there—" she gestured toward the

manila envelope on top of his bag "—and we'll get you on the road to relaxation."

He muttered something else she didn't quite understand.

"I'm sorry?"

"It was nothing," Jamie said quickly, offering her a smile she knew he'd conjured solely for her benefit. It might have been false, but it was still potent. At any rate, he clearly didn't want to be here and, as her grandfather had said, was only acting on the Colonel's orders. That was going to make things much more difficult, Audrey thought, but she'd promised her grandfather that she'd do her best to take care of him.

For the next week, this guy was hers—the mere thought made her insides quiver—and even with the wacky trumped up so-called hobbies her grandfather had supplied for Jamie, she fully expected to enjoy herself much more than she should.

# 4

*You Can Go On—Dealing with Erectile Dysfunction.*

*Coping with Incontinence.*

Jamie snorted and tossed the books aside, then pulled his cell from the clip at his waist and dialed Garrett directly. "What?" he asked when the Colonel answered the phone. "Was *Chicken Soup for the Psychopath's Soul* on backorder?"

Garrett chuckled, the twisted bastard. "I see you've arrived."

"I have."

"And everything's in order?"

"Everything but your sense of humor. Basket-weaving? Watercolors? Ballroom dancing? Just exactly when were you planning to have me guard her?" Jamie asked, completely exasperated. Hobbies, hell. "Because the *relaxing* schedule I'm looking at leaves very little time for that."

"Tsk, tsk," said the Colonel. "You make it sound like you're not going to have a good time."

Jamie moved his duffel out of the recliner and dropped heavily into it. He flicked a casual glance around the living room and deemed it to his liking. Comfortable furniture, natural gender-neutral decor. A nice view of the lake. Not bad at all. "I didn't think the purpose of this mission was to ensure that I had a good time. I thought I was here to protect Audrey."

"Ah, Audrey, is it?"

Jamie felt his fingers tighten around the cordless phone. "That's her name. You didn't expect me to call her Ms. Kincaid, did you?"

"No, and I don't want anyone calling her Mrs. Derrick Willis either, which is the real reason you are there. Take notes. You're about to receive orders."

Jamie blinked, stunned. "What? I thought you said you wanted me to protect her from a personal enemy."

"I do—that enemy is Derrick Willis."

Jamie leaned forward in his chair. *Derrick? How could Derrick be his personal enemy? What the fu—*

"I have it on good authority that he's asked my granddaughter to marry him and has given her until the end of the week to make up her mind," Garrett said.

Jamie stilled. So *that* was the question Derrick-the-ass had been referring to, Jamie realized, suddenly sickened. Though he'd barely had time to rub two thoughts together since he'd gotten here, he had to admit that Audrey choosing a boyfriend like that sonofabitch was a little disheartening. Quite frankly, he would have thought she'd had better taste.

What was the draw? he wondered. It damned sure wasn't personality or sex appeal. The guy was provokingly abrasive at best and Jamie had personally seen her cringe when Derrick had tried to hug her. That certainly wouldn't make a happy marriage. It didn't make any sense.

And he sure as hell didn't see how he was supposed to "protect" her from Derrick.

"I don't understand," Jamie told him, thoroughly confused. "Derrick's not even here."

"I know. He's on a business trip."

What? Jamie wondered. Did he have the place bugged? "How did you know th—"

"Suffice it to say I have an excellent source in place who also has my granddaughter's best interests at heart."

Ah. *Tewanda*.

He was beginning to get the picture—albeit a vastly different one to what had originally been painted—but he still didn't see how he figured in it. "Sir, with all due respect, I fail to see how I can—"

Garrett chuckled. "For someone with a genius-level IQ, you certainly aren't doing a bang-up job of putting things together, Flanagan."

He supposed not, Jamie thought, completely baffled. He couldn't hit a target that wasn't here. What the hell did Garrett want him to do? Follow Derrick? If so, then why had he arranged for Jamie to be in place here? It didn't make any sense. Exactly what did the Colonel have in mind—

"Oh, for heaven's sake," Garrett finally snapped. "You're bait."

If Jamie hadn't had a death grip on the phone he would have dropped it. He felt his eyes widen and his jaw drop. "I'm *what?*"

"Bait," Garrett repeated calmly. "Your reputation with the ladies makes you the perfect man for this mission, Flanagan. Oh, I suppose McCann or Payne would have done okay as well, but in order to make absolutely sure that Audrey doesn't permanently attach herself to that pompous moron, I thought I'd err on the side of caution and send you in."

Silence stretched across the line while Jamie tried to process what the Colonel had just told him.

"You see," Garrett continued, "if my granddaughter is even remotely attracted to you, she wouldn't dream of saying 'I do' to that gelled-up windbag. She has too much class. And it's no secret that you have a certain talent with women... So here are your orders and you'd better heed them to the letter," Garrett warned. "Otherwise, I assure you that you'll be very, *very* sorry." He paused, letting the threat sink in. "For the next five days I want you to shadow my granddaughter. Spend time with her, flirt with her, compliment her. Do whatever it is that you do to get women to fall all over you. But that is all. I'm not pimping you out to my grand-daughter, Flanagan," he said gruffly, some of that legendary piss and gravel in his voice. "Baseball's an all-American game, so I'll put it into terms I'm sure you'll understand. You are on-deck, but you will never get to bat, do you understand?"

Still in a state of shock, Jamie cleared his throat. "Yes, sir."

"First base is forbidden. Second base is forbid-den. Third base is forbidden. If you get anywhere near home plate, you'll *need* that book on erectile dysfunction. You'll also need a surgeon to remove my foot from your ass. Is there any part of this that's unclear?"

"No, sir."

"This is a pseudo-seduction, for lack of a better description. I don't want her to want *you*, per se. I just want her to want anyone but Derrick. You're there to instill doubt and I know you can make that happen."

He could, Jamie knew. He just didn't want to do it. Not to her. It was wrong and underhanded, a personal interference he knew that she wouldn't appreciate. "Sir, I realize that I don't know your granddaughter, but if she ever finds out that you've done something like this, she'll—"

"That's why she'll never find out," Garrett said in his typical omnipotent voice. "She's special," he told Jamie. "She deserves someone who will see that. That blowhard Derrick sees nothing beyond himself."

Jamie passed a hand over his face. "Yeah," he admitted. "I noticed."

"You met him?" he asked, surprised.

"He interrupted my check-in. He came in and demanded to see Audrey."

"Then certainly you can see why I've resorted to these somewhat…unorthodox measures."

Actually, though Jamie didn't appreciate being the means to which Garrett reached his end, he did see why the Colonel would take such a drastic approach to derailing the relationship. He couldn't imagine any woman being permanently interested in Derrick, much less Audrey. Why? he wondered, intrigued beyond what was appropriate. What was she doing with someone who was so obviously wrong for her?

Jamie's head began to hurt. "If I'm going to do this, then I need a little back story."

"There's no *if,* Flanagan," Garrett told him gruffly. "You owe me and you agreed to my terms."

And there it was, Jamie thought with a mental sigh. "Fine. Bring me up to speed. How long have they been dating?"

"Too long."

Anything beyond a minute would be too long,

but that wasn't the answer he'd been looking for. "Naturally. Could you be a little more specific?"

"A little more than a year and half."

So definitely long enough to know whether they wanted to take things to the next level. Clearly Derrick did, otherwise he wouldn't have issued an ultimatum. And it had to have been an ultimatum, otherwise he wouldn't have added a time frame into the mix. So what were the consequences of saying no? Jamie wondered. A break-up? Most likely. Derrick seemed like the type.

"Is Audrey aware of the fact that you don't approve of Derrick?" Jamie knew the answer to that question before it was even fully out of his mouth. The Colonel was always willing to share his opinion—whether a person wanted to hear it or not.

The Colonel laughed. "What do you think?"

"Right," Jamie said, feeling like an idiot. "And yet she's still seeing him. Why's she bucking you on this? What's so special about Derrick?"

"I don't think there's anything special about Derrick."

"You don't, but she obviously does. Surely she's given you an explanation as to why she's still with him."

The Colonel hesitated. "She has," he conceded. "But I'm not sure I should share her personal business with you."

A bark of laughter erupted from Jamie's throat. Oh, now this was rich. "You've got to be kidding me. You've sent me up here to practically seduce her away from this other guy and yet your conscience is giving you a problem with *this?*" He chuckled darkly. "You need to check your moral compass."

"*Practically* is the key word there, Flanagan," Garrett growled. "But—" he sighed "—I suppose you're right. The more information you have, the better armed you'll be to deal with the situation."

Exactly, Jamie thought. Besides, he was genuinely curious. What on earth would make a great girl like Audrey interested in someone as self-absorbed and shallow as Derrick?

"My granddaughter is a very caring person, Flanagan—unusually empathetic—and as such, has always had a habit of attracting people, most often men, who require a lot of her. So much of her, in fact, that she found herself emotionally bankrupt. And sick. Derrick's appeal is that he's not like that. He's arrogant, but not damaged. At least, that's what I got out of what she's shared with me," the Colonel said, his voice ringing with a hell-if-I-know sort of resignation. He blew out a breath. "Anyway, I don't blame her for wanting someone who doesn't suck the life out of her, but I think she's swung too far in the other direction. She needs to find a happy medium. If she marries Derrick, that'll never happen."

It took Jamie a few seconds to absorb and digest what Garrett had just shared. "So, in other words, Derrick's easy."

"That too," Garrett replied. "You have your orders, Flanagan. I'll call for updates." He disconnected.

Jamie turned the phone off, leaned back into the recliner and let out a breath. Ten seconds later he turned the phone back on and dialed Ranger Security.

"You aren't going to believe this shit," he said in way of greeting when Payne answered his direct line. Jamie briefed his friend on recent events and waited while Payne took it all in.

"Let me get this straight. The boyfriend is the personal threat and he's sent you in there to 'pseudo-seduce' her away from him?"

"In a nutshell, yes."

To Jamie's extreme annoyance, Payne laughed. Not just a small series of chuckles, but a gut-rolling guffaw that set Jamie's nerves on edge. "That's c-cracked, man. I feel for you."

"Yeah, it really sounds like it," Jamie griped.

"Look at it this way. It's not dangerous, right?"

If he kept his pecker in his pants, no, Jamie thought. But if he snapped and ended up giving her a real seduction, then mortal danger was almost certain. Garrett would most definitely kill him.

"Not in the traditional sense, no."

Payne paused, evidently reading the ambiguity in that statement. "Damn. She's pretty, isn't she?"

Pretty didn't begin to cover it. She was beautiful in every sense of the word. Jamie had noted those soul-soothing eyes in the photograph in Garrett's office, but actually looking into them and feeling that calming sensation in her presence was quite… disconcerting. Garrett's explanation as to why she was with Derrick made perfect sense. He could easily see a needy person sucking up her goodness like a greedy parasite attached to her soul.

She wasn't seeing Derrick because she was in love with him—it was an act of self-preservation.

But Garrett was right. There had to be a happy medium. Derrick might not be draining her at the moment, but eventually her own unhappiness and dissatisfaction with the relationship would do the very thing she was trying to avoid.

Though he didn't approve of how the Colonel had chosen to interfere—and the part he'd ultimately be playing in it—he had to admit that he could see where she'd be better off.

She needed protecting all right. She needed protection from herself.

The question was…who was going to protect him?

When he'd thought he was just supposed to guard her, he'd worried about keeping his hands to himself. He'd known that it was going to take a Herculean effort on his part to try and keep his distance. Now he was charged with the task of wooing her… with no reward. What sort of divinely twisted infernal hell was this? Jamie wondered. To seduce with no seduction?

To seduce *her,* of all people?
"Yeah, she's pretty," Jamie finally confirmed.
And he was screwed.

# 5

*Atlanta*

PAYNE TOOK A PULL from his beer, then finished bringing Guy up to speed on Jamie's current situation. He laughed. "Can you believe that shit?"

Looking just as mystified as he undoubtedly had when Jamie had told him the nature of Garrett's "favor," Guy shook his head and smiled faintly. "You know, I fully expected him to utilize our skills, but that was one of Jamie's I would have never dreamed Garrett would risk putting into use. Especially with his own granddaughter."

"He's got a helluva lot more trust in our friend than I do," Payne admitted. "He said she's pretty."

Guy winced. "Damn."

"I know."

"I smell trouble."

He did, too. It was like turning a bloodhound loose, then telling him not to follow the trail. Fur-

thermore, he'd heard a bit of I'm-screwed misery
in Jamie's voice that definitely didn't get his vote
of confidence. Garrett undoubtedly was banking
on Jamie's ability to take an order—or take one for
the team—but this was different.

Jamie wasn't a Ranger anymore.

He was still a man of his word, but more than
one man had broken a promise when it came to a
woman. Sex did something to a guy. Made him
weak in a way that nothing else could. Payne's lips
quirked. Hell, his father was a perfect example of
that.

*Which was why he'd never be.*

Guy shot him a considering look. "Makes me
wonder what he's got in store for us."

Him, too. Payne had been certain that Garrett
had planned to use them for Uncle Sam. He'd never
dreamed that the crafty old bastard had planned on
cashing in those favors for himself. Point of fact,
it shed a completely different light on things. He
paused, tracing a bead of moisture down the side
of his beer, and re-evaluating. Not that it would
have changed anything—they would have agreed
to his terms anyway. They'd wanted out at any cost.
Still...

"I know," he finally said. His lips curled into
a grim smile. "Let's just hope like hell he doesn't
have any more relatives in need of rescue."

"Oh, I don't think we have to worry about that,"
Guy said. A smile rolled around his lips and a bark

of dry laughter erupted from his throat. "Evidently you and I aren't sexy enough."

Payne chuckled. "Speak for yourself, you ugly bastard. He didn't send me because he was afraid she'd fall in love with me. I was *too* much man."

Guy smiled, grabbing his beer. "Go to hell."

Yeah, and he could tell Jamie hello when he got there. He had a grim suspicion his buddy had been sent straight into the bowels of darkness.

"So THAT'S A BRIEF OVERVIEW of what we do here at Unwind. Any questions?" Audrey glanced around the room, waited a couple of beats, then smiled. "Okay then. Remember…no worries."

Though she'd been trying not to stare at Jamie, her gaze kept inexplicably wandering over to where he stood in the back of the room. Even if she hadn't known he had a special forces military background, she would have recognized the signs.

Casual, but alert, he constantly scanned the room, observing. She'd watched him note the exits, the number of people present and his demeanor seemed to suggest he could be a protector or predator, whichever the case may be. For reasons which made her question her own sanity, she found that wholly thrilling. In fact, she could honestly say that she'd never had such an overwhelming reaction to a man before.

"God, that man is beautiful."

Audrey barely refrained from jumping. Damn

Tewanda. "Don't sneak up on me like that," she chided, tearing her gaze away from the beautiful man in question.

"If you hadn't been staring so hard at him, you would have seen me walk up."

Since she couldn't argue with that, she decided to change the subject. "So, what do you think about this group?"

Tewanda nodded. "Seems good." She inclined her head toward a tall balding man in the corner. "He's a crier. We'll need to watch him." Next she turned her attention to a petite blonde with blood-red nails who carried a Prada knockoff. "That one. She's going to be a problem. She's already called three times about things that she says are 'wrong' and aren't her preferences. But don't worry I have everything on file and you know I don't make mistakes like that."

No, she didn't. Given their satisfaction guarantee promise, Tewanda was neurotically meticulous about the details. In fact, in their four years in business, she'd never made a mistake. Needless to say, she was an invaluable asset to Unwind and to Audrey, in particular. She also had the uncanny ability to size people up. Tewanda could spot a potential problem guest with almost psychic accuracy.

Audrey nodded, accepting her assessment. "Anybody else?"

"Yeah, there's one more."

"Point 'em out," she said from the corner of her mouth, smiling warmly at passersby.

"No need," she said. "Here he comes."

"What? Who?"

*"Him,"* she said significantly as Jamie sidled through the crowd toward them.

"Jamie?" Audrey said, startled. "What makes you say a thing like that?" Had she missed something? she wondered. Granted she'd initially been too preoccupied by the rest of him to note the sadness lingering around and in those mesmerizing hazel eyes, but she'd glimpsed it tonight.

Big time.

"Don't you play dumb with me," Tewanda told her, chuckling under her breath. "I know you think he's hot. You want him."

*"Tewanda."*

"Tewanda, Tewanda," she mimicked, as though she got tired of hearing her name repeated in that exasperated tone. "You know I'm right. That boy isn't just going to be trouble. He *is* trouble. Especially for you."

"Why for me?" she asked, instinctively knowing her friend was right.

"Haven't you been listening to me? Because you want him," she said with the sort of exaggerated patience used to communicate something to a person who might be a little slow.

"I just met him," Audrey chided with a nervous eye roll, an almost, but not outright denial.

"Doesn't matter. It's the animal instinct, honey. And I predict that you two will be going at it like a couple of Viagra-crazed rabbits by the end of the week."

Before she could shape her lips to refute that outlandish comment, a vision of her and Jamie, tangled up and sweaty and doing precisely what Tewanda had suggested materialized in her mind's eye, making her momentarily breathless. Her nipples beaded behind her bra, her knees weakened and a melting tingle started low in her belly and settled in her sex.

Oh, sweet Jesus.

If thinking about making it with him did this to her, then she couldn't begin to imagine what being with him would really be like.

Actually, that wasn't true.

She *could* imagine, and the resulting vision had an almost virtual reality effect. In fact, if she didn't derail this line of thinking immediately, she was going to have an immaculate orgasm. Right here in the lodge, amid a roomful of people. Audrey released a shuddering breath.

Now that was some potent sex appeal.

He sidled over and smiled, unwittingly upping her heart rate. Then her gaze tangled with his and, in the nanosecond before he could put a guard firmly in place, Audrey glimpsed a pain so intense she felt it deep in her belly. Oh, sweet Lord, she thought, as nausea threatened and her vision blackened around the edges. She *had* missed something.

*A huge something.*

Stark pain, grief, regret—they were all there, a perfect cocktail of misery. Her grandfather had been right, Audrey thought, swallowing. Jamie Flanagan had one helluva demon shadowing him. He disguised it well beneath effortless sex appeal and lazy charm, but she saw it, and more importantly felt it. In fact, while she'd had vast experience in feeling other people's pain, she could honestly say that she'd never suffered from this sort of intensity.

"Ladies," he said, jerking Audrey from her disquieting reverie.

Tewanda grinned. "Are you ready to unwind?" she asked him. "You look a little tense."

"I'm fine, thanks," Jamie told her, eyes twinkling.

"Audrey's a licensed masseuse," Tewanda said, much to Audrey's annoyance. Still a bit shaken, she resisted the urge to pinch her friend.

Audrey summoned a tight smile. "True, however we have a regular masseuse on staff. Part of the luxury of an expanding clientele." She managed a chuckle.

"So you don't have to be so *hands-on,* then," Jamie said, obviously enjoying her discomfort.

"Right."

"But since Jamie here is a *special* guest of the Colonel and you're supposed to be taking care of him personally, surely you wouldn't mind working out a few of his kinks, right, Audrey?"

Did Maine have the death penalty? Audrey wondered, sending her friend a murderously sweet smile. "Not at all," she said in what she knew was far from a normal voice.

Looking entirely too pleased with herself, Tewanda leaned forward as though she was about to impart a kernel of significant advice. "In fact, I can't think of a better way to start your Unwind experience than with a relaxing massage." She bobbed her head in a brisk nod. "I have one every week."

Jamie's eyes twinkled with humor. "Really?"

"Oh, yes." She preened. "It does wonders for my complexion."

"I've never had one. At least from a professional, that is," he amended.

And on that singularly disturbing note, Audrey cleared her throat. "You know what I think is the best way to start your Unwind experience?" she asked Jamie. "With a nice session of water colors down by the lake. My grandfather says you're quite the artist."

A soft chuckle erupted from his throat. "Really? I didn't realize he was a fan of my work. I'll have to paint something *special* for him."

Actually, her grandfather had said no such thing and she fully suspected that Jamie hadn't painted any sort of picture, much less a watercolor, since primary school. Playing along, was he? Now that was interesting. And it would be fun, considering her grandfather had already explained his bizarre preferences and hobby choices for Jamie. With the exception of the whiskey and beer, the *preferences* had been jokes. As for the hobby choices, her grandfather had chosen them so that Jamie could learn certain virtues. Like patience.

Audrey grinned. "Oh, good. We can have it framed in town and ship it to him before you leave."

His eyes glinted with knowing humor. "Excellent."

Marginally relaxing, Audrey rocked back a little on her heels.

"But I'll still want that massage."

And every muscle atrophied again, particularly the ones in her face which controlled her smile. "Of course," she said because she couldn't think of any other response. Dissembling while visions of her hands on his warm, naked skin, kneading those impressive muscles was completely beyond her. Audrey released a silent quivering sigh.

Time to go home, she decided. "Well, if you don't have any more questions, I think I'm going to call it an evening."

"I'll go with you," Tewanda said. She did an admirable job of looking concerned. "I don't like you walking up that hill all alone."

Honestly, this was over the top, even for Tewanda. Exasperated, Audrey shook her head. "I have walked up that hill alone every night of every season since we opened, Tewanda," she told her through partially gritted teeth. "I think I can manage."

"That may be true but—"

*"Te*wan*da."*

"I'll walk you home," Jamie offered, playing right into her maniacal matchmaking friend's hands.

"Really," Audrey insisted. "It isn't necessary."

"But it'll relax me," he said with a half-smile that made her belly do an odd little jump.

Oh, well…how nice for him. She wished she could say the same for herself.

"BE SURE TO GIVE MY REGARDS to the Colonel," Jamie leaned in and whispered to Tewanda before following a somewhat irate Audrey out of the room.

"Sure thing, Ace," Tewanda told him. She grinned and twinkled her fingers at him as he walked away. She was clearly enjoying herself, Jamie thought, fighting a chuckle. No doubt she'd received her instructions from the Colonel as well and was taking her role as matchmaker quite seriously.

While it was easy to laugh at her machinations, Jamie knew better than to discount them. As Audrey's right-hand man, so to speak, and clearly a good friend, she was better positioned than anybody to know what was happening with Audrey. If she was trying this hard to make sure that Audrey didn't marry Derrick, she had to have good reason.

Which made the Colonel sending him in as he had all the more understandable.

Sure, Jamie didn't like it, and no doubt being with her without *being with her* was going to be sheer hell, but she had two very discerning people covertly interfering on her behalf—three, if he counted himself, which, for reasons he didn't understand, he wasn't prepared to do just yet—and that told him enough about what he was doing to make him feel marginally better about his role in the deception.

Besides, he didn't have any choice. He'd owed Garrett.

Jamie opened the door for her, ushering Audrey out into the cool autumn air. Dusk had come and gone, bringing darkness and a spattering of bright stars. Fluffy clouds glowed in the moonlight and drifted lazily across the deep navy sky.

"She's a piece of work, isn't she?" Jamie remarked lightly as they descended the steps onto the walk.

Audrey chuckled, the sound soft, soothing and feminine against his ears. "Tewanda? That's one way of describing her." She crossed her arms over her chest, huddling further into her jacket. "I'm thinking 'fired' would be another."

Jamie laughed. "Surely not?"

"Nah," she relented. "I couldn't do what I do

without her. She's invaluable—and insufferable. That's part of her charm."

"Look at it this way," Jamie told her. "I bet you never have to wonder what she thinks."

She shot him a pointedly wry look. "Much like my grandfather."

Jamie tilted his head back as another laugh rumbled up his throat. "I definitely wouldn't argue with that assessment."

"He strong-armed you into coming here, didn't he?"

That was one way of putting it, Jamie thought. "In a manner of speaking."

"In a manner of speaking? He filled out all of your paperwork, sent your itinerary and told you when to be here."

"What tipped you off?" Jamie teased. "The book on erectile dysfunction, the bottle of Metamucil or the package of adult diapers in the bathroom?"

"What?" she deadpanned with wide-eyed innocence. "You mean you aren't an impotent, incontinent bed wetter?"

Smiling, Jamie ducked his head toward his chest and shoved his hands into his front pockets. "Er… that would be a big fat negative."

"I asked him about all of that. He was only joking with those things, you know," she said. "Wanted to prep you to relax with a good laugh."

He figured she'd asked about Jamie's so-called "preferences", Jamie thought. He would have. He had to give the old guy a hand, though—he was quick on his feet. "I know," Jamie said. "He's always good for a laugh." Jamie scratched his head, pretended to be confused. "Did he happen to mention why he listed my hobbies as basket-weaving, watercolors and ballroom dancing?"

Audrey shot him a smile. "Ah…those are 'relaxing' things he thinks you ought to try. Basketweaving requires patience, watercolor skill, and every man needs to know how to dance. Or so sayeth the Colonel."

So he'd conjured an answer for everything, then. Jamie shook his head. Somehow he wasn't surprised. "And we, er… We have to adhere to that schedule while I'm here?"

Audrey turned onto the sidewalk which led up to her house. Her porch light glowed in the distance, illuminating potted plants—mums, mostly—and white wicker outdoor furniture outfitted with comfy cushions.

"We don't have to," she said. "The purpose of Unwind is to enable you to relax, but—" She hesitated, nervously chewed her bottom lip. "I was told to personally keep you on task and to 'expect resistance.'"

She mounted the steps to her front door and turned to face him. The wind toyed with the ends of her hair, sending a long lock against her neck. He was suddenly hit with the urge to wind that wayward lock around his finger and draw her to him.

"For obvious reasons, it would make my life a lot easier if you'd simply give them a try."

Check and checkmate, Jamie thought, realizing that he should simply bow to the master and accept defeat. The Colonel had thought of everything. How could he look into those calmly pleading gorgeous blue eyes and say no?

Did he want to basket weave? Er…no.

Did he think he'd enjoy painting? That was a bigger no.

And ballroom dancing? Hell n—

Actually, Jamie thought, stopping short. Upon further reflection that one would probably be nice. Particularly if he'd be taking lessons with Audrey as his partner. His gaze slid over her small feminine frame, lingering broodingly on her delightful breasts and swept up over her plump bottom lip.

A dart of heat landed squarely in his groin and his palms suddenly itched with the unfamiliar need to cup her cheeks and draw her face up for his kiss. The Colonel had told him to do whatever it was he did to make a woman fall all over him, right? Well, kissing played a very significant part in that.

Unfortunately the Colonel had also forbidden First Base.

Audrey's suddenly heavy-lidded gaze dropped to his own mouth and, though it could have merely been wishful thinking on his part, she seemed to have leaned closer to him.

Then again, Jamie thought as his heart began

to race and he lessened the distance between them a little more, the Colonel wasn't here. Jamie was on a mission and that mission was to prevent her from marrying the wrong guy. If he kissed her, that would help right?

Right.

Jamie stepped even closer, raised his hands and felt her hair slide across his knuckles. He hadn't even touched her, yet he could feel her warmth against his palms and the sensation made his stomach clutch. His hands found her face and—

*"Woof!"*

"Damn!" Jamie swore, startled by the deafening bark. He instinctively drew Audrey to him and frantically glanced around.

"Moses," she chided, turning to face her front door.

Jamie wilted—quite embarrassingly, considering he was supposed to be such a military bad-ass—and followed her gaze. The dog from the photo looked menacingly back at him. The enormous animal had both paws planted on the glass and stood an easy five and a half feet—taller than Audrey, he thought, wondering how the hell she controlled such a beast.

"He won't bite," she said. "He's just curious about you."

"Right," Jamie said warily, not trusting that assessment.

Cheeks pink, Audrey awkwardly peeled herself away from him and opened the door, allowing the dog outside. She patted his head. *"Friend,* Moses," she said sternly. *"Friend."*

The dog ambled toward Jamie.

"Offer your hand."

Jamie shot her a hesitating glance. "Are you sure he won't mistake it for a chew toy?"

Audrey laughed. "Trust me, if he thought you were a threat, he would have torn your throat out by now."

Oh, now wasn't that a comforting thought? Jamie obligingly offered his hand. The dog sniffed his palm. Then his leg. Then his butt. Then predictably zeroed in on his crotch.

Chuckling again, Audrey grabbed Moses by the collar and tugged him back. "Good enough, old boy. Leave Jamie alone." She tucked her hair behind her ear. "Sorry about that," she mumbled, an adorable blush painting her cheeks.

Jamie couldn't think of anything politically correct to say, so he merely shrugged it off. "No problem. He's just being a dog."

She patted the dog again, then looked up, her wary gaze tangled with his. "Thanks for walking me home. It wasn't necessary."

Jamie shoved his hands in his pockets. "I enjoyed it. Well, most of it," he amended. "Your dog scaring the shit out of me, then molesting me I could have done without, but otherwise…" He grinned and shrugged.

A playful smile caught the corner of her lush

mouth. "Too bad you aren't wearing one of those diapers, eh?"

Imp, Jamie thought, thoroughly enchanted and missing that might-have-been kiss. "Right."

"So I'll see you in the morning?"

"See you then," Jamie agreed. His heart curiously lighter than it'd been in months, Jamie loped down the steps and made his way toward his cottage. Adrenaline from the dog-scare still pumped through his veins, his dick throbbed painfully in his jeans and his body ached with the regret of leaving her.

But he was smiling. How screwed up was that?

# 6

AUDREY CLOSED THE DOOR behind her, dropped to her knees and gave Moses a grateful hug. A shaky breath leaked out of her lungs. "You saved me, big guy," she told him. "From doing something *really* stupid."

Moses licked her cheek in answer, causing an unexpected chuckle to break loose in her throat. "Oh, Moses," she said with a shaky laugh. "This isn't good."

And she was the master of understatement.

In fact, it was downright horrible.

Being attracted to Jamie Flanagan—and not just merely attracted, but devastatingly so—was so far wrong it should have been unthinkable— even though it wasn't.

In the first place, she was in a committed relationship, supposedly contemplating marriage to a man who expected an answer by the end of the week. And in the second place, this guy was a friend of her *grandfather's*.

And for whatever reason, that was the one that seemed like a bigger betrayal.

The Colonel had recommended and entrusted him into her care and she fully imagined that her seducing him, kissing him or having wild, wonderful sex with him was not the sort of relaxation therapy her grandfather'd had in mind. She knew all this and yet...

She couldn't seem to help herself from wanting it.

Audrey was a big girl. She was sexually experienced and sexually responsible. She didn't share her body with just anyone and she always made sure she was protected. She had too much self-respect to do otherwise. Though she longed to have a family of her own someday and imagined raising that family on this very shore, she instinctively knew that neither the time—nor sadly, the man—was right.

But nothing in her experience could have ever prepared her for the overwhelming do-or-die toe-curling attraction she felt for Jamie. He'd merely smiled at her and something about that lazy grin had tripped some sort of internal previously-undetected sexual trigger. Parts of her body which hadn't so much as tingled in years were suddenly vibrating with a twang of lust-ridden enthusiasm she could feel in her fillings...and other more erogenous places.

As for what almost happened on her porch, Audrey couldn't explain that either. One minute she'd been standing there, thinking about the rugged yet curiously vulnerable line of his cheek and the next, she'd found herself staring at his mouth.

Then gravitating toward that mouth.

But who could blame her? Honestly, the man had the most gorgeous lips she'd ever seen. They were surprisingly full for a guy, but masculine nonetheless. And when he smiled... Mercy, they were utterly devastating.

Those hungry eyes of his—an intriguing mixture of brown, gold and green—had boldly slid over her body, then sizzled a path over her breasts, up her neck and onto her lips. At that point, thinking for herself had become a thing of the past and she'd merely gotten caught up in the moment. The rest of the world had simply fallen away and nothing had existed but the two of them and the inevitable meeting of their mouths.

If Moses, God love his big drooling heart, hadn't barked when he had, who knows what might have happened? They might have kissed, then kissed some more, and then she might have dragged him into the house, thrown him down onto the floor and ridden him until his eyes rolled back in his head. She might have had the most powerful orgasm of her life.

Forget the bed, forget a romantic fire, forget all the so-called set-the-mood trappings. She didn't—

*wouldn't*—need them with him. She needed a hungry mouth, greedy talented hands and that impressive bulge she'd noticed when Moses had inspected his crotch. The mere memory made her laugh.

She pressed her forehead against his muzzle and lovingly scratched her dog behind the ears. "How was it?" she teased, stupidly envious of him.

All right, Audrey thought. Enough already.

Drawing in a cleansing breath, she reluctantly pushed herself to her feet, ambled over to her stereo and plugged in Anna Nalick, her newest artist obsession. She could listen to that melodious voice for hours on end and frequently did. Anna was young, but had a surprising maturity to her lyrics that rang truer than anything Audrey had heard in a long time.

"Breathe" came alive through the speakers and set the mood for her bath. By the time the final chord of the song sounded, Audrey was neck deep in apple-scented bubbles and she could feel the tension melting out of her body. At least most of it, at any rate. There was still a depressingly insistent throb in her sex, but it was nothing she couldn't take care of herself if it became downright unbearable.

Which was a distinct possibility, she thought, as her thighs tensed with the ache of unfulfilled expectation.

With a helpless half-laugh, half-sob, Audrey bit her bottom lip, then held her breath and sank beneath the water. She stayed there until her lungs burned and her focus had shifted to the ache in her chest, opposing the one in her loins. Ah, she thought, pushing the hair away from her face when she finally emerged from the water. Much better. Her lips formed a weak smile. Nothing like a little dunk to help one get their perspective in order. Drastic times called for drastic, not altogether sane, methods.

Did she still want Jamie? Of course. And she grimly suspected that the more time she spent with him, the more she could expect that malady to worsen. But at least her head was clear enough for the moment to try and put a defense in order, to get her head fully in the game, so to speak.

Because regardless of how badly she might want him, she'd never slept with a guest before and she damned sure wasn't going to start now.

Not this guy. Not this time.

Not Jamie Flanagan.

Yes, it was unfortunate that he'd mysteriously managed to awaken her inner porn star—when she hadn't known she'd even had one—but Audrey knew she'd simply have to wrestle her IPS back into submission with truckloads of guilt and a stringent professional attitude. Jamie was here because he needed help. Help, dammit, not sex.

Above all else, she needed to keep that in mind.

Furthermore, she needed to talk with her grandfather and find out exactly what had happened to Jamie's friend. Merely losing him couldn't account for that wretched sadness she'd glimpsed in those gorgeous eyes earlier this evening. Granted no doubt losing a close friend would have put it there, but not to the extent she'd seen—*or felt*. There was something more, something else that haunted him and dogged his every step. In fact, though the Colonel had sent him here, Audrey didn't think her grandfather was even aware of the full extent of Jamie's pain.

Clearly Jamie had gotten good at covering it up, but that's what most hurting guys did, right? If they couldn't beat the pain into submission, pound it into the ground or simply ignore it away, they hid it. God forbid they ask for help, she thought. Help indicated weakness. Jamie, in particular, she knew, wouldn't be able to stand that, perceived or otherwise. What the fool didn't realize was that it took strength to ask for help. Men, she thought with an eye roll. They had the emotional intelligence of a goat.

Audrey toed the drain open and levered herself out of the tub. She dried off, then wrapped herself in a towel and, rather than do the sensible thing like dress for bed, she strolled to her kitchen window, inexplicably drawn. After only a moment's hesitation, she nudged the curtain aside and stared down the hill toward Jamie's cottage.

To her surprise he was sitting on the topmost step of his porch. The light illuminated his impressive profile in stark relief, leaving the rest of him in dark shadow. A bottle of whiskey—the Jameson she'd had to special order for him—sat at his side, and he held a tumbler of the flickering amber liquid loosely in one hand, allowing it to dangle in the deep V between his thighs.

To a casual observer he appeared unguarded and relaxed, but for reasons which escaped her at the moment, she knew better. It was all part and parcel of the image he liked to portray. Or maybe *had* to portray to keep up the status quo? She sighed softly and rested her head against the glass. That seemed more likely.

If he held it together and pretended like nothing was wrong, then it wouldn't be. He'd be normal and the rest of the world could simply accept that he was fine, or they could go to hell. Audrey didn't have any idea where these impressions and feelings were coming from—she seemed to be more in tune with him than with anyone she'd ever met before—but she knew her instincts were right on. Felt the familiar weight of grief and emotion—*his grief and emotion*—seep into her very bones.

She was siphoning already, she realized with a flash of dread, and she'd barely spent any time with him. That certainly didn't bode well for the rest of the week.

God, why did this always happen to her? Audrey thought with a silent whimper of despair. Why was she attracted to guys who used her up? Why couldn't she feel this overwhelming attraction for

Derrick? Why didn't *he* make her heart squeeze with emotion and her thighs quiver with want?

Was she simply wired this way? she wondered. Could she only be attracted to men who needed her? How screwed up was that? How screwed up was *she?* It took very little insight to recognize that she was going to be taking a huge risk by working with Jamie. Between the off-the-Richter-scale attraction and this equally driving need to heal his hurts—even if that meant making them hers—she'd be a fool to think she wasn't teetering on a slippery slope.

And she was going to be damned lucky if she didn't fall.

Even worse…for him.

SINCE JAMIE HAD long ago learned to fall asleep in almost any position, in any condition, it was no surprise that he enjoyed a restful night. The mattress on his bed was just the perfect combination of soft and firm, the pillows were excellent and the sheets were quality—Egyptian cotton—and had been cool and soft with a hint of some kind of summer rain scented fabric softener.

And the quarter bottle of whiskey he'd had before stumbling into bed hadn't hurt either.

He would have smiled, but knew from past experience that his face would hurt, so he quelled the urge. Instead, he braced both hands against the shower wall, bent his head and allowed the almost-scalding water to beat down on the back of his head and neck. Between the steam and two fingers of the hair of the dog, he was beginning to feel marginally better.

Jamie liked a drink as much as the next guy, but he ordinarily knew his limit. Hell, he'd been drinking Jameson since his grandmother had made him his first hot toddy. He knew when to stop. So why hadn't he, then? Jamie wondered, knowing the question was rhetorical.

He would have liked to blame it on the clear, cool night, the nocturnal sounds and lapping lake against the shore. Even better if he could have blamed it on boredom—he'd had nothing better to do than sit in the dark and get hammered.

But he knew better—he'd kept drinking because it had taken the edge off. The way Jamie had seen it, he'd had two choices. He could have either hiked back up the hill and finished what Moses had interrupted—and then some—or he could drink until he could master the urge.

While he hadn't mastered it by any stretch of the imagination, he'd at least managed to keep his feet planted firmly on the front porch of his "relaxation" retreat. He smothered a snort. Hell, he'd been more relaxed behind enemy lines with rocket-powered grenades—RPG's in soldier speak—going off in his shadow.

Jamie turned the shower off, slicked his hair back from his face and snagged a towel from the rack. Now, in approximately sixteen minutes, if his internal clock could be trusted, he was supposed to continue this *relaxing* retreat painting watercolors—with Audrey, no less, so that she could personally witness his complete ineptitude—down by the lake.

Satan had a familiar and his name was Garrett, Jamie thought, with a bark of dry laughter which made his head threaten to split in two.

He'd fully expected a call from the devil last night, but he suspected a divine hand had intervened. Because if Garrett had dialed him up yesterday evening, considering the alcohol pumping through his system, he would have most likely unloaded on him. Jamie had needed an outlet for all of this pent-up anxiety and since his preferred method of dealing with angst—sex, of course—was off-limits, that only left picking a fight. His cheeks puffed as he exhaled loudly. And since there was no one here he could reasonably pick a fight with—too bad Derrick had left, Jamie thought, wincing with regret—he'd had no choice but to drink.

The way he figured it, he was going to need a lot of alcohol to combat the attraction. If he factored in the time-to-attraction-to-alcohol ratio, then that meant he'd need an additional say...million bottles of whiskey to go with what he had left? If that didn't work, he could always see about being chemically castrated for the week. His lips quirked with miserable humor. A man had to have a plan, after all.

Feeling decidedly uninterested in watercolors, but ridiculously pleased to know that he'd see Audrey, Jamie dressed quickly and made his way outside.

"Ah," the object of his recent lust said. "There you are." Looking fresh and well rested and entirely too sexy for a woman dressed in an ugly flannel shirt, Audrey gestured to a wide assortment of gear at her hiking-boot clad feet. "Would you mind helping me with this stuff?"

"Sure," Jamie told her. He easily gathered a couple folding chairs and wooden easels into his arms, leaving her to tote a small bag he assumed held the rest of their painting necessities.

She shot him a curiously hesitant look. "Have you been up long?"

"A grand total of twenty-two minutes. Twenty of which were spent in the shower."

She smiled and inclined her head. "Ah," she sighed. "Slept well or barely slept?"

"Oh, I slept well."

"Good. Did you have time for breakfast?"

"Er...does thinking about it count?"

"No."

"Then no, I didn't have time for breakfast."

She shook her head. "Bad soldier," she chided. "My grandfather wouldn't approve. How does a muffin and some fruit sound?"

Not as good as a half a pound of bacon and a Spanish omelet, but better than nothing, he supposed, grateful nonetheless. "Good, thanks." What? Was she packing breakfast in that bag? he wondered.

Giving him a look he grimly suspected meant she'd somehow read his mind, Audrey grinned and grabbed the radio attached to her waist. "Do you want anything to drink?"

"A beer would be nice."

"Not for breakfast. How does tomato juice sound?"

"Nasty. Can I have coffee?"

Eyes twinkling, she bit her lip. "Sure." She placed his order and asked that it be brought down to the lake. "There we go," she said. "Henry should be down in a few minutes."

"Thank you," he said, and meant it. It had been a long time since anyone had cared whether or not he'd eaten his Wheaties.

"No problem. Besides, it'll help metabolize that alcohol and get you over your hangover."

Startled, Jamie almost stumbled over his own feet. "I'm sorry."

She darted him a sly look over her shoulder. "No need to apologize."

"I wasn't apologizing. I just—" He chewed the inside of his cheek and, equally impressed and disturbed, considered her. "How did you know?"

She stopped at a level spot behind a rather thick copse of trees and dropped her bag, then took the chairs away from him. "Well, number one, you slept late and you're a military man—granted, one that's not currently in service—" she said before he could interrupt because he'd instantly readied his mouth for argument. "I know that's not the norm."

Good observation, he had to admit. Still, it wasn't enough to deduce a hangover.

She made quick work of setting up the chairs. "Secondly, you skipped breakfast and you appear entirely too health conscious to make that a regular habit."

On the money again, Jamie thought, feeling more and more transparent.

"Would you mind setting those up?"

He blinked. "Huh?"

She gestured toward the easels, forgotten in his hand. "Set those up, would you?"

Right, Jamie thought, jolting into action. His cheeks heated with embarrassment. Here she was doing all the work, while he stood rooted to the ground, marvelling over her ability to read him like a friggin' book. Good grief. He had to get his head out of his ass and into the game.

"And thirdly," she said, shooting him a mischievous smile. "You look like shit."

Since he was more accustomed to accepting compliments than criticism, the blunt insult took him completely by surprise, jarring a disbelieving chuckle loose from his throat. "Don't hold back," he told her dryly. "Tell me how you *really* feel."

She shrugged. "You asked me how I knew," she said. "Don't ask if you don't want to know."

Utterly intrigued by her, he pushed a hand through his hair and nodded. "Duly noted. Anything else I should know?"

"Nothing." She paused, then seemed to remember something important. "Oh, wait. Erm…I might have seen you on your front porch last night with that bottle of Jameson."

A slow smile spread across his lips. Ah, he thought. The heart of the matter. Now that made more sense. "You're a piece of work, you know that?"

She handed him a watercolor pad. "I might have heard that once or twice."

"Or more."

She nodded. "Or more."

Feeling like he'd moved back onto solid ground, Jamie flipped the pad open and arranged it onto the easel. He thought about pretending to know what to do next, but ultimately decided against it. What was the point? She knew perfectly well he didn't have any damned idea how to paint. "Okay. What now?"

Audrey bent down by the water's edge and filled two plastic cups. Now here was a perk, Jamie thought. She might be wearing the ugliest shirt in the Northern Hemisphere—one that was better suited to a lumberjack and not a woman who looked like a cover model—but that shirt was tucked into a pair of jeans which fitted her quite nicely. Her delectable ass presently tested the seams of the worn denim and he found himself silently wishing he had either X-ray vision or the ability to make her pants instantly vanish.

What the hell. Why not wish for both?

She'd tied her hair back into a long ponytail at the nape of her neck and the cool morning breeze flirted with the ends of her espresso curls. She looked sexy and competent and…wholesome, Jamie realized with a start.

Now there was a word he didn't usually associate with a woman he was attracted to. Stacked, sexy, dim—those were the qualities most of the women he hooked up with possessed. No muss, no fuss. Attraction, action, reaction, end of relationship.

Audrey, he knew, wasn't that kind of girl. And yet he wanted her more than he'd ever wanted another female in his life. Was it because he couldn't have her? The so-called thrill of the forbidden? Had Garrett's orders somehow made her even more attractive to him simply because he knew he wasn't supposed to touch her? His gaze slid over the delicate slope of her cheek, the curve of her brow, the dainty shell of her ear and his heart did a funny little squeeze he would have labeled indigestion had he eaten this morning.

That would have been the simple explanation— the one he wished like hell he could cling to—but he knew better. In an act of what he could only deduce as divine punishment for his mistreatment of women, the Almighty had placed him with the one woman in the world whom he instinctively knew could touch his soul...and had made her off-limits.

If that wasn't divine retribution he didn't know what was.

She straightened. "Now we paint," she said brightly.

Ah, yes. For a moment there he'd forgotten.

Audrey chuckled, the sound soft and curiously soothing to his ears. "Don't look so glum. Remember, this one is for my grandfather."

Jamie accepted his paints, brush and cup with a vengeful smile. "That's right," he told her. "He's got a fondness for orchids, right?"

"He does," she confirmed hesitantly. "But I thought you might want to paint the lake."

Jamie wet his brush and dipped it into the red, toyed around with the combination of pigment to water until he reached the right shade of pink. Pussy-pink, Jamie thought, stifling a chuckle. "Nope. I'll paint an orchid."

Clearly suspecting that he was up to something, Audrey slid him a guarded glance. "Suit yourself. I'm painting the lake."

"Good. It can be a gift for me."

A smile flirted with her lips while she played around with her paintbrush. "Why would I give it to you?"

He purposely let his gaze slide over her. "So I'll have a memento of you when I go home."

She cleared her throat. "And home's in Atlanta, right?"

"It is."

"My grandfather mentioned you'd left the military and had gone into a private security business with some friends. Also Rangers, right? In the same unit?"

He could only imagine what else he'd mentioned, Jamie thought. No doubt the sneaky bastard had told her about Danny, too. The thought had been offhand, but now that he truly considered it, Garrett would have most certainly told her about Danny. And if he'd told her about Jamie's friends, he'd *definitely* told her about Danny. Furthermore, he would have cited it as a reason for his visit. Jamie's fingers tensed around the brush and he mentally swore.

Repeatedly.

God, how could he not realize that before now? He suddenly felt exposed and vulnerable, two adjectives he'd just as soon not associate with himself. Danny's death was a private pain, one he had no intention of sharing with anybody. You know, it was one thing to send him up here to work some behind-the-scenes machinations to keep her from marrying an asshole, but to use his own grief as a means to that end was beyond the pale.

And Garrett had seriously underestimated him if he thought he would simply let that slide.

Belatedly remembering that he was supposed to be carrying on a conversation, Jamie finally managed to respond to her comment. "I *am* in the private security business," he confirmed. "With friends. Me and a couple of guys who were also under your grandfather's command opened up shop a few months ago."

"Congratulations."

"Thanks," he murmured, putting more effort into his painting. He wanted it to be *just* right for Garrett, the scheming bastard.

"And business is good?"

"Better than we expected," he told her, the pride evident in his voice.

"That's fantastic. It's nice when hard work pays off." She added a few strokes to her own work, then nibbled absently on the end of the brush. "Do you miss being a Ranger?"

That topic was still too raw and he didn't have a clear-cut answer he could give to himself, much less her. "Sometimes," he told her, for lack of anything better.

"I know what you mean." She cocked her head, studying her work. "In a previous life I was a commodities broker."

Now that was enough to draw him up short. Wearing what he knew had to be a dumbfounded look, Jamie paused and turned to stare at her. "You were a what?"

She chuckled at the look on his face. "A commodities broker. Had the whole Wall Street walk going on. The briefcase, the PDA, the BlackBerry."

"Seriously?"

"Seriously," she told him.

Jamie returned his attention to his orchid—which was beginning to finally resemble the female genitalia he'd been aiming for—and digested this newest bit of information about Audrey. He couldn't make it fit. "So how does a Wall Street commodities broker end up in Maine running a de-stressing camp?" he asked, genuinely intrigued. That was a big damned leap.

"If I told you that, I'd have to kill you," she teased. She sidled over next to him. "What are you—" She gasped, clasped her hand to her mouth to smother a laugh. "That looks like a—" Her shocked gaze swung to his.

Jamie quirked an eyebrow.

"I mean to say, that's… Well, that's—" She nodded, seemingly at a loss. "That's lovely."

Jamie grinned and chewed the inside of his cheek. "Is there something *wrong* with my orchid?"

She pressed her lips together, shook her head. "Not at all."

"I think he should hang it in a place of honor, don't you?" Jamie asked her sweetly. "Like behind his desk or maybe in his home office. Possibly even his bedroom."

Her cheeks pinkened adorably and she gazed at his vagina painting with something akin to humorous outrage. "I'm s-sure he'll find a g-good home for it."

"You look a little flushed," Jamie commented, thoroughly enjoying her discomfort. "Are you feeling all right?" he asked with faux concern.

Tearing her fascinated blue gaze away from his painting, she jerked her attention back to him. "Me? Oh, no. I'm fine. Look," she said, a little too brightly. "There's Henry with breakfast."

If she'd been drowning, Henry would have been the lone life preserver in dangerous waters, Jamie thought, his lips curling into a grim.

"Oh, good," he enthused. "After I eat, I think I'll paint a picture of a couple of mountains. You know, the Colonel was right. This painting is *very* relaxing."

# 7

"WHAT THE HELL do you think you're doing?" Tewanda said, under her breath. She gestured disgustedly at Audrey's clothes. "Flannel?" she asked, horrified. "*Flannel,* Audrey? Why on earth would you clothe yourself in the single greatest 'do-not-touch-me' fabric known to mankind when a hot man like that is here?"

That's exactly why she did it, Audrey thought, shooting a careful look at Jamie from the corner of her eye. He'd finished his *orchid* painting—she inwardly snorted—and was presently hard at work on his interpretation of "mountains." Despite the flannel shirt, she kept feeling his darting gaze study her breasts, then go back to work. It was enough to make a perfectly sane woman go a little crazy.

Though she'd been absolutely appalled at first, she had to admit the watercolors he was doing for her grandfather were excellent retribution for the various books and medications the Colonel had made sure were on hand for Jamie when he got here. She smiled and shook her head. Oh, but to be a fly on the wall when her grandfather opened those packages, she thought, stifling another chuckle.

"What the hell is wrong with you?" Tewanda snapped. "I'm not being funny. I'm serious. Stop smiling."

Audrey made an attempt to accommodate her overwrought friend. She flattened her lips and tried to pay attention.

She failed.

Tewanda shook her head. "I don't understand you," she said, seemingly summoning patience from a higher power. "You're either looking to replace the guy on *Home Improvement*, you've become a lesbian, or you're purposely dressing like this to make yourself unattractive." Her lips curled with knowing humor. "And my money's on the last one."

Then that was a good bet, Audrey thought. This morning when she'd gotten up, she'd actually agonized over what to wear. She'd tried on several outfits, made a mess of her closet and her room—which had taken a solid fifteen minutes to repair—and generally acted like a junior high drama queen getting ready for her first date.

Which was ridiculous when she already had a boyfriend, dammit, and was not under any circumstances going to act on this unholy attraction to

Jamie. If she could have clothed herself in burlap this morning, she would have done it.

That's how desperate she was.

And it wasn't that she didn't trust him. She didn't trust herself.

She'd stood at her kitchen window last night and gazed at him until that throb between her legs had beaten an insistent tattoo against her defenses and had, predictably, become unbearable. Audrey let go a small sigh. Thus, she'd ended up taking matters into her own hands.

Quite frankly, since Derrick wasn't an altogether guaranteed orgasm, self-service for her wasn't an uncommon occurrence. Furthermore, there was a distinct amount of satisfaction which came from knowing she wasn't dependent upon a man for her own release. Too bad that younger girls weren't encouraged to explore their bodies the way that young boys were expected to explore theirs, she thought.

Masturbation in guys was a forgone conclusion and yet for many girls, it was still considered taboo. Considering it took a great deal more finesse for a woman to achieve climax than a man, it would seem that girls should be encouraged to explore themselves with the same zeal in which boys did. But that was a whole other matter, Audrey thought, a double standard that she imagined was going to take decades to correct.

The point was, this was the first time Audrey had taken care of business with a specific man in mind and the result had been quite…spectacular. Beyond anything she could have expected. In addition, though it had dulled the edge, so to speak, the ache had immediately returned with a vengeance. If thinking about doing it with him could make her fly into a million pieces and melt against her mattress, then what would actually being with him do to her?

And if he didn't stop sending her those sexy half-smiles and sidelong glances, she wasn't merely going to have to wonder—she'd have to *know*.

And that, she knew, was out of the question.

Of course, it'd be easier to remember that if he'd quit flirting with her. She looked down at the ugly flannel shirt and winced. Clearly her plan wasn't working.

"Go change," Tewanda told her. "It's not too late. You're spending the whole day with him. Has he asked for that massage yet?"

"No," Audrey said, releasing a shaky breath at the mere thought of her hands sliding over that silky skin and muscle. "And I hope he doesn't." She whacked Tewanda against the arm.

"Ouch," Tewanda yelped accusingly, rubbing the spot. "What the hell was that for?"

"That was for suggesting I give him a massage. Carlos can give him a massage. Not me."

"Hunh." She shook her head. "That man is not going to let another man give him a massage."

"He will if he wants one bad enough," Audrey said. She needed to keep her hands to herself, thank you very much, and it was going to be hard enough without Tewanda's interference. Honestly, she'd known that her friend didn't care for Derrick, but she didn't realize just how much Tewanda hated him until Jamie had come along.

Derrick had called last night immediately following Audrey's help-yourself-orgasm buffet and she'd felt so guilty over fantasizing about Jamie that she hadn't answered the phone. Of course, the instant his accusatory "Where-are-you? Why-aren't-you-waiting-on-my-call?" tone had sounded through the small speaker, she'd immediately let go of any remorse.

"My mountains are done," Jamie called from over his shoulder.

Tewanda frowned. "Mountains?"

"Don't ask," Audrey said, laughing under her breath.

"Oh, now you can't laugh like that, then tell me not to ask." Tewanda squinted down the hill at Jamie, trying to make out his painting. "What's going on?"

Audrey nodded her head in Jamie's direction. "He's painted some special...*artwork* for my grandfather."

"How nice," Tewanda said, brightening. "The Colonel should like that."

"Mmm-hmm." Audrey crossed her arms over her chest. "Why don't you trot down there and take a look and then we'll see if you still think he'll like it."

With a haughty look of sheer bafflement, Tewanda did just that. Audrey quietly followed, looking forward to hearing her friend's take on Jamie's paintings.

"Do you mind if I take a look?" Tewanda asked him.

Jamie glanced past Tewanda and his twinkling gaze tangled with hers. "Not at all," he said. "Art is meant to be shared, after all," he drawled.

Still smiling, Tewanda sidled forward and inspected the painting on the easel. The smile froze comically and she cocked her head and squinted, seemingly trying to make Jamie's mountains into, well…mountains. Her eyes widened and a shocked laugh burst from her throat when she realized what she was looking at. "Oh, you did not!" she said, her voice equally flabbergasted and impressed.

Jamie chuckled at her. "Want to see my orchid?" he offered.

One look at the orchid made Tewanda dissolve into a fit of hysterical laughter. "He'll have your beautiful white ass drawn and quartered for this, you know," she finally told him when she could speak.

Jamie inclined his head. "Probably."

"You don't look nearly as worried as you should," she added.

"Nothing worries me much anymore," Jamie said

lightly, but there was a truth in the humor which somehow rang very honest. It was a telling statement, Audrey thought, and filed it away for future consideration.

Tewanda sighed regretfully. "I've got to get back to work," she said with one last look at Jamie's orchid.

"Radio me if you need me," Audrey told her.

She laughed. "Don't I always?"

Audrey sidled into her friend's vacated spot next to Jamie and inspected the mountains for herself. Like the orchid, there was a surprising amount of detail which told her that, while he definitely was a novice painter, he had quite a knack for capturing the female form. And since he was painting from memory, well... She instinctively knew he'd never leave a girl hanging.

*He would be a guaranteed orgasm.*

The mere knowledge made a shiver work its way through her.

"You cold?" Jamie asked.

Audrey shook her head, trying to clear it of before and after orgasmic visions of her and Jamie. "No, I'm fine." She drew a bracing breath. "So... are you finished painting or would you like to try your hand at a banana?"

His eyes crinkled at the corners. "I'll save the banana for later in the week."

A self-portrait? Audrey wondered, her mouth

watering. "All right, then. Let me take a look at your schedule and see what you're supposed to do next."

Jamie rinsed his brush off, then disposed of the water in the cup. "Aren't you going to ask me what I want to do next?" he asked. He'd lowered his voice an octave and a curious invitation, one that made the hairs on the back of her neck stand on end, rang through the deep, sexy baritone.

She paused, toying with the necklace around her throat. "I'm hoping you're going to want to follow along with the schedule, but if it makes you feel better to tell me what you want to do, then by all means, go ahead."

"Where's Moses?" he asked, moving closer to her.

Audrey felt her brow wrinkle. "He's at home."

"Locked up tight, then?"

"Er…yeah."

She lost a little more of her personal space as he crowded even closer in. "Can't escape and tear my throat out?"

"No," she said hesitantly.

Jamie's finger slid up her neck, tilting her face closer to his, and rested under her chin. "Can't interrupt?"

"R-right," she murmured shakily, utterly mesmerized and rooted to the spot.

"Then, if you have no objections, I'd like to pick up where we left off last night," he murmured softly, weaving his voice and the image he'd effortlessly conjured around her senses. His warm breath fanned against her lips and his body heat seemed to be magically absorbed into her own hot spots. Her nipples tingled, her belly grew muddled, and that throb in her womb hammered until she wasn't altogether sure remaining upright without his support was going to be possible.

"Can I kiss you, Audrey?" he whispered, asking permission, of all things, when he could surely tell she had no objections. Making the choice completely hers. It was old-fashioned and noble and her heart squeezed with the kindness behind the gesture.

"Y-yes," she breathed, unable to conjure the sane response.

And God help her, that was the last fully-formed thought before his lips touched hers and life as she'd known it abruptly ended.

JAMES AIDAN FLANAGAN had stolen his first kiss in third grade from a blue-eyed blonde who'd smiled with angelic wonder after his bold preemptive move—then immediately thereafter cold-cocked him for his impertinence. His nose had bled for half an hour and his mother—probably the hardest working person he'd ever known—had had to leave her job and come to the school for a "meeting" on his behalf.

Jamie had learned two important lessons from that singularly defining experience.

One, never take anything without asking first.

And two, there was no action without consequence and sometimes those consequences weren't your own.

As a result of his stunt, his mother had had to pay for that thirty minutes of lost time with an extra shift, or lose her job. Though his grandmother had insisted that he go to bed that night, Jamie hadn't slept, and when his mother's tired footsteps had brought her into his room later that evening and he'd felt her fingers brush his cheek and glimpsed her weary loving smile, his chest had ached with the weight of guilt.

Curiously, though tasting Audrey—savoring her sweet breath and the plum-soft texture of her lips— was one of the most phenomenal gut-wrenchingly perfect experiences of his life, that same weighty ball of guilt he'd noted at eight had taken up residence in his belly. The meaning was clear—he might not have taken her kiss without permission, but he had a grim suspicion that she'd be paying for the consequences of his actions.

A better man would stop now, wouldn't be dragging her closer to him, angling her head to more fully devour her. A better man would stop, or more importantly, would never have started. And let's face it, a better man wouldn't have agreed to the Colonel's scheme at all, admiring the purpose but refusing to participate.

But if being a better man meant he'd never feel

these small hands pushing into his hair, tasting the gentle pleasure of her breath, the silken slide of her tongue into his mouth, then Jamie would simply have to resign himself to being a self-serving bastard. Because he couldn't stop now if his life depended on it.

Unlike a lot of men who merely used kissing as a means to an end, Jamie had always enjoyed it. While he wouldn't go so far as to say that kissing was as good as sex, he would say that it was second in line to the most personal…and telling. A guy could learn a lot about what sort of lover a woman would be by her kiss. In fact, a sorry kisser almost always resulted in a sorry lover.

It was no surprise then, given how potent his initial attraction and curiosity about Audrey had been, that the meeting of their mouths could be anything short of extraordinary.

And it was also no surprise that she was the single most talented kisser he'd ever had the pleasure of tangling tongues with. Kissing her was a full-body experience. He felt the effects of her lips in every cell in his being. His hands shook, his dick throbbed, his belly inflated with what felt like fizzy air and the rest of him seemed to be melting. Her technique was flawless. She was ardent and energetic, sensual and sure.

But most importantly, she didn't try to pretend like she wasn't equally affected.

He could feel her beaded nipples through the

flannel, raking against his chest. Flannel suddenly
became his favorite fabric, Jamie decided as he slid
a hand down her tiny back, then over her sweetly
curved rump. She slithered and squirmed, posi-
tioning herself as closely to him as she possibly
could. Her hands alternately kneaded his scalp and
shaped his jaw, forcing him to accept her ministra-
tions. Every mewl and sigh of pleasure echoed off
his tongue and it took every iota of willpower he
possessed to not topple her to the ground and bury
himself inside her.

Just like their kiss, he knew it would be instinctively explosive.

Jamie wouldn't have thought a bolt of lightning
could have startled them apart, but ironically, a single ring of his cell phone did.

Audrey stilled in his arms, then quietly stepped
back. In a second, he watched the passion fade from
her gaze and a cloud of worry and regret take its
place.

He inwardly swore, checked the display, then
swore aloud when he recognized the caller.

*Garrett.*

The man clearly had some sort of psychic connection, Jamie thought, resisting the ridiculous urge
to scan the tree line. "Flanagan," he finally answered, his voice a bit rusty to his own ears.

"Where's my granddaughter?"

Jamie's gaze slid to Audrey. "Standing right
here," he replied. "Would you like to talk to her?"

"Now that was subtle, Flanagan," he said, annoyed.

"Sorry, sir," Jamie lied dutifully. "What can I do for you?"

An exasperated sigh hissed over the line. "I just wanted to check in and see how things were going. Are you making any progress yet?"

Oh, yeah, Jamie thought, his gaze sliding over Audrey's slightly swollen lips. He could say that. "Yes, sir. I'm enjoying myself," he said, opting to play along and keep up the ruse. In for a penny, in for a pound, he supposed.

Especially now.

"Excellent. Has she confided anything about Derrick yet? Told you that he's proposed?"

"No, sir. The weather's beautiful. We've been painting and I've—" Jamie smothered a chuckle. "I've made a couple of things for you." He aimed a smile at her and was relieved when a ghost of a grin caught her lips as well. "Audrey has kindly offered to have them framed and shipped to you."

"Well, just keep plugging along," Garrett told him. "You haven't been there a full twenty-four hours yet. Even with your legendary charm, I didn't expect her to fall at your feet."

How odd, Jamie thought, when just a second ago she'd been standing on them to get closer to his mouth. Somehow he didn't think Garrett would appreciate that little nugget of information, though, so he decided to keep it to himself.

"Right, sir."

"You've got to make this work, Flanagan," Garrett told him grimly. "Failure is not an option here. According to my sources, Derrick is so sure of Audrey's answer that he's already bought a ring and booked a venue." He growled low in throat. "The arrogant SOB."

Jamie silently concurred. He glanced at Audrey and tried to imagine her married to Derrick and discovered, quite disturbingly, that he couldn't imagine her married to anyone...but himself. Which was ridiculous when he had absolutely no intention of ever marrying anyone.

Period.

Furthermore, he'd just met her. Soul-soothing eyes and flaming attraction aside, thinking about any form of permanent attachment was *ex*tremely *premature*. He was losing his mind, Jamie decided. She'd gotten him so damned hot she'd evidently rewired his brain.

Garrett cleared his throat. "Do your job, Flanagan," he told him. "And don't forget my orders. On deck but never up to bat. You haven't forgotten, have you?"

Jamie's conscience twinged. He passed a hand over his face. "No, sir."

"Good," the Colonel groused. "I'm fond of you, Flanagan. I'd hate to have to kill you." With that, he disconnected.

Evidently unable to stand still, Audrey had gathered their watercolor gear while he'd been on the phone. She folded the final chair and added it to the stack. "Checking in on you, eh?" she asked, obviously going to pretend that their scorching kiss had never happened.

*Up* on him was more like, but Jamie merely nodded. "Yeah."

Audrey hefted the bag onto her shoulder and frowned. "He's been acting weird lately," she said. A droll smile tugged at her lips. "He and Tewanda have spent entirely too much time on the phone for my comfort recently."

Jamie grabbed the remaining painting paraphernalia and fell in behind her as she made her way back up the hill. "Oh?"

"Yeah." She started to say something, but quickly changed her mind. She gave her head a small shake. "It's nothing, I'm sure." She shot him a smile. "I'm just being paranoid."

No, she wasn't, Jamie thought, feeling even more like a snake in the grass. She was reading everything correctly, but the signals just weren't clear enough for her to realize what was going on. God help Garrett—and himself—if she ever *did* realize what they'd been up to. While Audrey might come across as easygoing and mild mannered, he had the distinct impression that she could very quickly unload…and hold a grudge.

She'd forgive the Colonel—he was her grandfa-

ther, after all, and had her best interests at heart—
but she would never forgive him, Jamie realized.

She'd hate him.

And the kicker was…he'd deserve it.

# 8

"DON'T BE GENTLE, CARLOS," Audrey said, sighing with pleasure as Unwind's resident masseur used his magic hands on her shoulders. The soothing sound of bubbling water and the pungent aroma of relaxing herb-scented candles wrapped around her senses. If she didn't have so much on her mind—namely a six and half foot Irish American with miracle lips and the best ass she'd ever seen—she'd undoubtedly take a little catnap. As it was…

"Okay, then," he said, upping the pressure. "You asked for it. Geez, I haven't seen you this tense since that week we had the Slim-It-Up Diet group here."

"God, don't remind me," she groaned, her face pressed into the hole of the massage table. "Those women were horrible." And that was an understatement. They'd driven Tewanda stark raving mad with their low-fat no-fat strictly-organic *screw-it-where-the-hell-are-the-candy-bars?* demands.

Carlos clucked his tongue. "Hungry women are bitches."

She grunted. "Hungry women are insane. They broke into the kitchen. Remember that?"

He chuckled, working on a particularly tense spot between her shoulder blades. "I'd forgotten about that," he mused aloud. "That diet was too stringent. No wonder they snapped." He sighed. "Everything in moderation, I always say."

Yeah, well, that only worked if you only liked things in moderation, Audrey thought, guiltily picturing the half-pound block of chocolate in her bedside drawer. No one ever wanted good stuff in moderation, and those who did were…boring, she decided. To her dismay, an image of Derrick leaped instantly to mind, bringing guilt right along with it. She determinedly pushed both away, unwilling to devote any brain-power to what she knew would be a sobering thought process.

Say what you wanted about those dieters, but at least they were *passionate*. They knew what they wanted and had the guts to go after it. What if Monet hadn't painted in excess? If Beethoven had only been moderately motivated to compose? What if she did exactly what she wanted and seduced the hell out of Jamie Flanagan without the slightest notion of right, wrong and consequences?

What if she threw every bit of good sense and caution to the wind and didn't consider the repercussions of her actions at all? As if there wasn't a Derrick? As if Jamie wasn't her grandfather's friend? What if she did exactly what those passionate dieters had done and just said to hell with all of it? She let go a whimper. Would that be so terribly wrong?

Carlos paused. "You say something?"

She blushed. "No."

She was in hell, Audrey decided. And considering parts of her were still feverish and she'd left Jamie more than an hour ago, she imagined things were only going to get worse. Honestly, finishing out the day with him after that meltdown of a kiss—hell, she'd practically scaled his body, trying to get closer to him—had been sheer torture. Rather than dealing with the situation like an adult, she'd pretended like it had never happened. Pathetic? Juvenile? Cowardly? Yes…but she couldn't help it.

That timely call from her grandfather had been like a well-planned, well-aimed hose. Nothing could snuff out a blaze of lust faster than a hefty dose of guilt, that was for damned sure. As a result of her grandfather's call, Audrey had forced herself to focus on helping Jamie, the real reason he was here, after all.

Granted it had been difficult—she couldn't look at his face without zeroing in on that mouth, particularly after what had happened down by the lake—but fortunately, the Lord had blessed her with a very stubborn nature. When she truly set her mind to something, she could typically make it work.

Besides, she was genuinely curious and, after glimpsing his pain, genuinely concerned. No doubt Jamie's special forces training had included how to handle an interrogation because every single time she'd attempted to bring the conversation back around to his military career, he'd shut down and charmingly changed the subject. At one point, he'd given her a probing gaze which led her to believe that he knew exactly what she was fishing for, but wasn't going to be baited into giving it to her. While he hadn't overtly smirked at her, that's exactly what it had felt like.

Ordinarily she'd opt for the patient approach, but for whatever reason, she knew that wasn't going to work with him. Audrey frowned, considering. He was too controlled, too far into denial. In too much pain. No, patience definitely wasn't going to be the key in his case. It would take persistence. She'd simply have to keep asking questions, keep hammering away, adding to the pressure and he'd tell her to go to hell.

Or he'd explode.

And who knew? Audrey thought with a silent chuckle. He might do both. But she wasn't going to stop until she got something from him. Whatever his problem, it was festering inside him and, whether he knew it or not—or wanted to or not—he needed to let it go. Did she expect him to forget his friend? No, of course not.

But Jamie's hurt went far deeper than typical

grief and holding onto that pain was much more destructive than allowing himself to heal. He was punishing himself, purposely, she suspected. Atonement for some sort of sin? Audrey wondered. Guilt? And if so, for what?

"Relax," Carlos chided.

Audrey frowned, unaware that she'd tensed back up. She took a deep breath, allowing her muscles to loosen once more. "Sorry," she mumbled.

Carlos's soft chuckle sounded in the relative silence. "No worries," he teased. "How can you expect the guests to adhere to our motto when the owner doesn't?"

A long futile sigh leaked out of her lungs. "The owner never does, otherwise people here wouldn't have 'no worries.'"

He tsked. "Now that doesn't sound fair."

Audrey felt her lids flutter shut and a small smile curled her lips. "Haven't you heard? Life's not fair."

Carlos slid his thumbs down her spine, his signature "massage over" ending. "There you go, sweetheart. I hope you feel better."

Audrey gingerly levered herself into a sitting position. "I do, thanks," she said, pushing her hair away from her face. She wrapped the sheet tighter around her body and slid off the table. The tile was cool beneath her bare feet.

"Man or money?"

She blinked. "I'm sorry?"

Carlos sent her a thoughtful glance. "When a

woman is as tense as you are, it's either a man or it's money." He smiled and shrugged. "Since business is good, I'm going to go out on a limb here and say that it's a man." He paused. "And since I know you need me, I'm going to saw it off and say it's not Derrick."

Audrey considered feigning outrage, but couldn't summon the energy. What was the point? Carlos was right. She *did* need him. He was a thirty-four-year-old Cuban American who was handsome enough to make her female clientele happy, but manly enough to put most of the men who came through camp at ease—and made some of the men who came through camp swoon. Frankly, Audrey had no idea whose team he batted for and she didn't care. He was charming, dependable and competent. Furthermore, he was a friend.

"What makes you so sure that it's not Derrick?" Audrey asked, intrigued.

"In my line of work, there's tension…and then there's *tension,*" he told her, his lips twisting with knowing humor. "You've been seeing Derrick for more than a year, but in all that time you've never been wound so tight that a quick trip over a set of railroad tracks would set you off. Derrick doesn't have that—" his lips twitched "—*effect* on you."

"Carlos!" Audrey admonished, feeling her face flame. Good grief. Was she that transparent? Did she have "I need an orgasm from Jamie Flanagan" plastered on her forehead?

"Save that tone for Tewanda," he said, tossing a towel over his shoulder. "Denial's bad for your complexion. Are you drinking enough water? You look a little flushed."

"Shut up," Audrey replied, exasperated.

"Get laid," Carlos shot back, chuckling. "You know you want to."

"What I want to do and what I should do are two completely different things."

"Cop-out."

"It's not a cop-out," she said shrilly. "It's—" She gestured wildly, searching for the correct response. "It's being an adult."

He shrugged, unconcerned. "It's being a coward."

Sending Carlos an annoyed look, Audrey took a deep breath, counted to five, then let it go. She definitely needed to check on that death penalty thing because throttling her help was becoming an almost overwhelming temptation.

"I'm not afraid," she said, chewing the words lest her temper get the better of her. "I'm cautious. There's a difference."

"Cautious, eh?" he asked, seriously now, his gaze soft and somehow pitying. "And where's that gotten you?"

Audrey swallowed, recognizing the truth that lay unspoken between them. They both knew where being cautious had gotten her—with an arrogant egomaniac who didn't ignite any of her passions and who planned to dump her at the end of the week if she refused to marry him. That's what being cautious had done for her. Audrey chuckled darkly, released a low sigh and dropped her head.

Carlos walked over, tilted her chin up and planted a sweet, friendly kiss on her forehead. The gesture made her eyes inexplicably water and a lump swell in her throat.

"Sorry to hold up a mirror, babe, but someone's gotta do it," he said. "You want him, take him," he urged. "What's the worst that can happen?"

Audrey laughed, shook her head at the futility of it all. "You hit the nail on the head, Carlos," she said with a melancholy smile. "*That's* what I'm afraid of."

FROM THE CORNER OF HIS EYE Jamie watched Audrey try to covertly study the basket he was presently— much to his displeasure—weaving. He was quite obviously not following the pattern which had come with his kit and, being as she was a very observant person, she'd no doubt noticed his…modifications. He waited, instinctively knowing that she wouldn't be able to resist "helping" him. His lips twitched with a smile.

After all, that's what she did, what she was best at. Thus far he'd managed to thwart every casually veiled attempt to draw him out, but as he was her new project, so to speak—and he was so obviously screwed up—he knew that she'd officially taken him under her wing and had become one of those damaged men she was self-destructively drawn to.

Needless to say, it galled him to no end.

And despite Garrett's assertion that he'd chosen Jamie for this mission because of his player reputation, Jamie fully believed now that Garrett had chosen him for another reason. He hadn't sent Jamie in solely because he'd thought Jamie could charm her—he'd sent him because he knew she wouldn't be able to resist *fixing him*. Amazing what sort of clarity could come from being half-loaded, Jamie thought.

Last night had been another drink-himself-into-numbness act of futility. Hell, even the best Irish whiskey couldn't dull this ache. If he'd been thinking clearly before he kissed her, he would have realized that, but considering that anything remotely resembling coherent judgment had eluded him since he'd met Audrey, that was equally pointless.

At any rate, he knew she wasn't going to stop trying to make him share his past—or God forbid, his feelings, Jamie thought, stifling a wave of panic—so he'd decided that she'd left him with no choice but to up his offensive.

In short, despite Garrett's warning, he was going to stage a full-out no-holds-barred seduction.

Let Garrett castrate him, Jamie thought, because it was definitely better than the alternative. He didn't want to be *fixed,* thank you very much. He was fine. He'd lost a friend. He was grieving, dammit. Why couldn't everyone just accept it and let him deal with things in his own time? If he tagged every woman from here to Borneo, it was nobody's damned business. His gaze slid to Audrey and he broodingly considered her.

Furthermore, he'd castrate his own damned self before he became her *pity* project.

The way Jamie figured it, she needed to focus her energy elsewhere. If she wasn't willing to do it on her own, then he'd simply have to help her. She wanted him. He knew it. He could feel it every time that clear blue gaze slid over him. His skin practically sizzled in its wake. He'd tasted it in her kiss, felt her breasts pearl against his chest. In fact, the only thing that made being here bearable was knowing that she wanted him as much as he wanted her.

Audrey hesitated, then predictably scooted closer to him and inspected his work. "Did you abandon your pattern on purpose?" she asked.

Jamie chewed the inside of his cheek. "I did."

"Oh," she said. "You're doing quite well. I thought you'd said you'd never done this before."

Jamie didn't look up, but continued to work. Hell, if he could assemble a weapon in under sixty seconds, he could weave a damned basket without following a pattern. Besides, this, too, was another gift to Garrett and he somehow didn't think that they made a pattern for one shaped like a pair of testicles. "I haven't."

She hesitated again, bit her lip. "Then don't you

think you'd be better off following the instructions the first time?" she asked gently.

"I don't follow instructions well."

"You were a Ranger. You're not like the typical man. You have to follow instructions."

"I followed *orders,*" Jamie clarified. "Not instructions."

A smile rolled around her lips. "And there's a difference?"

Jamie pulled in a deep breath, let it go with a whoosh and then smiled at her. "It's subtle."

"Oh," Audrey said, laughing. "Thanks for clearing that up for me. I had no idea."

"Most women don't."

"Ouch," she teased, feigning offense.

"Present company excluded, of course," Jamie told her. He continued to work the reed through his frame, and nodded in approval when his new present for the Colonel began to take proper shape.

"Does it come naturally to you, I wonder, or did you have to take a special class?" she asked conversationally, working on her own design. They presently sat at a table on her front porch. She'd ordered a nice breakfast this morning, which they'd shared, and Moses—who'd immediately gone for his crotch again the instant he'd arrived—currently lay sprawled across her feet. If he wasn't so sexually frustrated and constantly on guard, he would have said that this was…nice.

Jamie frowned. "Did I take what class?"

"Bullshit 101. Honestly, I don't think I've ever heard anyone quite as good at BS as you are."

A startled laugh bubbled up his throat. "Oh, I didn't have to take a class. I'm a natural when it comes to bullshit."

Blue eyes twinkling, she shot him a grin. "Well, I suppose everyone has to have a special talent."

Jamie help couldn't himself, that opening was just too perfect to resist. "BS is an art." He chuckled wickedly and lowered his voice. "You haven't seen *my* special talent...but I'd certainly be willing to show you."

In fact, he had every intention of showing her over and over again. Quite frankly, he'd like nothing better than to show her right now, but he suspected if he so much as made a move near her, dear old Moses would obligingly tear his throat out.

Predictably, she flushed. She blinked as though suddenly disoriented and he had the privilege of watching her pulse suddenly flutter wildly at the base of her throat. God, how he wished he could taste it. Taste her all over. His dick leaped in his jeans and a hot, achy throb pulsed in his loins, forcing him to grit his teeth. He wanted her so much that even his chest ached, in the vicinity of his heart if he could admit he had one. Did that scare the hell out of him? Most certainly. His heart had absolutely no business in this.

But if he'd ever wanted another woman more— had ever been so obsessed with marking her as his—Jamie couldn't recall it. This force that was pulling him toward her…it was more than mere attraction. Attraction he could deal with—*need,* on the other had, posed a problem and that's what this felt like.

He didn't just want her—he had to have her. He wanted to take her hard and fast, then slow and easy. He wanted to settle her over his thighs, impale her on his dick, then suckle her breasts until she screamed his name. He wanted to wring her dry, then whet her appetite again. He wanted to take her so hard that the idea of ever being with anyone else would be jarred right out of her beautiful head.

And for reasons which were absolutely beyond his understanding, he wanted to punish her for making him want her so much. When this was over, he may finally have to break down and see a shrink, Jamie decided. In the meantime, he was going back to what had worked before—sex therapy.

Audrey finally cleared her throat. "So," she said, in an unnatural high-pitched voice. "If you aren't making the Country Onion basket, then what sort are you making?" She frowned. "It looks like you've got an egg there that didn't split."

"Close," Jamie said. "It's a testicle basket."

Audrey's eyes widened in shock and she choked. "A what?"

Jamie grinned. "It's another gift for your grandfather. I was thinking about crocheting some little sperm to go in there for him, but since he didn't list needlework as one of my hobbies, I guess I'll have to settle for some sort of substitute. Any ideas?"

Still laughing, she sighed and shook her head. "Your last wishes, because if you send him this in addition to your orchid and mountains paintings, he's going to kill you." She paused. "Is it so bad being here?" she asked. The note of genuine interest and insecurity he detected in her voice prevented the glib comment he would have otherwise provided.

"No," Jamie said. He reached over and traced the pad of his thumb over her bottom lip. "Not when I'm with you." Now it was his turn to ask a question. "Do you regret kissing me yesterday?" For whatever reason, her answer was far more important to him than he'd ever care to admit.

A shadow passed over her eyes and she hesitated. "Regret isn't the right word."

"I just wondered, you know, 'cause you keep trying to pretend like it never happened."

"It shouldn't have happened."

"So you do regret it."

"No," she said, giving her head a small helpless shake. "I enjoyed it too much to regret it. But I *should* regret it. I'm—" She winced, seeming to weigh her words carefully. "I have a boyfriend," she finally blurted out. "He's asked me to marry him and instead of thinking about my answer, I'm here kissing you. Guilt," she told him, apparently seizing the right word. "Guilt but not regret."

Ah, guilt. Jamie knew a lot about that. Still…
"And there's a difference?" Jamie teased, throwing
her earlier question back at her.

She smiled, just a simple matter of rearranging
the muscles on her face, and yet he felt that grin tug
at his midsection. "It's subtle," she told him, eyes
twinkling with humor.

He inclined his head. "Looks like I'm not the
only one who's a bit of a bullshit artist."

She shrugged, unrepentant. "I try," she de-
murred.

Unable to help himself, Jamie leaned forward
and pressed a gentle kiss against her lips. Her sweet
breath stole his. "Do you have plans for tonight?"

She blinked drunkenly, then a slow smile caught
the corner of her mouth. "No."

"Excellent," Jamie told her. "I'll share my whiskey…and you can give me that massage."

# 9

"No, Gramps, he still hasn't told me anything," Audrey said, scattering olives over her salad. Dinner hadn't been part of the deal, but she'd been struck by the urge to cook. A blatant stall tactic, but what the hell? She was equally anxious and desperate.

"Nothing?" Evidently disheartened, the Colonel sighed. "I was hoping that he'd start to loosen up a little."

Oh, he had, Audrey thought, remembering that toe-curling kiss he'd given her this afternoon. Just not in the way that her grandfather had hoped for.

"It's going to take a little time, but I'm glad you called. I wanted to ask you something." She quickly washed her hands, then made her way into the living room.

"Sure. What's on your mind?"

Audrey hesitated. Now that she had the opportunity to find out a little more about Jamie's past, something about it felt wrong and intrusive. While she knew she'd be better able to help him if she had all of the information—and admittedly, she was curious—she nevertheless couldn't shake the feeling that she was mining for information he'd just as soon not share.

But the more time she spent with him, the more she saw how desperately he hurt. Had he told her anything? No. Trying to get that man to give her one single nugget of personal information beyond the superficial had been like trying to coax water from a stone—it wasn't happening.

He smiled, he laughed, he teased, he flirted.

And she lapped up every second of it, charmed in spite of her better judgment.

But he didn't give her anything he wasn't willing to share.

And while that might have worked with the average woman who was mesmerized by those gorgeous hazel eyes and bowled over by that extraordinary body and sex appeal, it wasn't working with her because she could *feel* his pain. And every second she spent in his company, every unguarded glimmer she caught—rare though they may be—only made the ache to soothe him worse. He might not know it, but he needed her.

"Sweetheart?"

Audrey blinked. "Yeah, I'm here. Listen, I need to know more. I know you told me that Jamie lost a friend, but I'm sensing there's more to it than that."

"What makes you say that?"

"I can feel it, Gramps," Audrey told him quietly. She didn't have to explain. He knew exactly what she was talking about. "A cold stone sits in my gut every time he slips up and lets me in." She plopped heavily onto her couch and patted the spot beside her for Moses. The great animal jumped up next to her and laid his enormous head on her thigh.

Her grandfather sighed heavily. "I was afraid of this. Is he too much, honey?"

"No," she assured him. "It's not that. It's—" How to explain? "I keep pressing and pressing, but I'm not getting anywhere. I need to know more."

"All right," he relented, clearly reluctant. "But this is strictly between us. If it comes down to it, I don't mind you telling him that I've told you that he lost a friend, but he would seriously object to my sharing the details."

"That's fine," Audrey said, bracing herself. Every muscle tensed in anticipation and she had to force her fingers to relax around the phone.

"Flanagan's unit was special," he began. "Elite. Secretive." He went on to tell her about how the four of them had met in ROTC in college, how they'd been more like brothers than friends, how their last mission had gone so terribly wrong, resulting in Daniel Levinson's death.

Her grandfather let out a tired breath, one that spoke eloquently to his age and burdens. "What I didn't tell you, Audie, is that it was Flanagan who went back to get Levinson when he went down.

Amid enemy fire, no less. Unfortunately, Levinson had taken a fatal hit and he bled out in Flanagan's arms before Flanagan could get him off that hill."

"Oh, God," Audrey whispered, her chest squeezing painfully. Nausea threatened, forcing her to swallow.

"The other two—Payne and McCann—they took it hard as well, but Flanagan... Well, understandably, Flanagan hasn't been right since it happened. He and Levinson were supposed to have each other's back. He feels like he failed him. All of them do. That's why they wanted out."

She could certainly understand that. And knowing what she knew now, she could definitely see why Jamie was hurting so terribly badly. Losing a friend would be hard enough, but feeling responsible, then having that friend die in your arms... She couldn't imagine. But she didn't have to because she could feel it emanating off of him.

"Thanks for telling me, Gramps. I, uh..." She scrubbed a hand over her face. "That, uh... That explains a lot."

"Keep me updated, would you?" the Colonel asked.

"I will," Audrey promised. She said goodbye, disconnected and then absently rubbed Moses' head, and continued to consider everything she'd just learned. Poor Jamie, Audrey thought, wincing for him. No wonder he was so closed-mouthed about all of it. Not only was it very private, but also, talking about it no doubt conjured images he'd just as soon forget. The trouble with that, though, was that he'd never forget. He might learn to deal with it—to cope, even—but the memories would always be there.

In fact, according to a recent study, memories in times of trauma were essentially *hard-wired* into the brain due to the additional adrenaline pumping through a person's body. Modern medicine was currently researching a pill which would ultimately help make traumatic memories fade. According to several well-known doctors, veterans, victims of horrific crimes such as rape and murder, would particularly benefit from it. Audrey let go a breath.

Unfortunately, there was no such magic pill yet for Jamie and he was simply going to have to learn to cope the old-fashioned way. She still felt guilty about asking her grandfather for that information, but she was glad that she did. It was easier to find something if you knew what you were looking for.

And she could start looking immediately, because Jamie would be here any minute now with his whiskey in tow. Despite everything she'd just found out, Audrey felt a half-hearted grin tease her lips. A miserable anxious laugh bubbled up her throat. Sweet Lord, what had she gotten herself into?

*I'll share my whiskey...and you can give me a massage.*

No doubt getting a buzz would help take the edge off the thought of putting her hands on him—just thinking about it made a quaking shiver rattle her belly—but she just hoped it didn't take the edge off too much. Oh, who the hell was she kidding? If he so much as crooked his little finger, she'd leap on him like a wild woman and he'd have a hell of a time getting her off.

They'd followed their basket-weaving lesson this morning with an amiable horseback ride around the lake, then had shared a late lunch in the lodge. Afterwards, Jamie had wanted to check out the gym and they'd spent the rest of the afternoon working out. Or rather, she had pretended to work out, and had watched him instead.

Mercy.

Watching Jamie Flanagan work out was like watching poetry in motion. He was efficient and methodical, like a well-oiled machine. He alternated time between the free weights and various machines, and by the time he'd finished, he'd been hot and sweaty, every muscle pumped and in beautiful form. Audrey sighed and bit her lip, remembering.

Ordinarily hot and sweaty didn't do it for her, but the entire time she'd watched him, she'd been muddled and warm, and hit with the inexplicable urge to lick him all over. The side of his neck, the V between his shoulder blades. She wanted to taste his skin, feel those muscles play beneath her fingertips. He might have been the one to work up a sweat, but she'd been the one on fire.

He knew it, too, the cocky jerk.

To her immense mortification, he'd caught her staring at him too often to even consider trying to be anything but a total wreck. He'd grinned, the wretch, then had pinned her to a mirror when no one was looking and kissed the hell out of her.

It was at that point that Audrey had come to a decision. Tewanda was right—she *did* want him. More than she'd ever wanted anybody and with an intensity that shook her to the very core. And Carlos had been right as well—what had being cautious ever done for her? Her entire life had been about helping others, pleasing others. With the exception of going to the college of her choosing and ultimately taking a risk on Unwind, what had she ever done strictly for herself? The answer was sobering.

Nothing.

She could list a dozen reasons she shouldn't sleep with Jamie—her grandfather's relationship with him, for starters. Not to mention Derrick, who would *not* get the answer he wanted from her this weekend. Even if he didn't follow through with his threat to break things off with her, she'd already decided that she'd end the relationship herself. It was a dead end. She didn't love him. Staying with him because he was safe—because he didn't make her feel anything—was a disservice to him and to herself.

Yes, there were a lot of legitimate reasons she shouldn't sleep with Jamie, and only one reason she should...and that was the one she was going with.

She wanted him.

He was the puppy in the window, the candy through the glass, the last piece of cake on the platter. He was every risk she'd never taken, every thanks-but-no-thanks, every missed opportunity.

But more importantly, tonight he was hers.

Moses lifted his head from her lap, signaling Jamie's timely arrival. The dog murmured a low woof, then lumbered off the sofa to the door. Audrey stood, felt a wild thrill whip through her midsection and her palms suddenly tingled in anticipation of what was to come. She grabbed Moses by the collar and opened the door.

Jamie smiled, a crooked sexy grin that made her heart do an odd little dance. He'd loaded the testicle basket with the bottle of whiskey and a bouquet of flowers he'd obviously snagged from the landscaping beds. Odd that she'd find that endearing. "For you," he said, offering it to her.

Chuckling, Audrey accepted the gift. "Come in," she told him. She gestured toward his gift. "Nice to see you found a purpose for your basket."

Jamie sidled forward, brushed his lips across hers and nuzzled her cheek. "I'm nothing if not resourceful."

Heaven help her, Audrey thought, because her heart was nothing if not doomed.

JAMIE HAD BARELY TAKEN A STEP into the room before Moses had once again gone for his crotch. He grunted, made a little "whoa-ho-ho" noise, and stepped back, awkwardly trying to avoid being victimized by the dog again. Honestly, he knew this was normal canine behavior, but couldn't help being embarrassed nonetheless. This was the third time, dammit. It was beginning to become a habit. "*Moses,* please, man," he said with a shaky laugh. "I don't know you well enough and, even if I did, you aren't my type."

Audrey's face pinkened and she hurriedly dragged the dog back once more, no small feat when the animal had to weigh in excess of 150 pounds. "Moses," she admonished through gritted teeth. *"Cut it out."* She pushed a hand through her long curly hair. "I've got a solution for this," she said. "Hold on." She disappeared into the kitchen, then returned a few seconds later with an aerosol can. "This won't stain," she told him, and before he knew what she was about to do, she aimed the can at his crotch and sprayed him with it. Jamie gaped. "What the—"

"Turn around."

"What?"

"Turn around," she repeated. "I need to put a shot of this on your—"

"Ass," he supplied helpfully. Jamie wrinkled his nose. "What is that? It smells."

"Exactly. It's a repellent." She stood once more, popped the lid back on the can. "It'll keep him from, you know—" she gestured toward his package "—checking you out."

Now this was a first, Jamie thought, absolutely stunned. He'd never had a *repellent* spayed upon his privates. He felt a slow grin tug at the corner of his mouth. "This only works on the dog, right?"

She laughed, the sound feminine and oddly gentle. "Right. I use it to keep him out of things I don't want him messing with."

Did that mean she wanted exclusive rights to his penis? Jamie wondered, resisting the urge to tease her further about it.

Seemingly following his line of thinking, she darted him a somewhat sheepish look. "Well, you know what I mean."

God, she was beautiful. Jamie grinned. "I do."

She turned and started back toward the kitchen. "I hope you like Italian."

Unexpected delight expanded in his chest. "You cooked for me?"

"Baked ziti," she said, neatly avoiding his question. "Caesar salad and chocolate pie for dessert."

"Sounds fabulous. You didn't have to go to all that trouble," he told her, and he meant it. In fact, though he appreciated the gesture, it made him feel downright uncomfortable knowing that he planned to use the massage as a seduction tool. He'd brought that bottle of whiskey, a bouquet of flowers and a handful of rubbers just to mark the occasion.

And she'd been busy cooking for him.

Though he knew it was ridiculous, her gesture pleased him far more than it should have. His mother and grandmother cooked for him all the time when he'd been at home and he'd had one serious girlfriend in college—Shelley-the-two-timing-bitch-Edwards—who'd cooked for him while they'd lived together. Since then, he hadn't gotten close enough to a woman to warrant something as domestic as cooking. This was nice, Jamie decided, inexplicably pleased.

"Make yourself at home," Audrey called. "I've got to pull this out of the oven."

"Can I help?"

"No, I've got it, thanks."

Rather than park himself on her sofa, Jamie wandered around her living room, inspecting various pictures which lined her mantel. Not surprisingly, there were several of her and the Colonel. A couple of candid shots of her down by the lake. Several chronicled Moses's growth, Jamie noted, resulting in a smile. Proud momma, eh? he thought with a shake of his head. Interestingly enough, there were no pictures of Derrick. He grimaced with pleasure and rocked back on his heels.

That had to be significant.

As for her house, it was a larger version of the cottages. White beadboard lined the bottom of the walls and she'd painted the top an interesting shade of blue, the color of an almost-but-not-quite night sky. Various vintage prints—Art Deco—were scattered around the room and a large antique mirror hung over her fireplace.

A comfy contemporary sofa had been dressed up with puffy floral pillows and instead of a traditional coffee table, she'd opted for an old seaman's trunk. It was an eclectic mix of old and new—the end result was not only a reflection of herself, but comfortable and homey as well. He could very easily see her and Moses curled up on her couch watching TV and snacking, and to his acute discomfort, his imagination obligingly Photoshopped himself into that picture.

Audrey chose that moment to peer around the kitchen wall. "Dinner's on," she said, smiling. That adorable dimple winked in her cheek.

Once again, he was struck by just how beautiful she really was. Something in his chest squeezed, almost painfully. She'd left her espresso curls down and loose and, if she wore any make-up aside from a coat of pinkish gloss on her lips, she'd applied it with a very light hand. She was fresh and open and those kind, soothing eyes twinkled with some sort of hidden joy. She was bright and infectious and sexy as hell—the total package. Jamie released a pent-up breath, one he hadn't realized he'd been holding. And the Colonel was right, he thought.

She *was* special.

And there was no way in hell he was going to let her marry Derrick.

*Seduction on,* he thought, purposely kicking the charm factor up a notch. Playtime was over.

# 10

AUDREY WATCHED Jamie's lips curl into that trademark bone-melting grin as he sidled into her kitchen, and she felt the abrupt shift in his intent. It was as though he'd flipped a switch, the change was so remarkable.

He wore a pair of faded denim jeans which were tight in all the right places and a brown cable-knit sweater which accentuated his broad, muscled shoulders and picked up the golden tones of those remarkably sexy eyes. From the looks of things, he'd attempted to gel his unruly curls into place, but had failed because they'd sprung free, a riot of loose and sexy locks she simply itched to push her fingers through. He obligingly pulled her chair out for her.

"Thank you," Audrey murmured.

"You're welcome," he said silkily. He took his own seat. "Thank you for cooking. It's been a long time since I've had a home-cooked meal."

"Oh?" Fishing again, but what the hell? By this

point he should expect it. Audrey filled his salad bowl first, then hers.

He grinned and his gaze twinkled with knowing humor. "You never give up, do you?"

She speared a forkful and shot him a smile. "No. It's part of my charm."

"Oh, I don't think I'd say that," Jamie told her, his gaze dropping with lingering accuracy to her lips. He finally relented with a sigh. "Let's just say that I have a roommate who isn't any better in the kitchen than I am, and my mother and grandmother live too far away to make dropping by their house for dinner do-able."

"How far out of Atlanta do they live?"

Jamie finished a bite of salad. "Five and half hours. They're in Alabama."

So that was the Roll Tide connection. Her grandfather had told her that they'd met at the University of Alabama. She should have realized that he still had family there.

In the process of carefully moving all of his olives to the side of his plate, Audrey frowned. "You don't like olives. I'm sorry," she said. "I should have asked."

Jamie glanced up. "No problem," he assured her with an easier grin. "They're easy to spot and easy to move."

"And—" Audrey forked one up from the side of his plate "—they are not meant to go to waste. I *love* olives."

Jamie stilled for a fraction of a second, watched the olive leave his plate via her fork and then land in her mouth. Audrey swallowed. "Is something wrong?" she asked. Maybe he didn't like them on salad, but preferred them otherwise? "Were you going to eat that?"

"No," he said, blinking out of whatever had bothered him. He made a face. "Olives are nasty. They're not in the ziti, are they?"

Audrey chuckled. "No."

Jamie ladled some of the Italian dish onto her plate, then his. "Good." He paused. "You know, if we were dating, this would be like our...third date, wouldn't it?"

The question came so far out of left field that Audrey choked on her wine. "Uh... Well, we aren't dating, so it's a moot point. But yeah, I suppose if we were, this would be considered our third date of sorts." Bewildered, she darted him a confused glance. "Why do you ask?"

"No reason," he said quickly, then shoved a forkful of ziti into his mouth. He looked curiously alarmed, though for the life of her, she couldn't imagine why.

Audrey frowned. "Are you all right? You look a little flushed."

"This is spicy."

No, it wasn't, Audrey thought, thoroughly baffled by his behavior. Rather than pursue it, though, she decided to continue their conversation. He'd finally given her a little bit of personal information. That was a start, at any rate.

"So your family lives too far away to cook for you. What about a girlfriend? There's no future Mrs. Flanagan wannabe who whips up meals in your honor?"

The comment drew a laugh, full and throaty, and seemed to ground him once more. He picked up his glass, inspected the contents. "Er. No."

Audrey shrugged, ridiculously pleased. Honestly, she had no vested interest in whether or not he had a girlfriend, but she couldn't deny that the idea that there might be another woman in his life irritated her beyond prudent reason. In fact, it made her downright ill. A significant revelation no doubt lurked in her disproportionate jealousy, but why ruin what was going to be a wonderful evening with expectations and what-might-have-beens?

"What about you?" Jamie asked, turning the probing conversation around on her. "Does the future Mr. Audrey Kincaid cook for you?" he drawled.

She grimaced, smiled. "There is no future Mr. Audrey Kincaid."

His gaze tangled with hers above the rim of his glass. "But I thought you said you were supposed to be considering a marriage proposal this week?"

She cocked her head, conceding the point. "I am. I've considered. I'm saying no."

Though she might have imagined it, something seemed to shift in Jamie's gaze. He hadn't moved, hadn't so much as blinked, and yet she felt him tune in more fully. "Really? What made you come to that conclusion?"

A laugh broke up in her throat and she rolled her eyes. "You mean aside from the fact that I can't keep myself from kissing you?" she said, grinning. "He's just not the man for me. It, uh... It wouldn't be fair to either of us."

"Would you have said no if you had been able to resist kissing me?" he asked, looking entirely too pleased with himself.

"No, I'd planned to say no all along." She scooted a cut glass tumbler toward him and gestured toward the Jameson. "I was just dreading it."

Jamie's eyes twinkled with some sort of secret humor. He poured her a shot of the whiskey and slid it back to her, then hefted his own glass. "Here you go," he said. "Liquid courage."

How timely, Audrey thought, as she brought the tumbler to her lips. She was going to need it because she grimly suspected he planned to call in his massage any minute now. *Her hands on that hot silky skin, shaping those incredible muscles...* She took a drink, allowed the smooth honey-like taste of the whiskey to caress her tongue before swallowing. He was right, she thought, immeasurably pleased—no burn. Just a pleasant warmth which quickly expanded in her belly, then gradually infected the rest of her body.

Audrey inclined her head. "This is good," she told him.

Jamie shrugged. "I like it."

"Are you ready for dessert?" she asked.

His sexy twinkling gaze told her he had other ideas in mind. "Maybe later," Jamie said. He leaned back in his chair and absently scratched his chest. "I thought I'd let you go ahead and give me that massage."

Audrey chuckled. "*Let* me, eh? How thoughtful of you," she said wryly.

"I'm nothing if not thoughtful."

"I thought you said you were nothing if not resourceful?"

Jamie nodded sanctimoniously. "That, too."

Audrey laughed, then stood and cleared their plates. "You're nothing if not full of shit, that's what you are."

"Let me help you," Jamie offered, chuckling. He stood and quickly helped her clear the table. It was nice, Audrey decided, warmed from a combination of his presence and the Jameson.

When the last dish was washed and dried, she took a deep breath, and then turned to face him. "Thank you," she said, feeling uncharacteristically sheepish.

Jamie nodded, pressing a shameless hand against his chest. "What can I say? I'm nothing if not helpful."

Actually, he was nothing if not gorgeous and

charming and wonderful and she wanted him more with each passing second. Her gaze tangled with his and the breath seemed to thin in her lungs. A hot cocktail of seduction and sex was imminent. She could feel it every time that somnolent gaze raked over her. Her skin prickled and her belly fluttered with unstable air. She was a wreck, Audrey decided. A sexually frustrated wreck.

"Where do you want me?" Jamie asked.

Audrey blinked. "What?"

He laughed, the sound intimate and darkly sexy. "For my massage," he explained.

Well, they could save a lot of time by merely moving things to her bedroom, but she supposed she should at least give the impression of not being a complete pushover and administer the massage in the living room on her massage table.

"I, uh…" She jerked her finger toward the other room. "I'll just go set it up."

"Audrey?"

She turned on her heel, but before she could take a single step, Jamie stopped her with a mere touch of his hand.

"Yes?"

"You don't have to do this if you don't want to," he said softly, the comment rife with double meaning. Though the smile was the same charming grin he always wore, there was a sweet sincerity in his gaze which made her silly heart melt like a pat of butter over a hot bun. He was giving her an out, a get-out-of-sex free card.

The trouble was…she didn't want one.

The first time he'd kissed her, he'd asked permission, but she wasn't gentleman enough to give him any such courtesy. Audrey leaned forward, wrapped her arms around his neck and laid a kiss on him she knew would dispel any doubts about what she wanted or her intentions. "Come on," she finally told him. "It's time for me to work some of those kinks out for you."

A wicked chuckle rumbled up his throat. "Be gentle."

"Oh, believe me," she assured him. "I'm nothing if not gentle."

FOR THE FIRST TIME in his life Jamie was stuck with a true moral dilemma. To seduce or not seduce? Technically, since she had no intention of marrying Derrick, he could dub this mission successful and go home. He'd be free, Jamie realized. He would have paid his debt to the Colonel, could officially cut ties with his past and move forward. That was the lie he'd been propagating, at any rate. There was nothing to gain for his so-called cause if he seduced her.

And yet for reasons he didn't dare explore, he knew—*knew*—that *he* had everything to gain… and even more to lose if he didn't.

Besides, the first touch of her cool fingers

against his back set a path into motion he didn't have a prayer of changing. It would have been like trying to route a detour in the middle of a bridge—pointless.

"Remind me to thank Tewanda," Jamie told her, his voice low and rusty to his own ears.

Audrey chuckled softly, kneading the muscles in his shoulders with small, competent, surprisingly strong hands. "Me, too," Audrey said. "Though I wanted to throttle her when she first suggested this."

"Really?" Jamie asked. "You mean speaking through gritted teeth isn't how you normally express excitement and joy?" he teased, remembering her murderous expression that first night in the lodge.

She laughed, skimmed her nails down his spine, eliciting a shiver of delight. "Noticed that, did you?"

He grunted wryly. "It was hard to miss."

"And yet you wouldn't let it go," Audrey added. "I wonder why," she mused aloud, her conversational tone rife with exaggerated humor.

Jamie felt another laugh rattle his belly. "I would think it would be obvious. I wanted your hands on my body," he murmured softly. "Like they are now."

He heard a stuttering breath leak out of her lungs, felt her touch grow a little bolder. She rubbed and kneaded, methodically working his muscles until they were melting under her exquisite touch. Meanwhile another muscle below his waistline was anything but melting. He felt her fingers trace an inverted heart, then linger and outline the tattoo on his right shoulder blade.

*Sonofabitch,* Jamie thought, involuntarily tensing. He squeezed his eyes tightly shut, braced himself, knowing she would ask. And knowing that he was in no shape to resist.

"Oh." She sighed softly, her heart in her voice. "Who was Danny?"

A fist of pain tightened in Jamie's chest. Unbidden images from that horrible night flashed like a broken projector through his brain. He tried to stop it, tried to push it away, but failed.

*Danny's bloodstained chest, a huge gaping wound littered with torn cloth and sand. "Leave me, dammit! Leave me! You know it's over!"*

*Panic, fear and adrenaline rushed through Jamie's bloodstream, making Danny's 240-plus pound body feel virtually weightless. Jamie's heart threatened to pound right out of his chest and the urge to weep was almost more than he could bear. He had to get Danny to the truck—if he could only get him to the truck, they'd be safe. He almost tripped. Righted himself. Kept going. "It's not over until I say it's over."*

*Bullets whizzed by, spraying up sand. "Goddammit, Jamie! Leave me. There's no p-point in us both d-dying out here."*

*"I won't leave you," Jamie had growled, running until his lungs had burned and he'd had to*

*swallow the urge to retch. Then he'd looked down into his friend's pale blood-speckled face and told the biggest lie of his life. "You aren't going to die, dammit. I've got you. Just hang on."*

"Jamie?"

Audrey's soft voice penetrated the waking nightmare.

"Are you okay?" she asked, her fingers still hovering over his tattoo, his memorial to a fallen friend—an eagle with a ribbon and the inscription "In Memory of Danny Boy" trailing from its beak.

No, he wasn't okay. He would never be okay. He'd failed to keep his friend's back. It was his fault Danny'd been hit and his fault that he hadn't gotten him to safety.

He was a murderer by default and nothing would ever change that.

"Oh, Jamie," she said, bending down to kiss his back. "Give it to me and let me help you," she implored softly. "Tell me about Danny."

For one blind horrifying instant he was struck with the impulse to do just that. That was her specialty, after all. Taking damaged people and fixing them. If he opened himself up to her, could she heal him? Jamie wondered. Could she mend the yawning hole in his soul? For whatever reason, he knew if there was a person on the planet who could do just that, it was her. Jamie swallowed. Being with Audrey, something as simple as sharing the same air, made him feel more human and more alive than he had in months.

Unfortunately he wasn't worthy of healing—he didn't deserve it—and even more importantly, he wouldn't become one of those "life-suckers" who drained her that the Colonel had told him about.

He wouldn't become her next pity project, dammit.

"Look, Jamie, I know this is hard, but sometimes talking about things—"

Enough already.

Before she could finish the sentence, Jamie turned over, rolled into a sitting position and pulled her into the open V between his thighs. Time to shut her up before he did something stupid, like spill his guts and cry. "No more talking," he told her.

Then he fitted his mouth to hers and kissed her until he felt every bit of the resistance melt from her body and felt a new kind of tension—the right kind—take its place. Ah, he thought, the panic lessening. Familiar ground.

She parlayed every bold thrust of his tongue and pushed her hands into his hair. A little sigh of pleasure leaked from her mouth into his and there was something so inherently erotic about that telling breath that he felt as though his chest and dick were both going to explode before he could get himself inside her.

Her long curls trickled over his shoulder, framed them in a world of their own making, one where nothing existed outside the meeting of their mouths and the inevitable joining of their bodies.

Jamie slid his hands down her back, found the hem of her shirt and tugged. One touch of his fingers against her soft bare skin made his penis jerk hard in his shorts. Oh, God, she was so perfect she made him ache. Supple and womanly, her scent an intriguing mixture of apple and spice—wholesomely wicked. He wanted to be gentle, wanted to prime her, make her so blind with need that she'd never imagine sharing her goodness with another man, and yet now that the time was upon them, Jamie didn't have the strength to hold back.

And it was equally—*gratifyingly*—obvious that she didn't either.

Her touch was sure, but impatient, her greedy palms sliding all over him, blazing a tingly trail of heat everywhere that she touched him. And she had the advantage because he was already half-naked, while she on the other hand was still fully clothed. That definitely needed rectifying, Jamie thought, setting himself to the task. He pulled her shirt up over her head, tossed it aside.

*Creamy skin, lacy pale pink bra, tiny waist.*

God help him.

He groaned, pulled her to him and licked a path over the rim of each cup, sampled the delectable spill-over flesh. His hands framed the small of her back, then pushed her pants down and over the sweet swell of her rump.

*Matching thong, barely the size of a postage stamp. Equally lacy and sheer, with a butterfly hovering expectantly over her dark curls.* Looking for nectar, no doubt, Jamie thought with a wicked chuckle, as every bit of the blood in his body suddenly gathered in his loins. His lips curled. He imagined he'd be more successful than the butterfly.

He fingered the lace riding high on her hip. "Nice," he murmured.

Audrey smiled. "Glad you approve." She slid a hand down the front of his boxers, boldly cupped him through the fabric, causing a hiss of air to push past his teeth. "This is nice as well."

A strangled laugh bubbled up his throat. "And I'm glad you approve."

"I'd approve even more if you'd put it to better use," she said, giving him a gentle squeeze.

Shocked, another chuckle vibrated his belly. "As you wish," Jamie told her. He punctuated the promise with a deft flick of his fingers which made her bra pop open, revealing her pert, lush breasts. Rosy nipples puckered, seemingly in waiting for his kiss. He bent his head and pulled one perfect peak into his mouth, suckled her soft, then hard, flattening the bud against the roof of his mouth.

Audrey whimpered, grasped his shoulders, her nails biting into his flesh. She moved closer to him, lightly skimmed a hand over his chest, down his belly and beneath the waistband of his shorts. Then she was touching him and everything else simply faded into a blur of frantic—frenetic—sexual energy. The incessant need, the drive, was stronger than anything he'd ever experienced and, he instinctively knew, ever would again.

His dick practically leaped into her hand, anxious for her touch. She worked the slippery skin up and down his shaft, nipped at his shoulder while he moved to her other breast. Kneading, sucking, licking. He wanted to taste her all over. Couldn't get enough of her. Fire licked through his veins and into hers. She was a fever inside him, an itch he couldn't scratch.

"I want you so damned bad," Jamie told her. He brushed his fingers past her butterfly and smiled against her neck when they came back wet.

"Then take me," she taunted, running a finger over his engorged head. She wriggled out of her panties.

A second later he'd located a condom, another three and he was ready. He whirled her around, sat her on the edge of the massage table, then spread her legs and in one solid thrust, pushed into her. Her breath caught in her throat, her lids fluttered closed and her head dropped back, seemingly too heavy for her neck.

Interminable seconds passed as Jamie absorbed the feel of her around him. His heart segued into an irregular rhythm, his legs shook, and he had to lock his jaw to keep from roaring in primal, almost caveman-like approval. Every hair on his body prickled with awareness and his stomach did a little pirouette of pleasure. Nothing in his past experience could have prepared him for the complete *rightness* of this moment. Everything began and ended here, Jamie thought, shaken—reformed and reborn—to the very core.

He looked down at her, bare breasts, sweet belly, his rod buried into her warmth, then his gaze tangled with hers—soothing and blue and heartbreakingly beautiful—and James Aidan Flanagan did the one thing he'd sworn he'd never do.

He fell head over heels in love.

# *11*

IT TOOK EVERY OUNCE of willpower Audrey possessed not to pass out. The feel of Jamie's body inside her—the desperate need in his eyes—was so intense it literally took her breath away.

So far, she hadn't been able to get it back.

He was big and solid and his presence consumed her. And those gorgeous hazel eyes… Tortured, anguished, wondering, wistful and curiously doomed. She didn't have to be psychic to know what he was thinking.

She could *feel* it.

He wanted her, but didn't want to. He needed her help, but would never willingly accept it. He was hurting and angry and bitter and hopeless.

She'd felt those emotions and more when she'd touched his tattoo, a permanent tribute to a man who'd given the ultimate sacrifice for his country. Naturally when she'd pressed for more information, he'd derailed her with sex. A blatant stall tactic, but how could she complain when he felt so right seated between her legs?

Audrey tightened around him, drew him even farther into her body. She watched the veins in his neck strain, watched him lock his jaw and a thrill of feminine power whipped through her, urging her to take even more. She angled her hips forward, pushing him even deeper inside her and saw little stars dance in her peripheral vision.

God, he felt good. Better than anything she could have ever imagined.

Jamie withdrew, then plunged back in sending shock waves of sexual delight pulsing through her. Her womb contracted, slickening her folds. They'd barely started and yet, amazingly, she could already feel the quickening of climax tingling in her clit. This felt so right and it had been so very long— *so very, very long*—since she'd had a proper orgasm, she couldn't bear to wait a second longer. She wanted to savor it, but couldn't summon the strength. She worked herself beneath him, forcing him to up the tempo to give her more.

Jamie answered with a wicked chuckle, wrapped a muscled arm around her waist and pounded into her. He was hot, hard and thrilling. Harder, harder, then faster and faster still. Deep then shallow, a fabulous combination designed to energize every nerve inside of her. She was coming apart, Audrey decided, as the tension inside her wound tighter and tighter. Any second now she was simply going to break and fly into a million pieces.

Jamie bent forward, licked a wild path over both nipples, then sucked one into the hot cavern of his mouth.

She fractured.

Her back bowed so hard off the massage table she feared it would break, her mouth opened in a silent scream and she dug her nails into his ass, holding him there while she convulsed around him. Every contraction around the hot, hard length of him made her limbs weaken. The orgasm tore through her, whipped her insides into an erupting volcano of sensation so perfect it brought tears to her eyes.

The force of her own release triggered Jamie's. His lips peeled away from his teeth and a feral growl of approval, which would have made a caveman proud, ripped from his throat. He lodged himself firmly into her, so tight and so deep you couldn't have gotten a toothpick between them.

It was more than just an orgasm, Audrey realized as her gaze tangled with his, it was a statement.

She was his. He'd claimed her.

For all intents and purposes, he'd just planted a no trespassing sign in her vagina. It was barbaric and romantic and her idiot heart soared with ridiculous joy. Chest heaving, she let her head fall back and a long peal of glorious laughter echoed up her throat.

Evidently pleased with himself, Jamie bent and kissed her forehead. "You look happy."

"What tipped you off? The smile or the orgasm?"

He chuckled, carefully withdrew, then helped her up, thank God, because she couldn't have managed it on her own strength. "Both." He cocked his head toward the back of her house. "Are you up for a little lather-rinse-repeat?" he asked.

Another dark thrill coursed through her. "You want to take a shower?"

His voice lowered an octave. "Among other things."

Ooh-la-la, Audrey thought as, unbelievably, her womb issued another greedy contraction. That must be where the "repeat" part came in. *Jamie, naked, wet, needy and hard...*

Oh, yeah. She could definitely go for that. Among other things.

HE'D DONE IT, Jamie thought. After a lifetime of being very careful—of always maintaining an emotional distance—in the course of the past four days he'd abandoned and broken every bachelor rule. He and Audrey had had more than three unofficial dates. She'd eaten off his plate. And, he thought, as his gaze traced the beautiful lines of her slumbering face, he'd spent the night with her.

In her bed, no less.

Strangely enough, no clap of thunder rent the heavens and the first rays of dawn peeking above the horizon didn't appear any different from any other he'd witnessed in his thirty-some-odd years on this earth.

And yet everything had changed.

Not in the world around him, Jamie thought. No, she'd changed his world from *within*. The world he lived in might not have changed, but the one inside him no longer remotely resembled the one he'd been a part of before.

Somehow, someway, when he hadn't been paying attention, he'd fallen in love with her. He wouldn't have knowingly done it—he was too much of a coward—but he couldn't deny that it had happened nonetheless. And never had that been more startlingly clear than when he'd pushed into her and looked into those calm clear blue eyes. She'd been so perfect that he'd felt the back of his lids burn with some unnamed emotion he hadn't had the courage to claim in years.

No doubt, he'd become the butt of his friends' jokes—oh, how the mighty have fallen, they'd tease—and Garrett would most likely make good on his threat, but this morning, in this very instant, frankly he just didn't give a damn.

So long as he was with her, the rest of the world could simply go to hell.

He wasn't going to worry about Garrett or what he would say. He wasn't going to worry about his role in meddling in her private business. He wasn't going to worry about falling in love and the resulting powerlessness that would no doubt bring. He just wanted to be with her.

Audrey's head was on his shoulder, her sweet hand curled palm down against his chest—his heart, specifically—and he could feel her plump breast resting against his side. Moses lay sprawled at the foot of the bed—on his feet, thank you very much—and from his vantage point beside the window, Jamie could see a couple of squirrels leaping from tree to tree. Their antics drew a smile. He felt Audrey stir and turned to watch her wake.

Her eyes were heavy-lidded with the last vestiges of sleep. She caught him watching her, smiled sleepily, then stretched like a cat. "Good-morning," she murmured groggily.

"Morning, beautiful," Jamie told her.

"I'm glad you stayed. I'd pegged you for the leaving type."

In another life, with any other woman—but not with her. His gaze tangled with hers. "You're worth waking up with."

She smiled at the compliment and a stain of pink washed over her cheeks. Amazing, Jamie thought. He'd taken her six ways to Sunday last night—on the massage table, in her shower, against the hall wall and in her bed…and yet she couldn't take a compliment from him without blushing. Odd that he should find that endearing.

"So are you." She reached up and tousled his hair. "Your curls are all mussed."

"So are yours."

She grimaced. "But yours are sexy, whereas mine look like they've been hit with a weed-whacker and styled with a garden rake."

"Not true," Jamie told her, fingering one long curl. He wrapped it around his index finger and tugged her toward him for a sweet kiss. "I love your hair. It makes me hot."

Another one of those nervous smiles. Intrigued, Jamie sat up on one elbow and stared at her. "Are you not accustomed to compliments, or do they just make you uncomfortable?"

"Both," Audrey told him.

He traced a finger down the achingly familiar slope of her cheek. "We'll have to work on that."

"You could stand a little work yourself," she told him, her gaze searching his.

Since he knew she was referring to his inability to open up, Jamie decided a subject change was in order. "We could stand to work on breakfast," he improvised. "Are you hungry?"

Though she clearly wrestled with pursuing the line of conversation she'd started, to Jamie's immense relief Audrey let it drop. Not permanently, he knew, but at least he'd gotten a reprieve. She nodded. "Yeah. Let me take Moses out, then I'll fix us something."

"Let me," Jamie offered. He pushed up and planted his feet on the floor. "You cooked last night."

"You don't have to do that," she said. "You don't know your way around my kitchen."

Jamie chuckled. "I think I can manage," he drawled, shooting her a wicked grin. For someone who was determined to help the world, she wasn't very good at accepting help herself, Jamie noted, intrigued.

Audrey chewed the corner of her lip and her eyes twinkled with humor. "Smart-ass."

"How about 'Thank you, Jamie, that sounds nice'?"

"Thank you, Jamie," she replied dutifully. "I like my eggs over medium and prefer strawberry jam on my toast."

Ah, now that was more like it. "What am I?" he teased. "Your short-order cook?"

Audrey stood, shrugged into her robe and shot him an unrepentant grin. "You asked for it."

What could he say to that? She was right.

"Come on, Moses," she said, her voice trailing off in a sigh. "Time to give your offering to Mother Earth." She paused, turned and shot him another smile. "And there's absolutely nothing *short* about you."

"Thank you," Jamie told her, feigning a humble nod. "*That's* how you take a compliment."

Rather than comment, Audrey merely shook her head and left. Though he dreaded it, Jamie waited until he heard the back door close, then checked the display on his cell phone. He cringed when he saw two missed calls—both were from the Colonel.

"Flanagan, I want an update. Give me a call back ASAP."

The second call was received at eleven-thirty and was a lot less cordial. "Flanagan, you'd better be taking a late-night basket-weaving lesson because if you are doing anything—*anything*—that you're not supposed to be doing with my granddaughter, I will be on the first available plane up there and will personally tear your nuts from your body. *Do not* toy with my granddaughter's affections."

Was it toying with her affections if he wanted to be the sole object of her affection? Jamie wondered. Didn't matter. He sincerely doubted that the Colonel would recognize the difference.

For a moment Jamie considered telling Audrey about the real reason for his visit. Given what they'd shared and everything he wanted to share in the future, it didn't seem right to keep it from her. She'd be pissed at first, of course, and he could hardly blame her, but she wasn't completely unreasonable. She'd recognize that her grandfather had only had her best interests at heart and that he'd merely been repaying a favor.

Ultimately, though, he decided against it. Audrey had never had any intention of shackling herself to that self-important blowhard, as the Colonel had put it. And she needn't ever know that anyone had interfered, least of all him. And this worked out nicely for him, as he wasn't altogether sure that she would see things the way that he wanted her to. Self-serving? Manipulative? Selfish?

Certainly.

But the end justified the means here, Jamie decided, because it would damned hard to love her properly if she hated him.

And the idea of Audrey hating him was…unthinkable. What were his plans? Aside from making her breakfast, then making love to her again, he didn't have any. But he knew that in any future plans he had, he wanted her in them.

"A-HA!"

In the process of coming around the corner of her house, Audrey started, swallowed a scream, then pressed a hand to her rapidly beating heart. "Tewanda, what the hell are you doing?" she snapped. "You scared the life out of me." She glared at Moses. "Some guard dog you are," she mumbled.

"I was waiting on you," Tewanda told her. "He's in there, isn't he? Stella got her groove back last night, eh?" she asked, her voice loaded with innuendo. She danced around in a little circle. "Uh-huh, uh-huh, uh-huh. I can tell. You've got the glow. The orgasm aura."

"Shut up," Audrey hissed, shooting a furtive look over her shoulder. "He'll hear you."

Tewanda sidled forward. "Well?" she asked pointedly, her eyes dancing with do-tell mischief.

"Well what?"

She let go an exasperated huff. *"How was it?"*

Audrey wanted to hold back, to make her auda-cious friend suffer, but ultimately she couldn't do it. She giggled—actually giggled. "It. Was. *Amazing."*

Tewanda did her little dance again. "I knew it! Some guys you can just tell, you know, and the two of you were casting sparks from the get-go." She paused. "So what are you going to do about Derrick? Cutting him lose, right? Telling him no? Adios, sayonara, goodbye, don't let the door hit you on the ass on your way out?"

*"Tewanda."* Honestly, Audrey thought, stifling the urge to laugh. She didn't know what had made her friend happier—that she'd finally had magnifi-cent sex or that she was breaking up with Derrick.

"Well, you can't mean to stay with him, right?" Tewanda asked. She paused, considered her. "There's more here with Jamie already than there's ever been with Derrick. Hell, even I can see that."

She was right, Audrey knew. Four days into a relationship with Jamie had yielded more emotion than fourteen months with Derrick. Jamie did it for her on all levels. He was brilliant and funny, a bit wounded but not damaged beyond repair, though she knew he didn't believe that. He was loyal and gorgeous and…and she'd fallen for him, Audrey realized helplessly.

It was that simple and that complicated.

The idea that he was supposed to leave tomorrow made her previously happy heart constrict with panic. She didn't want him to leave. Ever, she thought with a wry twist of her lips, though that might be a tad premature.

All she knew was that she wanted him. She wanted to share every dawn and every sunset, every victory and every setback. She wanted to always see those laughing hazel eyes and bask in that crooked sexy grin. She wanted more lather, rinse and repeat, Audrey thought with a small grin as her insides did another little meltdown.

But most importantly, she wanted to help him. She was close, she knew. She could tell they were teetering on the edge of a breakthrough. Meaning that she'd just about pushed him to the breaking point and every bit of that pent-up grief, regret and misplaced guilt was going to come boiling to the surface. He'd come dangerously close last night and, while she could have pushed this morning, intuition had told her to hold back.

Though he'd derailed her with sex last night, she didn't want anything coming between them in bed. Bed needed to be a safe zone, Audrey thought. For whatever reason, she got the distinct impression that it hadn't been for Jamie. That he rarely, if ever, lingered for any intimacy.

Moses did his business, then trotted back to her side.

"So what now?" Tewanda asked. "Are you still

sticking to the schedule or are you going to improvise?"

They were supposed to start ballroom dancing this morning, but given the time factor Audrey had working against her, she decided that adhering to the schedule wasn't a good idea. "We're improvising," she said.

Tewanda clearly took that as doublespeak for sex-all-day. "No worries," she said, smiling like a Cheshire cat. "Turn the walkie off. There's nothing here that can't go without your attention for one day. Go commando and incommunicado and get laid-o." She whooped joyously again, then started back toward the office.

Smiling, Audrey merely shook her head.

Tewanda paused, turned and shot her a look which was curiously serious and sincere for a person who'd only a moment ago told her to get laid-o, for pity's sake. "Audrey?"

"Yeah?"

"I'm happy for you. He's a good thing."

Audrey's chest warmed and a small smile tugged at her lips. "Yeah," she agreed, nodding. "He is."

And a girl could never have too much of a good thing.

# *12*

Now, HE COULD TRULY get used to this, Jamie thought contentedly. He and Audrey had said to hell with the schedule, she'd turned off her walkie-talkie and they'd spent the entire day doing whatever struck their fancy. He'd made breakfast, they'd eaten, then showered, then enjoyed another session of lather, rinse and repeat. His lips quirked.

Equally as frantic as last night—he couldn't get into her fast enough—but somehow more intense than before. In fact, every moment he spent with her seemed to be more powerful than the last. And yet she was easy company. He felt...complete in her presence. Go figure?

At the moment he was resting with his head in her lap while she rowed them around the lake. It was late afternoon and the sun melted like a big scoop of orange sherbet above the trees, painting their riotous fall foliage in fiery color. It was truly beautiful here, Jamie thought, dragging in a breath of cool crisp air. Though he'd lived all over the world, he'd always considered Alabama his home. But he could easily see making this his home as well.

Anywhere with her would be home, he realized, a bit startled by the epiphany.

The water lapped against the hull of the boat, birds sang and a gentle breeze whispered through the tops of the trees. Unwind was right, he thought, feeling his lids flutter shut.

Audrey's fingers skimmed his eyebrow, making a smile tug at his lips. "You look relaxed."

"I am," he said. "I like it here."

"You mean you like having your head in my lap or you like being at Unwind?"

He looked up at her. "Can I like both?"

She chuckled, the sound soft and intimate between them. "Certainly. I like them both as well."

Jamie frowned as a thought struck, a question he'd been meaning to ask but had kept forgetting. "You said you'd been a commodities broker in a past life," Jamie reminded her. "But you never told me how you ended up here."

She pretended she didn't know what he was talking about, the little nimrod. "Did you ask?"

"I did," Jamie confirmed, laughing. "You said if you told me that, you'd have to kill me. Permission granted. After you have satisfied my curiosity, you can take your best shot." It's not like she hadn't been taking shots at him all week. It wouldn't hurt her to reciprocate the gesture.

"It's not pretty," Audrey warned him.

"The truth rarely is. Come on. Tell me."

He heard her sigh, looked up and watched her gaze cloud over. "I had a heart attack," she said glibly, shrugging. "Stress. It was either lose the job or lose my life."

Jamie had to clamp his jaw to keep it from sagging. Out of all the reasons she could have listed as to why she'd made such an abrupt career change, a heart attack certainly would never have occurred to him.

Stunned, he sat up and turned around to face her. "But— But you're young. You're healthy." He frowned, gestured toward her chest. "How did—"

"A body can only take so much," she said, smiling sadly. "I put mine through hell. I was also with a guy who—" she paused, chose her words carefully "—required more of me than I could give. That relationship ended with a restraining order." She frowned with regret. "Not one of my better decisions, but we all have some we aren't proud of."

Jamie swore. He passed a hand over his face and his gaze inexplicably zeroed in once again on her chest. He got it, all right. The guy she'd been with had taken so much of her that he'd literally broken her heart. Not in the traditional sense, no, but damaged her all the same.

Christ. No wonder the Colonel had kept going on and on about how special she was. He'd known it, of course. A man couldn't spend half a second in her presence without feeling the healing, soul-soothing effects of her company. And hell, he'd even felt it from a friggin' picture, two thousand miles away from here. *A heart attack*, Jamie thought again, absolutely shaken.

"How are you doing now?" he asked quietly. "Taking meds? Watching your cholesterol?" Another thought struck. Surely to God all the wild sex they'd had in the past couple of days couldn't be good for her. The exertion, the orgasms… He could have killed her, Jamie thought, his own heart turning to lead and plummeting into his stomach. Sweet mother of—

Audrey chuckled. "I can see that your imagination is running away with you," she told him. "No, I am not on any medication, though I do watch my diet since I'll always be at risk." A small smile turned her lips. "And, for the record, there are no special limitations on my…physical activities you should concern yourself with."

"But—"

"I'm fine," Audrey insisted. "I take care of myself. I know it sounds like a big deal, but it really isn't."

The hell it wasn't, Jamie thought. "How old were you?"

"At the time it happened? Twenty-six."

"Then it was a big deal," Jamie said. Honestly, he'd heard of athletes who'd pushed themselves into a premature heart attack, but never a young healthy woman. The Colonel must have been out of his mind.

"Anyway," she said, releasing an end-of-subject sigh, one he recognized because he'd used it frequently himself. "That's how I got here. Who better to help stressed-out professionals than a former stressed-out professional, eh?"

He could certainly understand that, and there was no doubt she was in her element here. Still… "Do you miss your old job? Your old life?"

She smiled again, marginally lightening the load in his chest. "Not at all. I'm where I'm supposed to be. Everything happens for a reason." Her clear blue gaze tangled with his and a secret knowledge seemed to lurk there that he sincerely wished he was privy to. "You're here for a reason, too," she told him.

While he could have just as easily made a joke, Jamie didn't. "Do you really believe that?" he asked. "Or is that just a platitude people bandy about when they don't have an answer for something? It all comes down to fate," he said, a hint of bitterness he couldn't control seeping into his voice.

Audrey mulled it over, then ultimately nodded. "I think so. There's a point and purpose to everything. Just look at the way the world is designed. Even nature has a point, a goal, an end."

While he couldn't fault her reasoning, he couldn't accept it either. Accepting it meant that Danny had been destined to die on that hill, and that Jamie had been destined to fail when it had come to saving him. Fate? he scoffed. Then fate was an unfair bitch. He was bitter and angry and wanted to know why. *Why, dammit?* What possible good had come out of his friend losing his life?

Geez, God, he was losing it here. Until the past few days Jamie had done an admirable job of keeping a tight rein on his feelings. He'd put every ounce of grief, regret and anger into a neat box at the bottom of his soul and, while he'd suffer an occasional setback—nightmares, mostly—for the most part, he could go into lock-down mode and keep it together.

It was her, he realized. She was acting like a sponge, drawing to the surface everything inside him he wanted to keep hidden.

Audrey set the oars aside, leaned forward, framed his face and gave him a tender kiss. "I just gave you a painful piece of my history. Now I'm asking for one of yours. Tell me about Danny," she implored softly.

Jamie instinctively drew back, shut down. He knew what she was doing—she was trying to fix him, but there were some things that simply couldn't be fixed and he was one of them. She'd been doing this all week—picking, probing, question after question, trying to open him up and lay him bare. The mere thought turned his insides to ice, made bile rise in his throat.

"Leave it," Jamie told her, a warning he hoped like hell she heeded. He set his jaw and fought back a tide of angry emotion. More horrible memories from that night rushed rapid fire through his mind, making his gut clench with dread. *Leave me! You know it's over!* The backs of his lids burned.

Oh, God. He couldn't do this.

"He was a Ranger with you, right? In the same unit?"

Jamie shoved his hands into his hair, pushing it away from his face. He glanced around and realized that she'd rowed them all the way out into the middle of the lake. No escape. Panic sent acid churning through his belly. This had been a trap, he realized suddenly. She'd done this on purpose. His gaze flew to hers. Of all the sneaky, underhanded... If he wasn't so damned angry, he'd be impressed. Like a bear with a ring in its nose, she'd led him around all day, setting him up for this very moment.

And while this tactic might have worked on an ordinary man, it wasn't going to work on him, he thought grimly. He'd been a United States Ranger, by God. He was like Houdini, he could find his way out of anything.

Jamie stood, inadvertently rocking the boat.

Audrey inhaled sharply, grasped the sides. "What are you doing? Sit down! You're going to tip us over."

"News flash, baby," Jamie told her, his lips curled in an angry smile. "Your plan didn't work."

Then he leaped neatly over the side and started swimming toward shore.

She would not break him, dammit.

*She would not.*

His feelings were all he had left of his friend. He didn't want to share them. And he wouldn't.

UTTERLY SHOCKED, Audrey watched Jamie determinedly swim toward shore. When she'd concocted this trap-him-in-the-boat plan, she could honestly say that she'd never anticipated this scenario. She'd wanted to force him to open up, to let her help him. The small boat had seemed like a good choice because, logistically, it would have been hard to distract her with sex, his usual, admittedly excellent, method of shutting her up.

Her eyes narrowed on his rapidly shrinking form. This new development was a setback, but she'd be damned before she'd accept defeat. The more time she spent with Jamie, the more she knew he needed her. She could feel the ache inside him worsening. Hell, he hurt so much it made *her* nauseous. It was eating him up inside, Audrey knew, and the more it festered, the worse it was going to become.

She stood. "Jamie!"

When he didn't so much as look at her, Audrey did what seemed like the only plausible thing—she jumped in after him.

The shock of cold water stole her breath, but she pressed on. She was an excellent swimmer, after all, and frequently took a dip in the lake. She'd

never done it in late September, but what the hell.
New experiences were what made life interesting.
Between strokes, she looked for Jamie and had the
pleasure of seeing his outraged face when he saw
that she'd come in after him.

His eyes looked like they'd burst from their sock-
ets. "Have you lost your mind?" he shouted at her.

Audrey ignored him. No more than he had, the
stubborn jerk. But she'd lost something a whole lot
more precious—her heart. She'd given it to a tight-
lipped obstinate former Ranger who could swim
like a friggin' fish, Audrey thought, resisting the
inappropriate urge to laugh.

Jamie had doubled back and was suddenly next
to her. "Do you have a death wish?" he shouted angrily. "What the hell were you thinking?"

"I just followed your lead," she said, ignoring
his anger. "I'm not letting you run away from me."

"What about the boat?"

"Fuck the boat."

His feet found ground before hers did. He gaped
at her. "What is your deal?" he demanded, slog-
ging forward. He grabbed her arm and tugged her
with him.

"What's yours?" she answered back.

"I want you to lay off!"

"Why? So you can wallow in self-pity for the rest
of your life?" It was risky and mean, but he wasn't
mad enough yet and it was going to take anger to
make him break.

Five feet from shore, his face dripping wet, clothes clinging to him like a second skin, he stopped and glared daggers at her. "Self-pity?" he repeated in a voice so quiet it was thunderous. "That's what you think is wrong with me?"

"What choice do I have when you won't level with me?"

He crossed his arms over his chest and smirked at her. "Did it ever occur to you that it was none of your damned business?"

That dart found a mark, forcing her to swallow. "Maybe not," Audrey conceded. "But you made it my business when you showed up at my camp! Sure, my grandfather ordered you here, but you didn't have to come, did you?"

He opened his mouth, readying for a comeback, but stopped short. He released a weary breath, rubbed the bridge of his nose. "Just let it go," he said instead.

Shivering, Audrey shook her head. "I won't," she told him. She thumped a hand against her chest. "I can feel it in here. It *hurts,* dammit, and if it hurts me, it's got to be killing you. Just—" She blinked, determined not to cry. "Just tell me what happened."

Jamie blanched. His gaze dropped to her chest, then darted back up and tangled with hers. She didn't have any idea what was going on in that head of his, but she could feel more and more pain radiating off him.

A helpless laugh rumbled up his throat and he

shook his head. "You don't know what you're asking of me," he told her, his voice breaking.

No, she did, and that made pushing him for it even harder. Audrey fisted her hands in his shirt, looked up at him. "Nobody deserves to carry around what you're wrestling with. I may be little, but I'm tough. Share the load, Jamie," she implored, punctuating the statement with a soft kiss to his jaw.

And that did it.

Her bad-ass former Ranger closed his eyes tightly shut, rested his forehead against hers and a quiet sob shook his shoulders.

# 13

JAMIE FELT AUDREY'S ARMS tighten around him and he clung to her, sapping up her strength just like every other selfish bastard who'd come before him. God, he was pathetic. But he couldn't seem to help himself. She'd just kept on and on, and then when she'd told him that she could feel it too—that *his* pain was hurting *her*—that was just the last damned straw.

"Oh, Jamie," she said. She tugged him toward the cottage. "Come on. Let's go inside."

Jamie allowed her to guide him, numb from the cold, from arguing, from the grief he'd been carrying for so long. He should be taking care of her, not the other way around, and yet he wasn't strong enough to deny himself her comfort. Selfishly, he needed it. No, it was more than that—*he needed her.*

Audrey grabbed the bottle of Jameson from the kitchen counter, then led him toward the bathroom. She quickly adjusted the tap and started the shower.

One quick guzzle of whiskey later and they were both naked and under the spray. The hot water beat down like little needles of fire, warming his skin back up. She lathered him up, washing his hair in a way that was gentle but not overtly sexual. It was nice, Jamie thought, to be able to be with a naked woman—one he admittedly wanted more than any other on the planet—and yet be content not to act on that desire. He supposed that's what happened when you found the right one.

In short order, she had them both clean, warm, dressed and situated in front of a small fire. She'd tossed a couple of easy-start logs into the grate and a cozy warmth soon permeated the room.

Her hair still wet, she sat down beside him wearing one of his shirts, and offered him her hand. A simple gesture, but one that had a singularly profound effect on his heart. His throat clogged.

Okay, he thought, blowing out an uneasy breath. She wanted to know about Danny. Where to start? "You were right," Jamie told her. "Danny was in my unit. I'm assuming your grandfather told you a little bit about him and—" he cleared his throat "—what happened?"

She nodded once. "Some. He mentioned that you'd lost a good friend recently."

"That's the watered-down version." He traced a finger over her palm. Then he swallowed again. "Danny was more than a good friend. He was more like a brother. Our unit was like that. Tight. We met in college, the four of us. Me, Danny, Guy and Payne." Jamie smiled, remembering. Young and dumb, he thought, hell-bent on changing the world. "Guy and Payne are my business partners in Ranger Security," he added as an aside. The silence yawned between them, then he shook his head. "When Danny died, we... We all wanted out."

"That's certainly understandable," Audrey told him. "Surely you don't fault yourself for that?"

"No, not for that," Jamie said. "I fault myself for not saving him."

"Oh, Jamie," she sighed, smoothing the hair above his ear. "You can't fault yourself for that either."

He could and he did. Tears burned the backs of his lids, his chest ached with the pressure of guilt. Jamie swore, wiped his eyes. "I was supposed to have his back," he said, his voice cracking. "Not Payne. Not Guy. *Me*. I was the one who was supposed to make sure nothing happened to him."

In an instant, Audrey was in his lap. She straddled him, framed his face with her hands, forcing him to look her in the eye. "Jamie, your intentions were good, but we both know you were setting yourself up to do the impossible."

"But—"

She shushed him. "Let me ask you something. Did you follow procedure?"

"Of course."

"Didn't vary from what you were supposed to do and took every precautionary measure?"

"Yes, but—"

"Were you operating on good intelligence?"

She was definitely the Colonel's granddaughter, Jamie thought. He'd asked many of these same questions. "Yes."

"Then what went wrong?"

A cold chill slid down his back. "We were ambushed."

Her thumbs gently swept his cheeks. "Then how were you supposed to have his back?"

Jamie started to reply, but found he couldn't answer.

"You would have had to have been psychic to know what was going to happen," she said softly. She bent forward and kissed him, causing the flow he'd been holding back for eight months to come rushing forward in a cleansing torrent he didn't have a prayer of stopping. He cried for Danny, he cried for himself, he cried for his friends.

"Let it go," she said, hugging him tightly. She rocked him back and forth, the movement soothing and tender and heartbreakingly sweet. "I've got you," she murmured. "Just let it all go. If he was the kind of friend worthy of this grief, then he wouldn't want you holding on to it like this, would he?"

No, he wouldn't, Jamie thought. Odd how he'd never looked at it that way. It was sobering. He felt like an enormous weight had been lifted off his chest.

Audrey drew back, showered his face with healing kisses, sprinkled them along his jaw, lingered around the corner of his mouth. Jamie turned his head and caught her lips, fitted his hands on the small of her back. God, she tasted wonderful, he thought, savoring the flavor of her against his tongue. What had he ever done without her?

Knowing what he wanted—what he needed—she upped the intensity of the kiss, slid her hands down his chest, then back up again, over his neck and into his hair. An arrow of heat landed in his groin, stirring his dick beneath her.

Audrey groaned into his mouth—the sound desperate and erotic—and wriggled on top of him, rocking her hips forward to catch the ridge of his arousal. A sweet sigh stuttered out of her mouth and into his. He cupped her rump and smiled against her lips as he made a pleasant discovery—no panties. They were piled on the bathroom floor with the rest of their wet clothing.

Jamie found the hem of the shirt and tugged it up over her head, then cast it aside. Full creamy breasts crowned with rosy budded nipples. Tiny waist. A thatch of dark brown curls.

*Heaven.*

He bent his head forward and drew one perfect nipple into his mouth, and a commingled sigh of pleasure leaked from both his and Audrey's lungs.

"I love it when you do that," Audrey told him. "I can feel it all the way down *here,*" she said, rubbing herself against him. "It makes my belly all hot and muddled."

Jamie growled low in his throat as his dick jerked beneath her. The only thing that separated him from her was a pair of boxer shorts. She leaned forward and licked a hot path up his neck, sighed into his ear, causing a wave of gooseflesh to break out over his skin. He felt a single bead of moisture leak from his dick.

She rocked against him once more, gasped as the pleasure barbed through her. "I need you," she said, her voice throaty and broken and every bit as desperate as he was.

Jamie shifted beneath her, freeing himself from his shorts and felt her warm juices slide over the swollen head of his penis.

He set his jaw and gritted his teeth.

Audrey's mouth opened in a silent O of pleasure and she moved against him once more, bumping the head of him against her clit. "God, that feels good," she told him, arching her neck back.

Jamie pushed against her, deliberately coating the length of him with her wet heat. "It can feel even better."

A sexy chuckle rattled up her throat. "Oh, I know it can," she said confidently. Then she arched herself up, positioned him at her entrance and impaled herself upon him.

A smile of sublime satisfaction transformed her gorgeous face to something almost painfully beautiful. Her lids drooped and a gasp of sheer erotic delight slipped past her lips.

*Hot, wet, tight,* Jamie thought, struggling to keep from coming right then. He'd never been one to detonate upon entry, but nothing had ever felt so fabulous as the feel of Audrey's sweet little body hovering over his, balancing on his dick. He grasped her hips, thrust up, pushing himself even farther into her.

Her mouth found his once more, desperate, frantic, but confident and sure. She wasn't just making love to him, he realized, she was laying siege. For every parlay of her tongue, she rocked against him, tightened her feminine muscles. The combination made every one of his senses soar, made him buck frantically beneath her. She was everywhere. On top of his body, inside his mouth, inside his head… inside his heart.

"Oh, Jamie," she groaned, the throaty purr the sexiest thing he'd ever heard. "I'm going to— I think—"

The seed of climax had taken root, Jamie knew, upping his thrusts. He reached down between their joined bodies, found the bud nestled in the peak of her curls and stroked her.

Predictably, she went wild.

Her breath came in short broken gasps, she tightened around him, making his balls shrink and his dick threaten to explode. Jamie set his jaw and stroked her even harder. *Come on, baby,* he thought. *Give it to me so I can let it go.*

A second later, she went rigid with release, a long scream tore from her throat, and she convulsed around him. What she looked like in that instant would forever be burned into his heart. She was… amazing. A goddess.

Jamie's own release followed hers. The orgasm shot so hard from his loins, it would have blasted paint off the wall. He went weak—literally weak. His vision blackened around the edges, his breath came in ragged gasps and his legs felt like they were going to fall off.

*Sweet mother.*

Audrey sagged against his chest, rested her head against his shoulder and pressed a breathless kiss against his neck. "Can I tell you something?" she asked.

It took effort, but he managed to find his voice. "Sure."

"I think I'm in love with you."

Emotion clogged his throat, preventing him from immediately returning the sentiment. Danny may have died in his arms…but he'd just been reborn in hers.

# 14

ARMED WITH THE REMOTE and a bowl of popcorn, Audrey settled in next to Jamie on her couch. "You aren't a talker are you?"

Jamie's beer paused halfway to his mouth and he glanced at her. "What do you mean a 'talker'?"

"I mean, you aren't one of those people who has to inject commentary throughout the whole movie, right?" She faked a wince. "'Cause if you are, that's just going to ruin it for me."

He chuckled. "What? Are you going to dump me if I am?"

No, Audrey thought, shaking her head. Dumping one person today was enough, thank you very much. Rather than leave Derrick in the lurch, Audrey had taken the opportunity to call him this afternoon while Jamie had been at the camp's library selecting their movie. He'd nixed a chick flick and she'd vetoed blood and gore, so they'd reached a compromise with a nice comedy.

At any rate, Derrick had been surprised by her answer to his proposal and even more shocked that she hadn't put up an argument when he'd told her that they'd simply have to break up. Thankfully, Derrick's ego was substantial enough that her refusal didn't seem to have affected him that deeply.

Still, she just felt better knowing that she'd ended that chapter in her life and started a new one with Jamie. There was nothing quite so thrilling as the blush of new romance, she thought, snuggling in next to him as the previews rolled.

Ah, Audrey thought happily. Another similarity. He didn't want to fast-forward through them.

She cast a glance at him from the corner of her eye and felt her chest squeeze with secret joy. Honestly, she could just look at him all day. Her gaze was perpetually drawn to the masculine line of his jaw, the curiously vulnerable patch of soft skin next to those amazing eyes. He just did it for her, Audrey thought. Was he perfect? No. What person was? She was suddenly reminded of a quote by Sam Keen. "You come to love not by finding the perfect person, but by seeing an imperfect person perfectly." That fit, Audrey thought, smiling softly.

And Jamie had turned a corner today. This afternoon when he'd finally broken down and shared his tragedy with her… Her own chest had ached so much it had brought tears to her eyes. He'd been grieving for so long, and worse, blaming himself. She wasn't altogether sure that he'd let himself completely off the hook in that regard, but she knew she'd argued a significant enough point to make him doubt. That was a start, at least. Baby steps, Audrey told herself, and wondered if asking him to stay with her indefinitely was more along the lines of taking a giant leap.

Technically he was supposed to go home tomorrow and yet the idea of him leaving now, after everything they'd been through this week, made her belly tip in a nauseated roll. She missed him and he hadn't even left yet. That couldn't be good, considering he was based in Atlanta and she in the wilds of Maine. Logistics, she knew, but she couldn't keep from jumping ahead.

He was it. Jamie Flanagan was The One.

"Can I ask you something?" Audrey said, wanting to make sure they were on the same page. Or at the very least in the same chapter.

He tugged playfully on a lock of her hair. "I thought you said you didn't like to talk during the movie."

"Previews don't count."

"Ah," he sighed, inclining his head. "That's a handy piece of knowledge right there. Sure," he said in answer to her question. "Ask away."

Audrey hesitated. "Do you have to go home tomorrow?"

A slow smile tugged at the corner of his mouth and those golden green eyes softened. "Are you issuing an invitation?"

Audrey nodded. "An open one," she said, putting it all out there. In for a penny, in for a pound, she supposed.

Impossibly, those gorgeous eyes softened even more and he leaned over and brushed his lips across hers in a tender kiss that stole her breath. "I like the sound of that."

"I'm not scaring you, am I?" she asked, suddenly uncertain. She knew he cared about her—one of the only perks of this empathy thing, but… "I just—"

Jamie pressed a single finger against her mouth and his gaze searched hers. The emotion—the un-adulterated feeling he allowed her to see—made her pulse leap. "I'd only be scared if you didn't want me here."

"No worries then," Audrey told him. She leaned over and pressed her lips to his, sighed with plea-sure as the innocent gesture quickly morphed into something a lot more potent. A movie? she men-tally scoffed. Why watch a movie when there were other, more satisfying ways, to pass an evening.

Especially with him.

In the process of trying to crawl into his lap without upending her popcorn, Audrey jumped when a loud knock came at the door. Seconds later, it abruptly burst open.

Moses leaped off the recliner, 150 pounds of pissed-off growling canine, and barreled for the door.

*"Moses, heel!"* Audrey shouted at precisely the same instant she recognized her grandfather. There were two grim-faced men behind him whom she

couldn't identify, but she could hardly think about them at the moment. She was more concerned with keeping her dog from ripping the Colonel's throat out. *"Heel,"* she ordered again, jumping up after the dog.

Her grandfather scowled. "Moses," he scolded. "It's only me." He glared at Jamie. "It's him you should maul."

Confused, Audrey grabbed Moses by the collar and tugged him back. "Sit," she told him, patting him on the head. Her dog issued another warning growl, but did as she commanded.

Jamie had left the couch and had come to stand behind her. "Colonel," he acknowledged. His gaze darted to the men standing behind her grandfather and he gave them an up-nod, one of those male gestures of acknowledgment which seemed to indicate that he knew them.

Baffled, Audrey tucked her hair behind her ear. "Gramps, I didn't know you were coming," she said, for lack of anything better. She hadn't called with updates the way he'd asked her to—she'd been too busy sleeping with his friend, she thought, squirming—but surely that wouldn't warrant a personal visit.

He continued to bore a hole through Jamie. "That's because I wanted the element of surprise." He paused. "When you didn't return any of my phone calls, I began to get suspicious." His brows lowered even further. "Then Tewanda made an ominous comment about 'my plan working out even better than I anticipated' and I knew that I'd created a problem."

His plan? Audrey wondered, completely confused. What plan? "Gramps, I don't under—"

"I made the mistake of contacting your friends, here, Flanagan. As you can see they leaped to the same conclusion I did and have rushed here on your behalf to try and save you. Touching, but pointless." Unbelievably, his frown grew ever darker. "Because if you have done what I think you've done—if you have rounded any of the bases I warned you about— then no one will be able to save you. I want answers," he thundered. *"Now."*

He wasn't the only one, Audrey thought, growing increasingly worried. What the hell was going on? To hell with it. She didn't have to wonder. This was her house, dammit. "Gramps, what are you talking about? Plan? Bases? Why are you threatening a guest in my home?" Granted he was her grandfather, but this was uncalled for.

For the first time since he'd barged into her home, her grandfather paused to look at her. A flash of discomfort and oddly, contrition, momentarily claimed his features. "I have a confession to make, Audie. Do you remember last week when I told you that I would always have your best interests at heart, and to always remember it?"

A cold chill settled in her belly. She looked from a grim faced Jamie back to her grandfather. "I do," she replied cautiously.

He grimaced. "Well, remember it now because what I'm about to confess is most likely going to make you angry."

"Sir," Jamie butted in, speaking for the first time since this weird scenario had begun only minutes ago. "Let me tell her. Please," he added as an afterthought.

A throb started above her left eye and a sickening sensation swept through her midsection. Tell her what? What the hell was going on?

"You lost that option, Flanagan, and you're going to lose a lot more. I trusted you with someone I love, and you betrayed that trust. You've betrayed her. You were supposed to flirt with her, dammit!" He gestured wildly. "Not treat her like all those other tramps you whore around with."

The sickening sensation worsened, pushing panic into her throat. She squeezed her eyes tightly shut. *"Gramps, what are you talking about?"*

"Flanagan owed me a favor, Audrey, and I called it in on your behalf." He shifted uncomfortably. "You see, Tewanda had told me that Derrick had proposed and I was afraid that you would say yes." He jerked his head in Jamie's direction. "He was supposed to change your mind."

Floored, Audrey didn't know what to address first, her grandfather's manipulation or Jamie's part in it. The former pissed her off and the latter... Well, the latter felt like a well-placed punch straight to her heart. "You sent a man here to seduce me?"

she asked, thunderstruck. Her eyes narrowed into angry slits. "How dare—"

"Not seduce," the Colonel corrected swiftly. "He was supposed to flirt with you," he explained a bit sheepishly, unable to hold her gaze. "He was supposed to instill doubt." Her grandfather's wrath turned upon Jamie once more. "He was never supposed to touch you. Period."

Audrey went numb inside, absorbing what her grandfather had just said. She crossed her arms over her chest, chilled, and cleared her throat. "Is this true?" she asked, turning to Jamie.

"The simple answer is yes," Jamie admitted. "But I'm hoping you'll give me a chance to explain."

Audrey nodded, felt icicles lick through her veins. Any second now she'd be frozen completely, then simply shatter. She swallowed. "I, uh…" She winced, shook her head. "I just want to be clear on something. You were supposed to change my mind about marrying Derrick and then report back to my grandfather, right? Is that the gist of it?"

Jamie nodded. "But—"

"And yet you've known the answer to that for a while, haven't you, Jamie?" He'd seduced her, knowing that she'd never intended to marry Derrick. You knew, Audrey thought. She'd pegged Jamie Flanagan as many things—fierce, loyal, competent, hers, even, and yet an opportunistic player had never been one of them. He'd used her…and she'd made it easy for him.

Evidently reading her line of thinking, Jamie stepped toward her. "Audrey, I know that you're angry and you have every right to be, but if you'll just give me a chance to explain—"

She smirked, walked between his two friends— Payne and McCann, if she remembered correctly—and opened her door. "You've had plenty of opportunities to explain, Jamie, and no one is more disappointed, or feels more foolish right now than I do." She lowered her head to hide her watering eyes. "Please go."

"Audrey," he repeated softly, a say-you-don't-mean-it tone.

She merely opened the door wider.

"WE'VE BEEN TRYING to call you," Payne told him. "To warn you. When that didn't work…" He shrugged, not stating the obvious. They'd come to his rescue. Jamie was thankful, but couldn't find the words at the moment.

"You know this isn't over with Garrett," Guy pointed out. He jerked his head toward Audrey's cottage. "Once he gets finished covering his own ass up there, he'll be down here on yours."

Jamie tossed back another shot of whiskey, hoping like hell it would warm him up inside. Seeing the look on Audrey's face when she'd realized that he'd made love to her *after* she'd given him the information he'd needed had practically flash-frozen his insides. The duplicity had been bad enough, but this… This was an even bigger betrayal.

*You've had plenty of opportunities to explain, Jamie, and no one is more disappointed that you didn't or feels more foolish right now than I do.*

Anger was so much easier to accept than disappointment, he thought, remembering the look of complete regret on her hauntingly beautiful face.

"Let him come," Jamie said, spoiling for a fight. Everything about this damned favor had been wrong. It was Garrett's fault. Jamie hadn't wanted to trick her to start with. He'd known then that it was wrong, that it could only end in disaster. *His.* "I've got a few things I'd like to say to him."

Guy and Payne shared a look.

"I think you'd better start figuring out a way to keep Garrett from separating your stones from your shaft, if you know what I mean," Guy suggested. "This was his *granddaughter,* Jamie." He chuckled darkly. "This wasn't just some three-date disposable girl you messed around with."

Annoyed, Jamie looked up, glared menacingly at his friend and laced his voice with unmistakable lead. "She's not disposable."

Payne's gaze sharpened. "What are you saying?"

Guy stilled, studied him for a moment. Any trace of humor vanished from his gaze. "You're in love with her, aren't you?"

Jamie nodded. "She's…it," he finally finished, releasing a pent-up breath. And he'd blown the hell out of any chance with her. "I've screwed up. I should have told her and I didn't. And she was right. I've had plenty of time, I just…" He laughed bitterly.

"You just thought she'd never have to know," Payne finished.

"Stupid bastard," Guy chimed in. "Granted I am not the authority on women that you are, but even I know they don't like being lied to."

Payne peered out the window. "Or made a fool of. She thinks she fell for an act, and the longer she ruminates on that, the harder it's going to be to change her mind."

He was right, Jamie realized. Whether she'd wanted him to leave or not, by walking away he'd just made himself look all the more guilty. What the hell had he been thinking? Had he lost his freaking mind? He didn't retreat, dammit. He'd been a Ranger, for chrissakes. He didn't back down. He'd never walked away from a fight in his life and wasn't about to start now. Not when he had so much to lose.

Namely her.

Jamie sprang up from his chair and headed toward the door.

"Where are you going?" Guy asked, startled.

"I'm taking that hill," Jamie said, referencing the old military adage. And he was prepared to die on it if need be. His lips quirked with bitter humor.

Considering Garrett wanted to kill him, that was a distinct possibility.

## 15

"I DON'T GIVE A DAMN why you did it, Gramps. It was wrong," Audrey told him, giving him no quarter.

"Well, I never said I was right," the Colonel replied with a self-righteous sniff. "I said I did what I thought was right. There's a difference."

Though she was angry and aching, Audrey felt a smile pull at her lips. "Are you sure you shouldn't be an attorney? Because that sounds like a load of crap to me."

"Young lady," he scolded.

"Save it," she replied firmly. "You're not going to 'young lady' me on this. You had no right to do what you did. All of this could have been avoided if you had merely asked me if I was going to marry Derrick. I would have told you."

He blinked as though the idea had never occurred to him.

"Anyway, it doesn't matter now." She stood and pushed a hand through her hair. At this point she just wanted to be alone with her thoughts and properly nurse her wounds in private. "Come on," she said. "I'll put fresh sheets in the guest bedroom."

"Oh, I've got to go have a little chat with Flanagan before I go to bed," he said with an ominous chuckle.

Audrey drew up short. "No, you don't. I forbid it."

His eyebrows soared up his forehead. "You forbid it?"

"That's right. No more meddling." Honestly, Jamie deserved nothing better than a load of brimstone from her grandfather, but she needed to set a precedent here—the Colonel had to start butting out. "You are no longer permitted to meddle in my personal affairs."

"But—"

For the second time that evening, a knock sounded at her door, then someone burst through.

Only this time that person was Jamie.

Evidently used to it by now, Moses merely lifted his head, saw that it was Jamie and lay down once more. Her grandfather, however, wasn't so relaxed.

He scowled. "What the hell do you think you're doing here?" he demanded.

His face a mask of determination, Jamie pointed a finger at him. "Stay out of it."

"*What?* Have you forgotten who you're talking to?"

"My former boss," Jamie replied smoothly. "And

I didn't come here to talk to you." His gaze tangled with hers, causing the fine hairs on her arms to stand on end and an unwelcome bittersweet pang of joy to rattle her aching heart. "I came here to see you."

"Get out," the Colonel ordered.

"Hear me out, Audrey," Jamie said. "That's all I ask."

"You either get out or I'll put you out," her grandfather ordered, advancing on him.

*"I love her, dammit,"* Jamie snapped, rounding on him. "Either shut the hell up or I'll shut you up."

Audrey witnessed a phenomenon she'd never imagined she'd ever see—her grandfather speechless.

"Give us a minute, would you, Gramps?"

Though he looked like he wanted to argue, he didn't. "All right," he grumbled. He stalked to the back of the house, mumbling something under his breath about "mouthy upstarts" and "in my day…"

Had she really heard him correctly? Audrey wondered, shooting Jamie a questioning glance. Had he really just said he loved her? A hopeful sprout of happiness grew in her chest.

For the first time since he'd charged back into her living room, Jamie looked unsure of himself. It was curiously endearing.

"Audrey, I'm sorry," he said simply, the sincerest form of an apology. Regret painted his face with worry. "I'm not proud of going along with this. I just—" He paused. "I just wanted out of the military and your grandfather helped make that process easier than it should have been. I owed him. I agreed to a favor." He shook his head and his intense gaze tangled with hers. "But I never counted on anything like this. And I damned sure didn't count on coming up here and falling in love with you." He took a step toward her and grasped her shoulders. *"I love you."* A helpless laugh escaped him. "You are— You are the best thing that's ever happened to me. I know I was wrong, but— But don't cut me out over it. This evening you offered me an open invitation. Don't take it back. Please."

Audrey considered him a moment. "Why did you make love to me when you'd already gotten the answer you were sent here to get?"

Another helpless laugh rolled out his mouth. "Because I couldn't *not* make love to you. I need you."

A tremulous smile shook her mouth. That had been the answer she'd been hoping for. And she completely understood it, because she needed him, too. She needed that crooked grin and those sexy twinkling eyes. She needed his warmth and his strength and his loyalty and integrity. All of the qualities which had made him a good soldier also made him a good partner. He'd charged up the hill and taken on her grandfather for her, Audrey thought shaking her head. Now, *that* took courage.

Jamie caressed her cheek, sending a wave of

warmth and longing washing through her. Her lids fluttered shut, absorbing the feel of him.

"What do you say, Audrey? Can you forgive me?"

Audrey moved into the safe circle of his embrace, wrapped her arms around his waist, then looked up and pressed a kiss to his jaw. She smiled up at him. "Haven't you heard? I'm nothing if not forgiving."

Jamie chuckled, then lowered his mouth to hers. "No, you're nothing if not *mine*."

# *Epilogue*

"I WISH YOU COULD HAVE met him," Jamie said with a somber sigh. He and Audrey stood in Arlington National Cemetery, next to a plain white marble cross which marked the spot where Danny had been buried. More than a year later and Jamie was still grieving, but thanks to his wife—God, he was proud to call her that, Jamie thought, still in awe—he was allowing himself to mourn instead of blaming himself.

He glanced over his shoulder at Guy and Payne, who were standing a few markers down with the Colonel. The Colonel seemed to be in deep conversation with Payne and, judging from the unhappy look on his friend's face, he wasn't enjoying what he was hearing. Welcome to my world, Jamie thought, smiling. He didn't always enjoy his conversations with the Colonel either.

Garrett had received a commendation this morning and they'd all flown in to be there for him. Despite the interfering way he'd handled things, Jamie still owed him. The man had inadvertently introduced him to the love of his life, after all.

"I wish I could have met him, too." Audrey sighed. She squeezed his hand. "Daniel Garrett Flanagan," she announced matter-of-factly.

"What?"

"If we have a boy," she said. "We should name him after your friend and my grandfather."

It was a nice thought, but… Jamie grinned down at her. "I like it, but shouldn't we worry about that when you actually get pregnant?"

Audrey chewed the inside of her cheek, but didn't say anything.

Jamie stilled as hope leaped inside him. His heart began to race. "Audrey," he said slowly. "Are you?" he asked.

A huge grin spread across her lips and she nodded.

Jamie whooped with joy, snatched her up and whirled her around. My God, he thought. He was going to be a father. It was… It was… He shook his head. There were no words.

Except for these. "She's pregnant!" he bellowed to his baffled friends.

The Colonel beamed at them. "Audrey?" he asked for confirmation.

She nodded again. "Behave yourself and we'll name a boy after you."

Guy and Payne sidled over and slapped Jamie on the back. "Congratulations, man," Guy said, smiling. "We're honorary uncles, right?"

Jamie grinned. "Definitely."

Payne looked happy for him, but oddly distracted. And The Specialist rarely became distracted. "Is something wrong?" Jamie asked him, concerned.

"It'll keep."

"No," Jamie insisted. "You can tell me now. What's wrong?"

He glanced at Audrey, seemed to hesitate. "He just called my favor in."

So that's what they'd been talking about. "Where are you going?"

"I don't know. He's going to brief me on the return flight." He cast Audrey an uneasy look. "There aren't any more unattached women in your family I need to know about, are there?"

Audrey smiled. "Not that I know of."

Jamie laughed and wrapped an arm around Payne's shoulders. "Man, all I can say is, I hope you're as lucky with your mission as I was with mine."

Payne grimaced. From the look on his face, he hoped differently.

\* \* \* \* \*

# COMING NEXT MONTH from Harlequin® Blaze™

## AVAILABLE NOVEMBER 13, 2012

### #723 Let It Snow...
*A Christmas Blazing Bedtime Stories Collection*
**Leslie Kelly and Jennifer LaBrecque**

Ease into the hectic holiday season by indulging in a couple of delightfully naughty Christmas tales by two of Harlequin Blaze's bestselling authors. Can you think of a better way to spend a long winter's night?

### #724 HIS FIRST NOELLE
*Men Out of Uniform*
**Rhonda Nelson**

Judd Willingham is the ultimate protector—dedicated, determined and damned sexy. But when he's assigned to protect Noelle Montgomery, he knows his greatest challenge won't be keeping her safe, but keeping his hands to himself!

### #725 ON A SNOWY CHRISTMAS NIGHT
*Made in Montana*
**Debbi Rawlins**

Former air force pilot Jesse McAllister might be having trouble readjusting to his cowboy roots, but when shy computer programmer Shea Monroe shows up at the ranch, he's ready to get *her* back in the saddle....

### #726 NICE & NAUGHTY
**Tawny Weber**

All Jade Carson wants for Christmas is a little excitement. She's been a good girl *way* too long. So when sexy cop Diego Sandovol comes to town, she decides to change her ways. Because it looks as if being naughty with Diego will be very, *very* nice....

### #727 ALL I WANT FOR CHRISTMAS...
*A Hot Holiday Anthology*
**Lori Wilde, Kathleen O'Reilly, Candace Havens**

A landmark is torched in small-town Virginia and Santa's the main suspect! It's Christmas with a romantic twist for a local cop, fireman and EMT, when each meets his match!

### #728 HERS FOR THE HOLIDAYS
*The Berringers*
**Samantha Hunter**

Bodyguard Ely Berringer tracks a missing woman from the big city to big sky country. Not only does he find Lydia Hamilton, he's captivated by her—but will it last once he discovers her secret past?

# REQUEST YOUR FREE BOOKS!
## 2 FREE NOVELS PLUS 2 FREE GIFTS!

**◆ Harlequin®** *Blaze*™

### red-hot reads!

**YES!** Please send me 2 FREE Harlequin® Blaze™ novels and my 2 FREE gifts (gifts are worth about $10). After receiving them, if I don't wish to receive any more books, I can return the shipping statement marked "cancel." If I don't cancel, I will receive 6 brand-new novels every month and be billed just $4.49 per book in the U.S. or $4.96 per book in Canada. That's a saving of at least 14% off the cover price. It's quite a bargain. Shipping and handling is just 50¢ per book in the U.S. and 75¢ per book in Canada.* I understand that accepting the 2 free books and gifts places me under no obligation to buy anything. I can always return a shipment and cancel at any time. Even if I never buy another book, the two free books and gifts are mine to keep forever.

151/351 HDN FEQE

Name _____ (PLEASE PRINT) _____

Address _____ Apt. #

City _____ State/Prov. _____ Zip/Postal Code

Signature (if under 18, a parent or guardian must sign)

### Mail to the **Reader Service:**
**IN U.S.A.:** P.O. Box 1867, Buffalo, NY 14240-1867
**IN CANADA:** P.O. Box 609, Fort Erie, Ontario L2A 5X3

Not valid for current subscribers to Harlequin Blaze books.

**Want to try two free books from another line?**
**Call 1-800-873-8635 or visit www.ReaderService.com.**

\* Terms and prices subject to change without notice. Prices do not include applicable taxes. Sales tax applicable in N.Y. Canadian residents will be charged applicable taxes. Offer not valid in Quebec. This offer is limited to one order per household. All orders subject to credit approval. Credit or debit balances in a customer's account(s) may be offset by any other outstanding balance owed by or to the customer. Please allow 4 to 6 weeks for delivery. Offer available while quantities last.

**Your Privacy**—The Reader Service is committed to protecting your privacy. Our Privacy Policy is available online at www.ReaderService.com or upon request from the Reader Service.

We make a portion of our mailing list available to reputable third parties that offer products we believe may interest you. If you prefer that we not exchange your name with third parties, or if you wish to clarify or modify your communication preferences, please visit us at www.ReaderService.com/consumerschoice or write to us at Reader Service Preference Service, P.O. Box 9062, Buffalo, NY 14269. Include your complete name and address.

HBI1B

*Harlequin® Desire is proud to present*

*ONE WINTER'S NIGHT*

*by* New York Times *bestselling author*

## *Brenda Jackson*

Alpha Blake tightened her coat around her. Not only would she be late for her appointment with Riley Westmoreland, but because of her flat tire they would have to change the location of the meeting and Mr. Westmoreland would be the one driving her there. This was totally embarrassing, when she had been trying to make a good impression.

She turned up the heat in her car. Even with a steady stream of hot air coming in through the car vents, she still felt cold, too cold, and wondered if she would ever get used to the Denver weather. Of course, it was too late to think about that now. It was her first winter here, and she didn't have any choice but to grin and bear it. When she'd moved, she'd felt that getting as far away from Daytona Beach as she could was essential to her peace of mind. But who in her right mind would prefer blistering-cold Denver to sunny Daytona Beach? Only a person wanting to start a new life and put a painful past behind her.

Her attention was snagged by an SUV that pulled off the road and parked in front of her. The door swung open and long denim-clad, boot-wearing legs appeared before a man stepped out of the truck. She met his gaze through the windshield and forgot to breathe. Walking toward her car was a man who was so dangerously masculine, so heart-stoppingly virile, that her brain went momentarily numb.

He was tall, and the Stetson on his head made him appear taller. But his height was secondary to the sharp handsomeness of his features.

Her gaze slid all over him as he moved his long limbs toward her vehicle in a walk that was so agile and self-assured, she envied the confidence he exuded with every step. Her breasts suddenly peaked, and she could actually feel blood rushing through her veins.

She didn't have to guess who this man was.

He was Riley Westmoreland.

*Find out if Riley and Alpha mix business with pleasure in*

*ONE WINTER'S NIGHT*

*by Brenda Jackson*

*Available December 2012*

*Only from Harlequin® Desire*